They were going in.

Reid wiped sweat from his hand and replaced his finger on the trigger, triple-checking that the safety was off. His heart was beating so hard, he hoped he could aim if he had to. But more than that, he hoped he wouldn't have to. He couldn't imagine using a gun on a person.

Kayla turned into the doorway, crouching low, gun pointed. Reid followed immediately, sighting down his barrel. He braced against the doorjamb, scanning the dim room from right to left. Dresser. Mirror. Chair. Curtained window. Bed. *Someone under the covers.* He scanned past to a closed door, then back to the bed. Kayla approached with her gun pointed at the lump under the bedspread. With her other hand she motioned for Reid to check the closed door.

Reid crept over and, with his back to the wall, gingerly turned the knob and pushed. The door creaked open. After two beats he rushed in, pointing the gun high then low, willing his eyes to adjust to the darkness, scanning the rows of clothing and the closet's shadowed recesses.

"Clear," he said, just loud enough for Kayla to hear.

"She's sleeping," Kayla whispered.

"Who is it?"

"I have no idea."

Reid approached the bed and looked down at the first stranger he'd ever seen.

Also by Chris Mandeville:

52 WAYS TO GET UNSTUCK

Writers get stuck, but now they don't have to stay that way. This creative and comprehensive guide to overcoming writer's block is chock-full of innovative exercises, anecdotes, and advice from dozens of authors. It also includes practical "life prep" lessons to keep writers from becoming stuck in the first place. It's indispensable for all working writers—from newbies to pros. Want to get unstuck and stay that way? This book shows you how.

"Both practical and inspiring, Chris Mandeville's 52 Ways *is sure to become a writer's go-to guide for getting unstuck."*

~#1 NY Times Bestselling Author Susan Wiggs

QUAKE
Book One of IN REAL TIME

Fifteen-year-old Allie Bennett's a con artist, a pickpocket, and on her last chance at an end-of-the-line foster home. She learns her mom—who disappeared when she was ten—isn't a crazy but is actually a time traveler, and Allie's one, too. She joins a crew of time traveling thieves and goes back to the 1906 San Francisco earthquake to pull the heist of the century and find her mom. But time travelers are hunted, her crew might be killers, everyone has a secret agenda, and she must pull off the con of her life to make it out alive.

"An utterly original spin on time travel adventure, with heart-stopping action, laugh-out-loud humor, and featuring one heck of an engaging teen heroine. A roller-coaster of a read."

~Darby Karchut, award-winning author of
Del Toro Moon and *Finn Finnegan*

Seeds

a post-apocalyptic adventure

Chris Mandeville

To Elizabeth –
Always walk in the
sunshine ~ Cho!

PARKER
HAYDEN
MEDIA

DEDICATION

for my husband Jody
with gratitude for your love and support, your belief in me,
and your idea for this book

Parker Hayden Media
5740 N Carefree Cir, STE 120-1
Colorado Springs, CO 80917

ISBN: 978-1-941528-25-9

Cover art credits:
Cover design: LB Hayden
Cracked earth @ szefei/Shutterstock
Ferris wheel and sun @ Alexander Smulskiy/Shutterstock

Chapter 1

Reid Landers leaned against the brick wall in a sliver of shade, shifting his rifle uneasily as the transgressors threw trash on the fire. He belonged in the infirmary with his patients, but Commander Vega made everyone rotate through some form of guard duty—medics, clergy, even the Originals. Vega said everyone was a soldier. They had to be ready, prepared at all times.

Prepared? For what? No one had seen a stranger, much less a Raider, in forty years. The Mountain didn't need guards, and neither did the transgressors. They served their tours for swearing, being late to church, or whatever infraction they'd committed, trying to earn official forgiveness and get back inside the Mountain. Besides, where else would they go?

Reid knew what was beyond the fence. Nothing.

He hadn't seen much of it himself, but his brother Brian had. There were no plants, no animals, no people. Certainly no Raiders. Brian and Kayla had patrolled everything this side of the Burn and found only the bones of the people from the Before. There was nothing left but dust-filled houses, rusting cars, scuttling rats, and a dwindling supply of canned food.

There was nothing to run away *to*.

But even if there were, no matter how much Reid wanted to escape the confines of Vega's military and the oppression of his father's church, he wouldn't leave his patients.

"Reid!" Kayla ran toward him from the mouth of the tunnel, blond hair streaming behind her, not in its usual tight braid.

"What's wrong?" It had to be serious. She'd barely looked at him since Brian's funeral.

She stopped, out of breath, her face gaunt, her green eyes angry and red-rimmed. "It's Bethany. She's worse. A lot worse."

Reid pictured her little sister lying in the infirmary and had to clench his teeth to keep from cursing Vega out loud.

"She's asking for you," Kayla said.

There would be hell to pay, but he slung his rifle on his back and sprinted up the short stretch of Norad Road with Kayla matching his stride. At the checkpoint, the guards waved them into the tunnel. With each step, the air grew cooler, but at the same time heavier, more oppressive. They covered the quarter mile to the open blast door where Kayla's cousin stood guard. Her somber expression spurred Reid on.

On the other side of the door, the smells of antiseptic cleaner and trash assaulted his nostrils. They ran across the cavernous room past a squad of Remotes at their lockers gearing up for patrol. Someone shouted a warning, but Reid didn't slow. Vega was already going to sentence him to tours for leaving his post, but he didn't care if he got hit with another week, so long as he got to Bethany before it was too late.

He flung open the main door and ran faster, though he dreaded what waited at the end of the corridor. A week ago, Bethany broke her leg on the playground. Healthy people recovered from worse, but Bethany had never been one of the healthy ones. Without reserves to draw on, a broken bone could be a death sentence. Reid had requested extra nutrition for her, but it had been denied. The little girl was a fighter. He had hoped that would be enough.

At the end of the hall, a tech came out of the infirmary with a gurney. Bethany's gurney. She was being moved to the "family room," more commonly known as the *dying* room. Reid never called it that out loud, but that's what it was and everyone knew it.

Doc wasn't there, but Reid didn't really expect him to be. Doc rarely went in the dying room. Vega looked the other way while Doc hid in his office and drank, leaving Reid or another medic to tend to the families and pronounce the dead. It used to make Reid furious, but now he felt sorry for the old man.

As one of the Originals, Doc had seen more death than a sober man could bear: hundreds of thousands in Colorado Springs from radiation poisoning after the massive sun flare; more than half of the survivors slaughtered by Raiders; then the steady dying-off of the remainder since. Now they were down to a hundred souls and, for all they knew, the only ones alive on the planet. The last of humanity was dying out, and Doc couldn't watch anymore. So he did what he could for a patient while there was still hope, then drank till it was over.

Reid followed the gurney into the room where Kayla's mom stood wringing her hands, her thin gray face wet with tears.

"I can't do this," she said.

"Go home, Mom," Kayla said. "Reid and I will stay."

There was both anger and pity in Kayla's voice, and Reid couldn't blame her for either.

The tech handed him Bethany's chart as she followed Kayla's mother out, but Reid didn't open it. He already knew what it would say.

He joined Kayla at the bedside and took Bethany's hand. "Hey, sunshine."

"Where were you, Reid?" Bethany's voice was a hoarse whisper.

"It doesn't matter. I'm here now, and wild-eyed Raiders couldn't drag me away."

Bethany gave a weak smile and Reid forced himself to smile back. Her eyes closed and her breathing slowed.

Kayla dropped to her knees and buried her face in Bethany's blankets. Reid stroked her hair and wished there were something he could say. The best he could hope for was a quick passing. He didn't want Kayla to see what would happen if Bethany lingered. His cheeks burned as he pictured Vega pressuring him to hasten the process so the dying child wouldn't use up any more resources.

Reid wouldn't do it. He never had. Even if Vega bullied his father and Reid no longer had the protection of the church, he would stand his ground. Especially when it came to Bethany. Nothing could make him hurt Kayla like that.

"Reid?" Bethany's voice quavered.

"I'm here." He squeezed her hand.

"Tell me a story about the stars. The one about the princess."

Kayla lay down alongside her sister, slipped her arms around her and held her gently.

Reid settled into the chair by the bed. He held Bethany's hand and told the story of Cassiopeia until her pulse faded to nothing.

Kayla's eyes were closed, her chest slowly rising and falling. She looked so peaceful, Reid hated to wake her. He wished he could spare her the pain that would return the moment she knew Bethany was gone.

First Brian, and now Bethany. He didn't know how much more Kayla could take, how much more *he* could take. His brother's death had been an accident, a freak, tragic accident. But Bethany was the third child he'd lost to malnutrition in the last month. If they didn't find some other source of food soon, it wouldn't be long before they were all gone.

Reid leaned back in his chair and watched Kayla sleep. The news could wait a little longer.

Reid stood at attention and did a mental inventory. His hair was clean and cut above the ears, well within regs. His camouflage uniform was wrinkled and threadbare, but no more so than anyone else's. His cap was tucked in his waistband at the small of his back, and the revolver on his belt was cleaned, oiled, loaded, and locked. He kept his eyes forward, though he wanted to see how Kayla was holding up. Whatever penalty there would be for leaving his post yesterday should be his alone. Kayla should be allowed to grieve with her family.

"I'm disappointed in you both," Commander Renata Vega said, addressing Reid and Kayla from behind her desk. Vega's hair was short, a slick black version of Reid's blond crew cut. But unlike him, her uniform was pressed, and she wore a couple dozen ribbons and medals on her breast as if she'd earned them.

Reid kept silent, his face impassive. Kayla was silent too.

"It's been over a month," Vega said, "and nothing has been done about your matching."

What? This isn't about yesterday?

Vega motioned for someone to enter. Reid knew without looking it would be his father.

Bishop Peregrine Landers stepped inside. "What's the problem?"

He glanced at Reid, his face questioning, confirming what Reid had hoped. His father wasn't part of this—he had no idea why they'd been summoned. As the bishop, and as Reid's father, Peregrine had promised he wouldn't marry them, no matter how hard Vega pushed.

"These two were matched when Brian died. Why aren't they wed?" Vega demanded.

"I received your requisition," Peregrine said. "But Reid and Kayla are still grieving Brian's death. Now with the tragic loss of Kayla's sister—"

"That does not change my orders."

"I beg your pardon, Commander." Peregrine straightened his short frame and pushed out his chest. "You cannot order a wedding. That authority belongs to the church."

A hint of a smile played at the corners of Vega's lips. "I did not say I was ordering them to wed. I'm ordering them on brevet."

Reid's breath caught in his throat, and he sensed Kayla stiffen. Unmarrieds going on brevet was unheard of. This wasn't about him and Kayla at all. Vega was using them as leverage, trying to force his father's hand, escalating the pissing contest between the church and the military. He hoped Kayla knew they didn't need to worry. His father wouldn't let them down.

"Brevet is a rite of passage for the *married*. I implore you to reconsider," Peregrine said.

Vega raised one eyebrow. "And if I refuse?"

"I still won't marry them. I'm well within my rights per Article Three, Section Twenty-six, of the New Constitution, which plainly declares marriage solely a matter of religion."

"Don't quote me the Articles—my father wrote them," Vega growled. "And that knife cuts both ways, Bishop. Per Article Four, Section Five, I hereby order Lieutenant Reid Landers and Lieutenant Kayla Solomon to deploy on brevet, effective today."

"Today?" The surprise was evident in Peregrine's voice. "Respectfully, I request Kayla be allowed to bury her sister before any decisions are made."

"The decision has already been made. However, if you perform the marriage ceremony now, I'll defer deployment until after the funeral."

Reid considered it. Should he agree to the marriage so Kayla could attend the funeral? He risked a glance at her, and his heart constricted at the deadness in her eyes. He ached to take her in his arms, to make the rest of the world go away, to make everything okay again. But she'd never look at him without wishing he was Brian, and he couldn't do that to her or himself.

"Commander," Peregrine said. "*Renata*. Postponing would be the morally decent thing. But it does not change my decision."

"You still won't wed them?" Anger strangled Vega's voice and she gripped the edge of the desk so hard her hands blanched white.

"Not unless and until they desire it."

"Since when does what they want factor into the decision?"

"Since it's my son and my dead son's widow." Peregrine's face was flushed, his voice passionate. Reid rarely saw that much emotion in his father outside the pulpit. "I've given Reid my word."

Vega stood. "This is on your head, Bishop. Not mine." She glared at

Reid and Kayla. "Landers and Solomon. You will deploy on brevet at 1300 today, and you're not to return for one month."

"A month?" Reid blurted. No one ever stayed out a month. "What about my patients?"

"That's an order, lieutenants. Dismissed."

Reid clamped his teeth together, turned crisply, and followed Kayla out.

Kayla broke into a jog. Reid wanted to go after her, but he waited for his father. He had to tell him he didn't blame him. He knew there was nothing more he could have done.

Kayla would miss Bethany's funeral, but at least she didn't have to suffer a forced marriage. It was better this way. He'd rather love Kayla from afar than see up close day after day that she didn't love him. When they returned from brevet, they'd go back to their separate lives. They had his father's word, and Peregrine had never broken his word to either of his sons.

Chapter 2

Reid entered the mess minutes before lunch began. He hung his rifle on a hook and dropped his pack in the corner, then scanned for Kayla. He found her in the back, and slipped into the chair next to hers. She didn't acknowledge him.

"This taken?" Bartholomew Jones grinned at Reid, indicating the empty chair beside him.

"All yours." Reid always liked his brother's good-natured buddy, but it was hard to see him without Brian.

Kayla glanced up and cringed. It had to be even harder for her. Jones was a Remote, Brian and Kayla's teammate before the accident.

"I was in the orderly room, heard you two's going on brevet." Jones scooted his chair in.

"Yeah," Reid said. "But it's not what you think. We're not married."

"What? This place gets weirder and weirder." Jones's voice was low. "Now I suppose you're gonna tell me it's true you'll be gone for a month."

"Yep. I had no idea what to pack." Reid chuckled, trying to bring some levity to the table. "I've only been outside the fence once, and it was for a week. What do you bring for a *month?*"

Jones shrugged. "I don't guess packing for a month would be any different than for a day. What do you need besides a can opener, a knife, and a gun?"

"All rise for the bishop."

The room quieted and all forty-some people stood.

"Let us pray," Peregrine said. "Our Father, thank you for the bounty you have provided."

Reid glanced at the open can by his plate and wondered at his father's notion of bounty.

"As we mourn our dear daughter and sister, Bethany," Peregrine continued, "we humbly ask you to bless this food to nourish our spirits as well as our bodies. Amen."

Reid reached for his can of green beans as he took his seat. Jones was already dumping his can onto his plate, but Kayla slumped in her chair with her hands in her lap.

"Kay, you have to eat," Reid said. "Jonesy, what you got, carrots? Want to share?"

Jones shrugged and slid half the carrots from his plate to Reid's. Reid dumped some green beans onto each of their plates. Kayla hadn't moved, so Reid grabbed her can of lima beans and balked at the milky glob, wondering how it had gotten past the kitchen's inspection. He chucked the can in a collection tub at the back of the room and gave Kayla some of his food.

Kayla didn't seem to notice. Her eyes stared unfocused.

Reid swallowed a mouthful of green beans without really chewing. The vegetables got mushier each week, if that were possible. "Hey Jones, it's been two years since I was in the city. What's the story out there?"

Jones frowned. "You don't need my intel. Kayla knows everything there is to know."

Reid glanced at Kayla, but she hadn't engaged. "Yeah, but where would *you* go?"

"Me? I'd partake of the Honeymoon Suite at the Broadmoor, no question."

"It's not like that," Reid said. "Vega's making a point with my dad, that's all. We survive out there a month, then things go back to normal."

"Then you're missing the best part of brevet, man." Jones accepted a platter of barbequed rat from the person across the table and helped himself. "At least you won't have any trouble with the survival part. Kayla was the best Remote on our crew."

Reid took the platter and speared a portion of the bony meat. "I know." He glanced at Kayla again. "But I'd like to make it easier on her, if I can."

"Then how about the Academy? The commissary's empty, but nobody bothered much with the houses. There'll be more than enough supplies to last you. Those military families stocked up almost as good as Mormons."

"The Academy? I never made it that far north. Isn't it right at the edge of the Burn?"

"Yeah, but don't let that worry you. Burn or no Burn, you gotta respect the supplies. Man, it's to the point where only one out of four cans contains something edible."

"The Burn doesn't concern me," Reid said, though it actually did. "It's the hills. I remember Brian saying it was hell going north." Reid winced at Brian's name. He imagined it stung Kayla like a whip.

"Yeah, north's a bitch. Once you get down from the Mountain, it's uphill the whole hump, but that's probably why it ain't been cleaned out yet." Jones shoveled a forkful into his mouth and continued talking while he chewed. "If you want flat, head south or east. But it's a long-ass way before you find good pickin's."

"How far?"

"What's it matter?" Kayla stood. "It's not like we're in a hurry." She shouldered her pack, grabbed her rifle, and went out the door.

Reid shrugged at Jones and stood.

Jones shrugged back. "Good luck and God's favor."

Reid snagged his stuff and jogged after Kayla. He caught up as she passed the trash bins, but she didn't look over at him. It would be the longest month of his life if she kept this up.

The guard at the blast door watched them approach. When they stopped in front of him he took a clipboard from the holder on the wall and scowled at it through thick lenses.

"Landers and Solomon?" he asked, like he didn't know who they were.

"Stan," Kayla said. "I'm not in the mood."

Stan glowered at them. He was a young thirteen and still took guard duty very seriously. Reid watched him finger the butt of the M4 slung from his shoulder and questioned for the umpteenth time the wisdom of arming hormonal teens with automatic weapons.

"I'm giving the outbriefing, whether you like it or not." Stan was obviously trying to sound officious but came off like a bratty kid. "You are hereby ordered to remain inside the established perimeter. Stay out of the Burn at all times. Leave inedibles open for the rats, control your fires, and report any sign of Raiders immed—"

"Got it," Kayla said. "Let's go, Reid." She crossed the threshold into the tunnel.

"But—" Stan protested.

Reid hurried past. Kayla knew what she was doing, and the fresh air called to him.

At the mouth of the tunnel, Natalie and Wade were on guard duty. Reid figured it was no accident they'd been assigned together. They'd probably been matched. Wade's wife had died in childbirth two weeks ago, but the baby survived and needed a mother. Wade should be allowed to grieve for his wife and bond with his baby, but that's not how things were done.

Kayla passed the guard shack without stopping. "We know the drill."

"Fine by me," Wade mumbled.

Reid caught his eye. "Take care of yourself. I'll see you in a month."

"God's favor on the outside," Natalie said dutifully.

"Yeah. God's favor," Reid said under his breath.

Despite everyone else's fears, Reid wasn't scared of being on the outside. He didn't believe in the prophecy of a second solar storm any more than he believed Raiders still existed. The tickle in his belly wasn't fear, it was anticipation. Despite his regret at leaving his patients, he was excited. He'd be under the stars for a month.

A whole month, just him and Kayla. Relying on each other. No one else.

Even if Kayla didn't start to see him as something other than Brian's little brother, it would be more than enough time for her to come around and tell him the whole story of how Brian had died. He'd be patient. He was good at that. He'd had a lot of practice.

He watched Kayla ahead as she managed to look graceful traversing the crumbling asphalt and potholes that Norad Road had become. A few years back, Vega had ordered a team to repair the road, but they'd only made it worse. Now it was a sprained ankle waiting to happen.

Around a sharp bend, the road descended into neighborhoods. All of the houses looked equally dilapidated, even though some had been fixed up and occupied by families from the Mountain back in the beginning of the New World. Back before they knew Raiders existed.

His grandparents had lived in one of those houses with little Peregrine and another baby on the way. As a kid, Reid had begged his grandfather to tell him about the Raiders, but Tinker had refused and Reid knew better than to ask his grandmother. She didn't talk about the baby she'd lost, the scar on her face, or the Raiders who'd driven them back inside the Mountain.

Ahead at an overlook, Kayla drank from her canteen. Reid stopped beside her, but she stared past him. The landscape below was brown and silent and still. Reid couldn't imagine it any other way. He'd never shared Brian's conviction that the world would be reborn and green again. Kayla had. He wondered if she still did, now that Brian was gone.

14

Reid searched for something to say, to comfort her. But she resumed walking before he could find the words. He took a drink, then nearly dropped his canteen. Something had moved below. The hair on the back of his neck prickled as he stared at the city, but everything was still again. He told himself it had been a trick of the eye, but he knew he'd seen something.

"Kayla, wait up."

She stopped and turned around. Her expression was somewhere between misery and disgust. She hated being stuck with him. She couldn't even bring herself to look at him. "Yeah?"

"When Stan started to say something about Raiders . . . that was just routine, right?"

"If by routine you mean bullshit."

"That's what I thought. But from the overlook, I saw something move in the city."

Kayla rolled her eyes. "I'm sure it was a Remote, Reid. What, did you think we were the only ones out here?" She continued down the hill.

Reid's cheeks burned. What was wrong with him, getting all creeped out like a kid? Of course their own people were in the city. Besides, there weren't any Raiders. Brian had spent the last five years on patrol and hadn't seen a shred of evidence of anyone else left alive in the world. If he had, Reid would have been the first to hear.

Vega wanted everyone to believe Raiders lurked outside the perimeter, but it didn't add up. After the Raiders killed hundreds in the initial attacks, the remaining Originals had retaliated with a vengeance. They'd hunted down and killed every Raider they could find, then formed regular patrols in case more came. But none had come. Not then, and not in the forty years since.

Despite this, Reid's brother had become a Remote and gone on patrol at every opportunity. At first Reid hadn't understood it. Brian wasn't the bloodthirsty Raider-hunting type any more than he was. Then one day Brian had returned from patrol beaming. He'd pulled Reid into a private corner and shown him a handful of seeds. Then it all made sense. Brian was trying to grow things.

But after five years of finding and planting seeds, the only thing that had grown was Reid's fear his brother's heresy would be discovered. Even now, Reid kept the secret, safeguarding Brian's reputation and protecting Kayla.

Reid was surprised when Kayla turned off the main road, but he wasn't about to ask her anything. Halfway down the block, she went up a driveway. Reid looked at the house and stopped dead, watching in disbelief as Kayla opened the red front door and went inside.

It couldn't be coincidence.

The only people who knew what he'd done there were Tiffany and Brian. Tiffany would never tell, and Reid had thought Brian wouldn't either.

Chapter 3

Reid hadn't thought about that house since he and Tiffany had been granted a divorce. As he looked up at the red front door, the broken shutters, and the peeling paint, his cheeks burned again, but not from embarrassment. He understood Kayla lashing out because she was hurting, but she'd gone too far.

He climbed the steps and opened the door. Kayla was on the other side of the living room, standing at the picture window facing the backyard. Her head was angled toward the exact spot where he'd buried them.

"I don't know if I'm more pissed that Brian told you, or that you brought me here to throw it in my face."

Kayla turned. "What?"

"Look, I get that you need to blame someone for the brevet, for Bethany, even for Brian. So blame me. I can take it. But bringing me here—"

"What makes you think this is about you? This was a special place for Brian and me. I left something here. I came to get it."

"But this is where Tiffany and I came on our brevet. . . ."

"I know. That's why Brian brought me here. What you did meant something to him."

She turned back to the window, and he followed her gaze to the place where he'd buried the couple who lived there in the Before. He hadn't felt right tossing out their bones while he and Tiffany ate at their table and slept in their bed. So he'd dug a grave and said words over them, even though the church forbade it and Tiffany had been horrified.

"You're wrong about me," Kayla said in a small voice, still facing the window. "I don't blame you. Not for any of it."

"Then why can't you look at me?"

Kayla looked at him, really looked at him for the first time since Brian died. "It's just . . . you remind me of him. Your voice, your eyes, even the way you walk."

Reid wished he hadn't asked. This was worse than thinking she blamed him.

A tear spilled down Kayla's cheek. Reid hadn't seen her cry. Not when Bethany died, not even at Brian's funeral. Maybe she was finally ready to let out the pain she had walled inside. He took a step closer, willing to hold her, to comfort her, whatever she needed, despite his own feelings. But she wiped her face and gave a shuddering sigh.

"I'll be ready to go in a sec." She squeezed his arm, then crossed the room and disappeared down a hallway.

Reid touched his arm where Kayla's hand had been, and turned to the window, remembering when he and Tiffany had discovered the house and its inhabitants. The couple had been elderly, judging by the photos. Apparently devoted to each other. He and Tiff found them sitting on the couch facing that window, holding hands. He'd buried them like that, with her hand clasped in his. Even then he'd known what he felt for Tiffany was not that kind of enduring love. Not the kind Brian and Kayla had for each other.

"I know some apartments not far from here," Kayla called. "There's a bait station close by, so good hunting. If we hump it, we can make it by dark." She came out with her hair freshly pulled into a ponytail, the wisps around her face damp. "Okay by you?"

He nodded and followed her out, pulling on his cap to shield his face from the sun. They walked shoulder to shoulder, saying nothing. But the silence was different now. Not as heavy.

As the sun inched toward the mountains, they approached the apartments, rifles in hand. Two rats darted from behind the rusted hulk of a car, and Kayla nailed them both before Reid could squeeze off a single round.

"You better grab those, Landers," she said. "You'll be cooking tonight. Fair's fair."

"Fine by me, Solomon, but that means you scavenge the rest of dinner."

"I hope you're quick with the knife because I'm starving." She shoved him in the direction of her kills.

Reid smiled as he grabbed the rats. It was like he had the old Kayla back.

They found an acceptable unit on the second floor, tossed down their packs, and got to work. While Kayla rummaged through the kitchen cupboards, Reid gathered a pile of papers and a couple of books into a desk drawer and went out onto the balcony. The barbeque grill was dry, so he laid a fire with the papers, books, and some unvarnished pieces of the drawer, then lit it. In minutes, Reid had the rats gutted and cooking.

"This will be better hot," Kayla said, placing a pan of something gray-green on the grate next to the meat.

While the rats sizzled, Reid leaned back in a chair with his boots up on the balcony rail watching Kayla bring stuff out.

"Very fancy," Reid commented as she spread a tablecloth and topped it with blue-rimmed plates, cloth napkins, and a full complement of silverware.

"Just you wait, Lieutenant Landers." She went inside, then returned with a tray bearing a bowl of peaches, the candlesticks she'd been using in the kitchen, and two goblets. She handed him a glass. "That's the last of my water. You should have told me you were empty."

"Yeah, sorry." He hadn't even thought about it. It had been a long time since he'd been away from the Mountain where the underground spring provided an endless supply of fresh water. He'd have to pay more attention.

"It's okay," Kayla said. "We'll hit a rain barrel on our way out in the morning."

He rotated his goblet, watching the facets on the crystal reflect the candlelight like a diamond. "What, not drinking bottled water?" he teased.

"After the lectures your grandmother subjected us to? Right."

Reid grinned at the memory of his grandmother railing about the toxins that leached out of plastic bottles. Like it wasn't the same stuff lining the cans of food that they and the rats ate.

Kayla pulled out a chair and sat. He watched her fiddle with her napkin and straighten the silverware. The sunset framed her in an orange glow, and her face was relaxed, peaceful even. But when she looked at him the pain returned.

"Hey," she said, frowning. "Is that burning?"

"Shit." He hopped up and rescued their dinner from the flames. "It's not too bad," he said, placing meat on their plates, then scooping them each some of the vegetable stuff.

Kayla wrinkled her nose and put her hands in her lap. "I'm not that hungry anyway."

"At least eat the thymus. You can have both." He pointed to the raw organs he'd set aside when cleaning the rats.

"Ugh, no. I can't stomach those anymore."

"Since when?" Everyone was supposed to have at least one thymus a day, preferably two. "How long has it been? Are your teeth loose?"

"My teeth are fine. Here, I'll eat these." She took the bowl of peaches and slopped half onto her plate. "They have vitamin C, right?"

"Not much, but some."

They were silent while Reid devoured his food and Kayla picked at her peaches. He left the thymus glands in case she changed her mind, but when she put her feet up on the rail, he ate both, ignoring their minerally grittiness. He'd have to find her some mandarin oranges or it wouldn't be long before she started showing symptoms of scurvy.

Reid finished off both helpings of meat and then discarded the bones as he had the guts—by dropping them to the rats' cannibalistic brothers below. He drained his glass and kicked his feet up beside Kayla's, taking in the ruins of the city. A study in gray.

By the time Kayla spoke, the fire had died and the stars had come out.

"There's something I need to tell you."

He waited.

"Actually," she said after a moment. "It would be better if I showed you. First thing in the morning, all right?" She gave a sad half-smile and went inside.

It had only been a day, but she'd always known she could trust him. Tomorrow, he'd finally learn how Brian died. He leaned back and gazed at the stars.

"This is delicious," Reid said the next morning over hot oatmeal. "What's in it?"

"Honey and nutmeg," Kayla said, cinching her pack closed. "Don't worry, I didn't use bottled water. I went to the rain barrel while you were sleeping."

"Mmm," Reid replied, his mouth full. He felt like he hadn't slept at all. He'd tossed and turned all night thinking about Brian.

"Here's your canteen. I filled it for you." She tossed it to him.

"Thanks. You said you have something to show me this morning?"

"Uh huh." Kayla hefted her pack and headed for the door. "I'll wait outside."

"Be right there."

Reid opened his canteen, thankful Kayla had filled it, and quickly brushed his teeth and ran wet hands through his hair. After a glance around to be sure he had everything, he put on his pack and slung his rifle over his shoulder.

As he walked down the stairs, an odd mixture of excitement and dread built in his chest. He'd always thought Kayla's official explanation of Brian's death was bogus—Brian would never have strayed into the Burn accidentally. Vega hadn't swallowed that story either, but his father believed it. He said Kayla never backed down under questioning, never varied her account, even when Vega's questions were not strictly congenial requests for information.

Still, Reid was sure there was more to it.

He caught up to Kayla by the side of the road.

"So, where are we headed?" he asked, trying to sound casual.

"You'll see."

He followed her to the edge of the neighborhood where it butted up against a highway littered with decaying cars, the dinosaur bones of the last era.

Kayla climbed over the guardrail onto the asphalt and turned north. They were heading toward the Burn. She was taking him to the place where his brother died.

Reid avoided looking in the cars as he weaved his way past the heaps of rusting metal and disintegrating rubber. Some people had abandoned their vehicles wherever they'd been when the computers failed, but quite a few others had died in the initial blast of radiation. Normally it didn't bother Reid to see the dead, but there was something incredibly bleak about the endless, stationary caravan of skeletons.

Kayla moved at a quick clip, but Reid lagged behind, mentally preparing for a hard uphill hike. At least ten more miles, he figured. But when Kayla looked back at him somber-faced and turned up the next off-ramp, Reid's heart skipped. He hurried to catch up.

At the top of the off-ramp was a different world. Hollowed-out shells that used to be cars. Buildings gutted. Everything black.

Reid had no idea the Burn extended this far south.

He followed Kayla through the tangle of debris and rubble, knowing each step took him closer to the place where his brother had died.

Kayla stopped beside what had once been a yellow truck.

Brian died here?

Reid didn't know what he'd expected, but it hadn't been as mundane as his brother dying beside some rusted-out truck.

The wind gusted, throwing soot and dirt into the air. They turned away from the blast, pulling the bandanas from their necks to cover their mouths and noses. After a moment, the wind died as quickly as it had started, and the air cleared.

"I have something in my eye," Kayla said.

"Let me look." He grabbed his canteen and rinsed his hands vigorously, then held her eye open and flushed it with water from the canteen. "I guess that's why they say to stay out of the Burn," he joked, knowing it was the least of the dangers.

"What are you talking about?" Kayla wiped her face with the inside of her sleeve. "We're not anywhere near the Burn."

"Then what is this? Why'd you bring me here?"

"This is where that lightning fire was two years ago. Don't you remember how Brian latched on to that theory he read about fires cleansing the earth and allowing plants to grow?"

"Yeah." There had been a time when Brian would talk about nothing else whenever he caught Reid alone. Neither one of them bought into the belief that it was a sin to grow things before God sent the second storm, but they knew better than to say it openly.

"The fire here provided the perfect opportunity to test the theory because it was close enough to visit regularly. So we planted seeds. All kinds. But no matter how much or how little we watered them, no matter what time of year or type of weather, nothing sprouted. That was tough, even for our eternal optimist." She paused, and Reid had to look away from the pain on her face.

"Brian started thinking it was useless," she continued, her voice shaky. "That every seed on the planet had been exposed to too much radiation. He was ready to give up when we found a fire-safe full of seed packets. We planted those seeds here. That's when he gave me this."

She pulled a silver chain from her pocket and held it out. It had a small charm attached.

He lifted it from her hand. The pendant was a clear heart held by a silver bezel. In the center of the heart, suspended in the glass, was a brown dot. "A seed?"

"A mustard seed. In the Before, it was a symbol of Christian faith. Of course, now it would be viewed by your father and the church as exactly the opposite, so I couldn't wear it in the Mountain. I kept it at the house. That's what I stopped to get. Would you put it on me?"

Kayla turned her back and held up her hair. He draped the chain around and fumbled with the tiny clasp, managing to avoid all but the slightest brush of his hand against her neck. She shivered.

"Done," he said, pulling back his hands and shoving them in his pockets to try to erase the feel of her skin on his.

Kayla pushed at the dry, cracked earth with the toe of her boot. "The seeds we planted here didn't grow either. But it didn't matter— the optimist was back. He was sure eventually something would grow. He promised me he'd never stop believing. Never stop trying. That's what this necklace symbolized. His undying faith that we would have a future."

Reid blinked, focusing on a blackened building thirty yards behind Kayla. Had something moved? He didn't want to overreact again and look like an idiot. It was probably a rat, or more likely, his imagination. Then he saw it again and his heart leapt into his throat. *"Oh my God,"* he whispered. "Turn around, very slowly."

A black shape was moving at the base of the building, barely visible against the charcoal wall. Whatever it was, it was alive, and much bigger than a rat.

Chapter 4

W hat the hell *is* that?" Kayla whispered.

"You haven't seen one before?"

"Never." Kayla lifted her rifle to her shoulder. "It's enough meat for a week."

"Wait." Reid pushed the barrel toward the ground. "Could it have survived out here by itself since the sun flare? What if it's a descendant, like us—that would mean there's more of them."

"You're right. I wasn't thinking. Come on, we'll track it."

They inched away from the truck and into the shadow of the nearest building. Using it for cover, they crept forward and looked around the corner. The animal was still moving around at the base of the other building.

"Do you know what it is?" Kayla asked.

"A dog, but bigger than I would have guessed from pictures."

"I've seen a few skeletons that size, but I never knew what they were for sure."

The black dog was so well camouflaged amidst the burned buildings, it was luck Reid had spotted it at all. It nosed around the base of a cinderblock wall, then lifted one leg and a stream of liquid washed down the bricks.

"It's peeing," Reid said, laughing under his breath.

"It is?"

The dog looked over, and they ducked back behind the building.

"Did it see us?" Reid whispered.

"I don't know." Kayla took a peek. "It's on the move."

Reid followed Kayla around the corner in time to see the dog disappear around another building. He kept up with Kayla as stealthily as he could, though his footsteps were nowhere near as light as hers. When they reached the end of the building, she held up her hand in a fist, the signal to halt. Reid froze. Kayla peered around the corner, then motioned for him to look.

The dog was about twenty feet away with its nose in a basin. Reid heard water slopping and figured it was drinking. The dog lifted its head and looked around. Reid held his breath, afraid to move, afraid it would detect them and bolt. After a moment, the dog resumed walking, in no apparent hurry.

They followed it to a house that had only half burned, protected as it was between two larger structures. The dog jumped over the crumbling foundation wall and disappeared into the shadows. Reid started after it, but was stopped short by a tug on his pack.

Kayla scowled. "This isn't the time to break protocol. Who knows what's inside."

"I thought you said there were no Raiders."

"A few minutes ago I'd have said there were no dogs either. Let me take point."

Reid nodded. He didn't want to put her in harm's way, but they were both better off with the more experienced soldier in the lead.

She slung her rifle over her shoulder and pulled out her pistol as she stepped into the house. Reid followed, stopping when Kayla held up her fist. She pointed with two fingers to her eyes, then toward footprints in the dirt.

The dog's prints. *And a human's.*

The prints led down a hallway.

Reid nudged his pistol's safety to the *off* position. His heart thundered as he followed Kayla down the hall, and he wondered if she was nervous too. She seemed so confident, placing each step deliberately. Alert and vigilant. Deadly silent. She was a good Remote.

At the end of the hall, a door on the right hung partway open. The prints led inside.

Kayla stayed back from the doorway and pointed to her ear. After a few moments she shook her head. Reid hadn't heard anything either. She pointed to her eyes and then the door.

They were going in.

Reid wiped sweat from his hand and replaced his finger on the trigger, triple-checking that the safety was off. His heart was beating so hard, he hoped he could aim if he had to. But more than that, he hoped he wouldn't have to. He couldn't imagine using a gun on a person.

Kayla turned into the doorway, crouching low, gun pointed. Reid followed immediately, sighting down his barrel. He braced against the doorjamb, scanning the dim room from right to left. Dresser. Mirror.

Chair. Curtained window. Bed. *Someone under the covers.* He scanned past to a closed door, then back to the bed. The dog stood beside it, tail swinging. Kayla approached the bed with her gun pointed at the lump under the bedspread. With her other hand she motioned for Reid to check the closed door.

Reid crept over and, with his back to the wall, gingerly turned the knob and pushed. The door creaked open. After two beats he rushed in, pointing the gun high then low, willing his eyes to adjust to the darkness, scanning the rows of clothing and the closet's shadowed recesses.

"Clear," he said, just loud enough for Kayla to hear.

"She's sleeping," Kayla whispered.

"Who is it?"

"I have no idea."

Reid approached the bed and looked down at the first stranger he'd ever seen.

Chapter 5

Reid stared at the stranger. Tangled brown hair partially covered her face. Closed eyes were sunken in dark hollows. Bony fingers with broken nails clutched the blanket. The faint odor of rotting flesh hung in the air. But she was breathing. She was alive.

The implications of this, of a stranger, crowded Reid's mind. Was she a Raider? How many more were there? Where had they come from? How were they living—was it better than back in the Mountain?

Kayla looked over at him, her eyes wide with astonishment, her mouth open like she wanted to say something but didn't have the words.

The dog moved and they both jumped.

"Jesus, did I suddenly forget everything I know?" Kayla pointed her gun at the woman.

"I don't think you have to worry." Reid held the back of his hand to the woman's cheek and wasn't surprised to find her feverish. She didn't react to his touch. "She's in bad shape."

"Still, be on guard while I check the rest of the house." Kayla left, closing the door behind her.

Reid holstered his weapon and opened the drapes, flooding the room with light. Then he thought better of making himself an easy target for the stranger's friends, and closed them again.

He returned to the woman. "Ma'am, wake up." He shook the woman's shoulder. When she didn't respond, he used his thumb and index finger to open her eye. The iris was rolled back showing yellowed sclera. There was no resistance against his fingers. He let go and the lids drifted closed.

"Wake up," he said firmly, rocking his knuckles against her sternum, but she didn't stir.

He was about to try again when he realized he hadn't checked for weapons. He'd never had to think like a soldier and a medic at the same time before.

Reid pulled away the bedding, exposing a body that was mere skin over bones. She shivered as he checked around her meager frame for weapons. The odor was worse now, and when he saw her swollen, discolored feet, he knew the source.

He didn't find any weapons, but if she'd had one Reid doubted she could lift it.

There was a click behind him, and he fumbled for his pistol. The door opened before he had his gun fully drawn. Thank God it was Kayla.

"House is clear," she said. "I'm pretty sure she's the only one who's been here. No other footprints but hers and the dog's. *What's that smell?*"

"Her feet are infected."

"Did you try to wake her?"

"She's unconscious." He squeezed the woman's fingertips to test capillary refill, then pulled up the skin on the back of her hand to check turgor. He pressed his fingers against the inside of her wrist, confirming an elevated heart rate. All signs of severe dehydration.

"Weapons?"

"I didn't see any." He kept his fingers on the woman's wrist, concerned about the fever.

"That doesn't make sense—no one goes around alone and unarmed. You checked her stuff?" Kayla gestured to a pack propped against the dresser.

He shook his head. He hadn't even noticed it.

"I'll do it," Kayla said.

Reid took off his own pack and pulled out his med kit.

Kayla drew in a sharp breath. "I found something."

"A gun?"

"No. *Look.*" Kayla held out her hand.

Reid gasped. Kayla was holding a grown apple.

Chapter 6

Seattle, Washington

Nikolai Petrov bit into an apple as he walked the deck of the *Diplomat*. Around him, his crew scrubbed, polished, loaded, and stowed in preparation for the next cruise. He suppressed a sigh thinking about the arrival of yet another contingent of self-important senators and their prudish wives. Captaining pleasure cruises for statesmen was not what he had in mind when he signed on, but his own future was not the reason he was there.

He'd been employed by the Democracy for a year, but it felt like ten. The three additional years he'd promised them seemed like an eternity. He needed a better attitude. He needed a week off.

As he tossed the apple core into a collection bin, he overheard his bosun haranguing a young crewman for over-tightening a screw. When Nikolai caught his eye, his tone softened. He wasn't a bad guy. None of them were. They were simply worn down by the unreasonable schedule imposed on them by the Democracy.

Nikolai strode to his office to meet with the Governor's envoy, clenching his fists so hard his nails cut into his palms. It was an ugly, unpleasant habit, but one that proved difficult to break when he was under stress, and his weekly meetings with the envoy always came with a certain amount of stress.

From a pragmatic standpoint, as well as a friendly one, Nikolai had made numerous and varied attempts to build a rapport with the woman. He'd joked, complimented, and bestowed gifts. He'd appealed to their shared heritage—their fathers were both survivors from the same Russian submarine. He'd asked her advice on a birthday gift for his daughter. He'd offered to take her sailing. But none of his usual charming overtures had broken through her icy demeanor. He had no illusion anything he said this time would make a difference.

Outside his office, he ran a hand over his face to make sure there were no bits of apple in his beard, then he smoothed his unruly hair and summoned the patience to deal with the bureaucrat waiting inside. Drawing himself up to his full six feet, he pushed open the door and entered his office. A quick appraisal revealed no surprises. The angular woman stood beside his desk wearing her customary starched white blouse and gray skirt, the matching jacket tidily draped over a chair. Her unadorned hands clutched a briefcase, which he knew held the paperwork for the cruise along with the walking shoes she'd stowed when slipping on her ever-modest gray pumps.

Nikolai smiled broadly. "Good afternoon, Deputy Chief Svetskaya. How are you today?" He didn't bother extending his hand, as she'd be as unlikely to shake his as to offer him use of her first name.

"I'm well. And you, Captain Petrov?" Her melodic voice hinted at something human beneath the rigid exterior.

"I'm dandy," he said, hoping it didn't sound as sarcastic as he felt.

He pulled out a chair for her and she sat, briefcase perched on her knees while she reached inside for the manifest. Nikolai sunk into his chair on the opposite side of the desk.

"Captain, I have the documents for your signature, as well as copies for your records." She followed her script precisely as she held out two manila folders.

Nikolai was trying to decide whether to broach the subject of crew-rest, when something inside him shifted. Instead of taking the paperwork, he leaned back in the chair. "Deputy Chief, we have a problem."

"*Chevo?*" Her brow furrowed over her cold gray eyes.

"I must postpone this week's cruise due to safety concerns." He wasn't sure where the words came from, but they felt right as they rolled off his tongue. It wasn't exactly a lie. Exhausted crewmen weren't the safest sailors.

The Deputy Chief's face showed genuine shock. "*Nye govori.* That is not acceptable. Three senators and their families are scheduled to board in less than twenty-four hours."

"Would you have them sail in unsafe conditions?"

"I'm certain whatever it is can be fixed in time."

"But *I'm* certain it cannot. I'll go to the coast today to consult a specialist about the problem. I require the full crew for that. You can expect our return in one week, fit to sail."

Nikolai wished he could read the woman's thoughts because her face held no expression whatsoever. He'd made a statement, not a request.

With no request to deny, she might simply fire him. She had that power.

The silence stretched. He grew queasy knowing Tatiana could be summarily dismissed from University based on what this woman said next. He had gambled his daughter's future without first calculating the odds. Now he feared he was about to regret it.

Chapter 7

Colorado Springs

"Is that really an apple?" Reid asked.

"There's other stuff, too." Kayla pulled a baggie from the woman's pack and sniffed the contents. "These are nuts, but they don't smell rancid. Think they could be newly grown? And feel these." She thrust a bag of something orange at him.

"Carrots? I think they're carrots." Reid couldn't believe it. "They're *hard*. These have to be grown."

"Do you know what this means?" Kayla's face blossomed into a smile. "Someone did it! Someone got seeds to grow."

Reid opened the bag and smelled the unfamiliar earthy scent of what could only be freshly grown carrots, and still he could scarcely let himself believe it. Grown food meant no scurvy, no malnutrition, no more unnecessary deaths like Bethany's.

Kayla shook the woman by the arm. "Hey, where did you get this food?"

"Let me try." Reid rocked his knuckles against the woman's sternum, harder this time. "Ma'am, open your eyes. I need you to wake up."

She was unresponsive.

Reid took her wrist to check her pulse and it was cool to the touch. He thought her fever had broken, then realized he'd left the blankets off. He covered her and checked her temp in the crook of her arm—still burning up. "*Damn*." It had been a long time since he'd made such a rookie mistake.

"What is it?"

"She's shocky. Probably septic from the infection in her feet, and I've made things worse, if anything."

"Pull it together, Reid. We have to find out where she got the food."

Reid went to the foot of the bed and lifted the blanket. "I need more light."

Kayla flung open the curtains.

"Is that safe?" he asked.

"At this point I'd welcome another stranger, as long as he was conscious. But I didn't see evidence of anyone besides her and the dog."

Reid squatted to inspect the woman's feet. The swelling had burst the skin in several places, and the fissures were black with necrosis, oozing blood-tinged pus. The smell was so noxious he had to fight back vomit. "I've never seen anything this bad."

"What do you need? Water? Bandages?" Kayla handed him his med kit.

He racked his brain for an option that wouldn't be an automatic death sentence. Everything he was capable of doing himself would kill the woman as dead as leaving the infection untreated. No matter what he did, without antibiotics she would die. Soon.

"She needs antibiotics and surgery. Probably amputation. She needs Doc."

"We can't take her back to the Mountain. Even if we kept the food a secret, Vega's people would still think she was a Raider. You know what they'd do."

"I know. Besides, she wouldn't survive the trip. We need Doc to come here."

"I don't trust him. What about your grandmother? I don't know for sure, but I'd bet tours she has a stash of antibiotics."

"You know where my grandparents are?"

"I'm sorry Brian and I couldn't tell you."

Reid pushed aside the shock and sting for now. "How far are they? Farther than going back to the Mountain?"

"Yeah, almost twice as far."

Reid thought about it, weighing the odds. His grandmother had become almost as skilled a surgeon as Doc, but the chances she'd have antibiotics seemed slim—the whole city had been scoured and all the meds taken back to the infirmary. Any drugs his grandmother took with her when she left the Mountain two years ago would likely be gone by now.

He shook his head. "We can't risk it. We have to get Doc."

"I can get antibiotics out of the Mountain, no problem. But I can't get Doc out without Vega knowing."

"My father can. Go straight to him and tell him everything. He'll keep our secret and help you smuggle out Doc. We can trust him."

"No way. Your father *is* the church. He condemns people who even talk about growing food. I know he's your dad, but in this he's the enemy."

"You're wrong, Kay. He knows about Brian trying to grow food."

"What?"

"Enough people have died. Show my dad the apple. I know he'll help us."

Chapter 8

Seattle, Washington, aboard the Diplomat

"Captain Petrov," Deputy Chief Svetskaya said. "You have been with the Democracy for sixty-one weeks."

Nikolai braced himself for the dismissal that was coming.

"And during that time," she continued, "you've had no schedule disruptions for illness, injury, or mechanical problems."

"That's correct." Where was she going with this?

"It appears the State may have been shortsighted expecting the *Diplomat* to operate year-round. I will submit a requisition today for regular downtime once per year."

"Once per quarter would be my preference, Deputy Chief," Nikolai said, seizing the opportunity. "But I'm grateful for any downtime you can contract."

"Your input is appreciated, Captain, for who knows the ship's needs more intimately than you? I will appeal for a maintenance mandate of once per quarter."

Nikolai felt as if the sun had broken through the clouds after a month of rain. "Thank you, Deputy Chief."

She nodded. Her posture was stiff as ever, her demeanor still chilly, but her mouth had softened. It wasn't a smile, but clearly she was not one hundred percent bureaucrat.

After Nikolai escorted her to the dock, he ordered the crew to muster on the aft deck, then left them to wonder why they'd been summoned while he fetched Cook. He swung open the galley door, breathing in the powerful aroma of chili tea steeping, octopus simmering, and rat frying.

Cook's grand form was bent over a tub of fish. Nikolai swatted her behind and braced himself as she whipped around. He felt the whiff of air on his cheek as she stopped her meaty hand mid-slap.

"Captain Nikolai, you sly fox." Cook batted ridiculously long lashes and smoothed her upswept hair.

"I can't help myself, Finola," he said, wrapping his arms around her girth and planting a kiss on her powdered cheek. "I have a weakness for Skokomish women."

"Women? There are others? Show me these *dushuyay*." She shook her fist.

"There's no one but you. I daresay you are enough woman to equal any three others."

"Only three? I must be getting thin." She winked. "What can I do for you, Captain? Besides stoking the lusty fire in your loins."

"I want you and your staff to join us on deck. Bring a keg."

"You scoundrel. It's barely midday." She pinched his cheek and bellowed, "You heard the man!"

Cook's helper, Freia, stacked mugs on a tray while Denny—who Cook called "the dishes boy" even though he was in his forties—hefted a barrel onto his shoulder. Cook took off her limp apron, tugged at her turquoise dress, and patted at the tendrils that had escaped her hairpins.

"After you, Finola," Nikolai said, enjoying the sound of the name forbidden to all others.

"Wicked captain." Cook sauntered ahead, swaying her hips as wantonly as he'd seen.

He was sure she could tell there was something bigger afoot than cracking a keg in the afternoon. She always could read him.

"Cider all around." Nikolai's order was answered with a cheer, and the crew didn't yet know the half of it. When everyone had mugs in hand, Nikolai continued. "After we drain these glasses, we hoist sails for Port Townsend and a week of rest and debauchery." He raised his cider. "To Corinne's!"

"To Corinne's!" The crew clinked their mugs, sloshing cider.

In less time than it took to pour one glass, all twelve were emptied. The crew scattered, shouting taunts and reminders, while Denny and the women gathered up the vestiges. Cook sang loudly in her native tongue, a rare occurrence that warmed Nikolai more than the cider. He whistled as he headed for the helm, looking forward to the delights that were Corinne's specialty.

The bath was almost too hot, a luxury Nikolai did not deny himself when there was opportunity, which was not often enough. Bubbles blanketed the wide porcelain tub with a fragrant froth. He leaned back and closed his eyes, letting his mind go blank as Lisette did wonderful things beneath the water.

"Niko," a strident voice called from the Carriage House door.

Nikolai heard Lisette's sharp intake of breath and the clip, clip, clip of high heels on the tile. He sighed and opened his eyes. Poor Lisette had her arms wrapped across her breasts and was keeping to herself.

The fire-haired woman at the edge of the tub was vibrant in a green Chanel suit.

"Hello, Madame Corinne," Lisette said in a shy voice.

"Nice of you to come see me when you landed, Niko," Corinne said.

"Hello, Mother," Nikolai said.

"You're looking well," Corinne said.

"Mother, we've discussed this. It's awkward when you visit unannounced. Don't let her intimidate you, Lisette. She'll leave in a moment and we'll lock the doors."

His mother appeared to ignore how uncomfortable she made Lisette, but Nikolai had seen her wink at the girl. It had helped some, though not enough for Lisette to resume her earlier activity. All for the best, really. Despite having grown up in a busy whorehouse, Nikolai didn't enjoy the prospect of onlookers. Particularly not when the onlooker was his mother.

"I'd like to speak with you," Corinne said.

"I look forward to that, Mother. Say brunch tomorrow?"

"Dinner tonight. Don't be late." Corinne clipped out.

"Now where were we?" Nikolai asked Lisette.

Lisette looked worried. "I should go."

Nikolai pulled her to him and nuzzled her neck with his whiskers. "I can be a little late."

"Are you sure?"

"Oh, I'm sure," he said, nibbling her earlobe, though he wasn't entirely sure. Something about his mother had been a little off, but he pushed the thought to the back of his mind and gave his full attention to Lisette. "I apologize for Corinne's interruption. Tell me, how can I make you forget she was ever here? After that, I will make you forget she even exists."

Chapter 9

Colorado Springs

Reid had done everything he could think of to keep the woman alive. Cool compresses to reduce the fever. Dripping sugar-water into her mouth. Rinsing her feet with a hydrogen peroxide solution. Nothing had made a difference, but he hadn't really expected it to.

Her body was shutting down from the sepsis. She wasn't going to make it until Kayla got back with Doc. If she did, even with surgery and the proper meds, she probably wouldn't last the night.

At least she wasn't suffering.

He washed his hands, then pulled a chair alongside the bed to do what he always did when an adult was dying. Whether they were conscious or not, he told them what was coming. He believed that on some level they could hear him, that it helped them pass more peacefully.

"Ma'am?" He took her hand. It was dry and papery. Already lifeless. "I'm sorry I don't know your name, and I'm sorry to have to tell you this, but you have an infection. A very serious infection. I've done everything I can to the best of my ability, but—*hey!*"

The dog had shoved its nose under his arm, forcing itself between him and the woman.

Reid had forgotten all about the dog. "Where have you been?" He wasn't sure if people talked to dogs, or if dogs had any way of understanding, but he supposed it wasn't any odder than talking to a person who was unconscious.

The dog whimpered and nuzzled the woman's arm, as if it was trying to wake her.

"I'm sorry, Dog. She's not going to wake up." On impulse, Reid touched the dog's back. It was so soft. He'd expected it to feel like the pelt of a rat. He stroked it, and the dog's tail swung back and forth in an arc.

The dog looked at him with liquid eyes that seemed to hold as much understanding and compassion as any human, then it nosed the woman's arm again, bumping and nudging her while issuing a high-pitched whine.

"Can you understand me?" Reid asked it. "Do you know what's happening?"

"I'm dying."

Reid's gaze shot to the woman's face. "You're awake."

"If you can call it that," she rasped. "Come, Zeke. Up." She patted the bed.

The dog—Zeke—leapt onto the bed and lay with his body pressed alongside hers. She curled her arm around his neck, and he rested his head on her shoulder.

Reid realized he shouldn't be surprised. People near death sometimes had moments of lucidity, often to say goodbye to a loved one. Clearly, the woman loved the dog.

"My name's Reid. I'm a medic. I'm going to check your pulse." He slipped his fingers between her thin wrist and the dog's back. Her heart was beating even faster, spreading the infection throughout her body, letting it take hold in each of her vital systems.

"I'm dying," she said again. It wasn't a question.

Reid met her gaze and nodded. "Is there anything I can do to make you more comfortable? Are you cold? Are you in pain?"

"The pain's gone now." Her voice was a dry, throaty whisper. "Angels took it away."

Reid had heard this before. It meant she didn't have long. "Ma'am, where did you come from? Where did you get the apple?"

"Zeke brought you to me. The angels want you to hear my confession. There's not much time."

She was right. She didn't have much time left, and he felt bad robbing her of her last moments, but she wasn't the only one running out of time. "I'm sorry, but I have to ask. My people don't have grown food—"

She raised her hand, stopping him. "Come closer."

He slid the chair until it touched the bed, then took the hand she offered. She pulled him toward her until he was leaning over the dog, looking directly into her clear, hazel eyes.

She drew a breath. "I'm Cumorah. From the City of Angels."

Chapter 10

Port Townsend, Washington

Nikolai arrived in the formal dining room alone wearing the pressed shirt he'd found hanging on the Carriage House doorknob. He adjusted his tie, reflecting on how he'd much rather have dined in his own clothing—or in no clothing at all—in his room with Lisette. Ordinarily, he might have begged off, insisting his mother wait until morning. But her demeanor had nagged at him, so he stood waiting behind his chair in her dining room.

His mother breezed into the room. Now he knew something was on her mind—she normally kept him waiting at least five minutes.

"Niko, darling." Corinne extended her hand to be clasped and her cheek to be kissed.

Nikolai dutifully clasped then kissed. "Mother, I didn't think it possible, but you look even lovelier now than you did in the green Chanel."

She smiled, her fingers grazing the silk of the black cocktail dress. He held her chair for her, then returned to his end of the table, appraising her expression as he took his seat. He could usually read her mood by her eyes. They were invariably sparkling with joy or flashing with anger. He'd rarely seen them smoky and worried as they were now.

"I'm glad you're here, Niko." She rang the silver bell beside her empty wineglass.

"You're back in wine?" Nikolai's mouth watered at the thought of a good merlot.

"A delightful man from Tacoma brought some bottles from a decent cellar he came upon. I think tomorrow we should invite people for wine and dancing. I might even be persuaded to open a magnum of champagne."

"Champagne?"

"Of course we won't know if it's good until we open it."

"Drinking and dancing? You read my mind, Mother. My crew is in desperate need of frivolity. But save the champagne for a special occasion. The men are happy with cider, and you know you don't need these trappings for me." He gestured to the table adorned with more crystal and china than he'd use in a week. While he was grateful that Corinne's predilection for formality had prepared him for his State role, his personal tastes were simple.

"You think this is for you?" Her eyebrows arched and she laughed gently. "There's another man in the family now who thrives on my— what did you once call them? My 'haughty, pretentious dinner parties with no cause, purpose, or redeeming value.'"

"*Chevo?* Did I really say that?" He was puzzled, but not about the barely-recalled insults he'd issued as a teenager. He wondered about the man his mother considered "family." She'd never even considered his father family, though she had loved him.

"Ah, here's our wine, delivered by the very gentleman who appreciates my pomp and circumstance," she said with the first real smile that night.

Nikolai looked toward the entry, anxious to see who had accomplished what so many had tried before—to ensnare his mother's stalwartly independent spirit.

A boy strode into the room wearing a sharp black suit, a white towel draped over one arm. Nikolai recognized his nephew immediately, even though Josh had grown half a meter since he'd last seen him. He ached to leap from his chair and crush him in a hug, but he held back, waiting for Josh's reaction when he finally looked down the table.

"Madame." The boy made a slight bow to Corrinne. "I have a 1998 French merlot from the Mont Sainte Chapelle vineyard for your inspection."

"Very good, Joshua," Corinne said. "Why don't you pour a taste for my guest. I trust he will tell you more plainly than most if it's to his liking."

"As you wish, Madame." Josh turned and his eyes opened wide. "Uncle Niko!" All pretense vanished as he ran to the end of the table, setting down the wine at the last moment before Nikolai scooped him up.

"You've grown so much I almost didn't recognize you." Nikolai squeezed Josh tight, then released him.

"Grandma," Josh scolded. "Why didn't you tell me he was here?"

"And miss witnessing this? You know me better than that."

Corinne's face softened, a grandmother, not the mistress of the manor now.

"So this is the man who appreciates you, eh, Mother?" Nikolai was surprised to feel equal measures of relief and disappointment. He roughed Josh's slicked auburn locks. "You're quite handsome as a wine steward, but I was hoping you'd develop a yearning for the sea and become my apprentice."

"Like Will?" Josh's eyes sparkled, but Corinne's darkened.

"Yes, like Will." Nikolai flashed a smile at Josh while noting the abrupt change in Corinne's mood. He should have guessed. Will was probably at the root of another scandal. It wouldn't surprise him if his son were the sole source of Corinne's tension.

"I may have a nose for wine, Uncle Niko, but sailing's in my blood."

"That's my boy. I'll be expecting you when you turn fourteen, if you're not too busy being a diplomat or reinventing airplanes by then."

"Fourteen? I want to come now."

"Fourteen. Now, can I try that wine? I'm starting to wonder if your grandmother got taken and it's a bottle of vinegar." Nikolai winked.

Josh poured the glass one-quarter full, neatly rotating the decanter and catching the lone drop with his towel. "So far, only one bottle from this cellar has turned. Judging from the smell, I mean the bouquet, I'd wager a dozen silk scarves this is still good. If you swirl it, you'll see it has good legs. I trust you'll appreciate the woodsy flavor as well."

Nikolai tried to appear serious as he swirled his glass. Josh looked to Corinne for approval and received it in the form of a nod.

"How do you find it, sir?" Josh asked.

Nikolai held the glass below his nose and wafted the air across the bowl. "Very fine." He tipped the glass and touched the wine to his lips. "Very fine indeed. Not a hint of vinegar."

"Can I see you later, Uncle Niko? I've been practicing chess like you taught me, and I'm getting pretty good."

"Absolutely. Tomorrow morning we'll have a match."

"Fresh!" Josh ran across the room, shadow-boxing with the air. "See you first thing in the morning, Uncle Niko."

"Not before nine," Nikolai shouted as Josh disappeared through the doorway.

"He forgot my wine," Corinne said.

"I'd be happy to oblige." Nikolai carried the decanter to Corinne's end of the table and poured with panache, using a napkin as his *torchon de sommelier.* "Your wine, Madame. I trust it will be to your liking."

"You do a fine imitation of the boy."

"We had the same tutor." Nikolai returned to his seat and topped off his glass. "He's a great kid, huh?"

"I'm going to miss him."

"What do you mean?"

"I assumed you came home because you'd heard. Your sister is moving to San Francisco and taking Josh with her."

"Wait, what happened to Marseille taking over the business when you retire?" This was a whole new set of worries, but at least it had nothing to do with Will.

"A rebellion of sorts, though she's awfully old for it. She thinks I don't know she's been conspiring with that lot of colonists. I expect she'll break the news to me soon, now that the secret preparations have been completed."

"What are you going to do?"

"I don't know. I'm too old and too tired to run all this for much longer." She gestured to the lavish furnishings surrounding them, but she didn't mean the material things. They were never as important as the women and children who relied on her for their wellbeing.

"Nonsense, Mother. You're not old, and you look half your age at that. Even so, do you want me to speak to Marseille?"

"It won't do any good. What I need is a viable replacement. I've been thinking of little else since I learned of Marseille's defection, but there's no one with the head and the heart for it. Except your daughter, of course."

"We've been over this," Nikolai warned.

"But—"

"I'll be here a week. We'll figure out who to groom as your replacement. But leave Tatiana out of it."

"She'd be perfect."

"It's not what she wants."

"She doesn't know what she wants. She changes her mind like the wind."

"Not anymore." Nikolai never would have indentured himself to the Democracy if Tatiana weren't committed to studying at the University. "She's made her choice, and she's sticking to it. I wouldn't have chosen politics for her area of focus, but if that's what she wants, I support it."

"Politics?"

"Be glad of it. Some day she'll be our voice in the Democracy. I wouldn't be surprised if she fully legitimizes what we do here on the fringes. Your services, and bootlegging too."

"Don't tell me you're fool enough to believe she's gone to Lost Angeles for political reasons. She got Will to take her down there to look for seeds."

"What?" Why would Tatiana and Will have sailed straight into danger when they *knew* the seed bank in Southern California was destroyed?

"You didn't know?" Corinne asked.

"Of course I didn't know! Why the hell didn't anyone tell me? Why didn't you stop them?"

"I don't see why you're so upset. Will assured us he could handle the pirates. I'm sure everything's fine."

"Maybe I can catch them before it's too late. When did they leave?"

Corinne frowned, swirling the wine in her glass. "I think a month ago, more or less."

"A *month?* Jesus, why am I only learning about this now?" Nikolai stormed to the door, calculating how long it would take him and Creighton to get a ship under sail, and trying not to imagine what they'd find when they arrived in Lost Angeles.

Chapter 11

Colorado Springs

"Landers!"

Reid opened his eyes, surprised he'd fallen asleep.

"At attention!" One of Vega's soldiers, Beckum, stood in the doorway holding a lantern.

Reid came to his feet. Vega entered, followed by Kayla. Kayla's mouth was bloodied and one eye was swollen. Vasquez, another of Vega's men, had an M4 at Kayla's back.

"What happened?" Reid asked, but Kayla wouldn't look at him.

"She did what you said," Peregrine said, coming through the door with another lantern. "But I couldn't keep it from Commander Vega. Not something like this."

"*Dad, no.*" Reid's body felt hollow, like his insides had shriveled up and turned to ash.

"You had to know what I would do." Peregrine said. "It's for the greater good, son."

"Lieutenant Landers," Vega said, "I find it interesting you thought your father would keep such a secret from me."

Reid wanted to lash out, to reveal all the secrets Peregrine knew. But he held his tongue.

"Your father's complicity will be dealt with later," Vega continued. "Along with your treason."

"Renata, please," Peregrine said. "His actions were misguided, but not treasonous."

"Stay out of this, Bishop," Vega said. "This is a military matter."

"But Renata—"

"Shut him up," Vega said to a hulking silhouette in the doorway.

Leigh stepped into the lantern light. "You want I should take him outside, Commander?"

"No, he's going to watch. But if he makes another sound, shoot

45

him."

"You can't do that," Reid blurted.

"I can't?" Vega's eyes widened in mock surprise. "Who's going to stop me, you? Broken little Kayla? Now that I have evidence of Raiders, I can do whatever the hell I want."

She was right. A stranger gave her everything she wanted. With hard evidence of a "military threat," the balance of power shifted. The church was required to give full control to the military. To Vega.

"Commander," Beckum said from the other side of the bed. "The Raider's dead."

"Then Lieutenant Landers will tell me what I need to know."

"I don't have anything to say." Earlier, he'd begun to feel guilty about keeping the stranger and the grown food a secret. But now there was no way he was going to tell Vega anything. She'd never intended to help the stranger. She hadn't even brought the doctor.

"I suggest you rethink that, Lieutenant." Vega raised her Beretta. There was a click as she released the safety. "Where are the other Raiders?"

"I said I have nothing to tell you." He could almost see Vega's blood pressure rise. There was too much tension in the room, too many guns. He should say something to defuse the situation, but he refused to kowtow like his father.

"You *will* tell me," Vega said. "Everyone has a breaking point, and I'll find yours."

"It won't do any good," Kayla said. "She didn't say anything. She was unconscious."

"Get her out of here," Vega told Vasquez.

"My pleasure." A sick grin spread across Vasquez' face. He butted Kayla with the M4. "You and me, outside."

"Screw you," Kayla said, standing her ground.

"Bitch!" Vasquez backhanded her, and she staggered back.

"Kay!" Reid started toward her, but was stopped by the muzzle of Vega's Beretta.

"Wait," Vega barked. "We've struck a nerve. Whatever you were going to do outside, do it here."

"No! Stop this," Peregrine shouted.

A shot sounded and Peregrine crumpled to the ground, a small hole in his white shirt.

A primal cry came from deep inside as Reid tackled Vega, propelling her backward. They collided with Leigh, and the three of them fell in a tangle. Reid grabbed Vega's wrist and slammed it against the ground to dislodge the gun. The gun fired as it flew from her hand.

Kayla screamed. A snarling flash of black fur came from the shadows. From the corner of his eye, Reid saw the dog barrel into Vasquez, knocking him from where he sat astride Kayla.

Reid wrestled with Leigh for control of his gun. Leigh squeezed off several rounds, and Vega shrieked, grabbing her leg. Reid wrenched the gun away and cracked Leigh on the head with it. Leigh went limp. Reid dropped the gun, nauseated by what he'd done.

Vega writhed on the ground, clutching her knee to her chest. Reid knew he should tend to her, but not before he helped Kayla. He stood and turned, but Beckum was there, gun raised. *Shit*. He'd forgotten about Beckum.

A shot went off.

Reid looked down at his chest wondering why he felt no pain.

Then Beckum's uniform shirt blossomed red, his face went slack, and his knees buckled.

Kayla held a knife in one hand and Vega's Beretta in the other. She'd shot Beckum. Now she had the gun pointed at Vega.

"Don't, Kay," he said, his voice muffled by the ringing in his ears.

"*It's for the best.*" Kayla sounded like she was underwater.

"This is never the answer." Reid held out his hand. "Please, give me the gun."

"Everything would be different with her gone."

"I know." With Vega out of the picture, people could live outside the Mountain without the fictional threat of Raiders. They'd be free to speak up against leadership, even try to grow food. "But not like this." He stepped between Kayla and Vega and took the gun.

The disgust on Kayla's face was plain, even in the lantern light. "Then we run." She turned her glare on Vega. "Don't move. Don't even breathe."

Reid followed Kayla to the door, then looked back at the carnage. His father. Beckum dead in a pool of blood. Vasquez staring at the ceiling with unseeing eyes. Leigh unconscious. Vega grimacing, hugging her leg to her chest.

"Reid, we have to *go,*" Kayla said.

"Don't try to come after us," he told Vega, then followed Kayla into the night.

Reid didn't know how long they'd been running or how far they'd gone when Kayla stopped. She took her canteen from the clip on her belt and drank, then handed it to him.

"I had the chance to change our future. Everyone's future," she said. "Without Vega and your father, everything could be different."

"My father." Reid flashed to images he didn't want to remember. With horror he realized— "I didn't check. What if he was still alive?"

"He was dead before he hit the ground. You know that."

"But I didn't check. I should have checked." Reid's eyes prickled and his throat constricted. He knew his father was dead.

"We have to keep moving. They'll be coming."

She stepped into the moonlight and Reid thought that, even with blood crusted at the corner of her mouth and one eye swollen shut she looked beautiful.

"You should have let me kill her," she said.

Chapter 12

Port Townsend, Washington

Nikolai knew that his former partner, Simon Creighton, wouldn't arrive in the dark. Still, he paced the pier, watching the mouth of the inlet for the familiar silhouette of the *Juggernaut*. He'd come to the docks straight from Corinne's, and had been there all night getting soaked to the bone by a persistent drizzle and more enraged with every step.

Inside there would be dry clothes and a hot cup of tea, but he refused to step foot in his old office and see everything he'd given up for Tatiana to go to University. He couldn't face how casually she'd tossed aside his sacrifice and destroyed her future, at least not until he knew she was safe.

And his son? Nikolai's cheeks heated despite the cool rain. Will was oblivious to danger, ignorant of his own shortcomings, his own mortality. He'd risked not only his own life, but the lives of everyone else naïve enough to sail with him, including Tatiana. No, he couldn't think about Will now either, or how he'd throttle him if the boy made it back to land alive.

Instead, he focused his rage on his old business partner. Nikolai loved Creighton like a brother. But he'd entrusted him with his only son, and what had Creighton done? Stood by and watched as Will sailed into pirate-infested waters, taking Tatiana with him. For all Nikolai knew, Creighton had encouraged them to go, but more likely he'd been too caught up in his own desires to notice what they were doing. The thought twisted Nikolai's gut, and he seethed as he paced, scarcely aware of the chill and the blood trickling from his clenched fists.

At morning's first blush, the *Juggernaut* sailed into view. Even if Nikolai hadn't been expecting it, he'd know the schooner anywhere. He and Creighton had spent eighteen months restoring her, and he knew every inch and every nuance of that ship even after twenty years. He remembered their maiden voyage like it was yesterday—the smell of new varnish, the creaking of the masts and hull, the feel of the sheets in his hands and the sea spray in his face. More than that, he recalled the sense of accomplishment, the promise of future adventure, and the bond of brotherhood he shared with Creighton.

But Creighton had severed that bond.

Now as the *Juggernaut* glided up, Nikolai's muscles quivered and his body hummed. Creighton was going to pay.

"Niko, it *is* you," Creighton boomed as he bounded onto the dock, hand outstretched. "I thought I recognized your nervous pacing."

Nikolai hit him, a hard right to the jaw.

Creighton recovered quickly, holding his hands up in supplication. "Jeez, brother."

"Where are Will and Tatiana?"

"That's why you're ticked? Seriously, I was going to tell you. In fact, as soon as we offloaded, I was planning to find you. You can ask anyone." Creighton gestured to the half dozen crewmen who had gathered on the *Juggernaut's* deck.

Nikolai grabbed him by the jacket and jerked him closer, so close he could almost taste the bitter coffee on Creighton's breath. "I don't need excuses, *zhopa*. I need answers."

"Calm down, brother," Creighton said, pushing him away. "Can't we take this inside?"

"You're not my brother," Nikolai said in a low tone. He glanced at the crew lining the deck rail. "Fine. My office. Two minutes."

"Uh, Niko—"

"*Two minutes.*" Nikolai strode to the building.

At the door Nikolai stripped off his sodden shirt, tie, shoes, and socks, and walked in wearing only khakis. He grabbed a towel from the kitchenette and dried his beard and hair as he headed down the hall. Earlier he'd wanted to avoid his office, but now he was anxious to get the flannel shirt he kept in his desk. And his father's pipe. Even though Nikolai didn't smoke, there were many times the past year he'd regretted leaving it behind.

"Kakógo chërta?" What the hell?

His office was as he'd left it, except for the nautical charts spread on the desk and the man leaning over them.

The man looked up and straightened to a height greater than Nikolai expected. "Captain Petrov. I'm Kennedy Davis."

"I know who you are." Nikolai felt more than a little uncomfortable half-naked in front of the president's son. "What are you doing here?"

"I see you two have met," Creighton said, entering the room.

"Simon," Nikolai growled. "Tell me what's going on."

"This," Creighton said, indicating Kennedy, "is Tatiana's boyfriend."

"*What?* No." Nikolai shook his head. He hadn't heard correctly. Tatiana didn't have a boyfriend, but if she did, it wouldn't be a vacuous playboy ten years her senior.

"I would prefer to meet you under better circumstances, sir," Kennedy said. "But I'm glad you decided to come."

"What do you mean, *decided to come?*"

"I asked Mr. Creighton to invite you to assist in the rescue mission. There's no one more knowledgeable about pirates, and I expect we'll need every advantage to get Tatiana and Will back safely."

Nikolai turned away from the smug bastard—who was doing a decent job of sounding sincere—and glared at Creighton.

Creighton looked pleased with himself. "Corinne didn't tell you about Kennedy? I guess she doesn't know everything that goes on after all."

More likely she knows but didn't want to face my reaction, Nikolai thought. He turned back to Kennedy. "Tatiana and Will are my responsibility. I'll go after them. Now vacate my office."

"Of course." Kennedy came from behind the desk and stepped aside for Nikolai to pass.

"*How, Niko?*" Creighton asked. "How are you going after them? Will sailed on the *Belle,* so by my count you have no ship."

Nikolai couldn't believe what he was hearing. He clenched his teeth, trying to maintain his composure as he shrugged into the flannel shirt he'd pulled from the drawer. "Simon," he said, having trouble keeping his voice low. "You should be begging my forgiveness and insisting I take the *Juggernaut.* She's as much mine as yours."

"We both know that's bull."

"You owe me. I'm taking her."

"Over my dead body." Creighton leaned across the desk. The cool, laidback persona had fallen away revealing the scrapper at his core.

Creighton was no match for him, but Nikolai knew he would never back down. And no matter what happened between them, Nikolai wouldn't take his life, which was what he'd have to do to take the *Juggernaut.*

51

"Never mind." Nikolai found the oilskin pouch that held his father's pipe and slid it into his breast pocket. "I don't need the *Juggernaut* or anything else from you."

Nikolai edged past Creighton and out the door.

"Captain Petrov," Kennedy said. "If I may—"

"I don't need anything from you either," Nikolai called. "Except to stay of out my way."

Nikolai went down the hall and out the front door, leaving his former friend and his soggy shoes behind. He was going to sail the *Diplomat* south and bring his children back. To hell with it being the State's ship, to hell with the consequences.

Chapter 13

Manitou Springs, Colorado

Reid looked over his shoulder, surprised to find the sun peeking above the dead city behind them. He hadn't noticed the sky getting lighter.

"We're almost there," Kayla said.

His legs were leaden, but he kept moving. Soon he'd see his grandparents. "I have to tell them about my dad. And about Brian."

"They know about Brian. They were with us when it happened."

"Wait." Reid grabbed Kayla's elbow. "They were with you?"

"Not now." She shrugged away and picked up the pace.

"I deserve to know." Reid hurried to catch up, then froze as he heard the unmistakable ratchet of a shotgun being cocked.

"Tinker, it's me," Kayla called.

"I know." Reid's grandfather stepped from behind a house, shotgun to his shoulder. "I'm not aiming at you. The mother of all rats is in the shadows behind you."

"Don't shoot. It's a dog," Kayla said.

"You're shitting me." Tinker lowered his gun.

Reid turned to see the dog bounding toward them. "Where'd he come from?" he asked as the dog stopped beside Kayla, tail swinging wildly.

"It's been following us," Kayla said. "I thought you knew."

"I never thought I'd see the day," Tinker said. "A dog. *Damn.* Grandma will never believe it. Come here, you two."

Tinker hugged Kayla with one arm, his shotgun hanging from his other hand. He released her and pulled Reid into an embrace. Reid hugged him hard, inhaling of his aftershave.

"Pops," Reid said, his voice cracking with emotion. It had been too long since he'd seen his grandfather.

"It's damn good to see you kids. Damn good." Tinker sniffed. "Let's get inside. Then you can tell me and your grandma how you came about a dog, and what-all happened to you. She'll want to take a look at those cuts and bruises."

Reid swallowed, wanting to unburden himself of the news about his father, feeling it would be wrong to keep it from Tinker. But then he nodded. He might as well tell both his grandparents at the same time. "Come on, Zeke," he called to the dog.

"That's his name? Zeke?" Tinker asked.

"How do you know its name?" Kayla asked.

"The woman told me."

"She woke up? She talked to you?" Kayla exclaimed. "What did she say? Did she tell you where she got the grown food?"

"Whoa, hold up!" Tinker said. "Someone had grown food?"

"A stranger," Reid said. "She had carrots and nuts and an apple. And I know where she got them."

Chapter 14

Port Townsend, Washington, aboard the Diplomat

"Please understand," Nikolai told his confused crew. "I'm taking the ship, but I'm not asking you to come with me. I'll make arrangements to get you back to the capital, and I'll sign a statement saying you were not complicit in my actions."

Olexi, the First Mate, stepped forward. "Requesting permission to accompany you."

Nikolai nodded. Olexi was a good sailor, and a solid, loyal shipmate. The only crewman he considered a friend, besides Finola. Nikolai had hoped Olexi would sail with him.

The other men had families and would go back to the Democracy. He saw their apprehension and regretted what his actions would put them through. Despite his best efforts to clear them, they'd still face interrogations and sanctions, then be split up and assigned to new jobs. It was a shame because they'd become a real crew, but it couldn't be helped.

"Excuse me, Captain Petrov."

Nikolai turned. *Kennedy.*

There was a collective gasp from the crew. They were either shocked that an outsider had come aboard unnoticed or stunned by who the outsider was. Probably both.

"I'm sorry to intrude," Kennedy said. "But I'd like a word with you, Captain."

"I'm on a tight deadline," Nikolai said in a flat tone, then turned back to his crew. "Those of you not coming with me, pack up your personals. You'll be Corinne's guests tonight and can return to the capital tomorrow."

"Sir," Kennedy said. "If you'd belay that order for a moment, I have an alternative that may be less . . . detrimental."

Nikolai held back the retort that sprung to mind. Boarding his ship uninvited and then countermanding his order? He would throw the arrogant *parshivec* overboard except he saw how Kennedy's words raised hope in the crew. Nikolai decided he could agree to hear what he had to say without losing face. "Crewmen, belay that order while you check the riggings and fittings."

The crew dispersed, oddly silent. Nikolai headed for his office with Kennedy in his wake. At the door, Nikolai stepped aside for Kennedy to enter, noticing again how tall the man was. It was petty, but it rankled to have to look up to meet his eyes.

Nikolai remained standing. "I don't have much time."

"I'll be to the point," Kennedy said, also forgoing a chair. "We both know what it means—for you and your crew—if you sail south in the *Diplomat*. I'd like to offer an alternative that may be more palatable, at least to your crew and the government."

"You've got my attention."

"For the past week, I've been readying my boat to depart for Lost Angeles. My crew is well prepared but for one concern—pirates. I need someone with the expertise and experience to deal with them. That's why I asked Mr. Creighton to convey my invitation to you."

"The pirates are your only concern?" Nikolai laughed. "You'll never make it into pirate territory on a Hobie Cat. You need a real boat to nav those waters. Maybe you could talk to your daddy and get us permission to use the *Diplomat*."

"That won't be necessary. The *Emancipation* will be ready to sail tomorrow."

"The *Emancipation?*"

"A thirty-one meter Philippe Briand. Sloop-rigged. Not only fit for the open sea, but fast. And she's not government property." Kennedy smiled. "She's mine."

"What's the catch?"

"No catch. She's stocked and watered, and my crew is conducting the final checks now. We'll leave tomorrow morning."

"I can leave on the *Diplomat* within the hour."

Kennedy raised his eyebrows, and Nikolai realized he'd been caught in an overstatement. The *Diplomat* could be ready in an hour, but he couldn't sail without a crew. He'd lose precious time assembling men, and more time still to the inefficiencies of an untried team, plus several additional hours to gather up the necessary bribes now that he couldn't get them from Creighton.

"All other things being equal," Kennedy said, "at her top efficiency, the *Diplomat* is no match for the *Emancipation*. Even with a half-day head start, we'd overtake you before the California border."

Nikolai needed to pace, but there was no room. He clenched his fists, barely registering the pain in his palms. Worry was clouding his mind, and he needed to think clearly, to reason this out logically.

A faster ship with an established crew. Little or no repercussions for the crew of the *Diplomat*—they could return to the capital and be sailing under a new captain within a week.

More importantly, he'd be present to mitigate the damage Kennedy was certain to cause in pirate waters. The northern pirate king would not appreciate Kennedy's blue-blooded naiveté, and the king's cooperation was essential, especially if they had to deal with the southern pirates. A shiver ran up Nikolai's spine at the thought.

He met Kennedy's gaze. "I'll go with you. But we leave today."

Kennedy held his stare. "No, sir. Tomorrow."

Nikolai wasn't sure how he felt about Kennedy not backing down. It was mostly annoyance, but woven through it was a thread of respect. After a tense, silent moment he acquiesced. "Fine. Tomorrow." He gestured to the door, indicating Kennedy should leave. He'd give him this, but he wasn't going to grovel.

Chapter 15

Manitou Springs, Colorado

Tinker ushered them into a two-story house that looked no different on the outside than all the other houses on the street.

"Sarah, honey? We've got company," he called.

"What mischief are you up to, Tinker Landers?"

Reid smiled at the sound of his grandmother's voice. He rushed to her as she entered the living room.

"Oh my goodness," she said hugging him tight. "Oh, I've missed you." She released him and looked him up and down. "I think you've grown since I saw you last."

Reid laughed. "I think I'm done growing, Grandma."

"A man can still grow at nineteen. Don't you look at me like that. It's possible." She grinned but her expression grew serious when she opened her arms to Kayla. "Come here, darlin'." She squeezed Kayla, then held her at arm's length. "What happened to you? Let me look in the light."

"I'm okay," Kayla said as Sarah ushered her to a brown tweed sofa by the front window.

"Lordy, who's this?" Sarah exclaimed, seeing the dog by the door.

"That's Zeke," Tinker said, like they saw dogs every day. "Kids brought him along."

"Any more surprises?" Sarah asked, crossing to the kitchen. She pulled some gauze and ointment from a box on the counter.

"Yeah, Reid," Kayla said. "Is there anything else you haven't told me?"

"Kay, I—"

"We were only walking all night," Kayla said. "You couldn't take one minute to mention the stranger woke up?"

"What on earth? What stranger?" Sarah asked, dabbing at Kayla's cuts with the gauze.

"We found a woman in the city," Reid said. "Zeke led us to her. He was her dog."

"Was?" Sarah asked.

Reid nodded. "She was septic. Kay went for Doc and antibiotics."

"I should have come here instead," Kayla said.

"You made the right choice, honey," Sarah said. "My antibiotics are long gone."

"It was the wrong choice," Reid said. "I wish I'd never sent Kayla. The stranger died before she got back."

"But not before she woke up and talked to you." Kayla glared at Reid.

"I was going to tell you. I was in shock from—" Reid swallowed the next words. It wasn't the time to say his dad was dead. "The woman told me her people live in 'the City of Angels' where they grow all kinds of food. They have lots of dogs, and other animals too. Chickens, pigs, monkeys, cows."

Reid's grandparents exchanged a glance.

"Sounds like she was delirious," Sarah said.

Tinker scratched his nose. "You're sure she said monkeys?"

"Yes, I'm sure. But what does it matter? She had grown food and she got it from somewhere."

"But where?" Kayla said. "How do we even know 'City of Angels' is a real place? Maybe she *was* delirious."

"Well," Reid said, meeting his grandfather's gaze, "thanks to Pops for telling me all those stories when I was little, I'm pretty sure she was talking about *Ellay*. Right, Pops?"

"That is the City of Angels," Tinker said. "Or it was, once upon a time."

"But monkeys?" Sarah pursed her lips.

"Why is that so much harder to believe than dogs or chickens?" Reid asked.

"Well, for one thing, they're not farm animals," Sarah said. "And, for another, they don't normally live in this part of the world."

"Hang on," Tinker said. "They could have come from a zoo or something, so don't jump to conclusions. The important thing is, the stranger had grown food. You did see it for yourselves, right? It wasn't wax or plastic?"

"We both saw it," Kayla said. "I touched the apple. I smelled it. I can't imagine how it could have been a fake."

"She had carrots that were hard as rocks—they had to be grown.

There was also this slimy stuff called aloe she had me put on her wounds."

"Then it don't matter what she *said*," Tinker said. "She could be crazy as a loon, but the grown food speaks for itself." A grin spread across his face. "What do you say we go to Ellay to check it out?"

"I don't know, I'll have to check my day planner." Sarah winked.

"California, here we come," Tinker sang out.

"How far is it, Pops?" Reid tried to picture it on a map. His legs ached from last night's hike, but he'd gladly climb the Rockies twice if it meant bringing back viable seeds. "You figure it will take us a month to get there?"

Tinker's grin broadened. "More like a couple of days."

"But California's clear over by the ocean, isn't it?" Reid asked.

"You two haven't told him about the Humvee," Sarah chided.

"A Humvee, like a *car?*" Reid asked.

"On the money!" Tinker rocked back on his heels. "We're *driving* to Ellay!"

"Seriously?" Of *course* his grandfather had never stopped trying to get a car running. He hadn't given up at the Mountain even after he'd been put in jail for it. "What's it run on? Does it burn garbage like in that movie you talked about? Or did you end up going solar?"

"I tried the garbage thing—total fiction. I did have some encouraging results with solar and wind power, and I'd probably still be tinkering around with those if it hadn't been for your grandma. She remembered something out at Schriever that changed everything."

"Schriever?" Reid asked. The name wasn't familiar.

"A little air base annex on the other side of Peterson. It wasn't that well-known even in the Before. I'd never been there. Most of their projects were above my clearance. I'd forgotten all about it until one day something jogged your gram's memory about work she'd done at Schriever in the Before, and she mentioned the warhead."

"As in a *bomb?*" Reid asked.

Tinker chuckled. "Come see for yourself."

"That can wait until later," Sarah said. "Take them upstairs so they can get washed up while I turn breakfast for two into a feast for four."

"I guess we've got our marching orders," Tinker said.

"We need two more chairs," Sarah said pointing at a small round table with a red plaid tablecloth flanked by two wooden chairs with matching cushions.

Tinker pushed open a swinging door and entered an adjoining room. "Those chairs should be here somewhere."

Reid followed him in and whistled. The room brimmed with shelves upon shelves of food and supplies.

"This is only part of what we have stored," Tinker said. "This would ordinarily be a formal dining room, but you know your grandmother. She always says you can't be too prepared. I don't see any chairs, though, do you?"

"Nope," Reid said, glancing around.

"Would have made sense to store them here, but the old brain doesn't work quite like it used to."

"Don't sell yourself short, Pops," Kayla said. "You're still the smartest man I know."

Tinker grinned at her. "Hey, there's Zeke." The dog was behind Kayla, peeking around her leg into the storage room. "C'mere, buddy. I bet you've got to widdle." Tinker crossed the storage area, pulled open a sliding glass door, and headed across the yard toward a long-dead tree. Zeke trotted after him like he'd been following Tinker his whole life.

Kayla wandered into the yard, avoiding Reid's eyes.

"Okay, do your business," Tinker said. "Not there!" Zeke was shooting a stream of liquid onto the barbeque stand.

Reid tried not to laugh.

"I guess I'll have to be more specific with future requests," Tinker grumbled. "All right, pull that door shut, Reid. We'll circle around to the back door. It's best to stay out of your grandmother's space while she's cooking."

As Reid followed Tinker around the back of the house, he was ambushed by the memory of Vega's attack. Unwillingly, he replayed it, hearing the gunshots, seeing his father fall. He knew he had to tell his grandparents, but the thought filled him with dread.

"Where'd that dog get to? Is he still with us?" Tinker asked, glancing back.

"Right behind Kayla," Reid said.

"Good. All right, let's head upstairs." Tinker opened a door onto a mudroom with a wooden staircase. They climbed to the second story, a cluster of rooms attached to a narrow hallway. Tinker pointed at the first doorway. "We use this bedroom for storage. The adjacent bathroom, too. The bathroom we use is at the end of the hall. Here's our reading room." He opened a door. "Root around and take whatever books you want for the trip."

Reid poked his head in. The room was cozy with two easy chairs centered on a braided rug. Each wall was covered floor-to-ceiling with full bookcases, and he wondered how many of the books Tinker had read.

Tinker waved his hand at the doorway across the hall. "This is where your grandma and I sleep. Not flashy, but comfy." There was a large bed, nightstand, dresser, and more full bookcases.

"So many books," Reid said.

"Of course. Time to read is the greatest gift of the New World. In the Before, no one had time. Now I finish a book every other day."

"Was all this here from the Before?" Reid asked.

"The furniture was," Tinker said. "Can you imagine us two old folks trying to move beds? All we brought was the food and books and such, which was enough for us, believe me."

The next door was shut. Tinker rattled the knob and swung it open. "This is Kayla and Brian's room. Been closed up awhile. Hope it's not too stuffy." The bed was topped with three fluffy pillows and a pink quilt. A table held a lamp with a glass shade. There was no dresser, but the far wall held another stocked bookcase. "I guess I'll leave you two to settle in."

"Oh, we're not together, Pops," Reid said.

"Sorry, I wasn't sure." Tinker looked uncomfortable. "I knew Vega and your father had been pushing some wacky customs."

Reid winced at the mention of his father.

"The whole notion of arranged marriage is wacky, if you ask me," Tinker continued.

"Yeah," Reid said. Kayla was silent, looking out the window, but Reid knew she felt the same way. "This is Kayla's room. I'll find someplace else to bunk."

"There're plenty of other places to sleep. We picked this house hoping someday Brian and Kayla would fill it up with great-grandkids."

Kayla didn't say anything, but Reid saw her stiffen. It was wrong Brian wasn't there. Reid had no idea what to say, and the silence was awkward. He was relieved when Tinker cleared his throat.

"Oh, honey," Tinker said, crossing to Kayla. "I'm sorry I brought up Brian. I didn't mean to upset you."

"You didn't do anything wrong," she said. "It's good to have someone say his name. I miss him all the time, but no one ever talks about him, like he never existed."

"I didn't know that's how you felt," Reid said, chagrined he'd never thought of it that way.

Kayla issued something resembling a smile. "It's not your fault. It's hard to know what to say to me these days."

Tinker pulled her into a hug. After a moment, he patted her back. "Hey, Reid hasn't seen the facilities yet." He grinned. "Shall we?"

Kayla sniffed and nodded.

The bathroom was warm and bright with sun filtering through glass block windows. In addition to a sink and toilet, there was an oversized soaking tub, and a separate shower.

"Where's the water come from?" Reid asked. "I don't see a hose."

"This ain't no ordinary sun-shower, kiddo," Tinker said.

"Tinker doesn't do ordinary, remember?" Kayla said.

Tinker turned one of the knobs under the showerhead. There was a bubbling sound and water spurted out.

"How?" Reid said. They had running water in the Mountain, but that was due to an elaborate system of self-contained power generation, water heaters, and pumps.

"That's not all," Tinker said. He shut off the water, crossed the room, and pushed a lever on the toilet. The water whooshed from the bowl and new water flowed in. "Practically like living in the Before."

"How'd you manage that?" Reid asked.

"It's actually simpler than back at the Mountain," Tinker said. "We don't need pumps. The water collects in tanks on the roof and gravity takes care of the rest. Eventually the septic may stop working, but so far so good. Now you two get washed up while I figure out where those extra chairs are."

"Can I help with something?" Reid asked.

"No, your grandma likes to do things a certain way. It's smoother if we stay out of the kitchen. Take a few minutes to get settled. The bedroom by the stairs has a decent bed, though you may have to move a few boxes. Sheets and towels are in here." He pointed to a cabinet.

"Thanks, Pops," Reid said as Tinker shuffled out.

Kayla wiped at her eyes.

"Thinking about Brian?" It still felt weird to say his name.

"No. I mean, I'm always thinking about him, but what set me off was Tinker saying to get settled. It made me think of home. My sisters' paintings on the walls. My mom knitting and knitting and knitting while crying over Bethany. Ignoring her other kids who are right there."

"I'm sorry, Kay." He never should have trusted his father. "Do you want to go back?"

"No. But you know we can't go back now, even if we wanted to. It would be different if you'd let me kill Vega."

Chapter 16

Port Townsend, Washington, aboard the Diplomat

After informing his crew of the change in plans, Nikolai gathered his belongings. He loaded his briefcase with his sextant, compass, and charts, and his father's pipe, then tossed some clothing and toiletries into a duffle. The rest of his personals went into two trunks that would be stored at the Carriage House.

Olexi rapped on the doorjamb. "You asked to see me, sir?"

"Come in." Nikolai tossed the duffle on top of one of the trunks. "Are you packed?"

"Yes, sir. I wanted to thank you for bringing me with you."

"Thank *you* for agreeing to come. Kennedy was kind enough to allow it. We'll be bunkmates—sharing a room." Nikolai smiled as if this was a normal thing for him.

"*Yeshyo by?*"

"It will be fine." Sharing a room would be awkward, but the priority was getting his kids. "Olexi, I realize I'm no longer your commander, but I have a request." Nikolai shifted, uncomfortable with their new roles. "Would you mind delivering my bags to the *Emancipation* with your own? I'm not planning to board until tomorrow, but I'd like to clear these quarters."

"Of course, sir."

Nikolai appreciated the short reprieve that would buy him. He dreaded stepping foot on the *Emancipation* more than he cared to admit. It was one thing to be a guest aboard another man's boat. It was another thing entirely to sail under the command of someone too green to be a captain. It was ten times worse when the very sight of that captain made one's blood boil.

Concern lined Olexi's brow. "Is there something else?"

"No, that's it. I'll see you at the party this evening?"

"Wouldn't miss it." Olexi's weathered face drew into a grin exposing crooked teeth.

He wasn't a handsome guy, but he was charming in his own right, particularly when he played the harmonica. Nikolai wished Cook would notice, because the man thought she made the stars.

"Oh, there is one more thing," Nikolai said. "Have you seen Cook? I stopped by the galley but she wasn't there."

"Gone ashore."

"Ah, already in her mother's kitchen, I'd wager. I'll catch up with her there. She'd slit my throat if I left without saying goodbye."

"She's a spitfire, that one." Olexi's eyes had grown wistful.

Poor smitten bastard.

Nikolai sent the trunks to the Carriage House, then headed for the big kitchen to see Cook. It was obvious a feast was in the making. The kitchen had overflowed into the former kitchen gardens with tables of food being prepped by young apprentices, and barbeque grills and smokers being tended by a few older men. Nikolai waved to familiar faces. As he picked his way through the chaos, two girls stopped shucking clams to giggle behind their hands at him. He didn't recognize them, but gave a polite wave then promptly tripped over a log that had strayed from the woodpile. He barely managed to stay on his feet, which added to the girls' delight. Nikolai tipped an imaginary hat, happy to oblige.

He felt like he'd already crossed a battlefield, but looking into the kitchen, he realized the real battleground lay ahead. The air was thick with steam and smoke, and the heat pouring out the door soaked Nikolai's shirt in seconds. A dozen people were crowded inside, half of them shouting to be heard above the clanging of pots and each other. Nikolai's skin prickled against his sticky shirt, his beard itched, and his eyes burned, but he went in.

Cook wasn't there, but he spotted the old woman who presided over this kingdom—Finola's mother, "Mama Cook" Winnie Tucker. Sitting on the counter at her elbow, taking up precious workspace, was Josh.

Mat blyad. With all that had happened, Nikolai had missed their chess date.

Josh's face was long, but perked up when Winnie handed him something. Nikolai approached, trying to see what it was, hoping fervently it was a slice of apple.

Oh, hell. Mama Cook had broken out the chocolate, which meant one thing—somebody was in deep *dermo*. In this case, it was Nikolai.

"Uncle Niko!" Josh jumped off the counter and ran into Nikolai's arms.

Nikolai hugged him, saying the phrase his own father hadn't said often enough. "*Moy zolotoy mal'ch'ik.*" *My golden boy.* "I'm sorry." He didn't try to explain. Explanations and excuses don't matter to a boy who feels forgotten.

Nikolai noticed Mama Cook carefully not looking at him while she pulverized the dried fish on her cutting board. She didn't have to say anything for Nikolai to know what she was thinking, and his cheeks burned as only Mama Cook could make them.

"Winnie?" Nikolai said softly.

She shook her head.

"Goodness, boy, you're getting too big to hold," Nikolai said, shifting Josh in his arms. "How about we go for a swim?"

"Damn straight!" Josh said, kipping out of Nikolai's grasp.

"Josh," Nikolai said, trying to appear stern.

"Sorry."

"Thank Mama Cook, then grab your suit and meet me at the Carriage House."

"You promise you'll come?" Josh looked up at him, so vulnerable, wanting to trust.

"On my life."

"Fresh! Thanks, Mama Cook." Josh sprinted from the room, dodging buckets and people and the hot oven door on the way.

Mama Cook would not be as quick to forgive. Nikolai, of all people, should not have sent a little boy crying to her kitchen. Not after all the times he'd been that boy, running in for a hug and some chocolate after being left on the dock by his papa. Nikolai had sworn he'd never be that kind of father, and he felt ashamed for the many times he hadn't been there for his own children. He'd tried to do better with his nephew because he was the only father figure the boy had. Mama Cook was right to be disappointed in him.

"I'm sorry." He kissed the top of her head. "I'll make it up to him. To all of them."

Chapter 17

Manitou Springs, Colorado

Reid ate breakfast quickly, anxious to see the car. "You were kidding about the bomb, right?" He had to be kidding, didn't he?

"It's perfectly safe." Tinker opened a door off the kitchen, revealing a dark garage with a hulking shadow inside. "Stay here a sec while I get us some light."

Reid was surprised when the light came from inside the car. He'd expected Tinker to open the garage door.

"Go on," Sarah said, coming up behind him. "We'll go for a joyride."

"Kayla, you up for that?" Reid asked.

"I'm tired," Kayla said. "I'll stay and take a nap."

"Nonsense," Sarah said, shooing her through the door. "We'll all go. Be good for us. Get back on the horse and all that."

Reid looked at Kayla for an explanation, but Kayla didn't provide one.

"Sit up front with me, Reid," Tinker said, tapping a beat on the steering wheel. "Let the gals spread out in back."

Kayla and Sarah were already climbing through the back door, so Reid circled to the other side of the car. "I'll open the garage door."

"No need," Tinker said. The garage door rolled up by itself.

"How'd you do that?"

"Magic," Tinker said.

"There's Zeke," Reid said, seeing the dog in the front yard. "I'll get him."

"Why don't you whistle for him?" Tinker asked.

"How do you mean?"

Tinker whistled, loud and shrill. Zeke bounded into the garage and jumped into the car through the door Reid had left open, then leapt into the back and curled up on the seat beside Kayla.

"How'd you do that?" Kayla asked. "How could he have known what that meant? You just met him."

"Me and this dog, we have a special bond already," Tinker said. "We're simpatico. Amigos. The Lone Ranger and Tonto, Calvin and Hobbes, Batman and—"

"Phooey," Sarah said. "Whistling for a dog was as common as dirt in the Before. Besides, that dog's simpatico with Kayla, not you, you old fart."

As if on cue, Zeke nuzzled Kayla's arm aside and rested his head on her leg. The look on Kayla's face was almost happy as she ran her hand along Zeke's back. "He's so soft."

Tinker reached up and took a card from the visor. "This is the key," he told Reid, inserting it into a slot on the dash then punching a sequence of numbers on a keypad. "Ready?" He pulled a lever and the car started moving, silent as air.

They rolled down the driveway and onto the street.

"This is amazing!" Reid grinned at Kayla, but she was staring out the window, her arm draped across Zeke's back.

"Only took me forty-some years to make it happen," Tinker said. "I didn't realize at first how much I'd have to overcome. I knew the electronic components were rendered useless by the solar event, but I figured it wouldn't be long before I could get an older model car running, one that never had any electronics. Who knew that rubber would disintegrate and gasoline would turn to varnish in such a short time?"

"I don't understand how a bomb could change all that," Reid said.

"It was far more than the warhead. If I hadn't found this Hummer and a stockpile of experimental tires, I'd still be messing around putting train wheels on a Volkswagen Beetle."

"A what?"

"Doesn't matter. Point is, after we found the warhead, we were poking around at Schriever trying to decide which vehicle to try it on when we found a whole lab full of Hummers. I thought I'd stroked out or was hallucinating. I mean, who'd have thought the Air Force would be developing ground vehicles? It was the last thing I expected to see, but there they were. The R and D guys were doing all sorts of modifications and experimental stuff. Near as I could figure, some of the motors were made to run on corn oil, others looked to have carburetors designed to work underwater. All manner of crazy stuff."

"A whole lab full of Hummers." Reid's thoughts cascaded with the possibilities. "How many of them work?"

"None of them, at first. I thought it was because I didn't have the code that went with the keycard. Let me tell you, I spent a few days trying to crack it, then your grandma came in and figured it out in five minutes."

"Oh, don't make it sound like I'm some genius," Sarah said. "I just found the list of passwords hidden behind a photograph."

"So you punched the code in and the car worked?" Reid asked.

"There was a tad more to it," Tinker said. "None of the Hummers were rigged for nuclear power because in the Before there was no way people would drive something powered by a nuke. The Russians had lighthouses powered by them, and even we used them for satellites, so it wasn't an issue of scientific viability, it was fear."

"I can understand that," Reid said.

"Don't be such a worrywart. The nuke's shielded, and I disabled the part that makes it explode. Anyway, I messed around for a while trying to reconfigure the nuke as a power supply. After I found some NASA reports on the satellite nukes, I got this old beast purring like a kitten and drove right out of the lab."

"A few feet outside the lab, that is," Sarah said.

"Those goddamn tires!" Tinker pounded the steering wheel. "They're the biggest challenge of all, disintegrating right out from under the wheels. Every single set I tried. Must have been hundreds of tires from all over the city. Could be from the radiation, or maybe exposure since the buildings haven't been heated or cooled. Regardless, regular tires were never going to cut it."

"What did you do?" Reid asked.

"We figured our only chance was if the Army had been developing something, so we risked being seen and went down to Fort Carson."

"I thought Vega's father cleaned out Fort Carson long before I was born," Reid said.

"Yeah, of weapons and food and anything else he thought useful. But he didn't think tires were useful, so there they were—stacks of tires made of plastic. And nothing lasts like plastic."

"And with those tires, *then* it worked?" Reid asked.

"Like a dream."

"How many cars did you get running?"

"Just this one. I didn't want to build a whole fleet that could fall into Vega's hands. But I documented how to do it, and we've got enough components to build a half-dozen more."

"I should have known you'd never stop trying, Pops."

"The day I got this one on the road felt like a hundred Christmases rolled into one. Driving is one of the things I miss most. Feels mighty good to be behind the wheel again." Tinker's grin made him look decades younger, and Reid could imagine what he'd looked like in the Before. "Hang on to your hat, kid—here's the highway."

Reid wasn't sure what he meant, but the next second his head slammed back against the seat. "Jesus, Pops!" Reid grabbed a handle above the door.

"We're only doing forty," Tinker said. "Back in the day, I pushed seventy on this road."

"This is crazy." Reid had never gone so fast. He wondered if Kayla was enjoying the ride, but she was asleep with her head against the window and Zeke pressed against her side.

He looked back at Tinker, impressed how he handled the vehicle, weaving through the other cars.

"Dear?" Sarah called. "Stop squirreling around and go down the shoulder. You're making me sick back here."

"There's one operational car in the whole damn universe," Tinker grumbled. "And it has a backseat driver."

Chapter 18

Port Townsend, Washington

Nikolai's mouth watered at the spread. There was so much food, the usual buffet table had to be doubled to hold everything. Josh was in top form, working the room with a tray of champagne goblets. He grinned at Nikolai, and Nikolai saluted, thankful the chocolate and the swim had healed all.

Cook was still nowhere to be found. Olexi probably knew where she was, but he'd been scarce too. Nikolai scanned the partygoers for them now, paying particular attention to the area where the band was playing, as Olexi was apt to break out his harmonica once the green serpent of drink found him.

He finally spotted Cook and Olexi at the edge of the dance floor. *With Kennedy.*

Cook was batting her eyelashes at the young bourgeois, laying it on thick, swishing her orange gown and leaning forward to show her cleavage. Olexi gazed at her with rapt adoration, even though she was peacocking for someone else. Nikolai was making his way over when someone grabbed his elbow.

"Niko, darling." Corinne was bejeweled collar to toe in rhinestones so thick the silver fabric that held them was barely visible.

"Mother, you look gorgeous." He bussed her cheek.

"It's time for the toast, dear. Will you do the honors?"

"Happy to," Nikolai said, thankful she'd asked him and not someone more longwinded. The aroma of the buffet had him giddy with hunger, and all that stood between him and a full plate was a few of his own spare remarks.

The guests parted for them as they crossed the room. Corinne, ever the gracious host, murmured hellos and nodded, while Nikolai, ever the dutiful son, followed, grabbing two goblets of champagne as they approached the staircase.

They ascended to the first landing and faced the hushed room.

"Friends, welcome!" Corinne said, extending her arms to encompass everyone. "Grab a glass, gather round, and share a toast before we eat."

Nikolai handed Corinne a glass of champagne. When the room quieted again, he raised his glass for the customary first toast. "To the cooks!" he said, looking right at Finola.

"To the cooks!" the crowd repeated.

Nikolai sipped and was impressed by the tart flavor, as tasty as the best champagne he'd had. When he looked again, Finola was gone. Maybe her mother had told her about the incident with Josh, or maybe Olexi had finally worn her down and they were headed off to enjoy a passionate goodbye. More likely, she'd simply left, too worried about Tatiana and Will to enjoy the party. That's what Nikolai would like to do, but he continued with his duties.

"To the fishermen and the apple growers!" he called. "To the sommeliers and the wine!" This met with lots of cheers. "And to Corinne!"

"To Corinne," the crowd roared.

Corinne reveled in the adoration, but only for a moment. "The buffet is . . . open!"

Nikolai escorted her to the buffet and filled their plates with the items she wanted. After leaving her in a wingback chair in front of the fireplace, he went to the veranda to eat alone.

After a few bites, he found he didn't have an appetite after all. He set down his plate, frustrated by the empty hours ahead waiting for Kennedy. Leaning his forehead against a pillar, he groaned aloud— something he'd never do in front of his crew.

"Captain, is it so terrible?" a soft voice asked.

A smile crept across his face. "Ekaterina. It's been a long time."

"Too long." She was radiant in a strapless white dress that showed more of her silky skin than it covered. Her feet were bare, something indescribably more attractive to Nikolai than the sexiest of high heels. She tiptoed and draped her arms around his neck. "My poor Captain. So sad. Maybe Ekaterina can help?"

Chapter 19

Manitou Springs, Colorado

Reid flopped over in bed, too worried to sleep. Earlier at dinner, they'd been planning their trip to Ellay, when Kayla went pale and ran out covering her mouth. Reid had started after her, but his grandmother stopped him and went herself. He could hear Kayla retching outside. Was it something she'd eaten? No one else was sick.

Botulism from the canned food was a remote though deadly possibility. Ordinary food poisoning was less rare—a few cases each year caused by improperly cleaned rats—but still he was concerned.

He told himself Kayla would be fine, that his grandmother was right—Kayla had nothing more than a case of exhaustion. It did make sense. Kayla had just lost her husband and sister, and on top of that had killed Beckum and Vasquez. Now she couldn't go back to the only home she'd ever known. The fatigue and stress had simply caught up with her. He wished he could comfort her, tell her it would all be okay. But he wouldn't go to her. He'd made a promise.

He rolled over and tried to ignore the familiar ache of empty arms.

There was a click. His door opened.

"It's me," Kayla whispered, closing the door softly behind her.

He sat up. "Feeling better?"

"Shhhh." She put her finger to her lips as she approached.

"I've been worried—"

"Shh. Don't say anything." She pressed her hand against his bare chest, and he shivered as he eased back against the pillow. She stared at him a moment, then slid under the covers.

Her legs were cool against his as she settled beside him. She rested her hand on his shoulder and he felt her tremble.

"Kay?" He brushed her cheek with the back of his hand but felt no tears. She smelled of soap and toothpaste.

"Please," she whispered. "Don't talk."

She kissed him.

Reid's eyes widened. He didn't resist, he let her kiss him. She pulled back and kissed his cheek, his neck.

"*Kayla.*"

"Don't." She kissed him again, pressing her body against his, gripping his shoulder. "Kiss me," she whispered against his lips.

When she kissed him again, he pulled her closer, kissing her back. Gently, sweetly. Hardly daring to believe it was happening. She'd come to him. She wanted him.

Her breathing came faster and she kissed him harder, grabbing him by the hair, biting his lip. He turned her onto her back and kissed her neck. She moaned and arched against him. His fingers found the bottom of her shirt, and he pulled it up, skimming her nipple with his knuckles. She helped him pull the shirt over her head. Then he saw the look on her face.

"Kayla."

She opened her eyes. Tears streamed out the corners and down her temples.

"Kay, what are you doing?"

"You, you smell like him."

"God, I'm sorry," he said, rolling onto his back.

"It's not your fault. I thought I could . . . I tried . . . but I can't."

Reid stared at the ceiling, his cheeks burning. "Why would you do that?"

"You don't understand."

"So tell me."

She sat up, clutching her shirt in front of her. Tears spilled down her cheeks. She looked at him for a long moment then whispered, "I'm sorry."

She got up and left without looking back.

Chapter 20

Manitou Springs, Colorado

After a fitful sleep, Reid woke before dawn and lay in bed trying not to replay what had happened with Kayla. Everything felt mixed up and wrong. Like he'd been betrayed, but also like he was the betrayer.

When Kayla kissed him, he'd allowed himself to hope she could have feelings for him. For *him,* not Brian. He'd let his guard down. Now he was kicking himself for being so weak, so foolish. And on top of it all, he hadn't found out what had happened to Brian.

When it was finally light enough, he went for a walk to clear his head. The air was cool for summer, and he set a brisk pace to keep warm. He tried to see things from Kayla's perspective. What had she been thinking?

Maybe it was as simple as being held. Wanting to feel alive.

Allie.

He'd forgotten about the thing with Allie. She and his friend Nolan were definitely a love match, but Nolan had died when they were on brevet. Doc thought it was meningitis and said that even if he'd been at the Mountain there was nothing they could have done.

He remembered how shaken he'd been over Nolan's death, and that was nothing compared to how Allie took it. She wouldn't eat, talk, or leave her room. People wondered if she'd ever recover. Then one night she came to him. At first they held each other, then she kissed him. She kept wanting more, saying she needed to feel alive. He felt it too, like it was reawakening a part of his soul. After that night, they were never together again and never said a word about it. Later she was matched with Nolan's cousin and seemed okay, even happy.

That had to be it. Kayla needed to feel something again. It didn't have anything to do with him, but he'd been too blinded by his own desires to see it. He'd handled it all wrong.

What if she came to him again? He wanted to be there for her, but he'd loved her ever since he could remember. He wasn't sure he was strong enough to make love to her without hoping for more.

He returned to the house, wishing he'd come up with some sort of plan.

Inside, it was quiet. He headed for the stairs, hoping to sneak back to bed.

"Good morning," his grandmother's voice sang out from the kitchen.

"Morning," he called over his shoulder.

"You have a nice walk?"

"Yeah."

"Come here. This shouting is for the birds."

Reid wondered if he should protest and head for his room, but he knew his grandmother wouldn't let it go. She'd end up making a fuss and eventually get him to spill his guts, so he headed for the kitchen.

"What can I fix you?" Sarah asked, drying her hands. "Kayla's drinking herbal tea, but I can make coffee."

Reid glanced at Kayla sitting at the table with her hands wrapped around a mug. She looked away. His cheeks burned. He shoved his hands in his pockets and looked back at his grandmother who was still talking.

"We've got oatmeal packets. I remember how you like those."

"Nothing, thanks. I'm not hungry."

Zeke stirred under the table, readjusting his head on Kayla's foot.

Kayla stared at her tea, refusing to look at him. He felt like such a jerk. He knew he should say something, but he had no idea what.

"Well, if you're not going to eat, go see your grandpa," Sarah said. "He's in the garage. He wants to teach you to drive this morning."

"That's great," Reid said, perking up.

"Kayla, you should go, too," Sarah urged.

Reid couldn't help it—his whole body tensed. He needed some space to pull himself together.

"I don't think so." Kayla dropped her gaze back to her mug.

Reid was relieved, but immediately felt guilty. He was sure she'd seen his reaction. "Kay, come if you want." He needed space, but not at the expense of making her feel even worse.

She looked up again. Her eyes were sad, but she smiled. "Thanks, but I'll stay."

Reid headed for the garage, trying to convince himself they'd get past this.

After his driving lesson, Reid found Kayla throwing a stick. She'd toss it across the yard, then Zeke would bring it back.

"What's he doing?" Reid asked, fascinated.

"I never would have thought of it, but your grandma suggested it. Zeke seems to like it." Kayla threw the stick again.

There was an uncomfortable silence while Reid debated what to say. He decided to avoid the topic. "Driving is incredible. I can't get over how fast you can go. Pops said he already taught you. Said you're a natural."

Kayla shrugged. She took the stick from Zeke's mouth and threw it again.

"Still, practice can't hurt," he said. "You want to go out this afternoon? We can drive all we want before dark."

Kayla shook her head.

It was going to be a long drive to California if things stayed this way between them. He decided to face it head on. "Look, I'm sorry about last night—"

"Forget it." She hucked the stick again.

"No, we should talk, get it sorted out before we leave."

"I'm not going."

"What?"

"I'm not going with you." She met his gaze briefly then headed toward the house.

"What? *Why?*" he called.

She didn't answer.

Zeke dropped the stick and trotted after Kayla.

At the house, Kayla held the door as Zeke slipped inside. She hesitated a moment, staring at Reid, then went in.

What did she want from him? What was he supposed to do? He wanted to make things right, but she sure wasn't making it easy.

Chapter 21

Port Townsend, Washington

"Welcome," Kennedy said with a broad smile as Nikolai boarded the *Emancipation*.

Nikolai shook the proffered hand with a firmer grip than was necessary. "Your boat is a beauty." That was an understatement. The *Emancipation* was the most gorgeous yacht he'd ever seen. She was trim and sleek, with a gleaming teak deck, and aquamarine paint waxed to an icy glow.

"Thank you," Kennedy said. "It's taken years to bring her back to her original glory."

"You did the work yourself?"

"Primarily. I used tradesmen for skilled crafts like rehabilitating the hull, of course."

Nikolai nodded, appraising Kennedy a little differently knowing he'd put his own sweat into the restoration. He was glad to see the single mast looked solid and true, and the sails and riggings appeared properly cared for. The deck was pristine, with everything stowed and tidy the way Nikolai liked it. But a little too perfect. "This isn't her maiden voyage, is it?"

"Not exactly," Kennedy replied. "She's been on day sails. Several. She's seaworthy."

Several. Day sails. Nikolai had to clamp his teeth together to keep from listing what could go wrong on the first voyage. This wasn't his ship, it wasn't his place. He reminded himself that, broken in or not, the *Emancipation* was his best option.

"Is there a problem?" Kennedy asked.

"Not at all." Nikolai forced his jaw to relax.

"Excuse me." A stocky young man approached. "You asked for me, Captain?"

"No," Nikolai said.

"Yes," Kennedy said at the same time.

"My apologies." Nikolai clenched his teeth again. This would take getting used to.

Kennedy half-smiled. "Mike, would you show our guest the ship? Anything he'd like to see—galley, crew quarters, and his own cabin, of course."

"Yeah, sure," Mike said.

Kennedy extended his hand to Nikolai again. "Happy to have you aboard, sir."

Nikolai shook his hand, hoping his distaste wasn't as apparent as his earlier emotions had been. When Nikolai was in command, he made a point of issuing orders, not asking. He couldn't believe "yeah, sure" was an acceptable response. *What kind of leader is he?*

"Hey Kennedy, when do we sail?" Mike asked.

"Uh, I'd say in about . . . " Kennedy looked at his watch. "A half hour, give or take?"

"I'll be back in twenty." Mike gave a half salute. "Follow me," he told Nikolai, descending the lustrous wooden steps that led belowdecks.

Nikolai couldn't help shaking his head. *What kind of operation is this?*

Even given how immaculate the *Emancipation* was topside, Nikolai fully expected to see clutter below, a sure sign of an inexperienced captain. But everything was tidy. At least Kennedy had that going for him, even if he did allow his crew to call him by his first name.

"This is the library." Mike indicated an alcove filled with books.

"Impressive," Nikolai said, meaning it.

"This lounge area used to be the engine room, but since we didn't need all that stuff, Kennedy fixed it up for playing cards and such. Farther forward is the dining room and galley, plus a smaller lounge, a guest cabin, and Kennedy's office. For the crew quarters, you drop down one more deck. Your room is this way," he said, heading aft.

"Here?" Nikolai asked, pointing to a closed door.

"Nope." Mike lowered his voice. "Steer clear of that room."

"Why?"

"It's the cook's. I think she's daft. Scares me a bit. Here's your berth." He opened the door at the end of the hall, revealing a full-width room with portals high on both sides.

Nikolai followed him into the well-appointed chamber, which was larger than he expected given the size of the yacht. The floors were skillfully crafted from some kind of cork, and the vanity was black granite. A desk, a leather chair, and two beds occupied the space. One bed was substantial with a headboard built into the back wall, while the other was clearly a temporary addition. "This will be fine."

"I should hope so. It's Kennedy's stateroom, but he wanted you to have it."

"That's generous." Perhaps Kennedy wasn't as spoiled as he'd thought.

"Alrighty, then," Mike said, stuffing his hands in his pockets. "Anything else you want to see? I need to visit the head before I go topside."

Nikolai stifled a grimace. "No, thank you. I'll get acquainted with my quarters."

"Alrighty, then," Mike said again. "I'll see ya around."

Nikolai latched the door behind Mike, pondering the fact that there weren't many people he'd lend *his* quarters to. It indicated how serious Kennedy was about Tatiana, and Nikolai wished he'd been offered a bunk in the bilge instead.

The smaller bed held Olexi's bag, while the expansive one held Nikolai's. He might as well stow his gear, so he opened the door at the aft of the room thinking it was a closet. Instead, it provided access to a tender garage, bigger even than the one on the *Belle*. This one held not one but two vessels—a large skiff and a two-man racing scull. Nikolai peered into the skiff and found a mast, sails, oars, life vests, and jugs of water. Watertight, self-buoyant bags were strapped below the benches. Nikolai snooped inside one and found food, slickers, survival blankets, first aid supplies, fishing gear—everything he would have packed himself.

This was easily the most impressive thing about the fancy yacht. Any sailor who took such care with emergency preparedness had to have some sense. Kennedy inched higher in his esteem, though he was still too old for his daughter.

Nikolai tucked his belongings into the drawers under the bed, then headed topside to help out. There was always plenty to do when getting underway.

On deck, the crew was readying the sails. The sun was out and a breeze carried the scent of the open ocean. The familiar sounds of the ropes and riggings made Nikolai feel more right than he had since learning about his children.

"How can I help?" he asked Kennedy who was sitting in the shade of the wheelhouse, head bowed over a clipboard.

Kennedy looked up and glanced around. "No need, sir. We're about ready."

"Surely there's something?"

"Everything's in hand," Kennedy said. "Perhaps you'd like to read a book from the library? There's a vantage point far forward with good light and a comfortable chair."

Nikolai hesitated, but Kennedy didn't look up from his clipboard, so he headed for the stairs. It never would have occurred to him to go below and laze about. But he understood a captain not wanting a passenger underfoot. And that's what he was—a passenger.

"Sir?" Kennedy called.

"Yes?" Nikolai hoped he'd thought of a job.

"I'd like to meet to go over plans. In a day or two?"

"Certainly." Nikolai paused, but Kennedy had said all he had to say.

At the bottom of the stairs, he looked toward his room but couldn't stomach holing up in the ass-end of the boat where he'd have no idea what was going on. The forward vantage point sounded marginally better, so he grabbed a book from the library and headed that way.

In the corridor he heard singing. The familiar voice rang out from behind the galley door.

Nikolai flung open the door. "Finola?"

"What *Stibat-Ka* dares call me that name?" Cook wielded a knife like a baton. "Oh, it's you. I'm not speaking to you." She turned her back and hacked at something on a cutting board.

"Why didn't you tell me you were coming?" Nikolai remained in the doorway. It was wise to give her space when she was in a mood.

Finola ignored him.

"I looked for you to say goodbye." He figured that's why she wasn't speaking to him. When she didn't respond, he took his chances and crept up behind her. He blew lightly on her neck, making the hair that had escaped her updo dance across her skin.

Her hand flew up, and Nikolai dodged as she swatted her neck. He hoped she'd turn and grin, or at least scold him, but she resumed working. Apparently his transgression—whatever it was—was serious.

"*Finny*." He used the name he'd called her when they'd been children playing together outside Mama Cook's kitchen. "Finny, please."

"Out!" She wheeled around. "Get out of my kitchen!"

Nikolai stepped out of reach of the knife, though she wouldn't use it. At least he was pretty sure she wouldn't.

"Usali, dos-wail-opsh! Mos tsil! Mos tsil!" She came toward him, her face blazing red.

Nikolai backed away. When she swore in her native tongue, all bets were off. He didn't know for a fact they were swear words, but the meaning was clear, and he got the hell out.

As the door slammed closed he burst out laughing, realizing the "daft cook" Mike referred to was Finola.

Walking forward to the reading nook, he grinned so wide his face hurt. Even if Finola was roaring like a beluga, finding her aboard was the best thing that had happened all week.

Chapter 22

Southern California, the same morning

Pascal Worth stood just inside the closed door of his private office in City Hall, admiring his pale skin in the eighteenth century Baroque mirror he'd obtained from the Getty. He smoothed his hair, glad he'd told the girls at Services to leave the color natural. The silver looked dignified. Regal, even.

The King of Lost Angeles. That's what they'd been calling him.

He heard the muted pound of the gavel and faced the door, waiting for it to open.

"All rise for the honorable Chancellor Worth, Regent of Southern California," his secretary bellowed from the main hall.

The oak door swung open and Pascal remained still for a moment before stepping into the room. He was keenly aware of the two dozen people standing stiffly in front of their benches, and he took his time settling into the leather chair behind his massive desk.

"Good morning," he said, pleased with the deep hollow sound of his voice now that he'd had the rugs removed from the hall. He hadn't liked the acoustics since the day he'd had them brought from the art museum at USC. "Be seated."

Clothing whispered as the attendees took their seats.

"Chancellor." His secretary, Roberto Gomez, approached. He was a slight man, hair graying at the temples, and he'd taken to wearing wire-rimmed reading glasses all the time. He stopped beside the desk wearing one of his collection of sweater vests he was never seen without, no matter the season. He flipped open the notepad in his hand. "On your agenda today we have—"

"Later," Pascal said. "What's going on with the collectors?"

"Well, sir," Gomez said. "I regret to report that the collectors went on strike this morning after all."

"You were supposed to dispense with that," Pascal said in measured tones. "I'm *sure* there was an exceedingly important reason you did not."

"Yes, sir." Gomez adjusted his glasses, a nervous habit. "Last night I sat down with their Speaker and—"

"What is a *Speaker?*"

"The collectors elected him—"

"Elected?"

"His name's Giles Premovich," Gomez said. "He used to be a catcher on the train, so the collectors know and respect him. I think they'll listen to him no matter how we settle their case."

"What case is that?" Pascal said.

"They make a good argument for an additional hour to spend with their families. Only during the summer months when the days are longer. Premovich thinks it would actually increase productivity, and it certainly wouldn't hurt morale."

"Is this *Speaker* present?" Pascal asked.

Gomez nodded and gestured to a burly man in the front row. The man stood.

Pascal opened his desk drawer, drew out a handgun and shot Premovich in the chest.

A guttural sound emitted from the body as it crumbled to the floor. The crowd collectively drew in a breath.

"Is anyone unclear about the punishment for sedition?" Pascal asked, the gun still in his hand. His gaze swept across their faces, pausing pointedly on Gomez's, then he replaced the gun on its flannel pad.

"As for the collectors," Pascal continued. "There is no *case* and there will be no strike. The city will not grind to a stop because a few people want an hour to read a book. Gomez, where are the collectors now?"

Gomez stepped forward, his olive skin greener than usual. "Marching with signs outside the north depot. They are calling it 'the Daylight Hour strike.'"

"How many?" Pascal asked.

"About forty."

"Where's Minou?"

"Here, Chancellor." The major stepped forward from the back wall. Pascal appreciated the pressed uniform taut over her small muscular frame and her dark hair pulled in a tight bun. His gaze flicked over her angular face, noting the firm jaw, the hardness in her eyes. He would get no flack from Minou.

"Major, take your Blades and put a stop to this *strike*. Put the ringleaders in the Tank. Make sure my message is clear."

Minou saluted and marched out.

"Gomez, give me the report from the scientists." Pascal settled back in his chair.

"Sorry, Chancellor." Gomez wet his finger and turned a page. "We have Census, Security, and a written report from World Waste, but nothing from the lab."

"Nothing?" Pascal was not accustomed to being put off. "Who's the Dispatcher today?"

"Here, sir." Captain Aaron Brandt rose, towering over the others in the back row. Pascal had been keeping an eye on Brandt as he climbed the ranks. His level-headedness and loyalty were impressive, not to mention the speed the lanky man could produce on skates.

"Brandt. Good," Pascal said. "Send a second team of Blades out to Irvine to fetch Professor Emery. I want to see him right away. Go."

With no news from Irvine, nothing else seemed interesting. Pascal checked his Rolex and decided to get in a tennis match before lunch. "Gomez, unless there's something pressing, give me Census and put the rest in my office."

"Yes, sir. Census says three dead, one born overnight. Unfortunately one of the dead is the dentist," Gomez said.

"*The* dentist? Can I assume the apprentice is up to speed?"

"I'll find out, sir." Gomez took a pencil from over his ear and jotted something on the page. He continued. "One of Ms. Ford's girls tried to leave. She was reacquired without injury and is in Rehab House. The biggest news is that two new missionaries arrived late last night."

"Are they talking?" Pascal leaned forward, interested but not hopeful. Gomez shook his head. *Of course not. They never talked.* "Anything else that can't wait?"

"No, sir."

"Send for Ms. Ford. Have the massage table set up in the cabana by the tennis courts, and show her there. She'll be joining me for lunch. Tell Chef I want stew with carrots and potatoes." After some exercise and a massage, maybe he'd see a new way to go about solving the puzzle of the missionaries.

Chapter 23

Lost Angeles, Pascal's cabana

Pascal handed his tennis bag to an attendant who scurried away closing the cabana door behind him. "Ms. Ford—Ellianna—I'm glad to see you."

"You too, Chancellor."

Ellianna stood alongside the massage table in a sleeveless shift. Pascal's gaze slid down lithe arms whose grace belied their strength. The silk of her dress hung loosely, and he imagined tight thighs and firm breasts beneath. For a moment he allowed himself to consider running his hands along her curves, the feel of her lips and her long black hair hanging in his face as she sat astride him.

"Shall we begin?" she asked.

Pascal knew she would give herself, and not out of obligation.

He pulled off his shirt, dropped his athletic shorts, and wrapped the towel she offered around his waist. He sat on the table and closed his eyes as she sponged his chest with jasmine-scented water. Yielding to the pressure of her touch, he stretched out on his stomach along the table. His breathing slowed as she kneaded oil into his skin, erasing the tension in his neck.

Ellianna's hands worked down his legs and lingered on his feet, finding the pressure points that eased his mind as much as his muscles. He felt himself teetering on the edge of sleep, so he turned to his back and was awakened by the scent of lemongrass. Ellianna knew his desires as well as he. Her hands drifted across his chest and up his neck, then smoothed his forehead. As she worked on his temples and jaw, his thoughts cleared. In his mind's eye he saw all his concerns distilled down to essentials and filed away. Until only one remained.

"I haven't received an update from Irvine," he said without opening his eyes.

"No?" Ellianna said, her fingers still massaging.

"If there was progress to report, I'd have heard by now."

"Perhaps. But the scientists are not the only way to get what you're looking for."

Pascal opened his eyes. "The new missionaries? What have they said?"

"Nothing, of course. After everything we've tried, I'm convinced none of the girls know how to get back home. Except one."

"Who?"

"Justine, my assistant."

"She's been here for years. Why haven't I heard this before now?"

"Because there's been nothing to report. But I've always had a feeling she knows more than the others. That's why I've kept her close." She trailed her fingers down his cheek.

He grabbed her by the wrist. "You should have told me."

She winced and tried to pull away, but he didn't let go. "Pascal, I—"

"You have no idea the decisions I make, the complex machinery of my job. Everything is connected in ways you can't begin to understand."

"You're right, I had no idea. Please, accept my apology."

He let go of her wrist and relaxed back into the table. "It's just that, had I known this sooner, I might have approved the application for her to marry one of my up-and-coming officers. To keep her close."

"That's even more important now . . . since I found out she's *pregnant*. The arrival of healthy new missionaries could not have been timed better. Just as Justine learns she's responsible for a new life, evidence of her old home is waved before her."

This could be the breakthrough he'd been waiting for. A missionary highly motivated to return home, one who might well know how to get there. All the other times he'd allowed missionaries to leave Lost Angeles had rendered nothing. Just sad girls praying at churches, asking for God to show them the way home, and God never answering. But this time . . . this time could be different.

"Don't keep secrets from me anymore, Elli."

As her deft hands began massaging again, he allowed himself to visualize the road to the home of the missionaries. That road had always been shrouded in mist, but the mists were swirling, perhaps even beginning to clear.

Ellianna's fingers skimmed down his stomach, drawing tantalizingly close to the edge of his towel. For a moment, he was seized by the desire to pull her on top of him.

Their eyes met. Her hand froze and her smile dissolved. She raised one eyebrow. Asking.

No. She was the one person he could talk to. That was too important to risk.

Pascal closed his eyes again, forcing himself to relax into the table, forcing his desire to recede, locking it away again. He visualized withdrawing the key from the lock and pulling his arm back to hurl the key into the ocean. But at the last moment, he placed the key in his pocket.

Chapter 24

Manitou Springs, Colorado

R eid doubted Vega and her goons could find them, but still, he was anxious to leave for Ellay. He found Tinker in the garage.

"Hey, Pops. How can I help?"

"I'm done here. Got everything in the toolbox I think we might need."

"I need clothes, but I don't feel like rooting through houses. Is there a store nearby?"

"You kiddin'? We've got all kinds of clothing, clean and folded, sorted into bins by size and season."

"Really?"

"You remember how your grandma is. Have her show you where the backpacks are so you and Kayla can get packing."

"About that." Reid figured he might as well get it over with. "Kayla's not coming."

Tinker scowled. "Why on earth not?"

Reid shrugged. "She's been through a lot."

"Don't you think it's time you told me what-all happened? Your grandma and I have been patient, but we can see something's eating at you. At Kayla too."

Reid looked down at his hands. Tinker was right. It was time. "We were on brevet."

"I thought you two weren't a couple."

"We're not. When Dad refused to marry us, Vega got pissed and sent us anyway. It was the second day when we found the stranger. We needed Doc, so I sent Kayla to Dad. I was sure he'd help when he saw the apple."

"Instead, he betrayed you."

"How'd you know?"

"I know my son."

"But I was so sure."

"Don't be too hard on yourself," Tinker said. "The only thing you're guilty of is believing the best about people. There's no shame in that."

"I'm so . . . *furious* with him." Reid's throat constricted.

Tinker patted him on the back. "You and your dad will sort it out."

"No, Pops, we won't." Reid gritted his teeth so hard he thought they might break.

"Give it time."

Reid forced himself to meet Tinker's gaze. "It's too late. Dad was shot. He's dead."

"*No.*" Tinker closed his eyes and shook his head slowly back and forth. "How?"

"He and Vega came for the stranger, but she was already dead. I wouldn't tell Vega what the stranger said, so she was going to hurt Kayla to get me to talk. Dad tried to stop it, and one of Vega's men shot him. Then I don't know what came over me. I *reacted*. I launched into Vega, then guns were going off everywhere. Kayla, she killed Vasquez, then Beckum." Reid took a breath. "She saved my life."

"Jesus."

"Before that, before we left the Mountain, one of Kayla's sisters died. The littlest one. So with that, and everything else . . ."

"And Brian."

"Yeah." He wanted to ask what happened to Brian, but Tinker had just learned about his son's death. There'd be a better time later. "Kayla's pretty messed up, Pops. Can you talk to her? She has to come with us."

"I'm no good at that sort of thing. That's a job for your grandmother, don't you think?"

Reid started to answer, then realized Sarah still didn't know about Peregrine. He didn't think he had it in him to go through telling it a second time.

Tinker must have realized. "It's all right, son. I'll take her for a walk to her favorite place and tell her about your dad. Give her a chance to digest it. When we get back, she'll talk to Kayla. It'll work out the way it's meant to," he said, pawing his watery eyes. "You'll see."

His grandparents had been gone for over an hour, and Reid couldn't wait any longer. He knocked on Kayla's door.

"It's me," he said.

Silence.

"We need to talk."

More silence. He knocked again in the pattern kids liked to use. "You might as well let me in. I'm not going away."

No response.

He could be as stubborn as she was. He leaned back against the door, absently drumming his fingernails against the jamb.

The door opened and he fell backward, landing on his rear end. "Hey!"

Kayla glared at him, hands on her hips. "Are you trying to irritate me to death?"

"My strategy was persistence. The irritation was incidental. But whatever works." He held out a hand for help up, but she ignored it and went to the window.

Reid got to his feet and joined her. They stood, side by side, looking out. He figured more waiting was in order, but after a while it was clear she wasn't going to say anything, so he dove in.

"Kay, you not coming to Ellay—it's because of last night, right?" She didn't argue, so he forged ahead. "I want you to know, you didn't do anything wrong. I was caught off guard and I said the wrong thing. I'm still saying all the wrong things. But I want to do right by you, and by Brian." His brother's name was the tiniest bit easier each time he said it. "Please, will you accept my apology? You have to come with us."

"I'm the one who's sorry," she said, still staring out the window. "I never should have put you in that position. It was a dumb idea."

"It wasn't dumb. Hell, it's what everyone wants us to do, but I know it's not what *you* want."

"I don't know what I want. I can't have what I want, and I don't know anything anymore."

"That's okay," Reid said. "You don't have to know what you want. You don't have to decide anything. Just come with me to Ellay. I want you to."

He could tell what her answer would be before she shook her head. "I can't."

"Do you want me to stay?" He held his breath, not sure how he wanted her to answer.

"No, you have to go to Ellay and bring back seeds. It's what Brian lived for. Now you have to do it for him."

"He lived for *you*, Kayla."

Chapter 25

Pacific Ocean, aboard the Emancipation

Nikolai hadn't been able to get immersed in the book he'd grabbed, a poorly constructed science fiction about an alien invasion. So he'd browsed the library until he found something more appealing—a detective story that took place in the Hawaiian Islands. He'd gone back to his room to read, and ended up sleeping through lunch. Now he was hungry on top of being bored and out of sorts. He paced the tight space between his bed and the basin, wondering if the afternoon would stretch on forever.

Finally there was a knock and he swung open the door, hoping he didn't seem too eager.

"Dinner's on the table," Mike said. "Kennedy thought you might want to join us."

Nikolai followed him to the dining room where Kennedy sat with three men.

"Captain Petrov," Kennedy said, standing. "I'd like you to meet the crew. You know Mike Huffman."

Nikolai nodded at Mike.

"This is Ernesto Pilapil." Kennedy indicated a small man of Asian descent.

"Everyone calls me Ernie."

"Ernie, Mike, and I crew together on a four-man racing team," Kennedy said. "Ivan's the fourth, but he's at the helm right now. We're the principle sailing crew aboard the *Emancipation*. I brought Fahnestock and White along for their non-sailing expertise."

"I'm Fahnestock." A slender man with silver hair peered at Nikolai with hard, blue eyes. "This is White." He pointed to the very muscular, very black man beside him. "We specialize in weaponry, combat, military tactics, that kind of thing."

Neither Fahnestock nor White stood or offered a hand.

"Have we met before?" Nikolai asked.

"I don't think so," Fahnestock said.

White squinted his eyes. "No, I'd remember." His voice was soft.

"Strange," Nikolai said. "Given your area of expertise and my past, I'm surprised our paths didn't cross."

"Captain Petrov was a bootlegger before he went to work for the Democracy," Kennedy explained. "His expertise is more real-world. Including firsthand with pirates."

"Indeed," Fahnestock said. "White and I are scholars, here to obtain some firsthand knowledge of the Pirate Guard ourselves."

"It's why we agreed to come, in fact," White said, looking pointedly at Kennedy.

The slightest look of irritation crossed Kennedy's face, and Nikolai wondered what was behind it.

"It's a pleasure to meet you all," Nikolai said, pulling out a chair.

"There's someone else I want to introduce, Captain," Kennedy said.

Nikolai remained standing, uncomfortable that Kennedy kept referring to him as "captain," when that was Kennedy's role.

"This is Friday," Kennedy said, gesturing to the galley door.

Finola and Olexi stood in the doorway with a small man of indeterminate age. He had dark brown skin, deep-set black eyes, and pure black hair. His hands were gnarled and disproportionately large for his body.

"Friday doesn't speak," Kennedy said. "He's a Survivor. My family found him as a toddler and he's been with us ever since. His hearing is good, but he's never spoken and doesn't sign or write. He's a genius when it comes to boats."

"I've heard the stories," Nikolai said. "The legend of Friday is so grandiose, I'd assumed it was a fiction. It's good to meet you." He extended his hand to Friday, who clasped it with a surprising gentleness given his ropy musculature. "I'm glad you're aboard. I've heard you can fix anything that floats."

Friday nodded, and his bottomless eyes seemed to be smiling, though his placid expression hadn't changed.

"It's true," Kennedy said. "He can fix anything. But when nothing's broken, he likes to keep busy in the kitchen. I hope Cook won't mind having him underfoot."

"Underfoot?" Finola bellowed. "He's much too quick for that. No, he's no trouble, that one. No trouble at all. He's worth half a dozen of any helpers I've had."

Kennedy laughed. "Glad to hear it. Now, I believe it's time to eat."

"We'll bring the food right out, Captain," Olexi said.

Apparently Olexi was serving as kitchen help. A way to spend time with Finola, no doubt.

"When you come back, please join us," Kennedy said. "All three of you. We are one crew here, and you are more than welcome at this table."

Olexi looked to Finola.

"If it's the same to you, Captain Kennedy," she said, "I'd prefer not." She didn't offer an explanation, and though she didn't look at Nikolai, he felt her anger radiating toward him.

"I'll eat in the kitchen, too," Olexi said.

Nikolai had the uncharitable thought that his friend was a spineless bastard, but he reminded himself that a man silly in love did all manner of foolish things he wouldn't ordinarily do. Nikolai had felt that way once, but it was so long ago, it hardly seemed real anymore.

"We're easy here," Kennedy said with an annoying boyish grin. "Eat where you like, when you like."

"Your food will be out straight away." Finola disappeared into the galley with Olexi and Friday trailing behind like two parts of her imposing shadow.

"She is a national treasure," Kennedy said. "It's unbelievable what she can do with a few simple ingredients. I'm more astounded each time she cooks for me."

With a start Nikolai registered the implication of Kennedy's words. "How many times has she cooked for you?"

"She cooks for Tatiana and me whenever she comes into the capital. I think she knows our kitchen better than Tati does."

"*Our* kitchen?" Nikolai came to his feet, and his chair fell over behind him. It was all he could do not to fly across the table and separate Kennedy's too-pretty face from his head.

Kennedy froze with his glass halfway to his lips, then placed it back on the table without taking a drink. "My sincere apologies. That was careless. Tatiana and I—we did not intend for you to find out this way."

Kennedy had an appropriately contrite look on his face, but Nikolai still wanted to grab him by his preppy collar and give him a good shake. The only thing preventing it was the knowledge that he would not be able to stop.

The silence was thick with everyone waiting for his response. But he kept his mouth shut, afraid of what would come out if he dared open it. He was Kennedy's guest, like it or not, and if he wanted to remain so, it would not be prudent to insult the host at the host's own table.

"Captain?" Olexi asked from behind him.

Nikolai wheeled around, nearly knocking a plate from Olexi's hand. "I've lost my appetite." He angled his face toward the table, avoiding Kennedy's eyes. "If you'll excuse me."

He stormed back to his room, his heart and mind racing. *They're living together. Living together! Tatiana's a child, barely twenty. And living with that, that . . . superfluous boyar.*

Once safely behind his closed door, he paced as much as the space would allow.

His Tatiana, his baby, was living with a man and no one had told him. Not Tatiana. Not Creighton. Not Finola. Corinne probably knew, and Will, too. Yet no one had even bothered to mention that Tatiana had a boyfriend, let alone a lover.

There was a quiet knock at the door.

Nikolai hoped with all his being it was Kennedy so that Nikolai could strangle the life out of him. He stared at the door, grinding his teeth, torn between wanting to tell him to come in and knowing he shouldn't.

The door opened a crack and Olexi peeked in.

"Sir?" He stepped into the room and closed the door behind him. "You're bleeding."

Nikolai looked down at his hands. Blood dripped from his closed fists. Slowly he uncurled his fingers, revealing four bloody crescents in each palm.

"Hold your hands over the basin." Olexi grabbed a towel from the vanity and pumped the faucet handle.

Nikolai obediently held out his hands. After a moment, cool water cascaded over his wounds. As his palms began to sting, his cheeks heated. He'd compounded things by behaving like an idiot. *What kind of man gets so irate he makes himself bleed ?*

Olexi stopped the water and handed him the towel. "Better?"

Nikolai pressed the towel between his hands. "He's been sleeping with my daughter." He looked into Olexi's eyes and found compassion, but it was the pity he saw there that snapped him to his senses. He had to pull himself together. "Of course, there is nothing to be done now."

"There was nothing to be done before, either. Not anything that would have stopped it."

Nikolai looked more closely at Olexi. "You knew."

Olexi stared back at him, unblinking. "Yes, I did."

"Why didn't you tell me?"

"No good would have come of it."

"I might have been able to talk some sense into her."

"No, Tatiana knows her mind, and she believes she loves him." A small, sad smile crossed Olexi's lips. "She chose her path. And she is her father's daughter—more stubborn, I think, than even you."

"She's a child! Too young to be that involved. *Living* with someone." Nikolai twisted the towel, trying to keep his temper from boiling over again.

"Granted, I haven't known her long," Olexi said. "But I know a young woman, not a child. And she could do a whole lot worse than Kennedy."

"Don't tell me you're impressed by that highbrow."

Olexi shook his head. "Is that all you see?" He crossed to the door. "I'm going to walk the deck and throw back a few so you have time to think. It looks to me like you need it." Olexi left, slamming the door.

Nikolai spun and hurled the towel at the sink, clenching his teeth to keep from hurling profanities. Olexi was right about one thing—he did need time to think. Time to think about how to get rid of Kennedy Davis.

Chapter 26

Manitou Springs, Colorado

Reid was glad Kayla hadn't asked him to stay, because he would have. The truth was, he was excited to go. He rummaged through another bin for the last few things he'd need for the trip. He found two more T-shirts his size, and stuffed them in the pack. The only thing left to find was a hat, then he'd be ready to tackle the food supplies.

"Son?" Tinker stood in the doorway. "Your grandmother had a little chat with me, and now I need to have one with you."

"Sounds serious." Reid closed the bin and sat on it.

"Since Kayla is determined to stay here, your grandma's staying, too. Now, I don't want to leave her, but she's insisting."

"That's right." Sarah popped her head in the doorway. "No arguments."

"Reid, help me talk some sense—"

"Psht!" Sarah shushed Tinker. "You know you want to go."

"*Sarah—*"

"Psht!" She did it again.

A laugh escaped Reid's tightly sealed lips. "Sorry, I didn't mean to." He turned away, trying to stifle it, but a snort escaped. Then another laugh, and he couldn't stop. "I'm sorry, I can't help it." He bent over his knees, letting the laughter roll out of him.

Sarah giggled, then Tinker started to chuckle. After a moment, all three were howling. When Reid got control of himself, his eyes were watering and his stomach ached, but he felt a whole lot better.

Sarah sighed. "I needed that."

"Lordy, so did I," Tinker said.

"So it's settled?" Sarah looked from Reid to Tinker.

"It's settled." Tinker gave Sarah a sidelong look, then grinned at Reid. "We're going on a road trip!"

"I was hoping to leave tomorrow," Reid said. "But whenever you're ready."

"I assumed tomorrow was a foregone conclusion," Tinker said.

"How's that?"

"My wife told me to leave as soon as possible. You've seen what happens when I try to argue with her." Tinker poked Sarah with his elbow. "So we're leaving tomorrow. I guess I'd better gather up my clothes, huh?"

"I'm about done here, then I can get started on the food and other supplies." Reid sighed. It was going to be a long night. "Grandma, will you show me what foodstores we can take?"

"No need. Your pops and I took care of everything while we had our little discussion. Food, water, cooking gear, bedrolls."

"Tools, guns, ammo," Tinker continued. "Tarps, toiletries, and everything else we could think of. Water's the main thing, and we have lots."

"Wow," Reid said. "Thank you."

"See you bright and early," Tinker said, heading out.

"Goodnight, Pops." Reid spotted a bin of baseball caps on a low shelf. "That's what I've been looking for." He grabbed a hat and pulled it on.

"It suits you," Sarah said. "I always was partial to the Yankees."

"Then Yankees it is." He hooked the hat to his pack with a carabiner. "That's the last thing I needed, so I'm heading for a hot shower. Might be my last one for a while."

"I did want to ask you something," Sarah said, her expression serious.

Reid swallowed hard. "I'm sorry about Dad."

"He should have had a lot more years. But I don't blame you. It wasn't your fault."

But it was.

"Your father wanted you to be the next bishop, didn't he?" Sarah continued. "What will happen now?"

"He'd finally accepted that I wasn't going to do it. I'm no leader, and I'm certainly not a believer, not in his church, maybe not even in God. Dad had been training up a handful of others. I'm sure one of them has taken over already." *Or maybe not.* Vega said "proof" of Raiders changed everything. Maybe there would be no church. "That's what you wanted to ask me?"

"No, actually I wanted to know if you're taking Zeke with you."

The question surprised him. "I hadn't thought about it."

"Why don't you sleep on it, dear."

"No, he's attached himself to Kayla. Don't you think he'd be happier staying with her?"

"I was hoping you'd noticed. I think it would be good for her, too."

"Then Zeke stays." He gave her a peck on the cheek. "Goodnight."

Reid stood in the shower for at least twenty minutes. The water felt almost hot enough to cook with. He never wanted to get out, but his skin had started to shrivel. He toweled dry and slipped into baggy sweatpants, then padded down the hall toward his room.

He hesitated at Kayla's door. He'd been pointedly *not* thinking about her because every time he did he got confused. But on impulse he knocked.

"It's open," Kayla called.

He cracked the door. "Just saying goodnight."

She was reading in bed, propped against the pillows with a pink quilt tucked around her. She looked beautiful in the soft glow of the lamp, her hair flowing loose over one shoulder.

"Come in for a minute?" She put her book on the nightstand, scooted over, and patted the space she'd vacated.

Reid wondered if he should say no, but he couldn't. He crossed the room and sat on the foot of the bed, not sure what to do with his arms, wishing he'd put on a shirt.

"Reid . . . I've been trying to think what to say." Her eyes welled up.

He moved closer and took her hand. It was small and strong, and fit perfectly in his.

She pulled her hand back and folded her arms across her chest. There was determination in the set of her jaw. "No, don't be nice. I need to say . . . thank you. . . ." Her face wrinkled up, but she composed herself again. "Thank you for always being there for me, and for Brian. He knew that, and he loved you."

She half-smiled, half-grimaced. He reached out again but she stopped him.

"No, let me say this." She blew out a breath. "I don't want you to worry about me while you're gone. I'll be fine. Just come back. With seeds. That's what Brian would have wanted."

Reid opened his mouth to ask about Brian's death—he needed to know before he left—but Kayla burst into tears.

"I'm going to miss you." She sobbed, covering her face with her hands.

Reid felt like his own heart was breaking. He wrapped his arms around her and she clung to his chest, her face warm and moist against his bare skin. "Shhh. Shhh," he said, smoothing her hair. "It's going to be okay."

She cried harder, racked with sobs and ragged breaths. He held her tight and rocked her until she shuddered and pulled away, wiping her face.

"I'm sorry," she whispered. "I didn't expect that. I didn't know it would be so hard to say goodbye to you."

"Then don't."

"I don't want to." She touched his face. "Will you stay with me to-night?"

He stood and put out the lamp. In the moonlight her features looked porcelain, her hair like spun silver. He watched her, giving her a moment to change her mind.

She pulled back the covers and he climbed in, sliding his arm under her shoulders. She snuggled into the crook of his neck. He didn't know what she wanted from him or what it would do to him, but it didn't matter. He'd do anything she asked.

"I didn't want to be alone this last night," she said.

"You don't ever have to be alone."

She looked into his eyes. Her mouth was soft and her breathing was slow. He thought she was going to kiss him. Instead she took his hand and placed it palm down on her stomach.

"I'm pregnant."

Chapter 27

Lost Angeles, Pascal's living room

"**P**rofessor Emery, I am not accustomed to being kept waiting." Pascal's anger had been growing since sunset, and he had to remind himself he couldn't handle Emery like other men.

"I apologize, Chancellor," Emery said, pushing his glasses higher on his nose. "I was in the middle of an experiment. I opened the door for your men as soon as I could."

"From now on, you'll keep the doors unlocked."

"But that could be extremely detrimental. Some of the experiments require delicate conditions of light, temperature, and airflow. If one were disturbed at the wrong time, it would set us back weeks. Months, even."

"We wouldn't want that. Not as long as there is actually progress. You do have progress to report, don't you?"

"Yes, in fact I do. Quite exciting findings. The rat specimens are—"

"Rats?" Pascal rose from his chair before he realized. He made himself sit back down. "I believe I was quite clear on the subject of rats. We already *have* rats. We will never get milk or butter or eggs from *rats*."

"Yes, but the cow and goat experiments were going nowhere. There's not enough data to recreate that kind of animal. With rats, we have the advantage of living specimens, plus the substantial amount of research material from the world before. We've made real progress with rat DNA. Eventually we'll apply our findings to the preserved DNA of other species."

"Eventually." He saw it in his mind's eye—the path to the Irvine labs crumbling away. The scientists were never going to bring back animal life, not in his lifetime or his son's. Probably not ever.

"This is good news, Chancellor," Emery said.

"Is it?" *Not for you.* Pascal wanted to shove a pistol between the professor's yellow teeth. It would be satisfying to watch his brains spray out the back of his head. But the satisfaction would be fleeting. He visualized it on the scales, weighing that satisfaction against the possibility—however remote—that Emery would produce something useful. "Leave now, Professor. While I'm feeling generous."

After Emery scuttled out the door, Pascal rested his head back against the chair and closed his eyes. Only one path to the future remained. It was faint, but visible. Off in the murky distance was the home of the missionaries.

Chapter 28

Manitou Springs, Colorado

"Oh my God," Reid breathed. *A baby.*
Kayla let go of his hand, but he didn't move it from her stomach. There was a baby in there. Brian's baby.

"That's why I can't go with you to Ellay."

"No, of course you can't. You need to be on bed rest, monitored, taken care of. How far along are you?"

"More than three months."

"What? You had to have known before now. What the hell have you been doing running around in the city? If you'd only said something, they wouldn't have made you go on brevet."

"I know."

"Then why didn't you tell them? Why didn't you tell *me?* Kayla, you could have lost the baby."

"I know. I'm sorry."

"Did Brian know?"

She nodded. "I kept it from him at first. When I found out, Tinker had just gotten the car working and we were all going to leave together. I didn't want Brian to go without me."

"Go where?"

"Anywhere. Everywhere. Looking for seeds, looking for people. Brian was convinced there were other people alive in the world. I think Tinker believes it too, even though he's never heard anyone on those radios of his. Personally, I didn't care if we ever found anything as long as I was with Brian. If I'd let on about the baby, I'd have been left behind."

"No, you're wrong. Brian never would have left you."

"Don't you see? That would have been worse. I couldn't be the reason he didn't go. So I kept the pregnancy a secret. When we were getting ready for the trip, it was easy to hide the symptoms, but once we were driving, the motion of the car was too much. We were only a little way into the Burn when I needed to throw up. Your grandparents didn't know we'd stopped—they were so exhausted from packing, they were asleep in the backseat. After I puked, Brian asked point-blank if I was pregnant, and I couldn't lie. I've never seen him so angry. The things he said . . ."

Reid could imagine his brother's fury.

"I didn't want to wake your grandparents," Kayla continued, "so I walked away from the car. He followed, telling me I was irresponsible, that I could have lost our baby. He said we had to go back, that I couldn't travel until after the baby was born. I didn't want to hear it. I didn't want him to be right, so I kept walking. One second he was behind me. The next, the ground gave way beneath him and he fell into a basement. A piece of rebar went right through his side. There was so much *blood*." Her voice broke and she took a shuddering breath. "But he must have also hit his head because he never screamed. He was just gone. I don't think he even knew what happened."

Reid held tightly to Kayla's hand, trying not to squeeze it too hard, trying not to be angry with her, trying not to picture his brother lying bloody and broken. Sobs welled up in his chest, but he held them in. Brian was gone and nothing could change that. He took a deep breath, making sure he had control of his voice. "You were lucky. You could have been killed, too."

"I should have been! It should have been me. It's my fault he's dead. I was scared and stupid and selfish. *We both knew better.* But I wasn't thinking, and he was so angry, he wasn't looking. One wrong step and he was dead. It was my fault, but I blamed the baby. I know that's terrible, but I did, and I didn't want it."

"But you changed your mind?"

"I could hate it when it was only an idea. But I felt it move, and now it's real. It's a baby. Brian's baby. All I have left of him."

He let out a long breath, holding Kayla's hand gently now. His heart ached for Brian, but also for Kayla. She'd been through hell, alone. "I wish you'd told me sooner."

"I didn't want you to hate me. But tonight I realized I might never see you again, and you deserve to know the truth. About the baby, and about how Brian died. No matter how it makes you feel about me."

He squeezed her hand and looked into her eyes. "I could never hate you."

She broke eye contact, but still held onto his hand. "You should hate me. I was stupid and selfish. If I hadn't been, Brian would still be alive."

"No, look at me, Kay." He tipped her chin up, making it hard for her to look away. "It was an accident. It was horrible and tragic, and we'll never be the same. But it's not your fault."

"God, I want to feel normal again. Is anything ever going to feel normal again?"

He hugged her and she clung to him. He wasn't sure what normal was, but at least these secrets weren't between them anymore.

"Reid?" she whispered. "I'm scared."

He held her closer. He wanted to tell her that he was scared, too. Scared of his feelings for her. Scared what it meant that Brian was gone. Scared of her going through a pregnancy without him there to take care of her. Scared of leaving and maybe not ever coming back. But that's not what she needed to hear.

"It's going to be okay," he murmured in her ear. "My grandmother won't let anything happen to you or the baby while I'm gone, and when I come back I'll bring seeds. I'm going to make sure this baby has a future. I promise."

Chapter 29

Highway 285, Poncha Springs, Colorado

Tinker beat a rhythm on the steering wheel. "I should have rigged a way to play music."

"Do you miss it?" Reid asked, wondering what it would have been like to have music any time you wanted it.

"Yeah, particularly in the car. Still, it's great to be on the road again. So free. Almost like the good old days."

Reid let silence fall in the car again. He was worried about Kayla, but he didn't want to spoil Tinker's fun.

"Even going this route, we should make Albuquerque before dark," Tinker said.

They'd gone a back way to avoid being seen by Vega's men in Colorado Springs.

"Yeah, that's great, Pops."

"Try to sound a little excited," Tinker said. "This is a road trip. It's supposed to be fun."

"Sorry."

"A penny for your thoughts?"

"Another one of your ancient expressions?"

"No, I thought you could use a penny."

Reid couldn't help grinning. "Okay, if you must know, I was thinking about Kayla. I hate leaving her behind. I know Grandma will take good care of her, but . . ."

"You care about her."

"Yeah."

"But there's more to it. I get it. I know about the baby. That's a tough thing. A real joy to have that living memory of Brian, if it works out. But tough for you, I imagine. Hard to have a constant reminder of her dead husband if you're in love with her."

"What? Why would you think that?"

"Are you? In love with her?"

"It doesn't matter how I feel, Pops. What matters is I'm going to be there for her, and the baby too. I'm glad to have that reminder of Brian, and I'm going to do everything I can to give the baby a chance for a good life. We're that baby's family, and we should be Kayla's too."

"Kayla is family. Always will be," Tinker said. "I love her to pieces. I treat her like my own, and that won't change. But I gotta speak my mind on something."

Reid was pretty sure he didn't want to hear it, but Tinker wasn't likely to let it go. Might as well get it over with. "Okay, Pops. Spit it out."

"You need to be clear how you feel about her. With yourself and with her. If you love her, tell her. If you don't love her, you won't be doing her any favors, or yourself either, by marrying her."

"Marrying her? You don't have to worry about that. We're not going back to the Mountain, so even without Dad's protection, no one is going to force us to get married."

"Good. Because once you've walked in the sunshine, you can never go back to living in the dark."

"Huh? What are you talking about?"

"What I'm trying to say is, when you *care about* someone versus when you're *in love,* it's like night and day. Sure, you can live a pretty good life in the dark. You'll stumble around and bruise your shins, but you can be happy. But, once you've walked in the daylight and you can *see,* it's a whole different ballgame. After that, you'd wonder why you'd ever willingly live in the dark. You get my meaning?"

"I, I guess so."

"Kayla and Brian, they lived in the light. So if you two aren't in love, *you* might be able to make it work, but *she'd* know the difference. Be honest with yourself, and with her. Tell her how you feel."

"Sure, Pops." But he had no intention of ever telling Kayla how he felt. She'd always see him as a poor substitute for his brother. If he hoped for anything more, he'd only be disappointed. Besides, he'd made a promise.

Chapter 30

Pacific Ocean, aboard the Emancipation

Nikolai dressed for breakfast. Olexi hadn't returned since delivering his little lecture the night before, giving Nikolai more than enough time to think. He'd thought and paced all night, and made up his mind—he despised Kennedy. Hated him more than he thought possible to hate.

At one point, he concluded that throwing Kennedy overboard would be appropriate, but that would make Kennedy a martyr and Nikolai the villain in his daughter's eyes. Instead, Kennedy should experience the full agony of being dumped when Tatiana came to her senses.

With that image vivid in his mind, Nikolai could tolerate being on the same ship, at least for a little while. He headed out to beg forgiveness and breakfast from Finola. Olexi may have been snowed by Kennedy, but Finola was too good a judge of character.

"Hello?" Nikolai cautiously poked his head into the galley.

It was deserted. He hesitated. It wasn't his ship, but Kennedy had said to eat where and when he wanted. Certainly no one would begrudge him a snack. He went to the pantry where he tucked a couple of apples in his pockets and grabbed a handful of almonds. He tossed a few nuts in his mouth. Fifty-year-old semi-rancid almonds. Still edible, for now. But when they weren't, when all the old-world food ran out, there would still be rats, the endless bounty of the sea, and fresh apples due to the foresight of the Washington Apple Seed Storage Project. There was plenty of food. So why wasn't it enough for Tatiana? Why had it never been enough for Jess?

He popped the rest of the nuts in his mouth and turned to leave. Finola blocked his way with a cast-iron skillet in one hand and a large wooden spoon in the other.

He forced down the half-chewed nuts. "Finny." He stepped toward her.

She held up the spoon and shook her head.

"What?" Nikolai said, throwing up his hands. "At least tell me what I've done."

"I can't. I'm not speaking to you." She pointed to the door with her spoon. "Out."

"But—"

"*Out.*" She swatted his arm with the spoon.

"I—"

She raised the skillet.

"Fine." He left, feeling sorry for himself. But as he walked back to his quarters, he felt less sorry and more indignant. How dare she treat him like that? He might not be her captain now, but he'd been her boss for more than half her life, and her friend for longer. He deserved more respect.

When he arrived at his cabin door, he turned back around. He wasn't going to hide. He had nothing to be ashamed of. He was in the right. *Kennedy* should be ashamed, living with a young girl without her father's consent, without his knowledge.

Nikolai climbed the stairs to the deck and strode to the rail. *To hell with Kennedy,* he thought, gazing out across the vast water. He devoured the nuts and both apples down to the cores, telling himself the only thing that mattered was bringing Will and Tatiana home. For that, he could endure a lot worse than being a passenger aboard Kennedy's boat.

The sound of a sail luffing caught his attention. A crewman stood with the jib sheet in his hand, but did nothing to correct the luffing. The boat steered closer to the wind, but he hadn't heard anyone call the tack. Nikolai saw Kennedy at the helm, sailing merrily along, unaware his crewman wasn't trimming the sail.

"*Hooy na ny,*" Nikolai muttered. A boat was only as fast as her crew. He didn't have time for this. "Sailor!"

The crewman looked up. *Ernie.* that was his name.

"Ernie, see to the jib," Nikolai commanded. "Haul in the sheet for the tack."

Ernie stood frozen while the sail flapped about like a beached halibut.

"Fine, I'll do it," Nikolai barked, grabbing the ropes from Ernie's fists. He let down the jib, handed the ropes back to Ernie, then ran back to the other sail, muttering to himself. "If you want something done right . . ." He removed the sheet from the cleat and hollered, "Tack!"

then let the boom fly. The boat turned.

"Stop!" Kennedy grabbed the ropes.

There was the sound of an impact and the boat lurched, sending Nikolai to his knees.

What the hell? Nikolai stood. This was not good. No, in fact, this could be bad. Extremely bad.

"We were luffing on purpose, pinching through a shallow channel," Kennedy said.

Nikolai was mortified. "We're aground?"

Kennedy nodded, his expression grave.

Ernie locked eyes with Kennedy. "Get Friday," he said, then stripped down to his shorts and went over the rail.

"My sincere apologies." Nikolai wanted to sink through the deck. He should have stayed in his cabin. "What can I do? I'll get Friday."

"No, I will," Kennedy said. "In the future, I'd be grateful if you'd offer your opinions and concerns to me before acting."

"Of course," Nikolai said, humiliated that he was being chastised, and horrified because he deserved it. He cringed, thinking what serious damage might have been caused to the keel or hull. "It won't happen again. You have my word." Nikolai headed for his room, where he planned to stay.

Chapter 31

Lost Angeles, Pascal's office

The afternoon sun hit the oak desk at a slant. Pascal placed his fountain pen in the holder and leaned back in his chair. The day had been filled with pleasant anticipation. Linus was returning from the coast and would join him for dinner. He was anxious to hear how his son liked the gift he'd sent.

Living at the beach was good for a boy, and Pascal hadn't minded his son spending weeks at a time there when he was younger. But now that he was becoming a young man, Pascal needed more time with him, to groom and shape him. And the truth was, he missed him.

Raising Linus was his one true pleasure. The boy had spirit, something Pascal had been careful not to break. He was charismatic, opinionated, and brilliant. Pascal had seen to that by choosing Maybelline to bear his child, then paid the price for that choice many times over.

Maybelline's fierce protectiveness, keen appreciation for power, and superior intellect had been good for Linus, but only to a point. Recently, Linus had started showing signs of rebellion against her, which meant the time was drawing near when Pascal could be rid of her. Linus would miss her, but that could be turned into an advantage.

A rap at the door brought a smile to Pascal's face. Gomez was on an errand, and few people would dare knock on his office door without authorization from his secretary. Obviously, Linus could not wait until dinner to thank him for the gift. Pascal closed his portfolio and stood.

"Come in."

The door burst open. "I need a word with you."

Maybelline.

"I was expecting my son." Pascal sat, weary at the thought of yet another of Maybelline's demands. "What do you want?"

"How dare you give Linus command of a platoon of Blades? For God's sake, Pascal, he's a child."

"My son was born to lead. How do you expect him to run this city if he's mollycoddled through his formative years? Not that I have to explain myself to you. Tell me what you want and get out."

"What I want? What I want is for you to treat Linus appropriately for his age. He should be studying and swimming and taking music lessons, not skating around the city with trained killers pretending to lead them. He's fourteen, for God's sake. Not twenty."

"What's your point?"

"My point is, I'm taking Linus back to the coast first thing tomorrow morning. There he has boys his own age to play with. He can spend his time engaging in more suitable activities, like fishing and chess. He doesn't belong in the city as long as you insist on treating him like your second in command. Send us a message when you regain your senses and I'll consider coming back."

"You," Pascal said in a low growl, "will not take my son anywhere."

"I most certainly will. He's my son as much as yours."

Pascal came around the desk, grabbed her arm, and yanked her close. "He is not your son. He was never your son. You've served a purpose, but do not suppose you are anything more than a nursemaid. You are not indispensable."

Maybelline's raven eyes blazed. "He loves me, Pascal. If you do anything to me, you'll lose him, do you hear me? He's old enough now to see you for what you are. If you fight me, he'll take my side. I guarantee it."

"Do you. Clearly you underestimate me. I always thought your headstrong nature was stronger than your intellect. It's a shame I was correct, or things might have ended differently. At least the timing, anyway."

"You don't frighten me. Linus is everything to you. You wouldn't dare harm me, because he'd hate you for it. You'd never win him back, and you know it."

"Sir?" Gomez appeared in the doorway. "Is everything all right?"

"Escort Ms. Kagawa to the spa," Pascal said.

"Of course, sir."

"What are you doing?" Maybelline struggled as Pascal pulled her toward the door.

"Making sure you have an enjoyable time at the spa, dear." He released her arm, and was pleased to see her rub it. "Gomez, Ms. Kagawa is not to have any contact with Linus until further notice. If the boy attempts to see her, he's to be told she's ill. With womanly troubles."

"Yes, sir." Gomez took hold of Maybelline's arm where Pascal's prints still showed.

"Let go of me, I know the way." She shook free of Gomez's grip. "You won't get away with this, Pascal. Linus is smart. He'll see through this."

"Gomez, she's not to leave the spa without my express permission. And make sure she doesn't con anyone into delivering messages, particularly not to Linus."

"I'll see to it."

Pascal closed the door, smiling to himself. Never again would that bitch interfere with how he raised his son. He hadn't intended to initiate the plan this soon, but she'd given him no choice, and now he couldn't wait for it to be done.

He grabbed his fedora and went to notify the doctor. Soon he'd be rid of *that* annoying bottom feeder as well. Two for the price of one. Glorious efficiency.

As he crossed bustling New Orleans Court heading for the doctor's office, people stayed out of his way. He relished the wariness in their eyes. They knew he was the man who could make or break them.

He loved the power, loved being in charge. He loved it more because he was not one of them. He'd come as an outsider and made it his own. From the beginning, it had been obvious he was from a better class. His parents had been professors at CalTech, not some carnie folk who'd survived in the service tunnels like rats. Or perhaps *mice,* he thought as he tipped his hat to the statue of the park's creator and his godforsaken mascot.

As he strode past, he glanced down Main Street, recalling the first time he'd set foot in the park. It had been on that very street, that very first day, when he'd seen what the park could become. The necessary components had already been there. The only thing lacking was someone with the vision to assemble them. He'd stepped into the leadership void and rebuilt the park in a way its original "founder" never could have imagined. It was his legacy, and it was all for Linus. Anyone who got in the way would be dealt with swiftly, surely, and permanently.

At the doctor's office, nurses, attendants, and patients alike skittered out of his way.

"Where is Van Hooten?" he demanded of the waifish woman at the reception desk.

"I, I don't know," she said. "I'm s-s-sorry, s-sir." She looked ready to cry.

A slick-bunned nurse in a white uniform came up behind her. "He's in exam five, with a patient," she said.

"Where's that?" Pascal asked.

The woman looked surprised. "End of the hall. But as I said, he's with a patient."

Pascal wished someone would try to stop him, but of course no one did. He found the number "five" on the wall and opened the door without knocking. A pregnant woman lay on her back with her feet up in stirrups.

"Van Hooten," Pascal said to the man between her legs. "I need to see you."

"Chancellor, I'm in the middle of—"

"*Now.*"

Van Hooten patted the woman's knee. "I'll be back soon." He snapped off his gloves and tossed them in a receptacle.

Once inside the doctor's private office, Pascal locked the door. He sat on the edge of the desk, leaving Van Hooten standing awkwardly in the middle of the room.

"The personal matter we discussed some time ago," Pascal said. "You recall our conversation?"

"Of course, Chancellor." The loose flesh on Van Hooten's cheeks colored. He folded his arms across his chest and frowned, his eyes gazing in the general vicinity of Pascal's shoes.

"You will begin immediately."

"But Chancellor, I—"

Pascal raised his chin, which was enough to stop Van Hooten mid-excuse. "She's in a private room at the spa. You'll see her for 'womanly troubles.' I expect this to be concluded in a matter of days."

"I understand."

"Your service will be rewarded, as long as you remember—our business is to be kept strictly confidential. Don't breathe a word, even to your wife."

"Of course." Van Hooten unfolded then refolded his arms. "There is one problem. I examined Ms. Kagawa this morning and she was healthy. What if she doesn't want treatment?"

"I expect you to be convincing."

Pascal had no doubt the doctor was motivated enough to figure it out. He turned and left to go see Linus. It was time to step up his education, beginning with the assignment that would mark his son's entry into adulthood, and Maybelline's exit.

Chapter 32

Interstate 25 outside Algodones, New Mexico

"Sorry to wake you, son."

"Huh? What's that?" Reid rubbed his face. "How long have I been asleep?"

"Six hours or so," Tinker said.

"I guess I was tired."

"Guess so." Tinker drove the car onto the dirt on the side of the road and put it in park. "We're still a little ways from Albuquerque, but I've got to whiz so bad, I had to pull over."

Tinker jumped out of the Hummer and unzipped his pants as he walked to a dried-up scrub oak. A moment later, Reid heard him chuckle. Then laugh.

"What's so funny?" he called.

"Damn." Tinker started toward the car, erupting in a fit of guffaws.

"What? What happened?"

Tinker cleared his throat and wiped his eyes. "I pulled over."

"How's that funny?"

"There ain't another person alive on this highway. But I made sure to pull off the road to stop." He sighed. "Old habits die hard. It struck me funny." He got in the car and put it in gear.

"So where are we?" Reid asked, looking around at the plain dirt landscape.

"A little ways north of Albuquerque. I don't want to go in blind, so I'm fixin' to turn off the main highway and head up the mountain to get a view of the city. About a million years ago, I took a tram up there somewhere. I doubt I could find the exact spot, but I think I found a road on the map that should take us to a good vantage point."

"What do you think we'll see?"

"Damned if I know."

"Wouldn't it be great—awful but great—if we found grown food this close to home?"

"Don't get your hopes up, son. Nothing much grew in New Mexico in the Before, and I wouldn't think it a hotbed of agriculture now. I hope we find people, though, even if they're living like we're living."

"What do you think the chances are?"

"Who knows now, but I'd give good odds that some of them military guys at the air base made it through the initial event. There's these cave-like data processing and tactical centers totally sheltered from the outside. People in there would've had a good shot. What happened afterward is anyone's guess. I never heard a thing on the shortwave, so it could be a ghost town. I guess we'll find out soon enough."

As they turned off the road and headed into the mountains, fewer cars cluttered the road, and most had rolled into the guardrail or onto the shoulder due to the slope, but it was still slow-going. Eventually they reached a small plateau with good vantage point, and Tinker stopped the Hummer.

"Well, there's Albuquerque. I said not to get your hopes up."

Reid surveyed the city spread out below. There was no movement, no color. Just shades of brown as far as he could see.

Then something caught his eye. At the eastern edge of the city a lone spindle of smoke snaked skyward.

"Pops!" he pointed.

"Would you look at that," Tinker said. "There's nothing growing, but there's damn sure people down there."

Reid returned Tinker's wide grin. "Won't Grandma and Kayla be surprised we found people living this close to home? So what do we do? What's our plan?"

"Hell if I know. Truthfully, I didn't think we'd come across anyone this soon."

"I guess we don't go knock on the door."

"Guess not." Tinker scratched his head. "How about a little old-fashioned surveillance to help us come up with a plan?"

They headed back down to the Interstate, then crept south, hoping that anyone looking would mistake the Hummer for one of the old cars littering the highway. After a few miles, they took a side road east and skirted the foothills until they had a closer view of the smoke plume.

Tinker pulled into the parking lot of an adobe church, parked, and unfolded the map.

"If I had to bet, I'd say that smoke's coming from the general area of the air base," Tinker said. "What'd I tell ya? Hot damn, those boys did survive. Give me those binoculars, and I'll see if I can spot anything useful."

Reid handed him the binoculars, then folded up the map. While Tinker spied through the open side window, Reid surveyed the other cars in the lot for signs of recent use. They were all dilapidated, all equally covered in grime.

"Do you think they have cars that work?" he asked.

"They haven't come north to where we live, so it seems unlikely they have the means. But you never know. Either way, I'm anxious to see their faces when they get a load of us."

"Maybe they have contact with other groups of people. Maybe they know where to find grown food, even though it doesn't look like they grow it themselves."

"We can hope." Tinker put the binocs on the dash. "I got to whiz again. Can you believe it? The joys of getting old. Be right back."

"I don't think so, old-timer." A brown-skinned man inserted the muzzle of a shotgun through Tinker's window.

Reid felt the blood drain from his face. A similar man was outside his window with a revolver.

"Is this always how you welcome visitors?" Tinker asked, holding his hands up by his shoulders.

"Get out of the car. *Slowly,*" the first man said.

Reid glanced at Tinker. "No," he mouthed. "*Drive.*"

Tinker shook his head.

"No talking! Hurry up!" the second man shouted, gesturing with the revolver.

Reid's hand shook as he opened his door. The man grabbed him by the shirt and yanked him out of the car.

"Check him over good, Mario," the first man said.

Mario patted every inch of Reid with his free hand.

"We're friendly," Reid said, feeling ridiculous as soon as he said it.

"Found this." Mario pulled the Swiss Army knife from Reid's front pocket. "Other than that, he's clean."

"We didn't come to fight you," Reid said, hating the quiver in his voice.

"Shut up." Mario pointed his gun again. "Move."

Reid followed Tinker to the church, their hands atop their heads as instructed. Reid wasn't about to argue. He and Tinker sat on the crumbling cement steps. Mario and two other men held guns on them, while the first guy and several others swarmed over the Hummer.

"It'll be all right, son," Tinker said in a low voice.

"No talking! Shove over. Not so close," Mario said.

Reid met his grandpa's eyes then scooted a couple feet away. Were they going to kill them? His heart was beating fast, and sweat ran down his back and forehead. He wiped his face on his shoulder and tried to slow his pulse. They'd get out of this. They had to.

While Mario and his compatriots kept watch over them, the others pulled the supplies out of the Hummer. They found the pistols and rifles under the seats, and the extra ammo and shotguns in the back. They were already hauling the drums of water into the church.

"Let's talk about this," Tinker shouted toward the car. "I want to speak to whoever's in charge."

"Shut your hole." A man swung the butt of his shotgun into Tinker's face.

"Pops!"

Tinker fell back, blood pouring from his mouth. He tried to sit up, but he was dazed.

"Let me help him." Reid scrambled toward Tinker, but Mario's boot blocked his way. "Pops, stay still. Put pressure on your lip."

"Why can't you people *shut up?*" Mario's face was red, tendons bulging in his neck. He sounded on edge, like he'd love an excuse to pull the trigger.

Reid clamped his mouth shut, silently urging Tinker to do the same.

"Take the rest of the stuff inside," a man called, obviously an authority. "Bring the prisoners around back. We'll finish dealing with them there."

Reid's heart raced as he scanned for some way to escape. He tried to think like a soldier, like a Remote. What would Kayla do? There had to be a way out of this mess, but he couldn't see it.

Chapter 33

Lost Angeles, Pascal's private dining room

"Father, you should have seen it." Linus ate the meat from the back of the fork without putting down his knife or repositioning the fork to his other hand. He continued to talk while he chewed. "My Blades swooped in and grabbed the thief so fast he didn't even yell. His basket tipped over and cans went everywhere, but my men didn't stumble. The guy didn't know what hit him." He added another forkful of meat to the half-pulverized chunks still in his mouth.

Pascal didn't correct the boy. Why should he? Linus didn't need table manners to lead. He'd never need them to win a woman or an election. He would take his rightful office and ensure his position through his actions and prowess in the field. He need not ever worry about such petty things as etiquette. "They took the thief to the Tank?"

"I ordered them to." Linus took his last bite of meat and moved on to a large bowl of fruit.

"And?" Pascal added salt and pepper to his vegetables.

"They obeyed my command, of course. The sergeant, what's-his-name, he said 'yes, sir' and tied the guy's hands. Made him run all the way."

"You should know the names of your soldiers," Pascal admonished gently.

"It was . . . it was Navens. No, *Nathans*. Definitely Nathans. Sorry, I won't forget again."

"Good." Pascal took a long pull from his glass. Linus probably assumed it was water like his own, though Pascal would tell him the truth if he asked. He wondered when it would be time to introduce him to something stronger than wine. Better sooner than later so he'd gain a mastery over it rather than risking the other way around. The same was true for women, now that Linus was showing an interest. "What are your plans for tomorrow?"

"I wanted to take Mother for a carriage ride and show her what my platoon can do, but she's sick again."

"That's what I hear." Pascal chewed slowly. "With your mother indisposed, what will you do instead?"

"Why? Do you have a mission for me? My team is well-trained, I can tell already. We can do whatever you need."

"There is something . . . but I don't know if you're ready," Pascal said, baiting the hook. "It's more complicated than bringing in a thief."

"I'm ready. Give me the chance and I'll show you. My men and I can handle anything."

"This particular mission would be for you alone, and it requires guile and finesse. There is more to leading men than brute strength and barking orders."

"I know, Father. I can handle it."

Pascal took another slow drink, drawing the moment out as he gauged whether his son was as ready for the mission as he was eager. "Linus, this is a surveillance and information-gathering mission, and frankly, I was thinking about assigning someone a bit older, more seasoned."

"A person's age is not a good measure of his worth. I command Blades who are twice my age."

You've commanded them for a day, Pascal thought. Instead he said, "This is true. But the subject in question is closer to my age. A man of position."

"Who is he? Tell me the man and the mission, and I'll judge if I can handle it. You know I can keep a secret, so what harm is it to tell me?"

"That's a good answer." Pascal smiled, and Linus beamed back at him. "Come, we'll discuss it over a drink."

Linus followed him to the veranda, wisely holding his tongue until he had a drink in hand, though Pascal could sense his impatience bubbling beneath the surface.

"This isn't wine," Linus said, holding his snifter up to the sunset.

"It's cognac. What do you think?"

Linus smelled the cognac then tipped his glass to his lips. He held the liquid in his mouth a moment before swallowing, as he'd been taught to do with wine, then he tipped his head, looking thoughtful. "It's like wine, but stronger."

"Very perceptive. Keep that in mind when you enjoy brandy and other spirits. You must learn to gauge its effect and not let it get the better of you. A momentary lapse in judgment with a bottle, or a woman, can be more dangerous than a momentary lapse of attention in a fight with a skilled adversary."

"Yes, Father." Linus placed his glass on the patio table and sat on one of a pair of wooden slat rockers, looking at him expectantly.

Pascal sat in the other chair. He cradled his snifter in both hands, bringing it to his nose and appreciating the bouquet, then taking a slow sip. Linus had been patient long enough. "The mission is of the utmost importance, Linus. It concerns your mother."

"Mother? Why, what's wrong?" Linus came forward on his chair, his brow drawn in concern.

"I'm hoping you can shed some light on that. When you were at the coast, did she seem in good health to you?"

"She was fine."

"As I suspected. This is what's troubling. Does it concern you that when she's away she's well, and then immediately upon her return she becomes ill? Didn't the same thing happen when she returned from your excursion last month?"

"Now that you mention it. But what does this have to do with the mission?"

"Perhaps it's nothing, but . . ." Pascal savored his cognac, noting Linus's rapt attention. "I know you are familiar with Dr. Van Hooten, your mother's physician."

"Yes."

"I've noticed over the last several months that your mother has become ill *after* seeing the doctor. She had an appointment when you got back from the coast, correct?"

"Yes. So you think it's not a coincidence, that he's *causing* Mother to be sick?" Linus scooted to the edge of his chair, leaning forward, cognac forgotten.

"It crossed my mind."

"Have others become ill after seeing him? Or do you think it's something specifically to do with my mother? Why would he do something like that? What would he have to gain?"

"Those are good questions, and I don't know the answers. Which is the very reason I need someone to check into this."

"If he's making people sick on purpose, we have to stop him!"

"Yes, and while I appreciate your enthusiasm, we can't be too hasty. I don't have to tell you how few doctors we have. This could be coincidence. There are germs in a doctor's office. It's reasonable that someone would become ill afterward."

"But Mother doesn't go to his office. Dr. Van Hooten comes to her."

"Oh, is that so?" Of course, this was something Pascal was already well aware of, but he wanted Linus to put the pieces together himself.

"Besides, he's a *doctor*—he knows how to keep germs from spreading. I don't think it's a coincidence." Linus straightened, a determined look on his face.

"We can't afford to jump to conclusions, son. This must be handled deftly, delicately."

"I can be very shrewd and calculating, Father. Van Hooten still thinks of me as a child. I can find out what he's doing without him ever suspecting. I know I can. You *have* to give me this assignment. I said I'd tell you if I could handle it or not. There is no one better for this job."

"Linus." Pascal paused until Linus stopped fidgeting. "If our suspicions prove true, this is a grave matter. How we handle it will have broad-reaching effects."

"I *know*." The boy was impassioned, hands clenched, leaning forward in his chair.

"Do you?" This was the critical part. Did Linus actually understand what measures might be needed?

"Father, if it were revealed that a doctor was harming our citizens— especially my own mother—right under our noses, we'd have to respond with an iron fist. We would show the people that his actions did not go undetected and that no one can get away with such a heinous act."

"Yes." Pascal nodded. Linus did indeed have a grasp on the implications, but was he ready to take the necessary action *himself?* "But consider this. How such a criminal is dealt with after being caught reflects directly on the man who apprehends him. If this man is you—you who are to govern this city one day—how you respond to such an extreme crime will demonstrate what kind of leader you are. I won't put you in a position to appear weak before your people, so if you're not ready to see this through to the end, you must not participate at all."

"Father, I can handle it."

"There is no shame if you're not ready to mete out the necessary consequences."

"Let me do this. I promise, I won't let you down."

"I know you won't, son. The mission is yours."

And so it begins. Pascal leaned back and smiled to himself. Soon, he'd be able to savor a sunset and a cognac with his son, without interference from that bitch, Maybelline.

Chapter 34

Albuquerque, New Mexico

A cid pooled in Reid's gut as he and Tinker were taken behind the
church. They were outmanned twelve to one, and outgunned a
hundred to nothing. There was no possibility of overpowering their
captors, no way to escape. They'd have to talk, trick, or bargain their
way out, or they were going to die just one day into their journey, before they'd really even begun.

The wooden door to a small annex stood propped open with a brick.
The men shoved them into the small room toward two metal chairs in
the center of a cracked tile floor. Tinker stumbled forward and Reid
caught his elbow.

"Sit," someone commanded.

Reid tried to assess Tinker's condition as he helped him to a chair.
He'd taken a bad blow. He could have a concussion. Reid took the seat
next to him, racking his brain for some way to convince the men to let
them go.

A hulking man crossed the room. His hands were empty, and there
was no gun on him that Reid could see. Other men filed in, lining the
perimeter of the room. They all had guns. Additional men were visible
outside, and the occasional flash of sunlight on metal indicated they
were armed, too.

Mario sidled up to the big man and glared at Reid, fingering his
shiny revolver.

Reid took a deep breath and blew it out slowly, remembering his
grandpa's familiar admonition, "Never let 'em see you sweat." Reid was
determined to do Tinker proud, and tried his best to keep his terror
from showing, even though the prospect of getting out of there alive
was looking worse by the second.

The man without the gun scrutinized them. Reid tried to calm himself by assessing him like a patient. His brown skin had a healthy tone,
with the exception of sun damage and wrinkles around the eyes and

across the forehead. Though the man's hair and mustache were solid black, Reid placed him around fifty. His large hands were rough and calloused, and the back of his neck was darkened from hours under the sun. He was physically powerful, and obviously in charge. Reid didn't read anger in the firm set of his mouth, but he could tell the man was no one he wanted to tangle with. One word from him, and the others would do his bidding, whether that was to shoot them or to let them go.

Reid still didn't have a plan, but he had to say something. He took a breath, hoping the words would come to him as he went along. "Sir? My name's—"

"You the boss here?" Tinker interrupted, his tone unapologetic.

The unarmed man nodded. "My name is Manuel Garcia," he said with the quiet assuredness of someone who did not need to raise his voice. "I have not seen you among McClellan's men before."

"I don't know a McClellan. I'm Tinker Landers, and this is my grandson, Reid. We're from Cheyenne Mountain. Up north in Colorado Springs. We're not your enemy. You have no cause to hold us prisoner."

"You entered our land armed, and you are not one of us," Garcia said. "That makes you the enemy."

"Now what kind of enemy would drive up to your building and leave their weapons under the seat?" Tinker asked.

"A pretty stupid one," someone said. The remark was met by scattered laughter.

"*Pops.*" Reid tried to get his attention, to warn him to tone it down, but Tinker forged ahead, one hundred percent focused on Garcia.

"Listen to me," Tinker said. "What did I do when your men came at me? I said *hello*. We didn't attack, we didn't even defend ourselves."

"Since they didn't attack, I say that makes them *spies,*" the joker said. There was another smattering of laughter and some encouraging murmurs, but Garcia's expression didn't change.

"We're not spies, and we're not your enemy," Tinker continued. "We came from Colorado hoping to make contact with other human beings. From up on the ridge we saw smoke out at the air base. We stopped here to scope it out. We didn't see this McClellan or anyone else, but I wish to God we had. They might have been a bit more hospitable." Tinker thrust out his chin in a clear challenge.

Garcia narrowed his eyes.

The room was silent, like everyone was waiting for Garcia to rain down hell on the cocky intruders.

Shit. Whatever Tinker's plan was, it was backfiring.

Garcia took a step closer to Tinker. Reid braced himself, ready to defend his grandfather.

After a long pause, Garcia spoke. "Sir?" he asked Tinker, his tone deferential. "Are you a religious man?"

Oh no. Don't tell him how you really feel, Pops.

"We come from a deeply Christian community where my son—his father," Tinker pointed at Reid, "was the bishop. Why do you ask?"

Reid exhaled, silently thanking Tinker for not telling the whole truth. He sensed that voicing his contempt for organized religion would have been the exact wrong thing to do.

"I ask because," Garcia said, dropping to one knee, "I want to believe your story. Before you arrived, I was in church praying for a way to defeat our enemy. Then you drove up in that vehicle full of weapons, but none aimed at us. Now I ask myself, how could that *not* be a sign?" He stared earnestly at Tinker, who looked as dumbfounded as Reid felt.

"Father?" one of the armed men said, stepping forward.

"Domingo," Garcia said, standing. "I ask you, Domingo. Are these men, their weapons, and their vehicle not the answer to my prayers?"

"I . . . it would appear so," Domingo said.

"Is this the way we treat a gift from God?" Garcia asked the armed men at large.

The men looked at each other, seemingly as puzzled as Reid.

"Put away your weapons, everyone," Garcia continued. "These men are our guests. We will have a feast in their honor! But first, we give thanks to the Lord."

The men murmured to each other, shrugging and shaking their heads, then they started filing out. Reid stared, not quite believing it.

"Domingo, go tell your mother and your uncle," Garcia said. "They'll need time to cook the *pozole.*"

Reid leaned close to Tinker. "Is this for real?"

Tinker shrugged. "It's what *I* was praying for."

"Please, come with me," Garcia said.

Reid and Tinker followed him out. It still felt like they were under guard, but at least the abundant weapons were holstered or pointed at the ground.

They climbed the stairs at the front of the building. From the yawning double doorway of the church, women and children stared out at them. Feet scuffed on stone tile as the crowd pushed back to let them enter. Inside, the large room was cool, and Reid shivered as the sweat evaporated from his skin. He noted the colorful mural on the vaulted ceiling, the statues and stained glass windows lining the walls—he'd never seen a more beautiful room. He was surprised to find himself thinking it felt holy.

He'd expected to see people sitting or kneeling with their heads bowed, but the rows of carved wooden pews were empty. Instead, everyone walked up the main aisle in a kind of processional. After pausing briefly in front of an altar, each person exited through a side door.

Reid and Tinker joined the silent ranks, flanked by Garcia and Domingo. Garcia clapped a meaty hand on Reid's shoulder. Reid looked into his face and was inclined to believe the broad smile was genuine. As genuine as the distrust in Domingo's scowl. He locked eyes with Domingo and the hair on the back of his neck prickled.

When they stopped at the altar, Garcia bowed his head and pressed his hands together, whispering words in a language Reid didn't understand. Tinker bowed his head, too, and shot Reid a look to do the same.

After a moment, Garcia looked up. "Come. There are many people for you to meet."

Domingo stayed close as they followed Garcia through the side door. They passed an opening to a kitchen and entered a large room crowded with tables and benches made from wood so dark it looked black. There were dozens of people inside, and more pouring in from the church.

"Meet our new friends!" Garcia announced.

The room broke out in applause and cheers, and people started making their way over to them. Garcia steered Tinker to a chair at the head of a long table. Clearly it was a spot of importance. If Tinker was uncomfortable with this, he sure didn't look it. He was waving, saying hello, and shaking hands with people like he did it every day. Though he didn't appear to be seriously injured, Reid wanted to be sure.

"Excuse me," Reid said, getting Garcia's attention. "I'd like to take a look at my grandfather's injuries, if that's okay. My medical supplies were in the car."

"Yes, of course. We'll bring your things." Garcia spoke to another man who then left.

"You feeling okay, Pops?" Reid tried to get a closer look amidst the crush of people.

"Fine, don't worry," Tinker said. "Say hello to the nice folks, will ya?"

Reid smiled, saying hello more times than he could count, until finally people started claiming seats at the tables. The mood was boisterous and the noise level was high with people talking and laughing. Still, Reid felt uneasy. Tinker seemed to be having a grand time, trading stories with two men who looked about his age. But no one had brought Reid's belongings yet.

A woman set glasses of water and bowls of nuts on the table, and Reid's stomach growled. He figured the nuts weren't poisoned since everyone else was eating them. Besides, if they'd wanted to kill them, they'd simply have shot them.

He took a handful of nuts and tossed them in his mouth. After a moment, his tongue was on fire with a potent spice. He grabbed his glass and took a big gulp. Too late he realized it wasn't water. Somehow he managed to swallow, but his throat burned, and he coughed like he might hack up his lungs. The room went quiet, and everyone stared at him.

"Water," he managed to say.

The room erupted with laughter. Someone brought him a second glass of clear liquid, which he made sure to smell before drinking.

"I apologize," Garcia said. "For special guests we offer our finest tequila. I should have realized you would not know this."

"Mmm," Tinker said, sipping. "Smooth. I haven't had tequila like this, well, I don't think ever. Try sipping next time, Reid."

"Thanks for the tip," Reid croaked. "Mr. Garcia, you said I could have my medical kit?"

"I'm fine," Tinker said. "No need for the kit. I'm anxious to talk with these folks about their community, aren't you?"

"Yes," Garcia said. "Everyone wants to hear about you, too. Where you are from, what sorts of food you have, but there's no rush. That's not how we do things. We take our time with food, with drink, with conversation. My wife and my brother are preparing a meal. What do you say we eat and drink and talk into the night?"

"We'd be honored," Tinker said.

Reid didn't like it, but he didn't see how they could get out of it, and the smell of food had his mouth watering.

"Excellent," Garcia said, leaving Tinker at the head of the table and seating himself on the adjacent bench. "More tequila?"

Chapter 35

Albuquerque, New Mexico

A ll the food had been delicious, but Reid's favorite was the thin, warm bread called tortillas. He'd stuffed himself with so many— plain, with beans wrapped in them, with meat and tomatoes and chili peppers—he was sure he couldn't fit another bite. Then someone had brought a crispy version flavored with cinnamon, and he managed to eat more.

But in the end, the meal had been a disappointment. There was no grown food in Albuquerque. Only rats, canned food, and preserved grains for making tortillas. It was pretty much the same as back home, except here the resources were divided into two halves. In fact, the city itself was divided across the middle with McClellan's people on one side and Garcia's on the other. The warring factions were experiencing an uneasy peace, but preparing for the likelihood of war.

"So, I'm wondering," Tinker said, pushing back from the table. "Just how did you folks end up enemies with McClellan and his people?"

Uh oh. Reid suspected that was ground Tinker shouldn't be treading. But it was too late now.

Garcia frowned and shook his head. "A fundamental difference in belief. We believe the apocalypse was God's doing, a punishment, a message for man to heed. They do not."

"Oh?" Tinker said. "What do they believe?"

"That it was caused by the sun interacting with the North Pole, or some such nonsense," Garcia said. "What do your people believe?"

"There's a split at home, too," Reid injected. He looked pointedly at Tinker, hoping he'd catch a clue that this wasn't the right audience for his lecture about the magnetic poles swapping places.

"That's right," Tinker said. "Our religious folks say God sent the solar storm to punish mankind, and that another storm's coming. The military and scientists say a geomagnetic reversal weakened the magnetosphere, exposing the earth to massive amounts of radiation from the CME."

"The what?" Garcia asked.

"CME?" Tinker said. "Coronal Mass Ejection. A really big solar storm. Usually not a problem, but with the poles down, it fried the communications satellites, computers, the power grid—basically everything electronic."

"That's just what the scientists believe, right, Pops?" Reid asked, trying to keep Tinker on course.

"And you," Garcia said, scowling. "What do you believe, Mr. Tinker Landers?"

"Like I told you earlier," Tinker said. "My son was the bishop, the head of our church."

"He was killed recently," Reid said, trying to steer the conversation away from science, even if that meant talking about his father.

"You say he was killed?" Garcia asked.

"Yes," Tinker said. "By our military leader over a difference in beliefs. I guess things aren't that different between your people and ours."

"I am truly sorry for your loss," Garcia said.

Reid nodded, not having to act to put a grieving look on his face.

"Let's raise our glasses to my son," Tinker said, holding up his tequila. "To Bishop Peregrine Landers, God rest his soul."

"To their bishop." Garcia lifted his glass. "Amen."

"Amen" sounded around the table, then everyone quickly tossed back their tequila. Most people set down empty glasses, regardless of how full they'd been to start with, but Reid just took a small sip.

"Drink up!" Garcia said, topping off Reid's glass, and refilling the others.

The sun had gone down while they were eating, and the skylights were black with the night sky. The dining room was lit only by a fire in a stone fireplace and a smattering of candles on the tables, but even in the flickering light, Reid could tell Tinker was drunk. Throughout the meal, the tequila had never stopped coming, and Tinker'd kept drinking it. Reid had tried to refuse it, but they wouldn't take "no" for an answer, so he spit the tequila into his water glass whenever he could, and managed to remain mostly sober.

The conversation turned to the Humvee, and the way a few of the men were asking Tinker questions made Reid suspicious, so he pretend-ed to drink his tequila while listening. When Tinker mentioned their plans to go to Ellay, the men at the table exchanged glances. Something wasn't right.

Finally, talk turned to "the good old days," and Tinker and the older men and women laughed and joked about music and concerts and things they did in their youth. Garcia seemed happily inebriated and relatively harmless, but his son, Domingo, struck Reid as calculating and deadly. So when Domingo signaled for some men to follow him outside, Reid wanted to know what they were up to.

Reid eyed the girl who'd been flirting with him all night and ges-tured her closer. "Hey," he whispered loudly in her ear. "Wanna go outside?" He made a point of slurring, and hoped he sounded drunk.

The girl smiled and led him toward the same door Domingo had used.

Reid looked over his shoulder, trying to make eye contact with Tinker, but the old man was too busy reminiscing with his peers to notice. Hopefully, he wouldn't get into too much trouble while Reid was outside.

"What's your name again?" Reid asked the girl as they exited the church.

"Irma. You're Reid, right?"

She led him across a patio to an iron bench. They sat, thighs touch-ing.

"What d'you wanna do, Irma?" Reid asked.

Irma kissed him, and he kissed back while trying to look and listen for the men.

"Hey," he said, coming up for air.

She looked at him. "Something wrong?"

"No, I was thinking about those guys that came out here before us. Are any of them your boyfriend or brother or something? I mean, should I be worried about them seeing us?"

"Domingo is my uncle. He wouldn't like it."

"Uh oh. Do you know where they went?"

"Probably out by the old school. That's where they go to smoke."

"Where's that?"

"It's okay. They can't see us."

"I gotta, you know, I need to take a pee, but I don't want to stumble across them."

"I can show you where our facilities are."

"I'd better stay in the fresh air. I'm not feeling so great." Reid covered his mouth.

"Then stay away from that fat building over there." Irma pointed. "That's the school. You can go out behind one of the sheds."

"Will you do me a favor and stay here? I'm kinda embarrassed I drank too much."

"That's okay, it happens. But I'll wait for you inside, if you don't mind."

"Thanks, Irma."

He watched her go. She seemed nice. He felt bad for deceiving her.

Quietly, he headed for the school, choosing his steps as best he could in the moonlight. Thank goodness he wasn't actually drunk.

He sneaked to the corner of the building and stopped when he heard voices.

"Was good luck brought them here," a man said.

"God's grace," said another.

"I need to make that car work." *Domingo's voice.* "The old guy's tongue is so loose, he told us everything, but I couldn't turn it on."

Reid hadn't heard Tinker give them the code, and he hoped his grandfather would have enough sense not to, even as drunk as he was.

"I guess we shouldn't kill them until we can work the thing," Domingo continued.

"You think they might join us?" someone asked. "Your father seems to have accepted them already."

"No." Domingo's voice again. "They've got people back home to feed."

"Then for sure we can't trust them. They'll be gone the first chance they get. If we kill them now, at least we have the car."

Reid considered making a break for it. He was pretty sure he could get to the car without anyone seeing him, but there was no way he could get Tinker without provoking a shitstorm of gunfire.

"We can't kill them yet," Domingo said. "We don't know how to work that car."

"We can figure it out later. Don't take a chance, man. Dust 'em now."

"Have you seen how drunk they are?" Domingo asked. "The old man had a whole bottle, and the other one's just a kid, can't hold his liquor at all. They aren't going anywhere any time soon."

"So in the morning?"

"Yeah, we'll let them sleep it off, then get them to take us for a ride so we can figure out how the car works. It's no good to us against McClellan if we can't use it."

"I don't know, Domingo. Maybe we shouldn't chance it."

"You actually believe they pose a threat?" Domingo's voice boomed. "You saw how they drove up, no guns or anything. Didn't even ask for their guns back. They wouldn't have gotten so shit-faced if they suspected anything. I say we lay low, get what we want, then dust 'em."

Reid's heart hammered in his chest, the sound pounding in his temples, no doubt amplified by the tequila. He had to warn Tinker. They had to get out of there before morning.

He made it back to the church and slipped into the dining room unnoticed, as far as he could tell. He hoped he looked drunk and sick rather than scared sober. He slouched against the wall as he surveyed the room. The crowd had thinned, and most of the candles were out. Tinker was alone now, slumped over the table, his head cradled on his arms.

Irma caught his eye and flashed her dazzling smile. He staggered over to her.

"Shh. Don't tell anyone I was gone," he said in her ear. "I don't want anyone to know I'm sick."

"Are you better now?" she asked, though she didn't look hopeful.

"The room's spinning. I should lie down."

"I can find out where you're supposed to sleep."

"I should lie down here," Reid said, trying to look woozy. He couldn't afford to get trapped in a room with a bunch of roommates or locked behind closed doors.

"It's not comfortable. I'm sure there's a bed for you."

"Here's fine. Look, my grandpa's already passed out."

"If you insist. Let me get you a blanket at least."

"That would be nice." He reached out to her and feigned losing his balance. "Do you think you could find where they put our stuff? I'd like my sleeping bag, and they were supposed to bring me my medical kit." He didn't dare ask for the guns.

"Let me see what I can do. I'll be right back."

He watched her leave, then made a show of losing his balance again. He leaned against a table as a cover for checking out the people in the room. No one seemed to be paying attention to him. Several were passed out like Tinker. An older man lay flat on his back on a bench, snoring. There was a couple kissing. A woman rocking a baby. Garcia and his wife were gone, and Domingo hadn't come back. Yet.

Reid made his way to Tinker. "Pops," he said, shaking his arm.

No response.

"You gotta wake up, Pops." He shook him harder. He looked around, but no one was in earshot. "Wake up," he said directly in Tinker's ear.

Tinker lifted his head a few inches and opened one eye, then passed out again.

There was no way he was driving. There was no way he was *walking*. It'd be a couple of hours before he'd be good for anything. Would Domingo and his friends stay patient until morning?

"Reid." A touch on his shoulder.

He jumped. *Irma.* He hadn't heard her come up. "Hey, yeah, hi," he said.

"I startled you." She was holding their sleeping bags.

"Sorry, I guess I was dozing off. Thanks for bringing those. Can we put them on the ground here? My grandpa's in no shape to walk anywhere."

"Tequila seems like it's your friend at first. But later . . ." Irma shook her head and laid a sleeping bag out on the ground.

"I know what you mean," Reid said, grateful he hadn't ingested much. He'd feel sorry for Tinker in the morning. If they were still alive.

Reid grabbed Tinker under the arms while Irma took his feet. Together, they got him more or less settled on top of a sleeping bag. He seemed completely oblivious to the process.

Irma laid out the other bag. "I brought you a pillow," she said, placing it at the top of the bag. "To make up for not finding your medical supplies."

"Thanks." Reid wanted to ask about the rest of their gear, but was too scared he'd alert her. He assumed she'd been assigned to keep an eye on him. No one else was paying attention, at least as far as he could tell. Besides, most everything was replaceable, even the guns, though it would take some searching. The one thing he knew they couldn't go long without was water.

"Are you going to lie down?" she asked.

"I guess I'd better."

"Would you like for me to lie down with you?"

"That would be really nice, but," he looked around. "We won't have much privacy."

"Everyone's asleep, or soon will be," she said, raising one eyebrow.

"Good," he said, stretching out on the bag. "Whoa, dizzy," he said, holding his head. "I think I'm getting a headache, too."

"Hungover already?" She giggled, kneeling beside him.

"Is there water? That might help."

"I'll get some. Don't go anywhere." She gave him a quick kiss and disappeared into the darkness.

He couldn't have her stay with him, but he didn't know how to get rid of her without arousing suspicion. If a pretty girl wanted to lie down with you, you didn't send her away, no matter how drunk you were. There was no way to get out of it.

Unless he passed out.

Reid left his boots and belt on and flopped face down on the sleeping bag, head halfway off the pillow. He closed his eyes and hung his mouth open, breathing slow and loud. He hoped she'd fall for it. With any luck she'd leave the water and go.

After a few moments of pretending, Reid started to worry he'd actually fall asleep, then he felt a hand on his back.

"Reid?"

He tried not to alter his breathing.

"Reid, I'm back," she said, so close he could feel the heat of her breath. "You're not asleep are you?" She flicked her tongue around his ear.

He stayed still, hoping she'd give up.

"Wake up, lover," she said, shaking his arm. "Reid," she said louder.

He kept his breathing rhythmic, allowing a snore to rattle in his throat.

"He's out," Irma said.

"Think he'll stay passed out until morning?"

Domingo.

"Are you serious?" Irma said. "He's sopped. I can't believe he didn't pass out sooner. I thought I was going to have to lie down with him."

"No way, baby. We couldn't have that. I hate the fact that you even had to kiss him. Those lips are *mine*."

Reid heard them kissing. He hoped the part about him being her uncle had been a lie. He snored again. Why didn't they leave?

"Let's go to bed," Irma said, her voice husky.

"We can't leave them. *El Jefe* would be pissed."

"We'll come back at dawn and no one will know the difference. Please?" Irma whined. "I promise, they're so out of it, they won't even move."

Reid heard feet shuffle away, but continued pretending to sleep. His heart was beating so fast, there was no chance he'd fall asleep now. He listened for at least five minutes, but there was no movement in the room, no sound other than snores and sleepy groans. He rolled to his back, snuffling and pretending to snore while he opened his eyes the tiniest slit. As far as he could tell, he was the only one conscious.

He opened his eyes wider and glanced around, then sat up. Good, she left the water. He grabbed the glass bottle from the table, took off the cap, and drained a third of it. Swaying a little for effect, he took a good look around the room. There was a couple passed out in a pile in the corner. A woman was asleep on her arms at a table as Tinker had been. And the man laid out on the bench hadn't budged. This was as good as it was going to get.

"Pops, wake up," Reid said in his ear.

Tinker didn't move.

They didn't have time for this. Reid covered Tinker's mouth and plugged his nose. After what seemed like a full minute, Tinker's eyes shot open and he struggled, trying to yell. Reid muffled the sound the best he could.

"Shh," Reid said close to Tinker's face so Tinker could see it was him. "Don't make a sound." He let go of Tinker's mouth.

Tinker sat up, taking several deep breaths. "What the hell you doing?" he whispered.

"They're going to kill us. Do you have the key?"

"It's in the car."

"I hope you're right. Can you walk?"

Despite Tinker's assurance he could, Reid put his arm around him and helped him out of the room. Together they stumbled more or less quietly out of the building. Once outside, Reid kept to the shadows and moved as quickly as Tinker could manage.

When they reached the car, they were both breathing hard. Reid got Tinker into the backseat, then climbed behind the steering wheel, thanking all the gods that the car wasn't under guard. He reached to punch the code into the keypad and froze. The keycard was missing.

"Who's there?" a voice called.

Reid looked up. A man approached, pointing a gun.

"Pops, where's the key?"

"Sin the miser," Tinker mumbled.

"What?"

"The *visor.*"

Reid pulled down the visor, grabbed the card, and shoved it into the reader. His hand shook as he entered the code.

"Hey, who is that?" the man called. "You in the car, let me see your face."

Reid pressed the start button, but nothing happened. *"Shit!"* He panicked, pushing the button again and again. "Start, goddamn it, start."

The man was almost to the passenger door. Reid pushed the button that locked the doors, then punched in the code again. He jabbed the start button once more and the engine came alive just as the man grabbed for the door.

"Get out now or I shoot." The muzzle of the gun was pressed against the window.

Reid slammed the car in gear and pressed the pedal to the floor. The car lurched forward. The gun fired. But there was no sound of breaking glass.

"Come on, come on, *faster,*" Reid urged the Hummer. His breath was still coming hard, and sweat made his hands slick on the steering wheel.

"They're getting away!" the man shouted.

A barrage of bullets pelted the car, but the metal and glass held. Reid risked a glance back. Tinker was still slumped across the backseat where Reid had tossed him.

"Pops! Pops, you okay?"

"Mmmm." He sounded drunk, not shot.

The gunfire receded into the distance as the Hummer gained speed. He'd done it. He'd saved them. They'd made it out alive.

Reid's breathing slowed and he wiped his palms on his jeans, but he kept the pedal to the floor long after the light from the church had vanished from the rearview mirror.

Chapter 36

Pacific Ocean, aboard the Emancipation

The boat had been under repair for twenty-four hours, and every one of those hours had taken its toll on Nikolai. After all his concern about the *Emancipation's* maiden voyage, the delay was due to his own arrogance and impatience. He vowed to stay in his quarters for the rest of the trip, no matter how badly he wanted to know the status of the repairs, no matter how bored he got.

At least Finola was sending him food. He tried to take comfort that perhaps she was approaching forgiveness for whatever she thought he'd done, but he suspected she simply felt sorry for him. Olexi hadn't even been to see him. Not that he blamed him. He'd behaved like a *zhopa*. It was best he keep to himself.

He turned to pace the familiar route when there was a loud knock on the hatch.

He froze. Was it Olexi? Finola? *Kennedy?* He realized he didn't want to see any of them. Maybe they'd go away.

There was a second knock.

"The captain would like to see you," a voice called.

Nikolai hung his head. Just when he thought it couldn't get any worse, he was being summoned for further humiliation.

Another knock. "Are you coming?"

Nikolai sighed. He deserved the scolding. He opened the door to find Kennedy's lackey, Mike, pity and accusation painted across his face. Nikolai nodded, not meeting his eye.

Mike led him forward to Kennedy's office and issued two brisk knocks at the open door.

Kennedy looked up from his desk. "Thank you for coming, Captain Petrov. Do you take coffee or tea?"

"Tea." Nikolai liked *Kennedy* more than he liked coffee.

"Mike, ask Cook for a pot, would you? Anything but swamp tea."
Mike nodded and left.

"That swamp tea tastes as bad as coffee." Kennedy motioned for Nikolai to enter.

"Worse, if that's possible," Nikolai said, taking a seat. "Cook swears the mere smell of it eases seasickness, but I think it causes more ills than it cures."

"She does have interesting remedies." Kennedy smiled. "But that's not why I asked you here. The other day——"

"It won't happen again. You have my word." Nikolai's cheeks burned and he fidgeted in his chair. Though Kennedy had every right to chastise him, Nikolai wished he'd get it over with.

"Actually, I wanted to apologize."

"What?"

"For making you uncomfortable at dinner. When you found out Tati and I are living together."

Nikolai looked down at his hands. He was a guest on this boat, and had already violated that relationship in the worst way. He would keep his mouth shut.

"But that's not why I asked you here," Kennedy continued. "Our repairs are complete and we'll be crossing into California waters soon, so the time is ripe to discuss the pirates."

At the thought of his daughter in the hands of pirates, Nikolai's contriteness evaporated. He gritted his teeth and dug his fingernails into his palms, trying to keep the pressure inside from blowing. "How could you?" he growled.

"Pardon?"

"How could you let Tatiana go down there? You had to know it was a bad idea."

"*Let* her go?" Kennedy chuckled. The bastard actually laughed. "Do you know your daughter at all? Because if you did, you'd know I don't *let* her do anything."

"Then why didn't you go with her?"

"Tati insisted I stay behind to tend to other things, and I knew she was in good hands. Will said he had everything under control."

"Will said? *Will said?*" Nikolai slammed his palms against the desk, enjoying the start he gave Kennedy. "My son, God love him, has an over-inflated sense of his abilities. In other words, he's a cocky little shit who doesn't know what he's doing. And you entrusted Tatiana to him, so that both of my children could sail right into Pirate Central. What were you thinking?" Nikolai knew he'd crossed the line of decorum, but he didn't care. "Have you no sense at all? If you couldn't stop them, why didn't you come to me?"

"I did. When they hadn't returned two weeks ago, I asked Creighton to approach you on my behalf, but I heard nothing until you showed up at the office."

"That's because Creighton couldn't be bothered to tell me," Nikolai said through gritted teeth. He splayed his hands on the desktop and leaned toward Kennedy. "Creighton is a lying sack who cares only about himself. I found out that Will and Tatiana were missing through happenstance—a spontaneous trip to Corinne's. When I got there, my own mother—another shining example of self-centeredness—didn't bother to tell me my daughter had a boyfriend, much less that it was *you,* and that you were living together!" Spit flew from Nikolai's lips as he shouted the last word inches from Kennedy's face.

"As I said, I apologize for the way you learned about us," Kennedy said, holding his ground. "I'd planned to address the matter differently."

"So tell me now. What are your intentions with my daughter?"

"Captain Petrov, I love your daughter. She's smart and impetuous and beautiful. She has grand, grand plans that would seem preposterous coming from anyone else, but she makes them sound reasonable, possible. She makes me believe in them, too."

Kennedy paused. Nikolai glared, willing the jerk to burst into flames.

"What I'm saying is," Kennedy continued. "Tati's hopes and dreams have become my hopes and dreams. We're going to re-settle Sausalito and eventually San Francisco, too, with a government based on the real U.S. Constitution. Tati has taken up her mother's plans—trade relations with other economies, and real farming with more than just apples. That's why she had to go south."

"Does no one have any sense at all?" Nikolai couldn't understand why his otherwise intelligent daughter would risk her life on a theory disproved years ago. "My wife was wrong. There are no seed banks in Southern California. Tatiana knows that as well as anyone."

"She uncovered new evidence that a seed vault exists. Evidence you and your late wife never saw. I know Tati will find seeds and bring them back, so we can provide hope and a future for our children."

"Your *what?*" Nikolai reached across the desk and grabbed Kennedy by the front of his shirt. "Don't tell me she's—"

"No, but we want children. What I'm trying to say, sir, is that Tati and I want to get married and have a family, and we'd like your blessing."

Nikolai shoved Kennedy back into the chair. "*No fucking way.*"

Chapter 37

Holbrook, Arizona

Reid woke mid-morning, stiff and achy in the driver's seat. His mouth was cottony and his bladder full. He stretched the kink in his neck, but nothing would fix the dull pounding behind his temples, except finding water.

Tinker snored, sprawled half-hanging off the back seat. His grandfather was going to feel a lot worse than Reid did.

"Pops, wake up." Reid got out of the car and the door fell shut.

"Oooh," Tinker moaned.

"Sorry," Reid called from where he was pissing on the tire of another car.

"What the hell'd you do to me? I feel more dead than alive."

"The good news is you're not dead. You're dehydrated. We need to find water. The bastards didn't leave us anything."

"Bastards. So why'd we stop here?"

Reid hated having to tell him. "I put as much distance behind us as I could, but then something happened. I don't know what I did, but the Hummer won't go fast anymore."

"You didn't do anything wrong. See, the faster you go, the more battery it uses. When you got my sorry butt outta that lion's den, you must've put the pedal to the metal and used up the juice faster than the nuke could replenish it. When the battery level drops below a certain point, the car's programmed to go into limp-along mode while the battery recharges."

"Thank God," Reid said, relieved he hadn't broken it.

"So where in blazes are we?"

"Outside a town called Holbrook. I figured parking at this junkyard with the other cars would be good camouflage. I didn't see any signs of life, but it was the middle of the night. There could be people here."

"How far are we from those bastards in Albuquerque?"

Reid leaned in the driver's window and looked at the control panel. "A little over two hundred miles. Good thing, too. They were so riled up, I'm sure they'd do more than shoot us if they caught us."

"Seems I recall some kind of shooting." Tinker stretched his legs across the backseat.

"Yeah, they fired off some shots." Reid fingered a pockmark on the back of the Hummer. "We got lucky."

"So they were gonna kill us and use the Hummer in their little war, huh? I screwed the pooch on that one."

"You wanted to believe them."

"I'm damn grateful you got me outta there, son. I really am. But you've got to promise me—if there's a next time that I get stupid and get myself into trouble, don't stick around for me. Get the hell outta Dodge."

"No way, Pops. I wouldn't leave you."

"I'm an old man. It's been a good life, but there's no denying I'm at the tail end. You and Kayla have your whole lives ahead. You gotta get back to her and that baby. Don't risk that, not for me, not for anything."

"Let's make sure it doesn't come to that. What do you say we stay away from any place that looks inhabited till we get to Ellay?"

"Sounds good to me," Tinker said. "Jesus H. Christ, my head hurts something fierce."

"You need water. Think you're up to taking a walk, old man?"

"Better than dying here." Tinker got out of the backseat, groaning. "The goddamn sun's too bright and those goddamn bastards didn't even leave me a goddamn ball cap."

They walked down the gravel-strewn road toward Holbrook. Reid hoped there'd be no one there to greet them, and it occurred to him that in Ellay people might not be any more hospitable than in Albuquerque.

"Hey, Pops? The stranger—Cumorah—she didn't tell me anything about the City of Angels or why she left. Her people might not be . . . friendly."

"I don't recall folks from Ellay ever being what I'd call friendly."

"Something must have been pretty bad for her to leave a place with grown food, especially alone and on foot."

"She didn't say anything?" Tinker asked. "No detail that might help us make a plan?"

Reid thought back, trying to remember. Had it only been a few days? It felt like weeks. "When I asked where she got the apple, she wouldn't tell me. I had to hear her confession first."

"Did she confess anything that might help?"

"She said she came to Colorado because she couldn't get pregnant and she believed that praying at Garden of the Gods would cure her."

"Anything else?"

"She was adamant about one thing—Zeke is not meat. She repeated it several times and made me promise to protect him. She loved that dog."

"What about the monkeys? You're sure that's what she said?"

"She talked about their leader gathering up animals of every kind in the Before. I know she said monkeys right along with chickens and cows. She did say something weird about there not being any birds, that they had to be sacrificed to keep the secret."

"But she said they had chickens?"

"Yeah, a lot of what she said didn't make sense. It was lucky I recognized 'City of Angels' from your stories or I'd have assumed she was having a near-death hallucination."

"The real luck was finding that dog. That woman could have died within feet of you without you ever knowing she was there."

"More like Zeke found us." Reid pictured Zeke sticking close to Kayla, and was comforted he was looking after her.

They trudged up a slight incline at the edge of town and stopped beside a metal building that provided little cover and even less shade. Tinker groaned and rubbed his head.

"Headache worse?" Reid asked, pain still throbbing behind his own temples.

"Like my eyes are going to pop outta their sockets."

Reid looked up and down the road. "We need water."

"First, let's be sure we're alone. Then we'll find water and restock the supplies that them Albuquerquan bastards stole from us."

"Then maybe a nap before we start driving again?"

"If this place is safe, I vote we find some real damn beds and spend the night. I'm about crippled from sleeping in the car."

"It's a good idea to lay low for a day. Besides, it's going to take time to round up new supplies."

"Yeah, those bastards even took my sunglasses. Hey, check it out," Tinker said, shielding his eyes and pointing down the road. "A 7-11."

"A what?"

"Convenience store. They always have Twinkies, and those last forever. Breakfast of champions. And they'll probably have ball caps to keep this effing sun off our mother-effing faces. C'mon."

Reid laughed to himself. Tinker sure cussed and complained a lot more when he was hungover. Perhaps the prohibition on alcohol in the Mountain made some sense after all.

Chapter 38

Lost Angeles, the Grand Hotel

Pascal straightened his tie as he approached the Grand. It was a bit early in the afternoon, but he had nothing pressing on the docket and he deserved a celebration. He'd soon be rid of Maybelline and the repulsive Van Hooten.

He entered the spacious lobby and handed his hat to the attendant. His eyes adjusted to the artificial light and he spotted Ellianna by the stone fireplace, smiling as she spoke to two men across from her.

Pascal didn't recognize the men, at least not in their present condition with matted hair and several days' worth of beard. He vaguely wondered why these particular men rated the personal attention of the director, but that was Ellianna's business. He made a point to stay out of the day-to-day operations of his directors unless it was necessary. With Ellianna, it never was. He appreciated having at least one person he could rely on to make sound decisions without him looking over her shoulder.

As he walked past the reception station toward the fireplace, a voice called out.

"Sir? Sir, can I help you?"

He turned to see a girl in her late teens scurrying toward him.

"I'm sorry, sir, but you must check in at reception first. Right this way." The perky, shorthaired girl linked her arm in his and steered him to the desk.

Her fresh, unfamiliar face was as intriguing as her assertiveness. It was too soon for her to be one of the new missionaries, but she had that wholesomeness about her. "I apologize," Pascal said as he was deposited in a chair.

"There we go." The girl marched to her place on the opposite side of the desk. "My name is Devon and I'd like to welcome you to the

Grand."

"Pleased to meet you, Devon. My name is Pascal Worth."

Horror registered on her face. "Oh my goodness, I didn't realize. Please forgive me."

"I find your directness refreshing." He found it more than refreshing. "You're forgiven."

"Thank you, sir." There was nothing coy about her smile. "What can I do for you today, Chancellor Worth? Are you here to see Ms. Ford? Shall I get her for you?"

Pascal had planned to see Bianca, but that seemed boring now. "Actually, Devon, I'd like to spend time with you. Then you'll be sure to remember me next time I visit."

The girl stiffened. "I'm brand new. I'm not, uh, not . . . trained yet."

"Chancellor, how nice to see you." The soft voice was accompanied by the subtle aroma of patchouli.

He turned. "Ms. Ford."

"I see you've met our new receptionist," Ellianna said.

"Yes, I'm quite taken with her. We're going to spend some time getting acquainted."

"Good. I did have someone to introduce you to, but . . . another time." Ellianna smiled, but he knew her nuances so well, it was obvious she was disappointed.

Devon was plainly afraid, and not nearly as attractive now that her confidence had evaporated. Hardly worth disappointing Ellianna.

"That won't be necessary," he said. "I'm at your disposal."

Ten minutes later, Pascal stepped into his personal shower. As the steaming water cascaded over him, he wondered what pleasures awaited him in the adjacent room of his suite. Ellianna would not have chosen someone for him unless she was special.

He turned his face into the water, feeling it wash away the stresses of his job, the responsibilities of his office. He found the ritual of the shower so freeing, he almost always partook, even though he alone was exempt from the requirement.

There was a whisper of cool air and then hands on his sides. No one—*no one*—had ever joined him in the shower. For a fleeting second he hoped it was Ellianna, but of course it wouldn't be.

An exquisite young woman appraised him with intelligent brown eyes. His gaze followed her chocolate tresses to where they tumbled across flawless mocha breasts. Her hand trailed up his side and she stepped closer. Her nipples grazed his chest and she looked up into his eyes.

"Hello." Her voice was quiet but confident. "I'm Mia."

The girl had nerve. This was going to be fun.

Chapter 39

Lost Angeles, Club Three, the next day

The evening breeze wafted through the open balcony doors, flickering candles that burned at every table, though there'd be no other diners. It was pleasant. Romantic. Pascal thought perhaps he'd like to bring Mia sometime. He couldn't recall the last time he'd thought to take a woman out. Mia was different. He couldn't stop thinking about her. He wanted to see her again. Soon.

The waitress placed a basket of bread on the table between him and Linus.

"We'd like red wine, and my son will have fruit to start," Pascal said, placing his burgundy napkin across his lap. "What does Chef have for me today?"

"Cutlets with mushroom gravy, mashed potatoes, and green beans, or your son's favorite Shepherd's Pie. Unless you have another request, of course," the waitress said. *Ashley.* That was her name. "But we only have white wine. No red."

"None? Send the steward, and tell Chef we'll both have Shepherd's Pie."

"Anything else, sir?"

"Yes, Ashley, thank you for asking. I'd like music. Instrumental, no singing. Find out who's available to play."

"My pleasure." She smiled warmly and left.

"Did you notice her change in demeanor?" Pascal asked Linus. "Though we would receive excellent service either way, it made her feel good that I recalled her name."

"Yeah, I noticed. She's cuter when she smiles." Linus helped himself to a piece of bread. He snapped it in half, as he liked to do, covering the tablecloth with crumbs.

"So you're becoming interested in women." Pascal bit into his own

151

dry biscuit. "Anyone in particular? Not, Ashley, of course."

"Not really." Linus reached for his second piece of bread.

Pascal appraised his son, wondering just how ready he was to become a man. "I can ask Ms. Ford about someone suitable for you to spend time with."

"I don't have to wait until my birthday?" Linus's eyes widened, his lips curved in a smile.

Pascal was gratified. Linus seemed a bit nervous, but more excited than afraid. Just as he'd hoped. "I don't see why you should have to wait when you're already doing the job of a man. I'll make the arrangements."

"When? Soon?"

"When your current mission's concluded. I wouldn't want anything distracting you."

"I can handle both."

"I'm sure, but what kind of example would that set for the men under your command? A wise leader knows when to bend the rules and when not to. Ah, here's the wine steward now."

"Good evening, sir. How can I be of service?"

"Is it true you're out of red wine?" Pascal asked.

"Yes, sir. Shall I bring you a chardonnay instead?"

"I don't like white wine, which is something you should know."

"Uh, yes. My apologies, sir."

"Now what about the red."

"As I said, we are out."

Pascal was curious how Linus would handle this. "Son, is this an acceptable answer?"

"No," Linus said smugly. "Rankin, you will have red wine available for the chancellor *tomorrow,* do you understand?"

"I understand what you're saying, but drinkable wine is becoming more scarce every day. Of the last twenty bottles of red brought to Club Three, only a handful were good. We may be nearing the end of it."

"Are you saying you've searched all over Lost Angeles and you're certain there's no drinkable red wine left?" Linus asked.

"Not personally." The steward cast a sidelong glance at Pascal, but Pascal looked away and sipped his water.

"Then I suggest you get on the train and look for it yourself, is that clear?" Linus said.

"Yes, but there will come a day soon when we've exhausted the city's supply."

"Of course. But when you tell your chancellor the supply is exhausted, you'd better be sure not a single person in the city has a drinkable bottle of red wine. And then you'd better find a new supply. San Diego, perhaps?"

"Yes, I suppose, sir."

"You are the wine steward, right? It is your job to keep my father supplied with wine. We won't accept any more excuses. Get the job done or we'll replace you with someone who will. But don't expect to wear those nice clothes to the Tank." Linus took another biscuit. "That will be all, Rankin."

"Yes, sir." He turned to Pascal. "Is there anything else, Chancellor?"

"No. You're dismissed." Pascal couldn't help smiling as the steward fled the restaurant. It was obvious Linus was born to lead. "You handled that well, son. I'm proud of you."

"Really?" Linus beamed under his praise.

The boy had probably been craving his attention the whole time he was away with Maybelline. Well, no more. "Yes, Linus. You used his name, told him what you expect, and what the consequences will be if he lets you down. I think you are indeed ready to become a man. As soon as your mission is complete. By the way, how is the mission going?"

"I confirmed that Van Hooten saw my mother right before she got sick, and then several times at the spa. I need to talk to her, but she won't see me."

"You must be worried. Shall I try to convince her to allow you to visit?"

"That would be great. Tonight?"

"No, I have an obligation outside the city first thing tomorrow." He needed to give Van Hooten another day. "I'm paying a surprise visit to World Waste. You could come."

"I can't neglect my mission, even for one day. Someone's got to keep an eye on Van Hooten. I'm thinking I'll go to his office and pretend to have a hurt knee or something. I'll find out what I can, then follow him to see if he goes to the spa."

That was a good answer, and it shouldn't prevent Van Hooten from completing *his* mission, so Pascal didn't insist on Linus's company. Perhaps he'd bring Mia instead.

Pascal looked toward the kitchen. "We should have your fruit by now."

"I really need to ask Mother about Van Hooten. Can't you talk to her before you leave?"

"I'm afraid not, but I'll see her when I return."

"Tomorrow evening?"

"Or the next morning."

"But what if Van Hooten does something? What if that's too late?"

"Do you think it will be?"

Linus appeared to be thinking seriously. "Well . . . no, probably not."

"What do you think you should do?"

Linus pursed his lips. "Stay the course. Continue to observe and collect evidence. I apologize for being impatient."

"Good man. You realized your mistake before you made it. Here comes your fruit. I was wondering what happened to Ashley."

As Linus dug into his food, Pascal turned his thoughts to the next task at hand: the visit to World Waste. The visit itself was unnecessary, other than to give Van Hooten time. The World Waste director was loyal and reliable to a fault. But it never hurt to keep the good ones on their toes, too.

But first he'd return to Services. He drummed his fingers on the table, impatient for the meal to be over already. The way Mia had surprised him in the shower—he couldn't remember the last time he'd been surprised. By anyone. Now he wanted to surprise her. He wondered just what might surprise a girl like Mia, and he realized he knew nothing about her.

Less than fifteen minutes later, Pascal scanned the lobby for Mia. On the short walk over, his suspicions had grown. Where had she come from? Why hadn't he seen her before? She was far too skilled to be one of the newly arrived missionaries. The only explanation was that Ellianna had been keeping her from him. But he couldn't fathom to what purpose.

Devon was at reception again. It was hard to imagine he'd ever found her attractive.

"Hello Chancellor Worth," she said.

"I'd like to see Mia," Pascal said, wasting no time on pleasantries.

Devon ran her finger down a list. "I'm sorry, but she's not available at the moment."

Anger flashed through his veins. "Unavailable because she's not here, or because she's with someone else? Get Ms. Ford. *Now.*"

He strode to the bar, breathing deeply to calm what he knew was an overreaction.

"The usual, sir?" the bartender asked.

"No, give me your best Scotch." Pascal drummed his fingers on the polished wood until a tumbler arrived containing two fingers of the caramel anesthetic. He tossed it back and held it out for the bartender. "Fill it this time."

Halfway through his second Scotch, he began to mellow, though if Ellianna didn't show up before his glass was empty, that would change.

"Chancellor." Ellianna's satiny voice came from behind him.

Pascal turned. "I'd like a word with you. In private."

"Of course, sir. Come with me."

Pascal finished his drink and slammed the glass on the bar. Ellianna jumped, almost imperceptibly, but enough to be gratifying. *Good.* She should be a little on edge. She shouldn't take it for granted she'd be in his good graces forever. Anyone could fall from grace. Even her.

He strode across the lobby and up the stairs to his suite, not speaking a word to Ellianna. Once they stepped inside, he closed the door and turned on her.

"I came to see Mia, and she was not immediately available." He knew it was unreasonable for him to be angry, but he didn't care. "I want her on reserve for me to use or to loan out as I choose. I no longer require Bianca's services—you can release her back to the general public."

"Isn't this a bit soon?"

"Are you questioning me?"

"Of course not." She edged closer to him. "You seem tense. Would you like a massage?" Her voice was low and conspiratorial.

"No," he snapped, and she recoiled. "What I want is answers. Then I want Mia."

"What do you want to know?"

"Where did Mia come from? Why have I never seen her before?" He didn't like being suspicious of Ellianna, but the feeling was there nonetheless.

"You've seen her many times. At the clothiers."

"No, I'd remember her."

"Mia worked at the clothiers her entire life. She's Andrea's daughter."

"Andrea . . . the hideous woman who does the ironing?"

"Yes."

"I remember a gangly, awkward girl named *Hermia* who worked in the back, but that can't have been . . ."

"That was Mia. She seemed destined to look like her mother. Then puberty hit—granted it was rather late—and she was transformed into a beauty."

"So you brought her to work for you?"

"Actually, *she* came to *me*. I was doubtful given her history, but once she started, I saw enormous potential. In fact, I've been grooming her for you. I thought she would please you."

"Then why are you surprised I asked to reserve her?"

"I'm not, Pascal. I expected it. I'm simply surprised she captured your interest so quickly, and to the extent that you've released Bianca."

Pascal thought she had a point. He was moving a bit fast, but he would not give Ellianna the satisfaction of backing down. Besides, there was a tinge of sadness, perhaps even jealousy, in Ellianna's eyes, and he liked that.

"See to it that Mia is cleaned up and sent to me at once."

There was a tap at the door.

"It's already done, Chancellor. That will be her now."

Chapter 40

Pacific Ocean, aboard the Emancipation

Nikolai paced, growing more agitated with each passing hour. He hadn't left his quarters since that *zhopa* had asked to marry his daughter. What was Tatiana thinking, getting involved with him? Nikolai thought he'd raised her with more sense.

His stomach growled, which fueled his indignation. No more meals had shown up outside his door, which meant Finola must have heard about his altercation with Kennedy. Well, screw Finola and her misplaced loyalties. He was hungry, and he was going to get something to eat.

He flung open his door and stomped down the hall. He wasn't going to let that traitorous windbag keep him out of the galley. He thrust the door open, bracing himself for Finola's wrath, but the kitchen was vacant. Everything was buttoned up, no leftovers on the stove.

After poking around the larder, cooking seemed like too much trouble. He grabbed some apples and devoured them on the way back to his room. He'd had his fill of reading, and there was nothing else to do, so he climbed into bed.

He watched the sky outside the portal grow dark, then he marked the time on his watch, the hours ticking by more slowly than he thought possible. If only he could sleep, perhaps then he could stop picturing his children lost and alone, calling for him. Or injured and bloody, unable to call out. Or worse.

At sea Nikolai usually slept like the dead, but as exhausted as his body was, he couldn't rest. He gave up trying and returned to pacing.

There was a knock. He yanked the door open.

"Sorry to disturb you." It was Ernie, the guy he'd scolded about the sail. The sight of him made Nikolai's cheeks burn. "We're dropping anchor and I need to ready the scull to go ashore." He pointed timidly at the door to the tender garage.

"Why are we dropping anchor?" Nikolai boomed.

"Can I?" Ernie asked, pointing again.

Nikolai stepped out of the way, and Ernie scurried across the room.

"Hey there." Mike strolled in after Ernie, casual as could be.

"Where are we?" Nikolai demanded. "Why are we stopping?"

"We're checking if Tatiana and Will returned to the Sausalito settlement. We've got to row in because the Bay is too dangerous for the ship in the dark."

Nikolai remembered the waters of San Francisco Bay. They were treacherous even in daylight. "I'm going with you."

"Uh, no, you're not," Mike said. "Captain's orders."

"We'll see about that." Nikolai raced down the hall and burst into Kennedy's office. Then he remembered himself. "Excuse me, Captain. Requesting permission to go ashore."

Kennedy peered overtop his glasses. "Denied. I'm sending my fastest scullers. We'll have news in an hour. If Tati and Will are here, we go ashore at first light. If not, we go south."

He was right, but Nikolai still had to clench his teeth to keep from hurling profanities.

"In the meantime, here's some reading." Kennedy held out a notebook. "Plans for resettling Sausalito. There've been a few changes since you and your wife were here. I thought you might be interested."

Nikolai snatched the notebook and left.

The egotistical gasbag. How dare he give me a reading assignment. How dare he mention Jess.

He fumed back to his quarters and tossed the notebook on the desk without opening it. He paced the floor a half-dozen times, then decided he couldn't take it anymore, and went topside to wait for the scullers to return.

Nikolai crossed the deck to the rail, breathing in the salt air, letting it dampen his anger. The sky was resplendent with stars, and he gazed west imagining the islands of Hawaii far in the distance. Their siren song called so loudly, he was sure he could find the tiny specks of land in the vast Pacific even without the stars to guide him. Someday he would follow it, and see what remained of the island nation.

Despite his efforts to think of palm trees and hula girls dancing to ukulele music, his mind was drawn to Tatiana like his tongue to a sore tooth. His daughter was following her mother's path, and he wondered if that was the life she would have chosen if Jess were still alive.

God knew he tried his best to steer his daughter in other directions, encouraging her in any pursuit not related to seeds. He'd arranged for her to shadow a grade-school teacher and to intern at a museum. He'd sent her on visiting studies in ballet and art restoration. Hell, he'd given up everything so she could study at University. When she'd finally found her passion in politics—or at least it seemed like she had—he was supportive, even if it was the last career on the planet Nikolai would have pursued himself. Because anything, even politics, was better than Tatiana going 'round a bewitched circle searching for seeds that didn't exist.

But apparently it wasn't politics so much as a *politician* that had enraptured his daughter. A politician who had circled her back to the obsession with seeds.

Was it possible she'd inherited the obsession from her mother? It sure seemed that Will had inherited his love for the sea from Nikolai. From the time Will could toddle down the pier, there'd never been any doubt he'd be a sailor. But was that because Nikolai never questioned it? Would Tatiana have followed this one dream from the beginning if Nikolai hadn't kept steering her off course?

Maybe Jess's ambitions and dreams had resided in Tatiana from the moment she was conceived. Or maybe they'd taken root when Jess's soul had left the world.

He thought back to happier days when the children were small and Jess was a vibrant young mother. They'd had so many dreams for the future, for the world their children would live in as adults. And Jess had made those dreams into plans. She was the driving force behind the settlement in Sausalito. She'd talked nonstop about what it would be like, her face animated, hands gesturing as she walked through the town with their children skipping behind her. He'd never seen her so happy. He'd never been so happy.

He tried to hold that image in his mind, but against his will it evolved, tumbling forward through the years without Jess, the children aging without a mother. He focused on the faces of his children as young teens, trying to slow down the progression, trying to hang on to them, but they disappeared as he knew they would. As Jess had.

No. He stopped himself. Maybe it wasn't too late. He didn't *know* they were gone. Good news could be on its way right now from the settlement.

"Please?" he whispered, looking at the brightest star. "Let them be here. Let them be safe."

Clearing his throat, he pulled himself together and turned from the rail. Looking toward the stern, Nikolai couldn't make out the features of the man at watch, but he recognized his posture and the cant of his hat. He unclenched his fists and walked to the wheel-house.

"It's good to see you, Olexi," Nikolai said. "Kennedy gave you the watch?"

"I requested a shift," Olexi said. "Seems like the right thing to do."

The words Olexi spoke were benign, but Nikolai could read their meaning.

"You're angry with me," Nikolai said. "Speak your soul, old friend. I'm not your captain here."

Olexi didn't respond, but Nikolai sensed he was on the verge. Perhaps he needed a shove.

"Don't hide behind closed lips like Finola," Nikolai chided. "Be a man and tell me."

Olexi raised his chin, and the gray light penetrated the shadow of his hat, etching deep wrinkles in his face. "Since you asked, you're acting like an uncultured *govniuk*."

"Oh! Do I embarrass you in front of your refined new friends?"

"You embarrass yourself, Nikolai."

"I'm in the right! I've earned my way in life, not had it handed to me. I'm not some yacht-racing playboy who preys on a girl half his age. I'm that girl's father!"

"Kennedy is not what you think."

"He's exactly what I think—spoiled and superficial with no concept of the real world. Tatiana doesn't see it, but I can forgive that because she's young and naïve. What excuse do you have for your blindness?"

"You are the blind one, friend. Or perhaps you are merely ignorant, so I will educate you with a story. It was more than ten years ago, my brother and I sailed his Logan up to the Broken Islands to fish. A storm came up sudden, and we were too close to shore, so we pulled into a starboard tack and the mast snapped. All hell rained down. The boom broke my brother's leg and the mast barely missed us before smashing into the deck."

"I've heard this story from your brother himself. What does this have to do with—"

"Listen." Olexi's voice was stern.

Nikolai clamped his teeth together and folded his arms.

"My brother was down, screaming in agony. The sails and the sheets were whipping about like mad, but I strapped a life jacket on him, then ran to get the inflatable. That's when I realized how much water we'd taken on. My brother yelled something, so I turned. Then everything went black. When I came to, I was on the shore with this scrawny, wet kid standing over me, and my brother saying how this boy *swam out* and brought us in one at a time. You know how cold those waters are. Add a storm and a sinking boat to that, and it's not a stretch to say he risked his life to save ours. But the kid didn't want any credit. He left without telling us his name."

"I suppose you want me to believe that your brave young rescuer was Kennedy."

"It's the truth."

"Kennedy doesn't possess half the mettle as the boy in your story. He always comes out of the water dry, lathered in the trappings of privilege with all the world delivered as his birthright. It's time someone told him *no*." Nikolai stormed back to his quarters.

Chapter 41

Southern California

"Pops, wake up!" Reid smacked Tinker's chest with the back of his hand. *"Pops!"*

"What?" Tinker bolted upright. "Jesus H. Christ, Reid, what's wrong?"

"Lights."

"Stop the car. Turn off the headlights. Now."

Reid doused the lights and put on the brakes. "I couldn't believe it. I came around the bend, and there they were."

"If we can see them, they can see us," Tinker said. "Put it in park and take your foot off the brake so they can't see the brake lights. What is that, some kind of factory? Where are we? How far down the 210 did you get while I slept? Arcadia? Pasadena?"

"Not the 210. You said the 215."

"The hell I did. The 210 goes to Ellay. The 215 goes to Orange County, *past* Ellay."

"It doesn't matter. We found them." Reid pointed toward the lights.

"Well, we found someone," Tinker grumbled. "Until we know more, we lay low. Let's get off the freeway. We're sitting ducks up here. Keep the lights off and use the brake as little as possible."

Reid put the car in drive and inched forward. "It's starting to get light out."

"I guess it's good I got some sleep. Once I get you settled, I'll see what I can find out about these people."

"I don't think that's the best plan, Pops."

"No, we agreed. One of us has to stay with the car."

"No offense, but you're getting up in years. I should go."

"Son, I've at least been in this part of the country before. I've got better odds of getting around without getting caught, and better odds at improvising if they see me."

"Why not let me get the lay of the land and gather some basic intel first?"

"Well. . . ." Tinker appeared to be considering it.

"Come on, Pops, I've been drilling for years. I can handle a little recon mission. I'll be careful. No one will see me."

"The reality is, this whole thing is your mission. You should call the shots." Tinker sounded tired. Almost sad. "Let's hide the car and figure out what city this is. Then we gotta get you a map and some kind of cover story. Just in case."

Chapter 42

Pacific Ocean, aboard the Emancipation

They were underway again. The anchor had been pulled before the scull had even been secured. Nikolai knew he should try to sleep, but it was impossible. He paced his room and focused on Kennedy to keep from imagining his children's fate.

How did Olexi think it even possible that Kennedy was the boy from his story? He had to be misremembering the event. It would not be the first time a simple tale had been inflated to heroic proportions over years of retelling and large quantities of cider.

No, there was no backbone hidden beneath Kennedy's veneer of entitlement. Nikolai knew what Kennedy was, and he'd thought Olexi called things by their names, too. But his friend had been duped, as Cook apparently had, too.

What had Kennedy said to convince her to abandon her oldest friend in his time of need? Whatever it was, Nikolai was full up to the throat with it, and he was going to set her straight.

He yanked open his door and went to her room. As he waited for her to answer his knock, he glanced at his watch and blanched at the hour.

No matter. It was time to settle things.

Finola opened the door and scowled at him from beneath large pink curlers. "Go away."

Nikolai pushed past her and entered the candlelit room. "We need to talk."

"I'm not talking to you." Finola crossed her arms.

"Then listen." Nikolai noticed the empty bed and was surprised Olexi wasn't there. "I can't fathom why you're so mad at me, but it's got to stop. You're my oldest and dearest friend, and if I can forgive you for not telling me about Tatiana and Kennedy . . ." He dug his nails into his palms and took a deep breath. "Then surely you can forgive me for whatever it is you imagine I've done."

"Imagine?" Finola's face was as big and red as a sunset. "*Imagine?* I did not imagine you inviting me to go with you to rescue the children. Did I imagine you changing your mind and leaving me behind at Corinne's? *You* did not even have the decency to tell me you'd changed your plans. You did not even say goodbye!"

"Finny, I—"

"Those children. You know what they mean to me. These last years I've been more of a parent to them than you have." She stopped, her eyes wide and her nostrils flaring.

He staggered back, as if he'd taken a physical blow. She was right. After Jess died, Finny had been there for the children whenever they were sad, or sick, or lonely. She'd taken care of Will after every broken bone, and Tatiana after every broken heart. As much as he loved his children, he couldn't do it himself. Seeing them hurt made him miss Jess so fiercely, he thought it might consume him. So he'd let Finny do it.

He looked at her now, her sweet face scrunched in a scowl beneath her curlers. She wasn't going to forgive him, and he didn't deserve it anyway. He'd been selfish, self-centered, insensitive, and unappreciative. The truth was a stone on his heart, and he had no words of rebuttal.

"You're right," he said simply, and he went for the door.

"Nikolai Evgeny Petrov!" she shouted.

He froze.

"Look at me when I speak to you," she said.

At least she was speaking to him now. He turned.

"You are sorry," she said.

He nodded.

"That was not a question," she said. "I see you are sorry. . . . *Okay.*" Her expression softened. She grabbed him by the elbow, drew him into her arms, and clutched him to her ample bosom. "*Okaaaay,* okay, there now."

He rested his chin atop her curlers as she hugged her forgiveness.

"I know," she cooed. "You have been an idiot. Your anger got in the way of seeing your own nose. But you see now. You are sorry, and you are forgiven." She patted his back heartily.

"I'm sorry," Nikolai said.

"I already said you are forgiven. Go so Finola can get her beauty sleep." She pointed to the door. "Go on, get out of here, and stop being a half-sighted tomfool."

He kissed her cheek and left, thankful at least one thing was right with his world again. Soon, Finny would come around to his way of thinking and see through Kennedy's bloated pretensions. Then Olexi wouldn't be far behind. By the time they rescued Tatiana, Kennedy wouldn't stand a fighting chance.

Chapter 43

Lost Angeles, the Grand Hotel

Pascal woke in his suite and caressed the vacant place in the bed where Mia had been.

Last night, he hadn't felt like returning to his house and had told her to go back to her own room so he could sleep alone. He'd needed a few hours of rest after all the *surprises* they'd exchanged.

To think he'd almost missed out due to a brief infatuation with fresh-faced Devon. He was thankful Ellianna knew him so well. An encounter with Mia compared to a moment with Devon was like the difference between Cognac and water. While both quenched a thirst, they were not the same at all.

According to his Rolex, he had time for a shower before meeting Mia for breakfast. He was taking her on her first train ride. As he stepped into the scalding shower, he recalled again how Mia had surprised him there. He hoped this trip would prove as entertaining.

Two hours later, Mia sat in the front row of the empty train car, her hair tied back with a ribbon. "How long will the ride be?"

"Normally it takes several hours to make this trip," Pascal said, standing behind her. He rarely sat on the train, preferring instead to stand at the window or walk the aisle. "They usually stop every couple of blocks to load cargo. But I don't have the time or patience for that, so we'll be at World Waste in twenty minutes or less—I told them to push it. I like the speed."

"I like it, too. It's exhilarating."

"You'll ride home tomorrow on the regular route. From World Waste, the train heads south all the way to Angel Stadium. From there it swings back to Services, completing a circle."

"I want to see everything."

"There's not much to see. Inside the circle is worker housing. Outside is where the collectors work. They gather goods in wagons and wheelbarrows and deposit them at the train stops. Inside the circle, workers haul trash to load-holds on their side of the tracks. When the train stops, loaders toss the stuff from both sides to catchers on the train."

"The trash goes to World Waste and the supplies go to Services?"

"Correct."

"Will I get to see how the trash gets converted into electricity?"

"Would you like that? I'll be in meetings, so you'll be free for a few hours. I can arrange a tour, though I thought you might want to nap."

"What makes you think that?" Mia stood and looked coyly at him, steady on her feet for never having ridden a train before.

"You didn't get much sleep last night, nor will you tonight."

"I don't need much. Why waste time in a new place with my eyes closed?"

"Some things are better with eyes closed, and I don't consider them a waste of time."

"I prefer everything with my eyes wide open." She kissed him, long and slow.

He looked, and she did have her eyes open.

He lifted her and she wrapped her legs around him, taking his tongue deep in her mouth. He told himself not to get carried away by a girl he'd just met. Then again, why shouldn't he? He was the chancellor. The King of Lost Angeles.

When the train pulled in to the station at World Waste, the director himself was waiting at the stop. Pascal was impressed.

"Chancellor, welcome," the director said, a bit out of breath. He must have run all the way from his office when the train was spotted arriving without cargo. "We weren't expecting you."

"That was my intent, Tom," Pascal said. He stepped from the train and shook the man's hand. "No need to disrupt work preparing for a V.I.P. visit. Besides, I want to see your operation on a regular day. I trust you have nothing to hide."

"Our doors are always open to you, Chancellor." Tom's smile was relaxed, which told Pascal the inspection was indeed unnecessary.

"Tom, I'd like to introduce Mia." Pascal helped her down from the train.

"It's nice to meet you, Director Gould." Mia clasped the director's hand. Pascal was impressed she remembered his name—he'd only mentioned it in passing.

"It's a privilege to have you and the chancellor here," Tom said.

"I'm excited to be here," Mia said. "I've always wondered how you make electricity."

"She's a bright young woman, Tom. She's interested in your operation. Can she have a tour while we meet? I have some development issues to go over with you."

"Yes, of course," Tom said.

Whatever plans Tom had for the day, Pascal was pleased he'd set them aside without hesitation.

"I'll have my secretary bring tea to the conference room," Tom continued. "Mia, will you join us while I find a lucky volunteer to show you around?"

"If it's all the same to you, Tom, I'd rather take a walk on my own. I seldom have the opportunity to be alone, so as long as you don't mind, there's no need to take a worker away from his job." She looked at Pascal for approval.

"That's a fine idea," Pascal said, pleased she was so thoughtful. "She shouldn't need an escort. It's not particularly dangerous if she stays clear of the tracks and the incinerator, right?"

"Correct. Absolutely, Chancellor," Tom said. "Please go and enjoy yourself, Mia."

"Do you have a watch?" Pascal asked her. She shook her head. "I'll have to get you one, but for now take mine. Be back by two o'clock."

Pascal was glad to see her tuck his Rolex in the front pocket of her snug shorts. It would be inconvenient if she lost it.

"Mia, first let me get you something to eat," Tom said. "You'll be out over lunchtime."

"No need." Mia grabbed her bag from the floorboard of the train. "I have everything I need in here. Thank you, though."

Pascal watched her walk away with almost as much appreciation as Tom did.

So far the visit was going precisely as Pascal had hoped.

Chapter 44

Southern California

Reid was hot, tired, and thirsty. It was only mid-morning, but he needed to rest. He sat in the shade of a brick building, partially hidden by a dumpster and a crumbling cement staircase. He leaned against the cool bricks and drank half a bottle of water, wondering what Kayla was doing at that moment. Was she feeling okay? Was she lonely? Did she miss him?

There was an emptiness in the pit of his stomach when he thought about her, more hollow now than before. She'd finally come to his bed, but it wasn't him she wanted. It never had been, and no matter what happened between them, he'd always know he was second best.

Tinker was right. It would be too painful to be with her, to love her like he did, knowing she didn't feel the same. He wished they'd never kissed. Somehow that made it worse.

God, California was hot. It sapped the energy right out of him. He leaned his head back against the bricks and closed his eyes, just for a minute. . . .

Clunk. Reid startled awake. He listened, trying to figure out what he'd heard.

The sun was straight up. Crap, two hours or more had passed.

A hollow *clunk,* followed by *clatter.*

Reid used the dumpster as cover and peeked around it.

About fifteen yards away, a woman walked down the road, away from his position. Dark hair hung down her back. A tank top and shorts hugged her figure.

Thunk, clatter. She was kicking a can.

She must have passed right by while he was asleep. He was lucky she hadn't seen him. Stupid rookie move, falling asleep.

Thunk, clatter.

What was she doing out here alone? She carried a bag, but it was small for scavenging. She wasn't hunting—no apparent gun. Was she out for a leisurely walk? Were these people so well off they didn't need to work in the middle of the day?

She was the only person he'd seen all morning, and he wasn't going to let her walk out of sight. When she was thirty yards away, he grabbed his pack and followed.

He hugged the building, staying in its slim shadow. When she turned a corner out of sight, he sprinted. At the corner, he peeked around.

Shit! She was four feet away, looking right at him. Like she was waiting for him. Should he try to talk his way out of it? Should he run? Would she call in the troops? So much for being able to handle a recon mission. So much for not being seen.

"It's okay," the girl called. "You can come out."

Reid swallowed hard and made his decision. He stepped out where she could see him.

"Hi," the girl said. She had deep brown eyes that were in perfect harmony with her light brown skin, and the most beautiful face he had ever seen. She looked near his age, but it was hard to tell.

"Hi," Reid croaked. He felt like a total goofus, like he'd never talked to a girl before.

"I'm Mia. It's nice to meet you." She came forward, extending her hand.

Her grasp was warm and firm, her skin soft, not the calloused grip of a worker. He held her hand a little longer than he should have. "I'm Reid," he remembered to say.

"I'm glad I ran into you," she said. "It's hotter here than I'm used to. Do you know somewhere we could get out of the sun?"

"I, uh," Reid stammered, trying to assimilate what she'd revealed. She wasn't from here either. He thought back to the buildings he'd explored that morning. "Sure, I know a place. You're not from around here?"

"It's that obvious, huh? I took the train from Services this morning and I'm looking around while I wait for a friend. What are you doing? Am I keeping you from collecting?"

Collecting. She said it like it was a job. Think, *think.* "I'm, um, taking a break."

"Where I'm from we call it taking a nap," she said with a hint of laughter.

She'd seen him. She'd known he was there all along.

"Don't worry," she said, her smile radiant. "I won't tell your boss. But if he sees us standing here, he might make you work and I'd miss the opportunity to get to know you."

She reached out, her hand grazing his arm.

Reid felt his cheeks warm. "We wouldn't want that."

"So you know a place we can sit in the shade?"

"Yeah, over there," he said, pointing toward an apartment building he remembered had a pavilion. "Unless you saw my boss over that way."

"No, you're the only person I've seen in the last hour. Lead the way."

"So," Reid said, trying to think what he might learn from her, trying to think like a soldier instead of a boy flustered by an attractive girl. "You said you're from 'services'?"

"Yes, I'm a Ford girl. Have you ever been?"

He didn't know what she meant, but she said it like it would be acceptable to say he hadn't, so he shook his head.

"Well, hopefully you will someday." She smiled. "What about your job? Your pack seems awfully small for collecting, and I don't see a wagon. Are you really a collector?

"Well, not exactly." *Think.* "Uh, there's, uh, different aspects to the job. Different responsibilities." He paused, hoping she'd fill in the blanks.

"Like what, a scout or a supervisor?"

"Yeah, like that." *Quick, change the subject.* "What do you do?"

"I told you, I'm a Ford girl. Is this where you wanted to sit?" she pointed at a splintery picnic table in a ramshackle pavilion. It was in worse shape than he'd recalled.

"Sorry, I guess this isn't very nice."

"Could we go inside? I've always wanted to collect something myself instead of getting it from Services. I've been trying to get up the nerve."

He hadn't gone inside this particular building, but the ones he'd been in seemed safe enough. "Sure, I don't see why not."

"Okay, boss, lead the way."

Reid hesitated. She expected him to be the expert, and he didn't want to give himself away. He had a brainstorm. "How about *you* be the collector? You can lead the way."

"How fun! Let's see . . ." Mia wiggled the doorknob. "Locked. What do we do now?"

"You're not even trying. Think like a collector." Reid knew enough about scavenging to figure they'd find a way in before too long. Sliding glass doors were usually a good bet.

"Should we check around back?" She looked pleased when he nodded.

Mia was thrilled when the slider creaked open on its track. "Is there any good stuff left?"

"You're the collector. You tell me."

She poked her head in. "Let's find out."

Reid followed her into a dingy kitchen. The vinyl floor was dark and cracking, blackened near the door. The cupboards hung open, already picked clean.

"Kitchens are boring." She moved into the living area. "I'd rather have a book or a statue." She ran her finger along dusty framed photos that lined the mantel, stopping at a figurine of a chubby angel. "Not my taste. Can we try the bedroom?"

Reid's heart skipped. "What?"

She grinned, then her eyes went wide.

He followed her gaze to the couch. Bones. A skull, with hair and all, was grinning at them. "Oh God, I'm sorry." He ushered her back to the kitchen. "I should have realized you wouldn't be used to that."

"I was surprised, that's all. Are they everywhere?"

"Yeah—" Reid stopped himself. Back home there were skeletons everywhere, but he didn't know about here. In Colorado, people had died faster than the living could bury them. Some of those who'd died in the initial blast had been buried, but as more succumbed to radiation poisoning, the hospitals were overrun, and people stopped trying. Tinker said that when the survivors in Cheyenne Mountain finally came outside, the city was full of bodies. It would have taken decades to bury them all. Tinker always said *that* was why the Church forbade it—not because it was a sin to hide reminders of God's warning, but because it was impractical.

Maybe the sun flare hadn't been as strong in Ellay, and not as many people had died. Until he knew more, he'd better keep his mouth shut.

"Are you okay?" Mia asked. "I'm the one who's supposed to be shaken up."

"Sorry, just remembering something. Should we go?"

"No, I want to collect something." She twirled a strand of hair around her finger and stepped a little closer to him. "I was starting to say

173

we should look in the bedroom when you got embarrassed."

"Oh." His face flushed again.

"You're so cute." She touched his nose with her finger. "Let's go look. Maybe I'll find a scarf or a purse or jewelry."

"You want me to take the lead?"

"Not a chance." She led him past a pink bathroom and an office to an open door at the end of the hall. She stepped inside. "Oh, hello."

"Hello yourself," a deep voice replied.

Chapter 45

Pacific Ocean, aboard the Emancipation

A rap at the door roused Nikolai from a dream where he was frolicking in the tide with bronzed Hawaiian beauties. He considered ignoring the knock, but a glance at his watch sent him shooting out of bed.

Vot eto da! The exhaustion had caught up with him. He never slept past noon. He stepped into his trousers and zipped them as he fumbled for the door.

Outside was a tray of food. He smiled, inhaling the aroma of steaming nut porridge. He picked up the tray and latched the door, then sat down at the desk to eat. He noticed the notebook Kennedy had given him and figured he might as well have a look while he ate. No harm in that.

After ten minutes of reading, Nikolai had forgotten all about his food. The breadth, the scope, *the genius* of the plans for the settlement at Sausalito stunned him. He could see Tatiana's hand in the descriptions of horticulture and fishing, and he shook his head, thinking how proud her mother would have been. The outlines of the governmental structure were equally impressive, filled with common sense details—something completely foreign to the Democracy. Schools and apprenticeships, cooperative childcare, artisans and craftsmen, entertainment, cider production. Even guidelines for legal prostitution.

But what impressed Nikolai the most was the plan for trading with other settlements. It was brilliant. And it also cast light on the importance of finding seeds. No wonder Tatiana had risked her life to go south.

Nikolai pushed aside his tray, washed, and dressed, then went to find Kennedy.

Kennedy was in his office, sitting behind a desk piled with neat stacks of papers and charts. He rose as Nikolai entered, slipping his reading glasses into his breast pocket.

"Welcome, Captain," Kennedy said. "It's good to see you. Are you here to discuss the pirates? I expect we should encounter them late in the day tomorrow."

Nikolai knew if they discussed the pirates he'd blow and wouldn't be able to say what he'd come to say. "I reviewed the documents you gave me," he said, settling into a chair.

"What do you think?"

"Impressive," Nikolai said honestly. "Beyond anything I could have imagined."

"That's due to your daughter, sir. She's got a lot of ideas, and the brains to back up her enthusiasm. She impresses me every time we talk about it."

Nikolai appraised Kennedy, appreciating the high esteem with which he seemed to hold Tatiana. If only the man weren't so much older than his daughter, perhaps Nikolai could learn to see beyond his privileged upbringing. "There's one thing that bothers me."

Kennedy raised his eyebrows in question.

"It was a mistake the way you handled the situation with Corinne," Nikolai said. "Keeping the colony a secret."

"Ah, that," Kennedy said, leaning back in his chair with a sigh. "I don't know your mother personally, but from what I know *of* her, I questioned the wisdom of hiding our plans. But she's Tati's grandmother, so it was Tati's call."

Kennedy's pet name for Tatiana grated on Nikolai's nerves, but he did his best to set that aside. "It was the wrong call. Tatiana is bright, but she's young. What good is the wisdom of *your* years if you keep it from her when she's making a mistake?"

"But isn't that how we gain wisdom? By learning from our mistakes?"

"We only learn from mistakes we survive! The situation with Corinne was trivial compared to my children sailing on a fool's errand." Nikolai rose from his chair and towered over Kennedy.

"I understand you're upset—"

"Do you? Because 'upset' doesn't quite capture it." Nikolai tried to pace, but there wasn't enough room. "Okay," he said, trying to calm down. "It's clear from the plans that the new settlement is based upon farming and trade, but why look for seeds in Southern California, for

God's sake? We already know there are no seeds there."

"I beg to differ, sir," Kennedy said, his voice and demeanor calm. "Tati spent a great deal of time poring over the research your late wife left, as well as doing additional research on her own. There is strong evidence that there *are* seeds in Southern California."

"I don't care about all the damned book research on the globe. I've been to the ruins of the Seed Repository in San Diego. I've seen it with my own eyes. There are no seeds."

"Tati didn't go to San Diego." Kennedy's brow furrowed. "I thought you knew."

"There seems to be a lot no one has bothered to tell me." Nikolai looked Kennedy square in his too-perfect face. "So tell me—where did my daughter go?"

"The evidence . . . all the research showed . . ." For the first time, Kennedy seemed hesitant.

Nikolai leaned across the desk, daring him to continue.

Kennedy cleared his throat. "San Clemente Island."

"What? In God's name, *why?* No, don't answer that. There's no reason good enough." Nikolai spun around to leave, the tops of his ears burning and his palms throbbing where nails bit into already raw flesh.

"Wait," Kennedy called. "I don't understand. What's the big deal with San Clemente?"

Nikolai turned around to rail at Kennedy, but saw on his face that he really had no idea. He took a breath, trying to compose himself. "San Clemente is the base of the southern pirates, and those pirates are a bit . . . *different* than the northern ones. They like to cut designs in themselves. And others."

"Cut what, *skin?*"

Nikolai nodded. "To mark themselves as belonging to their 'tribe.' What they do to captives is unbelievably painful, and not at all pretty *if* the captive survives the process." He noted that Kennedy looked as horrified as he himself felt.

"Tati didn't . . . I never would have . . . she didn't tell me."

Kennedy looked both betrayed and confused. Nikolai briefly felt bad for him, but the fear and anger raging through his own veins quickly blotted out his compassion.

"It all comes back to those God damned *seeds,*" Nikolai spat as he wheeled around and stomped out.

Why the importance on seeds? He shook his head as he stalked to his quarters. Wasn't everyone doing just fine with apples and fish? He didn't comprehend how vegetable seeds warranted such risk. Jess would have understood, even supported Tatiana's decision. And that just made him madder. Nothing good had ever come of the search for seeds.

Chapter 46

Southern California

Reid froze in the hall. The man Mia was talking to in the bedroom hadn't seen him. He should run. He felt like a coward, but he couldn't get caught. He told himself Mia would be fine, and he turned to flee.

A small man in dirty coveralls blocked his way. "Hey, who are you?"

"Reid, come in here," Mia called. "This collector wants to see you."

Reid braced himself. He wasn't going to have the chance to act like a coward. He hoped to God he could talk his way out of this somehow. He nodded to the man in the hall, then went into the bedroom.

"That's who I'm with," Mia said.

"I never seen him before, lady," said the burly man beside Mia. "He's not one of us. You don't know this kid, do you, Frank?"

The small man stepped in blocking the door. "Nope. He ain't a collector."

"I thought you said you was with a collector," the first man said. "What's going on here?"

Shit. Reid couldn't think of anything to say. He gauged the distance to the door. The little man—Frank—was in the way, but Reid outweighed him by a few. He could probably run right over him and keep going.

"You misunderstood me," Mia said. "I said we were *pretending* to be collectors."

"Pretending?" the first man said.

"Yes, I'm sure it seems silly to you," Mia said with a self-deprecating smile. "You see, I'm visiting from Services where I'm a Ford girl." She paused for effect and the big man did seem impressed. "I've always wanted to collect something. I think what you do is so interesting and exciting. Tom—I mean Director Gould— gave me permission to wander around. He said I could go wherever I want. I hope I haven't done something wrong."

"Oh, that's right," Frank said. "The Supe told me there was a girl out here. Friend of the chancellor's. He didn't mention nothing about a kid with her."

"He came with me to carry the treasures I find," she said, drawing closer to the big man. "I have to tell you, I don't see how you collectors do it. I was horribly frightened when I saw that dead person in the living room. Doesn't it get to you?"

"Naw," he said, allowing her to steer him toward the door. Frank was forced backward into the hall. "You get used to it. It's not like they smell or anything."

"Very sophisticated, Roger," Frank said.

"Shut up," Roger spat. "So you like collecting, huh?" he asked Mia.

Reid followed quietly, hoping they'd forget about him.

"Oh yes, I've always wanted to try it. But I haven't found anything pretty yet to take home as a souvenir."

"I got something in my bag," Frank said. "It's a real nice shirt. I bet it would fit you."

"You're too sweet," Mia purred. "But I was hoping to collect something myself. I know you do it all the time, but it's a dream of mine, and now I'm afraid it will never be fulfilled." She sighed. "Unless . . ."

"Unless what?" Roger asked, like he'd do anything she wanted.

"Unless I can collect something before I have to go back to Director Gould's office."

"There's a much better complex on the next block," Roger said. "The people who lived there must have been rich. I could help you find something special."

"Don't be dense, Roger," Frank said. "She wants to do it herself."

"Then why's this kid with her?"

Both men looked at Reid.

"He carries things for me, remember?" Mia squeezed up to Roger. Reid suspected she pressed her breasts against his arm on purpose.

"*I* could carry things," Roger said.

"I wouldn't want to get you in trouble." Mia swayed her hips as she went to the front door. "I mean, you're supposed to be doing *real* collecting."

"Yeah, I guess," Roger said.

"Which way do I go?" Mia stepped into the sunshine.

"See that greenish store?" Roger pointed. "Turn there, go one block and it's on the left. The Royal Terrace. Sounds nice, don't it?"

"Yes, I bet I'll find something wonderful and I'll remember you every time I see it."

Roger beamed.

Reid tried not to roll his eyes.

"Oh, Roger?" Mia said. "There is one tiny favor you could do for me."

"Name it."

"Don't mention to anyone you saw me. When people hear there's a Ford girl, they get curious, and they're not always as gentlemanly as you two."

"No problem, Miss. We won't say a thing, will we Frank?"

"Not a thing," Frank said. "Have fun collecting."

"Thank you so much. Goodbye, now." Mia waved, and walked toward the green building. She handed Reid her bag. Nice touch.

As soon as they turned the corner, Mia grabbed his arm. "All right, who are you?"

"What do you mean?"

"I saved your ass back there. Now come clean."

"I, I . . ." What was his cover story? "I'm from up north. I'm looking for a job."

She stared, chin down, hands on her hips. "How about the truth?"

"That is the truth."

"Bull. Your accent isn't like any Northerner I've met. From the moment you opened your mouth, I knew you were an outsider. You're lucky those collectors weren't real swift or you'd be headed for the Tank, and they'd be enjoying their reward."

"Are you going to turn me in?"

"I covered for you, didn't I? Look, when I first saw you, I was having a little fun. Now, I like you. So I'm giving you a chance. Go home while you can." She took her bag and turned. "Don't worry, Reid—if that's really your name. I won't tell anyone about you."

"Wait." He wasn't sure what made him call out. "I can't tell you everything."

"I didn't ask you to."

"I can't say how I got here, but I came to find something, and I'm not leaving until I do."

"That's a big challenge, finding something in a city where strangers aren't welcome." She walked back to him, swaying her hips again. "It would be dangerous, but I like you, and I'm willing to help."

She was trying to play him like she'd played Roger, but it wasn't going to work.

"What's in it for you?" he asked.

"Everyone thinks a Ford girl's life is glamorous and exciting. I did, until I became one. But I'm already bored. I've always been bored. That's why I became a Ford girl to begin with, but turns out it's not enough."

"You'd risk helping me because you're bored? That doesn't add up."

"It would if you knew what it was like. My life consists of waiting around and looking pretty. I don't want to be another decoration in an elegant room. I want to explore. Lost Angeles is too small and contained. Predictable. I want adventure."

"If you want out so bad, leave. You don't need me."

"Oh, you're obviously not from around here." She laughed without humor. "I'd never make it far enough fast enough. My last hope was the train, and I found out today it doesn't go anywhere but around in a circle. Besides, I wouldn't know where to go."

"What do you want, a map to where I came from? What makes you think it's better there?"

"Then take me someplace else. Someplace new." She caressed his arm. "You're different. I bet you could show me things no one else can. In fact, I'm willing to bet my life on it."

She looked at him from under long dark lashes, the slightest pout on her moist pink lips. She tucked a lock of hair behind her ear, then trailed her fingers down her cheek and neck, along the edge of her shirt past her collarbone, stopping at her cleavage.

He could tell she was playing him, but knowing that didn't completely immunize him from the effects.

She pulled a watch from her pocket. "I don't have much time. The deal I'm offering is, I help you blend in and find what you're looking for, then you get me far enough away from Lost Angeles that the Blades can't reach me. After that we can go our separate ways if you want."

"What are blades?"

She shook her head. "If you don't know that, you *do* need my help." She looked at the watch again. "I have to go."

"Wait—you're right, I need your help." He hadn't known he was going to take the gamble until he said it. "When can you come back?"

"I can't. Not here."

"Then where? When?" He didn't want to waste time waiting for her, but it was becoming apparent he wouldn't make it very far on his own.

"I go back to the city tomorrow. You'll have to meet me there. The Grand Hotel."

"Is that safe? You said everyone would know I'm an outsider."

"You have a better option?" She pulled something from her bag and held it out to him. A card. "Don't lose this. It's a voucher for services. Give it to the receptionist and ask for me. Talk as little as possible. Make sure you're dirty and wear ratty clothes so you look like the other pirates."

"Pirates?"

"If they ask what ship, say you're looking for a new berth. Hopefully, they won't press."

"Can't we meet someplace where I don't have to talk to anyone?"

She shook her head. "I have no idea when I'll be allowed to leave the Grand again."

He didn't like meeting in such a public place, but she might be their best chance at navigating Ellay. And he wanted to see her again. "Okay, maybe. I can't promise though. How do I find it?" He and Tinker could always decide against it.

"Go to the amusement park complex in the middle of Anaheim. The Grand is the big hotel at the south end. It's on every map."

"When?"

"Tomorrow afternoon." She kissed him long and sweet. "Goodbye, Reid. I truly hope I see you again."

Reid gripped the card. She was definitely playing him, but that kiss made him want to believe she wasn't.

Chapter 47

Lost Angeles, World Waste

Pascal was pleased to find Mia waiting, radiant in a low-cut dress, her hair tousled and sexy. "Mia, you look like a kiss of sunshine. Did you enjoy your adventure?"

She smiled with her eyes and clasped his extended hands. "It left me energized. Wanting more." She raised an eyebrow.

Pascal considered changing his plans, but decided it would be short-sighted. Tom could prove a valuable ally. "You'll be spending tonight with Tom." He looked for any sign of reluctance or apprehension, and was rewarded with a knowing smile.

"Do you have anything in particular in mind? I can be very . . . *persuasive* if there's any way I can be of service to you."

He wanted to take her right there as he had on the train. She'd embraced the assignment *and* understood its implications. "Consider this laying a foundation of . . . indebtedness."

"I'll be thinking of you," she whispered in his ear. She drew against him, her hand on his thigh. "Will I get to have the real thing tomorrow?"

"I have some pressing matters to attend to, so it will be a few days. Your train leaves tomorrow at nine. Take it back to the Grand, and I'll see you when I can."

"I'm already looking forward to it."

An hour later, Pascal was back on the train. Leaving Mia behind was a small sacrifice for a sound investment. His focus should be on Van Hooten, anyway. The results promised to be more gratifying and long-lasting than even Mia could offer. He disembarked near the doctor's home.

Gloria Van Hooten was visibly shocked when she opened the door. "Chancellor Worth, what a pleasant surprise! Please come in."

Pascal followed her into a dark paneled room with overstuffed chairs, Persian rugs, and weighty paintings. Thick drapes trapped in the heat, exacerbating the cloying floral scent. Pascal loosened his collar and visualized sparse furnishings of stainless steel and Danish teak so he didn't suffocate.

"Lovely home, Mrs. Van Hooten."

"Why, thank you. We like it. Upstairs I went with Victorian antiques, cabbage roses and such, but this is Jerome's den. His haven. It's a man thing, I suppose, reading dusty old books and drinking whiskey. Speaking of which, where are my manners? Can I get you a drink? Bourbon? Water? Bourbon and water?" She wrung her hands and attempted to laugh.

"No need. I've brought something special." He indicated the bottle tucked under his arm.

Her eyes and smile grew wide. Even if he hadn't known about her *fondness,* it was readily apparent.

"How thoughtful," she said, fluttering her hands about her sallow face.

"A token of gratitude for your husband's service. A reminder, you might say. Can I have a word with him?"

"Oh, yes, of course. I should have gotten him right away, I don't know why I didn't. You are so kind to bring a gift. And to come here personally. My goodness. Well, you make yourself right at home. I'll be back in a jiffy." She scurried away.

Pascal wondered how the doctor managed to be around her five minutes without killing her or himself. He wouldn't be surprised if the den door had a lock and the doctor kept a large stash of booze inside.

He avoided the furniture and stood in front of a heavy-handed oil painting of a fox hunt, thinking it a violation of the laws of physics how slowly time was passing. Finally he heard the tromping of feet.

"I found him! We're coming!" Mrs. Van Hooten's voice had grown more shrill, if that were possible.

"Chancellor." The doctor made no effort to disguise his displeasure at Pascal's unannounced visit.

"Oh, silly me," Mrs. Van Hooten cooed. "I've forgotten the glasses."

"That won't be necessary. I'm not staying. But keep the gift." Pascal extended the bottle and she clutched it to her breast.

"I don't know how to thank you," she gushed.

"Give us a moment, dear?" Van Hooten shooed his wife out.

"Wonderful to see you, Chancellor! Thank you!" she called as he closed the door, which was, in fact, equipped with a deadbolt.

Van Hooten faced him, arms folded. "What can I do for you?"

"What, no offer to sit? Not even the pretense of camaraderie?"

"You said you weren't staying."

Pascal was half-tempted to take a seat and prolong the man's agony, but it would also prolong his own. "I'll get to the point. My son wishes to see his mother tomorrow. I'd like to accommodate him, but it would be inconvenient if she spoke to him. Is she conscious?"

"Uh, yes, I believe so."

Pascal frowned. "What about tomorrow morning? Will she be conscious then?"

"I really don't know."

"But you'll check on her tonight. Because I'd like for my son to have one last *quiet* visit with her tomorrow morning. Then we can be done with this business. Do I make myself clear?"

A flash of rage crossed Van Hooten's face. "It's awfully late to see a patient."

Pascal stepped closer and spoke softly. "You have such a lovely wife. It would be a shame if her thirst got the better of her."

It only took a moment for Van Hooten's rage to turn to resignation. He nodded. One brief nod, but all that was necessary.

"Enjoy the gift. I'll see myself out."

On the stoop, Pascal took a deep breath of the fresh evening air and congratulated himself. That had gone quite well.

Chapter 48

Pacific Ocean, aboard the Emancipation

Nikolai soaked his hands in the sink. Pacing hadn't helped. All it had gotten him was thinner boot soles and bloody palms. If anything, he was more furious now. Furious at himself for mutilating his hands and raising stubborn children, furious at his children for being as foolish as they were stubborn, and beyond furious at Kennedy and Creighton for not averting the disaster.

How had Tatiana become convinced there were seeds at the headquarters of the southern pirates? Nothing he or Jess had read suggested any such thing.

He couldn't think of a worse place for his children to be. The northern pirates were at least human. He wondered if Will had the sense to seek their help in dealing with the southern pirates. But Nikolai knew Will lengthwise and crosswise. His son was far too cocky and independent for that. The boy could sail but lacked a healthy sense of his own shortcomings, his own mortality. His overconfidence would be the end of him some day.

If it hadn't been already.

The thought took him by the soul.

A knock at the door brought him out of it. His children were not dead. Unless he saw their cold bodies, he would believe they were alive and wouldn't stop trying to find them.

He pulled the plug and watched the pink water spiral down the drain, in no hurry to answer the door. His days had become an endless cycle of loneliness and boredom, broken only by the occasional knock signaling a delivery of food.

When he opened the door, he was surprised to see Olexi.

"Sorry for the delay." Nikolai stepped aside for Olexi to enter. "I thought it was supper."

"You're not eating with the captain?"

"I can't look at him now. Do *you* know where we're headed?"

"I didn't think it my place to ask specifics."

"San Clemente." The very name was like acid on Nikolai's tongue.

Olexi gasped. "*Voobshye?*"

"I wouldn't joke about that." Nikolai took his father's pipe from his pocket and turned it over in his hands to keep from clenching his fists.

"*Kakógo chërta.* Why there?"

"Seeds. Am I to lose everyone I love to that bewitched pursuit? Creighton should have come to me, or Kennedy should have talked them out of it."

Olexi shook his head. "You know your daughter."

"Right, I've heard it—she has her own mind, Kennedy *couldn't* stop her. Sorry, but that's not good enough. I'd have tied them up in the cargo hold, or told the Democracy they'd committed murder—anything to prevent my children from going to San Clemente."

"You have a point," Olexi said. "But Kennedy's still a good man."

"I know you're his fan," Nikolai said. "Forgive me if I'm not."

"It's your children—no forgiveness necessary."

"Not even for how I treated you, old friend?"

"Much water has flowed by. Let's say we forget it." Olexi clapped him on the shoulder, and Nikolai felt an immense sense of relief.

"Shall we forget with a cider?"

Olexi grinned. "Perhaps more than one."

Chapter 49

Southern California, the next morning

Reid scratched the stubble on his face, wishing he could shave, but if he was going to see Mia, he had to let it grow. "What do you think, Pops? Do we trust her?"

"It's risky. But what's not?"

"I'm open to other ideas." Reid meant it, though he wanted to see her again.

"If we can't blend in, that limits our options. How sure are you about that?"

"Not completely sure. I mean, it's not like people here look like they're from another planet, but Mia said it's obvious I'm an outsider. Especially when I talk. And there's all sorts of stuff that was totally foreign to me. She said there are *pirates*."

"Who'd have thought so much of a difference would evolve between Colorado and here. Then again, Los Angeles always was a different kind of place."

"It's funny, I'd swear Mia called it *Lost* Angeles."

"Lost? Huh. Well, maybe that fits." Tinker rubbed his eyes and stretched. "So you said they have trains. What about cars?"

"I have no idea."

"Well, the fact is, they already have power. I was hoping to barter, to trade something for the seeds, like how to convert warheads."

"They have power, but maybe not cars."

"True, they could be interested in that technology. But we can't go in revealing our whole hand. If they want the Hummer, what's to stop them from taking it?"

"Good point. Mia made it sound worse than back home, but all we have is her word."

Tinker scratched his chin. "Only way to know for sure what we're dealing with is to get intel firsthand. So the question is, with Mia or on our own?"

Reid pictured Mia and his heart skipped remembering that kiss.

"You met the girl," Tinker continued. "What's your gut tell you?"

"To go to Mia." Reid thought it was his gut, but it could very well be another part of his anatomy. He just hoped it wouldn't lead them into trouble they couldn't get out of.

Chapter 50

Lost Angeles

"You're early," Pascal said. "Tea?"

"No thanks," Linus said, fidgeting. "How is Mother? Will she see me?"

"First things first. I want to know what you learned while I was away. How about breakfast while we talk?"

"All right, if you want." The boy managed to keep most of the dejection from his voice. "But it won't take long."

From the look on Linus's face, the idea of sitting through breakfast had been almost too much for him. But he'd handled it well. Pascal glanced at his watch. It was late enough. He wouldn't torture the boy. "Breakfast isn't necessary. Tell me what you found out."

"When Mother is in town, Van Hooten usually goes to her house every other day. But lately it's more often, sometimes twice a day."

"Interesting."

"There's more. This one junior nurse I've been talking to—Jenna— she said it seems like whenever Mother starts to get better, suddenly she gets worse again, always right after Van Hooten visits."

"Jenna noticed that?"

"She agreed when I pointed it out." Linus scowled. "I wish I knew what Van Hooten was *doing*. No one knows. He won't allow anyone in the room, and Mother's chart only says 'treatments.' I know he's hurting her."

"You're convinced?"

"Totally. But I couldn't figure out *why*."

Pascal frowned. He hadn't expected the boy to look beyond the surface. "Sometimes motivation remains a mystery."

"No, I figured it out."

Pascal relaxed. Linus had filled in the blanks himself. "Go on."

"I kept thinking about it, why he'd want to hurt her. Then I remembered—more than a few times he's been at her house at weird hours. Late at night, I'd come out of my room and he'd be there. A few times he snuck out the back door, looking around like he didn't want anyone to see him."

"And you think what? That they were a couple?" *That would be a laugh.*

"No, I think he *wanted* to, but Mother didn't. He'd be humiliated, enough to want revenge. Or maybe Mother threatened to tell his wife, and he's trying to keep her quiet."

"Do you think he would go so far as to kill her?"

"Yes—we have to protect her! You should forbid him to be her doctor."

"You know your mother. She is accustomed to getting what she wants. If I forbid Van Hooten to be her doctor, how do you think she will react?" He raised his hands in question, letting Linus make the conclusion himself. "Son, do yourself a favor and consider very carefully before you get involved with a woman who's *that* headstrong and independent."

"Okay, then we'll have to convince *her* to fire him. If I could talk to her, I know I could make her see reason."

Good luck with that, even if she were conscious.

"*Please,*" Linus continued. "You've got to get me in to see her. I *know* you *can.*"

Pascal placed his hand on Linus's shoulder. "Your mother and I have our differences, and I know she guards her autonomy fiercely, but I couldn't live with myself if I did nothing when her life may be in danger. The least I can do is get you in to see her."

"Thank you, Father!" Linus hugged him.

Pascal embraced him, remembering the days when Linus would impulsively leap into his arms. "Of course, son. Of course I'll do whatever is in my power. In fact, let's go right now. I'll make sure she agrees to see you."

"You were right about Van Hooten all along. Promise we won't let him get away with it."

"I promise."

They took the short walk to the spa at a brisk clip. Pascal's heart swelled at his son's ferocity and determination, and he was glad Linus was too focused on getting there to notice the pride on his face.

Linus flung open the front doors and stormed in like he owned the place. Pascal stayed a few paces behind to give his son a moment to assert his power.

"I demand to see my mother," Linus told the woman at the reception desk. "*Now.*"

"I'm sorry but I have strict orders she's to have no visitors," the woman said.

"I don't care! I *need* to talk to her." Linus turned to him, pleading. "Father?"

Pascal stepped forward, knowing he'd get no argument, but wanting to put on a good show for Linus. "My son needs to see his mother. I am the Chancellor. You don't have the authority to keep us out." He pounded the counter for effect.

The nurse shrugged. "Then I guess there's nothing I can do."

"What room is she in?" Pascal demanded.

A perky teenaged girl in a junior nurse's uniform appeared at Pascal's elbow. "Sir, I can take you." She exchanged a meaningful look with Linus. "Follow me. She's right down this hall."

Pascal assumed the girl was Jenna and hung back to give Linus a moment. He joined them at Maybelline's door where they were huddled with their heads together.

"Father, Jenna says Van Hooten visited Mother late last night."

"Oh?" Pascal crafted a look of surprise and concern. "How has she been since then?"

"I don't know, sir," Jenna said. "I just came on duty."

"Let's find out." Linus pushed open the door.

Maybelline was on her back in bed, eyes closed, mouth open, a withered version of herself.

"*Mother!*" Linus dashed over and took her hand. "It's me. Wake up."

Jenna circled to the other side of the bed and shook Maybelline's arm. "Miss Kagawa, can you hear me?"

Maybelline didn't stir.

"Oh my God, she's not . . . no, she can't be, her hand's warm." Emotion clogged Linus's voice. "Why won't she wake up?"

She'd better not wake up.

"I don't know. I'm so sorry." Jenna's voice oozed compassion. Her crush on Linus was going to prove useful.

"Jenna," Pascal said. "We need your help."

"Anything, sir."

"If someone wanted to hurt Ms. Kagawa and did something to *cause* this, how would he do it? Assuming he's smart and doesn't want to get caught."

"Gosh, there are lots of ways." Jenna frowned and bit her lip. "I guess the most likely would be a drug, like a sedative."

"How would he administer that? A pill?"

"If she was awake. Otherwise, an injection."

"Has she had injections? Can you tell?"

"I checked her chart because I wondered why she doesn't have an I.V. We usually inject meds directly into the I.V. line, but without it we go through the skin, usually the arm."

"Did the chart say she'd been given any shots?" Linus asked.

"That's the weird thing," Jenna said. "It didn't list any medication at all. Not even the vitamins she always takes when she's here."

"Van Hooten probably gives her all kinds of stuff without recording it," Linus said. "He's in here by himself. He can do whatever he wants and no one knows the difference."

"If he gave injections, I might be able to tell." Jenna ran her finger along the inside of Maybelline's arm.

"What's that?" Linus pointed to the crook of Maybelline's elbow.

Jenna leaned over, her face inches from Linus's. "It looks like a puncture. Here's another spot that could be one, too."

"He can't be her doctor anymore," Linus growled. "I don't care about her wishes. I'm her son and I say he can't see her."

"You're right," Pascal said. "We'll get your mother out of this spa and to the hospital for proper care. I'll station guards at her door, and I'll handpick staff we can trust. Jenna, I'd like for you accompany her and be her personal nurse. I'll make the arrangements." Of course, Maybelline would probably not make it to the hospital alive, but he had to let the little drama play out. "Don't worry, son. Van Hooten will be suspended pending an investigation."

"I already did an investigation and we know he's guilty." The veins bulged at Linus's temples. "*You* make the rules. He's guilty and he has to be punished."

"One thing at a time, son. I'll go take care of the transfer to the hospital."

"I'm staying right by her side to make sure nothing happens to her." Linus held his mother's hand with the fierce loyalty of a child and the conviction of the man he was becoming.

This would indeed shape him, and Pascal was pleased with how it was unfolding.

"Good, yes, you stay with her, Linus. When the transport team comes, accompany her to the hospital. I have to go into the office for a few hours, but I'll be over to see you this afternoon." Pascal turned to leave, but changed his mind. His son would soon experience the grief of losing a mother. For now, he should revel in a victory. "You do know that your actions saved your mother's life."

Linus looked at him with full eyes. "Yeah?"

"What do you think, Jenna? Would she survive another of Van Hooten's 'treatments'?"

Jenna shook her head.

"I agree," Pascal said. He took Linus by both shoulders. "I'm proud of you. Very proud."

Chapter 51

The Pacific Ocean, aboard the Emancipation

"I like it. I think it will work," Kennedy said.

"Olexi and I were inspired over cider last night." Nikolai rubbed at the dull ache behind his forehead. Perhaps less cider would have been better. He wasn't as young as he used to be.

"So that's why you brought so many barrels." Kennedy grinned.

Nikolai wasn't sure if Kennedy was referring to the inspiration or the plan. "Do you know where the pirates' boundary lies? It may have changed since I was here last."

"Not for certain, but they've been spotted as far north as thirty-four degrees."

"Then we should make ready."

"I agree. Would you see to the crew while I finish here?"

Nikolai held back a smile. "Right away, Captain. I've never liked sitting by with my arms folded."

Chapter 52

Lost Angeles, the Grand Hotel

Reid kept his head down, trying not to show the awe he felt. He'd never seen anything so magnificent. Enormous chandeliers with glowing bulbs shaped like flames. Red and gold-patterned carpet so elaborate it could be framed as art. Dark wood tables and leather sofas. Fancy people drinking from fancy glasses in front of a huge stone fireplace.

If it weren't for a couple of other guys who looked as grubby as he did, he'd have left. But no one acted like *they* didn't belong, so he gathered his courage and shuffled to the sign that read "Reception" where a freckled girl in a navy blue suit flashed a toothy smile.

"Welcome to the Grand, sir. My name is Devon. How may I help you today?"

"I'm here to see Mia," he mumbled, hoping he sounded like everyone else.

"Very good. Your voucher?"

He gave her Mia's card. It was bent and dirty from so much handling, one thing that hadn't needed fabrication.

"Follow me," Devon said.

He couldn't believe it was that easy. He'd been worried for nothing. The girl held open a door. "Here you are. Enjoy your stay."

In the next room, instead of Mia he found a well-groomed man in a blue suit.

"Good afternoon, sir. I'm Logan. Please empty your pockets and place all belongings here." He indicated a clear plastic bin.

What? He wasn't giving up his stuff. "Excuse me?" He'd forgotten to mumble.

"It's required for all appointments."

"My bag?" The gun he'd worked so hard to find was in it.

"Everything. It will be returned unmolested upon your departure. Many new guests feel similarly, but it's a perfectly safe and normal procedure, I assure you."

Reid placed his pack in the bin.

"Your clothing, too," Logan said. "Anything you wish to keep, put in the bin. Otherwise . . ." He pointed to a large trashcan. "After you shower, you'll receive new clothes."

They were making him shower? The trashcan was half-full of dirty clothes, so apparently that's what they made everyone do, or at least the dirty pirates. It would be nice to get cleaned up before Mia saw him, but it did seem excessive.

He put his boots and belt in the bin with his pack. The grimy T-shirt, jeans and socks went in the trash. The man looked pointedly at Reid's underwear. Apparently, those had to go, too.

The guy didn't seem particularly interested in his privates, but Reid held his hands over the shrunken parts anyway.

"You shower here." He held a door for Reid.

Reid went through, hoping the guy didn't get off seeing his naked butt.

The shower was more grand than any he'd ever seen. The pristine white alcove had showerheads everyplace imaginable. He turned a lever and hot pulsing water hit him from all sides. Forget Mia, seeds, Kayla, his mission. He wanted to stay in the shower forever.

"Stay in as long as you like, sir," a woman's voice said.

Were they reading his mind? He covered himself and turned. The grandmotherly woman kept her gaze on his face, but his parts still objected to the lack of privacy.

"Logan said you're new, so I came to tell you the soap comes out of that dispenser." She pointed to a fixture. "Here's your towel." She hung it from a hook. "But take your time. I'll be outside whenever you're ready."

He squirted soap from the dispenser and lathered up his head and body with suds that smelled like fruit cocktail, only better. After rinsing, he reluctantly turned off the water and wrapped himself in the enormous towel. He stepped into the next room, where the woman waited as promised.

"Hello again," she said kindly. "Would you like a robe?"

Reid wrapped the heavy white robe around himself before removing the towel.

"Sit right here." She indicated a chair with oversized arms and a foot-rest that reminded him of the dentist's chair back home. "Relax. We'll take care of everything."

Reid wondered what "everything" was. These people seemed to have an obsession with cleanliness and grooming.

More women entered. One sat on a low stool in front of him and tended to his feet. Another rubbed his hands with oil up to his elbows and trimmed his nails.

The grandmotherly woman trimmed his hair, then placed a hot tow-el on the lower part of his face.

"Ready for your shave, sir?"

No one had ever shaved him but *him*. It was weird, but nice too. He could get used to it.

When she finished, he rinsed his face at the sink. She handed him a toothbrush and some green liquid. It was almost as potent as tequila, but it made his teeth clean and minty.

"Come this way." She indicated yet another door.

As he went through, she took his robe and he stepped naked into a tiled room, empty except for a man in a long white coat.

What was going on? This wasn't right. Had Mia lured him into a trap?

Chapter 53

Lost Angeles

Pascal sat at his desk in City Hall, squinting at the report in front of him. He couldn't bear the thought of reading glasses. Silver hair was dignified, but glasses were a sign of frailty. Gomez would have to write bigger.

He signed the paper and handed it back to Gomez. "What's next?"

The benches were lined with people waiting to see him. He'd hoped for a tryst with Mia, but the business with Maybelline had taken all morning, and now he was backlogged.

Gomez looked at his notebook. "Next is the Chief of Security with the weapons report. After that, someone from Supply, and the two dental apprentices you wanted to see."

"Father!" The double doors flew open and Linus stumbled in, covered in blood.

Pascal's heart stopped. "Linus!" What had gone wrong? How could this have happened? "Linus, come here. Everyone, clear the courtroom. Gomez, get a medic," Pascal shouted. "*You*—" Pascal pointed at the Chief of Security, blanking on his name. "Secure the building. Post guards at the doors until further notice."

"Yes sir."

"Father." Linus collapsed on the dais steps.

"Was it Van Hooten? What did the bastard do to you?" Pascal looked him over, trying to find the wound. "Where is the medic?"

"Father, it's not my blood."

"Thank God." Pascal exhaled, feeling his tension fall away. He glanced around to be sure everyone else had left the room. Only Gomez remained, standing by obediently, waiting to be of service. "Gomez, cancel the medic. Bring us whiskey. Then privacy."

"Right away." Gomez left.

Pascal sat on the step beside his son, relieved beyond measure that he wasn't hurt. He'd give the boy a moment to collect himself, but no more than that. He was anxious to hear how he'd come to be covered in blood. And if the blood belonged to Van Hooten. "Tell me what happened," he said gently.

Linus threw his arms around Pascal and sobbed. Pascal held him while he cried out the worst of it. Gomez placed a bottle and two glasses on the floor near Pascal's feet, then scurried away. Pascal waited until the door closed, then disentangled himself from Linus's grasp and poured two drinks.

Linus was hyperventilating, but accepted the glass.

"Toss it back in one swallow." Pascal watched the boy do it, then emptied his own before refilling both. "Again."

The boy did as he was told then set down the glass. He was calm now. "I'm sorry I got blood on you."

"It doesn't matter. Can I assume it's Van Hooten's?"

"Yes, the bastard!"

"Do you need another drink?"

Linus took a shaky breath. "No, I'm fine."

"Can you tell me what happened now?"

Linus nodded. "I only left Mother for a minute. Jenna was out getting me something to eat, and I stepped out to use the facilities. When I came back, Van Hooten was there."

"And Jenna, had she come back, too?" That would be a stroke of good fortune.

"She walked in right behind me. We both saw him leaning over Mother with a needle. I tackled him and the needle went flying, but it was too late. He'd already injected something. I kept hitting and hitting him, and he kept yelling at me, saying it wasn't what it seemed, the liar."

"Maybe he was telling the truth. Are you sure—"

"He killed her! She stopped breathing, so Jenna blew into her mouth. Van Hooten said he could help and pounded on Mother's chest. But I couldn't let him, I couldn't." Linus's voice broke.

Pascal handed him another drink and watched him slug it back. He held Linus's shoulder and waited. The boy needed to say it like a man, not have it coaxed out of him.

After a moment, Linus continued, his voice steadier. "I stabbed him. This is his blood. I stabbed him until he was dead."

"Are you sure?"

"Yes."

"And your mother?" Pascal asked quietly. "Were they able to revive her?"

"No. It was too late." The boy's shoulders shook with silent sobs.

Pascal poured himself another two fingers and turned away so the boy wouldn't see his elation. Finally, the bitch was dead. And it had gone better than he'd hoped. Jenna had witnessed not only the stabbing, but also the suspicious actions and investigation leading up to it. Of course, Pascal's word would suffice to clear Linus, but it would be much easier to paint him a hero now.

His boy had become a man. Killed his mother's murderer with his own hand. Not coldly with a gun. *A knife.* That made it personal. This would shape him, fuel him better than Pascal could have hoped.

It was time to celebrate. He tossed back his whiskey and slammed down the glass. "Come with me, Linus."

"What?"

"You're a hero. Heroes don't sit inside crying."

"My mother's dead."

"Yes, but you avenged her death. I'm so proud. I want everyone to know. Stand up."

Linus stood and wiped his nose with his sleeve.

Pascal wrapped his arm around Linus's shoulders. "The whole city will know you brought a killer to justice. You will mourn your mother, of course. She was your mother, you loved her. But today you did the work of not just a man but a leader. Well done."

"Okay." Linus was subdued, but he'd come around.

"Bart," Pascal called to the Chief of Security, now remembering his name. "My son is a hero. When he discovered Dr. Van Hooten poisoning his mother, he defended her, killing the doctor with his own hand. Have guards take Van Hooten's wife into custody and send the news to all directors. Dispatch your fastest man to the Grand to have Ms. Ford prepare a hero's welcome for my son."

"Yes sir!" The Chief saluted Pascal, then saluted Linus.

"We're going to the Grand?" Linus asked. "Covered in blood?"

"You're a hero decorated with the blood of the enemy. Wear it proudly."

Linus stood taller.

"Trust me, son, you'll remember this day long after Ms. Ford's beautiful women have cleansed the blood from your body and the grief from your soul. Not as the day you first killed or the day your mother died, but as the day you became a man."

Maybelline and Van Hooten were gone. His son was becoming a man. And Pascal would get to see Mia after all. It was turning into the perfect day.

Chapter 54

Lost Angeles, the Grand Hotel

The man in the white coat beckoned Reid over.

Reid's heart thudded as he looked for an exit. The small white room had two doors, but both were closed. Probably locked. If they wanted him as a prisoner, it was already too late. He didn't want to think Mia had betrayed him, but . . .

"Come on over, son," the man said. Reid liked it better when they called him *sir.* "I'm Dr. Levine, and I'll give you a quick exam before you get dressed."

An exam? "I don't need a doctor," Reid mumbled. These people were overly concerned about germs and disease. Had there been some kind of epidemic?

"It's standard. Please remove your hands from your genitals."

It wasn't much of an exam. The doctor didn't listen to his heart or lungs, or look in his ears. He focused on Reid's penis. He lifted it with gloved hands and looked at the end, then felt his testicles.

"Any burning when you pee? Any itching? Foul odor?"

"No."

"Any problem achieving or maintaining an erection?"

"No." *What?* Had venereal disease mutated to where it was infectious via casual contact? He sure as hell would ask the doctor if it wouldn't risk giving himself away.

"Any pain or discomfort with ejaculation?"

"*No.*"

"You're done. Go through there."

Reid was through the door before the doctor's gloves hit the trash.

He was met by an attractive middle-aged woman.

"Let's get you dressed." She looked him over and he covered his privates again. "Size thirty-two, I think," she said. "You seem like a man who could wear red." She made a selection from a wall of shelves and handed him a pair of red boxers.

Reid had never worn red underwear in his life, but he put them on, happy to have something.

"Those fit well, sir?"

He nodded.

"Okay, the thirty-twos fit. Would you like slacks? Or jeans? Maybe some silk pajamas?"

Pajamas? This place is some kind of weird. "Jeans."

"Excellent." She retrieved a pair that looked like they'd never been worn. "Now how about a starched dress shirt in cobalt blue to complement your eyes?"

He shook his head.

"Are you sure? You want to look nice for your appointment."

Reid remembered the nicely dressed people in the lobby. "Uh, okay." Blending in was more important than being comfortable.

She handed him a shirt, which he quickly put on.

"Very handsome. Have a look."

Reid looked in the mirror and was surprised he was looking at himself. The haircut was the best he'd ever had, and the clothes looked nice, if a bit fancy.

"What about—" He cleared his throat and made sure to mumble. "My belt and shoes?"

"You'll get those later. I have slippers for you now. What size, ten?" She gave him leather moccasins that fit well enough. "I think you're set, except for a little cologne."

Before he could stop her, she squirted him. It smelled good. Maybe Mia would like it.

In the hall, a pony-tailed girl who looked twelve years old was waiting. She wore a navy blue uniform like everyone else, just smaller. "Please come with me, sir."

Reid followed her up two flights of stairs and down a long corridor. They passed a dozen or more doors before she unlocked one.

"Here you are."

Reid stepped into a foyer and the door closed behind him. "Hello?"

"Come in."

He walked through an archway, and there she was—more beautiful than he remembered. She was wearing a man's dress shirt that hung to the tops of her thighs, the white fabric in sharp contrast to her skin.

Reid gulped. His heart pounded. He couldn't form words, couldn't remember why he was there.

Time slowed as she came toward him. The shirt parted slightly as she walked, hinting she had nothing else on.

She came closer, so close her breasts grazed the front of his shirt. His palms were sweating and he forgot to breathe.

"I'm glad you're here." Her voice was low and husky. "I haven't been able to stop thinking about you. I don't know what I would have done if I never saw you again." She touched his nose with hers, brushed her lips against his.

He kissed her, just a touch, a test. Was he dreaming?

She looked at him, and he got lost in her eyes, then her lips were on his, urgent and demanding. She leapt into his arms, wrapping her legs around his waist.

The room swam. Her fingers gripped his hair. She kissed him harder. He slid his hands beneath her shirt and found nothing but satiny skin.

She squeezed him with her thighs. "We don't have to rush," she whispered, untangling herself. She led him past the bed to an oversized chair and pushed him into it.

He sunk into the cushions, breathing fast, heart fluttering. She tossed her head and her hair fell in waves, dark and shiny against the white shirt as she knelt in front of him. Her hands traveled up his legs, gliding along the denim. He shivered as they slid under his shirt.

"Mia, I—"

She stopped him with a kiss. Her hands traced his waistband to the front where she undid his jeans.

"But Mia, we—"

"Later," she said.

She climbed astride him and the thought of talking didn't cross Reid's mind again.

Chapter 55

California waters, aboard the Emancipation

"Pirates!" the watch called from the crow's nest.

"Location and number," Nikolai shouted from the helm.

"Due south. About twenty boats. Intercept in fifteen minutes."

"Alert the captain and ready the crew below," Nikolai told Olexi. He caught the grim expression on his face but brushed it aside. They had a good plan, providing Kennedy's crew played their parts. It was hard not knowing the men, their strengths and weaknesses, who he could trust under pressure. But it was too late for second thoughts.

He looked over their charade, noting that the crewmen appeared more keyed up than sloppy drunk. Thankfully, the pirates had shown sooner rather than later. Anticipation was often more difficult than the actual encounter, especially for those who'd never seen a pirate.

"Report," Nikolai called to the watch.

"Five minutes," he bellowed. "The largest is maybe a twenty-seven footer. Quite a few appear to be two-seaters."

Nikolai nodded to himself. Fortunately, not much had changed in these waters.

"Are we ready, Captain?" Kennedy asked, emerging from below with Olexi.

"As we can be," Nikolai replied. "The crew belowdecks?"

"Yes sir," Olexi said.

"Let's get the party started." Nikolai released the helm to Kennedy and headed to his post at the bow, nodding to each of the crewmen he passed, trying to assure them all would end well.

Nikolai stood at the bow with the yeoman, and when the pirates were in earshot, he nodded, indicating it was time for the yeoman to start the show.

"Ahoy! Ahoy, there, pirates," the yeoman shouted, managing to sound quite drunk as the largest of the boats, a Coronado, approached the *Emancipation.*

The deck of the pirates' Coronado was littered with men pointing guns. Nikolai held his breath. It was a deadly situation, a powder keg waiting for a spark, but when he saw "Jolly Roger" scrawled in black paint across the bow he breathed a sigh of relief—these were northern pirates, not southern.

"Prepare to be boarded, you bilge-sucking swabs!" the pirate yeoman called.

Nikolai stifled a guffaw at the ludicrous pirate talk, reminding himself that even this breed of pirate could be deadly.

"Helloooo," he called out, raising his mug. Cider sloshed out, splashing on the deck. "Oops!" He brought his other hand to his lips in mock drama as he sashayed across the bow to the other rail. "I'm so clumsy," he slurred to the pirate who was lashing the boats together. He ignored the other six men with guns trained on him.

"Stand down or you'll be meeting Davy Jones hisself," one commanded.

"Us?" Nikolai stopped, making sure to wobble noticeably. "We're standed down already, see? No weapons." He sloshed cider again as he gestured to the deck of the *Emancipation,* displaying what appeared to be a drunk, unarmed crew.

He stepped aside as pirates poured aboard, bearing automatic weapons.

Steady, men, Nikolai thought, hoping Kennedy's crew would hold up under the stress.

The pirates swarmed the ship, pointing their guns from crewman to crewman—Mike "passed out" on an untidy pile of rope, Ernie leaning lazily against the rear mast, Kennedy sprawled in the cockpit.

"They're drunk. Every last scab," a pirate called.

"Nooooo, we're not drunk." Nikolai hiccupped and followed it up with a burp.

"I'll see for myself," a voice boomed.

A pot-bellied bald man stepped onto the deck of the *Emancipation.*

Nikolai had been banking on this man's appearance. Apparently, the king had not yet recognized Nikolai.

Wait . . . wait.

When the king reached his "mark," Nikolai went into action.

"What kind of welcome is this, men?" Nikolai called. "These fine pirates look thirsty. Get them some drinks. Here, sir, take mine." Nikolai gestured with a flourish, sloshing cider on the pirate king's boots.

"*Blaggard,*" the king barked, wiping at his boots.

When he looked back up, the "drunk" crew had guns trained on the pirates.

As the rest of Kennedy's armed crew emerged from below, the pirate king smiled.

"Captain Petrov, you old scallywag."

"Good to see you, Captain Markoff."

"Looks like you win this one, Nikolai. Well played." Markoff chuckled and slapped Nikolai on the back. "Men, stow your weapons," he bellowed. "We've been bested by my old friend."

The pirates did as they were told, smiling and elbowing each other.

"Stand down," Nikolai called to the crew of the *Emancipation.*

Mike, Ernie, and the rest lowered their weapons, the relief evident on their faces. Nikolai was relieved, too. It could very easily have gone another way if they'd come across someone other than Markoff.

"You look thirsty, friend," Nikolai said. "What do you say I introduce you to the real captain of this vessel, then we share a drink or three?"

He turned him toward the helm, but between them and Kennedy stood two men with weapons trained on Markoff.

Oh hell. Just when things were well in hand. He'd forgotten all about Fahnestock and White, or he'd have had them bound and gagged. They were about to ruin everything.

Chapter 56

Lost Angeles

"You're a hero," Pascal told Linus. "Stand tall and enjoy this moment."

"Sir!" Gomez ran toward them.

Pascal had never seen Gomez out of breath, much less seen him run. "What is it?"

"Sorry, but this can't wait," Gomez said.

"Linus, go with the escort. Ms. Ford is expecting you. I'll be along when I can."

Linus looked lost, then smiled as if realizing what awaited him. He saluted—something he hadn't done since he was a toddler—and marched off, shoulders back, blood and all.

Pascal was swept by a wave of pride, followed by regret that he was not going with him. But if Gomez said it couldn't wait, it couldn't.

He turned to Gomez, who looked about to burst. "Tell me before you stroke out."

"A messenger from World Waste. He says that two nights ago—the night before your arrival—a couple of men spotted lights that didn't belong to any known source."

"What do you mean? What kind of lights?"

"At first they thought they were headlamps, but then they realized they were bigger."

"It probably *was* headlamps, closer than they thought. Or they were drunker than usual."

"That's what the director thought, but there was another sighting last night. It was definitely a moving vehicle."

A vehicle would be a huge coup. He could extend his reach, expand his holdings. "Tell me they captured it."

"No sir, but the director has everyone looking."

"Why am I only learning about this now! Institute Intruder Alert and get every available Blade searching for that vehicle."

"Right away, sir."

"I'm going to World Waste. I want to see the director and get the information firsthand."

Chapter 57

Lost Angeles, the Grand Hotel

R eid rolled to his back. "That was amazing."

Mia draped her arm across his chest. Her tongue traced his earlobe.

"We need to talk," he said, mostly meaning it.

"I know," she said, her breath warm on his cheek. "You haven't told
me what you came to Lost Angeles to find."

"Right." There was no reason *not* to tell her.

"The sooner you tell me, the sooner we can find it and you can take
me away from here."

"I came here to get seeds."

"What?"

"Seeds for growing food."

"I know what they're for. Why would you think we have them?"

"A woman came to Colorado—where I'm from—and she had
grown food. She told me she was from here."

"I'm sorry, but she lied to you. I've never seen grown food. There
are stories about a seed bank in San Diego, but the seeds were all bad.
The only food I've ever had is from the ocean or from a can. And rats,
of course."

"But she said 'City of Angels.'" Reid propped himself up on his elbows. "Ellay—Los Angeles—is the City of Angels, right?"

"Did you actually see the grown food? She wasn't conning you?"

"I saw it myself. Smelled it."

"Well, I guarantee it wasn't from here. If we had fresh food, the
Chancellor would be eating it."

"Oh my God." Reid slumped back on the bed. "We came all this
way."

"We?"

There was a soft knock at the door.

"Roll on your stomach," Mia commanded in a whisper. "Turn your head toward the wall. Do it now."

The door opened as Reid got into position. His heart was pounding so hard, he thought he might pass out. Mia laid a hand on his back, but it did little to calm him.

"Mia?" a thin male voice said.

"Shhh, you'll wake him," Mia said. "You're lucky he's asleep. What is it?"

"Sorry." The man sounded contrite. "I had to risk it. I had to see if you were okay. We're on alert for intruders."

Reid tried not to react, but he was scared out of his mind. He was sure the visitor could tell he wasn't asleep.

"I'm fine," Mia said, sounding a little cross. "He's a regular, but it was sweet of you to check on me."

"Mia? Do you think I could see you sometime, when we're both off duty?"

"Sure, maybe tomorrow. You'd better go before he wakes up, unless you want us both to get in trouble."

"Okay, I'll see you tomorrow." The door clicked shut.

"*Shit.*" Reid bolted up.

"Are you trying to get us both killed?" Mia said. "Who did you bring with you? What haven't you told me?"

Hot guilt washed over him. "I'm sorry. My grandfather. He's downstairs waiting." He'd forgotten about Tinker and now had endangered them all.

"I doubt he's downstairs any more. We need to get out of here, and we don't have much time. Once they get him to talk, we're dead."

Reid put on the moccasins, wishing he had his boots. *Damn.* His gun was tucked away "somewhere safe" too.

Mia dressed in a flowing gown and high heels, more like a fancy robe and slippers than clothing. She peeked into the hall. "Do exactly as I say."

They walked arm in arm the length of the hallway. Reid was so worried about Tinker, he was practically dragging her.

"Slow down, and don't look so nervous," she said as they descended the stairs. "When we get to the lobby, don't talk, and don't make it obvious you're looking for someone."

"I know what I'm doing."

She shot him a look that said she knew otherwise. "Going out for a smoke is as good a cover as we'll get, but even that's pushing it on Intruder Alert. I'll go ask for a cigarette, and you keep walking straight across the lobby and through the main door. Even if you see your grandfather, don't stop. If he has any sense, he'll follow you. Wait for me outside the door."

Mia's demeanor changed as they entered the lobby. She walked elegantly, her long legs slipping through a slit in her gown. Her smile was bright, her gestures sweeping. Everyone looked at her like she was someone important.

Reid let go of her arm to head for the door, but Mia grabbed him.

"Change of plans," she whispered through a smile. "It's worse than I thought. Armed guards at the doors. Wait here." She deposited him next to a large plastic tree. He leaned against the wall, trying to look nonchalant as he scanned the lobby. There was no sign of Tinker.

Mia breezed to the reception area and chatted with yet another young girl in a navy blue uniform. The girl handed her something, then Mia sauntered back.

"He's not here," Reid whispered.

"Shut up and try to look relaxed." She linked her arm in the crook of his elbow and steered him around behind the staircase. "Please be unlocked," she said under her breath as she reached for a door.

The door swung open, and they slipped into a long, narrow hall lit only by sunlight from a glass door at the far end. They hurried toward it.

"Remember, we're going out for a smoke," Mia said. "Follow my lead and don't talk."

The door opened onto an alley crowded with smelly dumpsters, but no guards.

"Do I really have to smoke?" Reid whispered.

"Yes."

Reid put the cigarette between his lips, lit a match, and held it to the end, cupping his hand around the flame as he'd seen smokers do. He sucked on the cigarette until the end glowed orange, coughing as the smoke hit his throat.

Mia clutched his elbow again, steering him down the alley. As he pretended to smoke, he prayed Tinker would be waiting back at the car.

At the end of the alley, a muscular soldier stepped from the shadows. "Halt." He pointed a gun at Reid's chest.

Chapter 58

Aboard the Emancipation

Nikolai squeezed Captain Markoff's shoulder in what he hoped was a reassuring gesture. *Damn Fahnestock and his beefy sidekick.* Apparently they wanted real-world action so badly, they were willing to start an all-out war with the pirates.

He prayed Markoff and his men would remain cool until he could get the situation in hand. He looked to Kennedy for support, and his stomach dropped as Kennedy joined Fahnestock and White.

Jesus, what have I done?

"Well done, men," Kennedy said to Fahnestock and White. "May I?" He extended his hand for White's weapon.

White handed over the gun, and Kennedy pointed it at Fahnestock. "Yours, too."

Fahnestock started to protest, but Kennedy stepped closer and he handed over the gun.

Nikolai let out his breath. Thank God Kennedy had some sense after all.

"Olexi," Kennedy said, "would you secure Fahnestock and White below?"

"Not a problem, sir." Olexi gestured with his gun. "Go on, you heard the captain."

As the upstarts were escorted away, Kennedy put down the weapons. "Captain Markoff, I apologize for my overzealous men. Those two are academics without a whole lot of real-world sense." He offered his hand to Markoff. "I'm Kennedy Davis."

Markoff looked at Nikolai. For a split second Nikolai considered shaking his head, but instead he nodded, and Markoff shook Kennedy's hand. He would not have his daughter's boyfriend gunned down. Besides, as much as Nikolai hated to admit it, he was starting not to hate the man.

"Now, how about that drink?" Markoff said, rubbing his hands together.

After cider had been doled out to both crews, save for Fahnestock and White who were tied up in their cabin, Nikolai figured he'd waited long enough. He gestured for Kennedy to join him at the rail where Markoff was drinking cider like water.

"Markoff, we're here about my children," Nikolai said.

"I figured as much."

Nikolai's heart skipped a beat. "What do you know?"

"Not as much as you'd like," he said, wiping cider from his mouth with the back of his hand. "Your old ship, the *Belle Jewel,* is under guard at Newport Harbor, so I figured you'd be coming through my waters sooner or later."

"My son, Will, was captaining her."

"That shark, Pascal, has him. Probably in the Tank."

Nikolai shuddered. He'd heard of the Tank, but it was better than the alternative. "And my daughter. She's there, too?"

Kennedy leaned closer.

"Your daughter's another story." Markoff chuckled, then took a long swig of cider.

Nikolai almost came unhinged. "What could *possibly* be *funny*—" A nudge from Kennedy stopped him. A day ago he might have slugged the man for as much, but now he was appreciative and took a breath. "My daughter?" he prompted Markoff.

"She's a wily one." Markoff took another drink.

Nikolai gathered all the patience he could muster. Clearly Markoff enjoyed prolonging his agony, and Nikolai resolved not to give him the satisfaction of another outburst. He leaned against the rail and took a sip of his own cider. Kennedy did the same.

"As far as I know, they never found her." Markoff grinned, showing straight brown teeth.

"*They?* The southern pirates?" Nikolai managed to keep most of the emotion from his voice.

"Didn't you teach her anything?" Markoff said. "You know what they're like. They give pirates a bad name. And they've gotten worse since you were last here. It's not just skin carving any more. They started splitting their tongues and using captives for slave labor. I'd say your girl didn't have much sense looking for seeds or some such on their island, but seems she's got sense enough to outwit them. She's right under their noses, but they can't find her. Ha! Can you believe it?"

Hope surged in Nikolai's breast. "How old is this information?"

"About forty-eight hours, ain't that right, Bud?" Markoff called over his shoulder, motioning for a skinny man with a scabby beard to join them.

"What's that, Cap'n?" Bud approached, and Nikolai saw the telltale designs of a southern pirate carved into his cheeks and forehead.

"When did you defect? Day before yesterday?" Markoff asked.

"Yeah, Cap'n."

"That girl that you were looking for, had she been caught?"

"Nope. We were thinking maybe she wasn't there after all because there hadn't been no sign of her. But then a gun and some food went missing, so she's there all right."

Nikolai let out the breath he'd been holding. "This is good news."

Markoff indicated Bud could return to his card game.

"What about Will?" Kennedy asked Markoff.

"I don't have any sources inside the Tank," Markoff replied, emptying his mug. "But I'll tell you something funny. That old boat of yours, the *Belle?* Seems Pascal has put a bounty on my head with the *Belle* as the reward. Ain't that something? Hey, can I have a refill?"

"Of course," Nikolai said, rising to fill the mug. An idea sparked in his mind—the seed of a rescue plan—and he wanted a moment to himself to see if it would germinate.

Chapter 59

Outside the Grand Hotel

"I said *halt,*" the guard shouted.

Adrenaline shot through Reid. His muscles clenched to make a run for it, but there was nowhere to go.

Mia pulled Reid to a stop and whispered in his ear. "Don't talk." She giggled, then turned to the man who blocked their way. "Tony, it's me."

"Mia?" The man lowered his gun. "Didn't you hear? No one is supposed to be out now."

"He wanted a smoke," Mia said. "You know how I take care of my regulars. Besides, I'm sure it's only a drill." She touched Tony's arm. "Come on, Tony. One cigarette while we circle around to the front door. We'll act like we're arriving. No one will know."

"All right, but only because it's you."

Mia smiled. She linked her hand in the crook of Reid's elbow again.

Reid tried to look nonchalant but his whole body was quivering. He kept his face angled away as Tony let them pass.

"Hey," Tony called after them. "Who is that you're with, anyway?"

Reid's heart sank.

Mia turned her head but kept walking. "Oh, you know Jimmy. From the *Gull Cruiser.*"

"Jimmy? You sure grew up," Tony said. "Good on you, son."

Reid nodded and waved, remembering not to speak.

"Thank you, Tony. I won't forget this," Mia sang over her shoulder.

Reid wanted to sprint, but Mia forced a slow pace. He let out a controlled breath, trying to stop trembling. "Can't we go any faster?" he said in her ear.

Mia stopped and draped her arms around his neck. "Oh, you." She kissed him, then spoke into his ear. "He's not following, but this is serious. We need to hide until dark."

Reid pulled back and glanced around.

Mia held his face with both hands. "Stop it," she said through gritted teeth. "You'll call attention to us." She kissed him hard on the mouth, then gripped his elbow and began walking slowly again.

"Do you think my grandfather's been caught?"

"Yes. Now shut up and smoke."

Reid dragged on the cigarette and tried to scan the shadows for Tinker while keeping his face aimed straight ahead. The hair on the back of his neck prickled and sweat ran down his spine. It felt like armed men were watching him from every window and doorway.

Why was everyone suddenly looking for intruders? Was it possible it had nothing to do with Tinker? Reid had a sick feeling Tinker would not be waiting at the car.

"The cigarette's gone," Reid said, dropping it and grinding it into the cement with his toe.

"Well, darling," Mia said, picking up the stub and putting it in the pocket of her robe. "We'll have to get you some more. It will only take a minute. I know you can't live without them."

Reid let Mia lead him along the street, then down an alleyway. She darted into the shadow of a building, pressing her back against the brick wall. He started to ask something, but she held her finger to his lips. They waited in silence for a full minute, then for some reason not apparent to Reid, she decided it was time to go again.

After several more of these maneuvers, Mia stopped at a squat, square building and pulled a loose brick from the wall. She took a key out of the gap and unlocked the door.

The steel door opened silently, and Mia slipped off her high heels as she stepped inside and beckoned Reid to follow. She closed the door and stood completely still. The only sound was their breathing. Reid's eyesight adjusted and he could make out the walls of a hallway. A change in gray tones indicated an opening at the end. After what seemed an eternity, Mia inched toward it with him in tow.

"Where are we?" he whispered. He didn't like being at her mercy, not knowing what the plan was or where they were going.

"My friend Justine's place. We should be safe here. We can't go back out until after dark. Hopefully no one will realize I'm missing."

His skin prickled like someone was sighting down a rifle at him. "Your friend's not going to come out with a gun, is she?"

"No, but her boyfriend might. He's a Blade."

"Jesus, isn't that who we're trying to avoid?" He grabbed her arm and turned for the door.

"Cut it out. They owe me. We can trust them," Mia said.

"I don't like it."

"Well I don't, either. I didn't plan to involve my friends, but now we're in a jam because something's put the whole town on alert for strangers. Think that might have been your grandfather's doing?"

"I hope not. I need to get to the car to see if he's there."

"Not until after dark," Mia said. "Until then, you're going to tell me more about this car."

A giant emerged from a room at the end of the hall. "What the hell are you doing in my house?"

Chapter 60

World Waste

Pascal leapt from the train before it stopped.

"Wait here," he told the driver.

He jogged to World Waste and demanded to see the director. A teenaged boy sprinted off, and in less than five minutes Tom arrived, sweaty and out of breath.

"Chancellor," Tom said, wiping his hand on his slacks before offering it to Pascal. "Sorry for the wait. I was at the plant."

"Your office," Pascal said, letting himself in without waiting for a reply. He seated himself behind the desk in Tom's chair.

Tom closed the door. If he was perturbed, he didn't show it. He handed Pascal a bottle of water, then drank from a second bottle as he sat in the chair opposite.

"Is there really a vehicle? How reliable is your information?" Pascal asked.

Tom nodded, wiping his forehead with a hanky. "I questioned the witnesses myself. The one last night was a young mother up with her baby. Not a drunk or a crazy."

"I want to speak with her."

"I already sent for her. She'll be here soon."

This was the kind of competence Pascal expected. "What about the first sighting?"

"At the time, I deemed it less than reliable." Tom put down his empty bottle, concern tingeing his brow. "A known drunk who swore he was sober. It hardly seemed legitimate. But when the mother came forward, I questioned the drunk again. Would you like to speak to him?"

"Do I need to?"

"I don't think so. All he saw was lights on the 215. Nothing useful beyond that."

"Any other news since your last report?"

"No, but all shifts are out searching for the car. Even the families."

The office door creaked open.

"Excuse me?" A skinny girl with sunken eyes and drab, stringy hair stepped through the doorway. A baby was bundled to her chest with a faded orange cloth.

Tom ushered her in and shut the door. "You didn't need to bring the baby."

"I can't leave him," the girl said. "He cries so much, no one will watch him."

"That's fine," Pascal barked.

The girl jumped, her eyes wide.

"Here, sit down." Tom showed her to a chair.

"If I do, he might cry." She looked like *she* might cry. "Can I stand?"

"I don't care," Pascal said. "Tell me what you saw."

The girl nodded. "The baby had been crying all night. That's why we live so far away from everyone. Because he cries all the time, and people complain. I was changing his diaper when I saw something moving in the street. At first I thought I imagined it."

"What did it look like?" Pascal wondered if the girl *had* been hallucinating from lack of sleep. If this was all a mistake, someone would pay.

"It was a big car. Dark colored. Boxy. Normal looking, but big," she said, a quaver in her voice. "I wouldn't have given it a second thought if it hadn't been moving."

A loud knock sounded at the door. The baby squawked and started to bawl. The girl bounced it, trying to hush it, while Tom spoke with someone in the hall. The child squalled louder, and Pascal's patience grew thin. No wonder the girl's neighbors had complained. That baby was the spawn of the devil.

"There's news," Tom shouted over the wailing. "Should the girl wait down the hall?"

Pascal nodded, and Tom sent her out. The wailing receded but didn't disappear completely. Pascal rubbed his temples, hoping the pounding didn't turn into a migraine.

"Sir," Tom said, excitement plain on his face. "There's been a stranger sighting."

"Tell me."

"That's all I know, but the men who saw the stranger are here now." Tom motioned to someone in the hall. "Come in. Yes, both of you."

A small weathered man and a stocky bear of a man, both dirty as pirates, entered. The small one took off his hat, then smacked the big one who then removed his cap, too.

"Frank Cox and Roger Walker." Tom gestured to the smaller man, then the larger.

"Tell me what you saw," Pascal said.

"Yesterday morning," the smaller man said, "me and Roger were collecting in Sector Twelve when we met a girl. She was real pretty. Said she was a Ford girl."

"Damn it," Pascal said, coming forward in the chair. "There *was* a Ford girl here yesterday. You're wasting my time."

"That's not it," Frank continued. "We didn't think nothing at first because the Supe had said there was a Ford girl looking around. But nobody said nothing about a guy being with her."

"What guy?" Pascal asked.

"The girl said he was helping her, that he came with her from Services."

Had Mia deceived him? "Are you certain he wasn't one of your men?" Pascal asked.

"We never seen him before," Roger said.

"And he talked funny," Frank said. "So this morning when we heard we were supposed to search for strangers, we got to wondering if those people weren't from Services after all."

"What did the girl look like?" Pascal demanded.

"Brown hair, big boobs," Roger said.

Frank elbowed him. "She was about as tall as me. Clean. I don't remember what she was wearing."

"Me neither," Roger said, scratching his sparse hair.

"Would you recognize her if you saw her again?" Pascal stood.

Both men nodded.

"Come with me," Pascal said, heading for the door. "You too, Tom. I want you stationed on the train until this is resolved. I don't trust anyone else to bring me information."

"I'll be on the train," Tom told his secretary as they passed her desk. "Any news, bring it to the train stop immediately."

Pascal gritted his teeth as he hurried toward the train. Either there was a female imposter or Mia had deceived him.

Chapter 61

Lost Angeles

R eid had the feeling they'd made a terrible mistake.

"Mia, who the hell is this?" the giant boomed.

"Keep your pants on, Brandt," Mia said. "You'll thank me when you hear his story."

"Honey, quit acting like such a tough guy." A tall brunette shoved Brandt aside and kissed Mia's cheek. "Hiya, sweetie." Her freckled nose wrinkled as she grinned.

"Reid," Mia said. "I'd like you to meet my best friend Justine and her pet ogre, Brandt. Reid has a car that works."

"Oh my God." Justine clung to Brandt, whose expression had softened.

"It's what you've been wishing for," Mia said. "With a car, you can go home."

"Wait a minute," Reid said. "I never agreed to this."

"Do you have a choice?" Mia asked.

"Hold on, Mia," Brandt said. "Who is this guy?"

There was banging on the door. "Brandt, open up."

"*Trust me*," Mia said to Brandt. She pulled Reid through a bedroom and into a closet.

"What's going on?" Brandt's booming voice was barely muffled by the thin walls.

"Everyone has to report to their stations."

"What for?"

"Intruder Alert. Could be a drill. Who the hell knows."

"I'll put on my uniform and be right behind you," Brandt said.

Reid's stomach clenched. Had they found Tinker?

In a moment, Brandt filled the closet doorway. "Convince me I made the right choice."

Reid followed Mia out, thinking he might vomit.

Mia climbed onto the bed with Justine, leaving Reid standing with Brandt.

Reid looked up—the guy had to be seven feet tall—then back at Mia. She raised her eyebrows and kept her mouth shut. Apparently it was up to him to convince the ogre.

"I'm from Colorado," Reid said. "I came here with my grandfather."

"In a car." Brandt said it like he didn't believe it.

"Yes. My people won't make it much longer on canned food and rats. We came here because we thought you had grown food."

"Then you screwed up 'cause we don't," Brandt said.

"Mia told me. Now we're in this huge mess, and for nothing."

"Can I assume the Intruder Alert is about you?"

"I don't know," Reid said. "My grandfather was waiting in the lobby of the Grand while I saw Mia. When we came down, he was gone."

"We barely got out of there," Mia said.

"They have the grandfather?" Brandt asked.

"Probably," Mia said.

"We don't know for sure," Reid said. "He's smart. He could have gotten out of there. Didn't you say this could be a drill?"

Brandt shrugged. "If I had to bet, I'd say they have him."

"If *I* had to bet, he's at the car." Reid wasn't as sure as he sounded. "I need to go see."

"It's too risky in broad daylight," Mia said.

"It's too risky *not* to go," Brandt said. "If they have the grandfather, it won't be long before he tells them about the car. We have to get there first."

"He wouldn't tell them," Reid said.

"He'll talk with Pascal's methods, I promise you," Brandt said.

Reid grew queasy at the thought of what could be happening to his grandfather right now because he'd gotten distracted by Mia. "Who's Pascal?"

"The chancellor," Mia said. "The leader of Lost Angeles."

"The most ruthless son of a bitch you'll ever meet," Brandt said. "The other day, I saw him shoot a man in cold blood because he dared to have a different opinion."

A shiver ran up Reid's spine. "Can you get me to my car?"

Brandt nodded. "Or get us killed trying."

Chapter 62

The Grand Hotel

"What do you mean, you can't find her?" Pascal knew in his gut now that Mia was involved. "Is she here and you haven't found her yet, or is she gone?"

"I don't know," Ellianna said. "She was assigned a client, but the room's empty."

Pascal grabbed her arm. "I gave specific orders she was to be on reserve for me."

"I'm sorry, Pascal. When I put in the paperwork, she was already with someone. I realize now I should have seen to it personally last night when you told me."

"I want Mia *found*. Search door-to-door until you locate her or can say with certainty she's not here."

Pascal could almost see Ellianna's thoughts as she processed them. She was loathe to disturb her clientele, but without him there'd be no clientele, no Ford girls, no Services at all.

"Of course, Chancellor Worth. Right away."

He hated how weary she looked. How old.

"Father!" Linus burst into Ellianna's office. "Why didn't anyone tell me?"

"There was no need," Pascal said. "Go back to your girl."

"But I can help!"

"*Linus,*" Pascal said, more sternly than his son was accustomed to.

"I can help, Father. I'll prove it." Linus stomped away, and Pascal decided not to call him back. As long as the boy didn't get in the way, why not let him think he was contributing?

Pascal took over Ellianna's office, with Gomez manning an impromptu command post immediately outside. The filthy World Waste workers, Frank and Roger, were reportedly asleep on lobby couches.

He'd considered sending them through intake to get cleaned up, but opted instead to keep them nearby—just not so close that he could smell them—so they could take a look at Mia as soon as she was located. He wanted Mia found so he could clear her. Or condemn her. Either would be better than not knowing.

Could he have been so wrong about Mia? Was he getting old, losing his edge? The idea that the wiles of a woman could have influenced him—

"Father!" Linus burst in again. "Mia left. About an hour ago."

Pascal came to his feet. "How do you know?"

"A guard saw her."

Gomez slipped into the room behind Linus, a guard at his side.

Pascal turned his attention to Gomez. "Why am I only learning this now?"

"This is him," Linus said. "Sergeant Tony Costello. He saw her."

"I didn't realize it was Mia you were looking for," the sergeant said. "I saw her a block from the east door, an hour and twenty-two minutes ago."

"We've lost a whole hour." Pascal kicked the chair aside and strode to the window. If the guard had been properly instructed, they'd have Mia right now. Had his whole operation gone to shit? He wheeled around. "Was she alone?"

"No, sir. She went out for a smoke with a young man. A regular client, a sailor from the *Gull Cruiser*, she said. Jimmy something."

"Are you sure? Did you recognize him?" Pascal demanded, wondering how many strangers had infiltrated his city.

"He looked familiar. But begging your pardon, sir, I believed what Mia said because it was Mia. I had no cause to distrust her."

"Did they return?"

"Not past my post. She said they were going around to the front door."

"Father, I already checked with the guards at the other doors. They haven't seen her."

"Damn it! She's got over an hour head start on us." Heads were going to roll when this was done. "I want a platoon combing the streets. Gomez, send the fastest runner for the Blades. Sergeant, give Gomez all the details you can recall—what the fugitives were wearing, what direction they went, everything they said."

"Understood, sir." The sergeant turned crisply and followed Gomez into the hall.

"Well done, Linus," Pascal said, sorry he'd underestimated the boy.

Linus was beaming. "What's my next assignment?"

Pascal considered for a moment. He had indeed proven himself valuable. "Take over for the guard watching the World Waste workers in the lobby—they are not to leave. As soon as Mia is found, bring her and the workers to me."

"Yes sir." Linus grinned, then marched into the hallway, barking orders for someone to give him a gun.

Good. Linus was rising to the occasion, Pascal thought, returning to the desk.

Gomez reappeared in the doorway.

"What do you want?" Pascal barked.

"Major Minou says the prisoner is ready to talk."

"It's about time. Bring him to me."

Chapter 63

Lost Angeles

"Here, put these on." Mia handed Reid a pair of dark glasses and a hat as dirty as the overalls he was now wearing.

He turned and his heart stopped at the sight of a man in police uniform. Thank God, it was only Brandt.

"Aren't you ready yet?" Brandt asked.

"What's to get ready?" Mia asked. "I'm climbing in the trashcan, right?"

"Yeah, but you need garbage on top of you. For realism," Brandt said.

"Sadist," Mia said.

"Here's the trashcan. I got it as clean as I could." Justine deposited it on the living room floor. She was wearing a pair of overalls grubbier than the ones she'd given Reid. She wore a long blond wig fastened into two ponytails that hung in front of her shoulders, and the effect was completed with a red kerchief. He'd never have recognized her.

"Get in." Brandt lifted the lid from the can.

"You were kidding about the garbage, right?" Mia asked.

"Don't worry, princess," Brandt said as Mia climbed in. "If they suspect us enough to open the can, we're done for anyway."

"That's reassuring." Sweat ran down Reid's neck. He hoped to God Tinker was at the car, but he wasn't feeling optimistic.

"I guess I'm ready," Mia said, settling cross-legged in the can. "Though I still say I could walk with you guys and no one would recognize me."

Justine snorted. "Wrong. There's no way we could make you ugly enough. Even if no one recognized you, they'd see you were too pretty to be a collector. Services takes any girls half as attractive as you."

"I'd have you in a trashcan, too," Brandt told Reid. "But Justine can't pull you both."

"It smells in here." Mia half-smiled. She looked so vulnerable, Reid had the urge to kiss her, but winked at her instead.

Brandt put the lid on the can, and Justine held open the front door while Reid helped Brandt carry Mia out. They set the can in the back of a wagon and secured it with a yellow nylon rope. Justine loaded a full black trash bag in front of the can and tied it on, too.

"Reid, you pull," Brandt said. "You're sure you know where the car is?"

"As sure as I can be." Reid pulled the wagon to the road.

"Slow down," Justine said under her breath. "Collectors don't move that fast, even with a police escort. Look more bored and less terrified."

Though his heart hammered in his chest, Reid attempted to traipse lazily down the road. There were only a few other people out, and he wondered if that was normal or because of the Intruder Alert.

Justine walked next to the wagon, her hand resting on the lid to Mia's trashcan. When there was garbage in the street, she picked it up and deposited it in a bag she carried.

Brandt whistled tunelessly a couple of paces behind the wagon. Reid worried it would call undue attention to them, but told himself Brandt knew what he was doing.

"Why did you think there were seeds in Lost Angeles?" Justine asked in a low voice.

"A stranger with grown food. She said she was from the City of Angels. Apparently she didn't mean Ellay."

"Out of curiosity, what was her name?"

They came to a crossroad and Reid turned right. "Cumorah," he said, wondering why Justine cared.

"Quit foolin' around, joker," Brandt said loudly.

"Laugh like you're kidding and turn the other way," Justine whispered.

"Ha! Just playin' with you," Reid said, turning the wagon around.

Brandt spoke into his ear. "If we don't head for a trash pickup, we're dead. And stop talking. If someone hears you, you sure to hell don't sound like one of us." Brandt resumed his place behind them.

As they walked, more people trickled onto the road, pulling wagons and pushing wheelbarrows. They were all ages, but mostly kids and a few elderly. Reid hoped he looked like he was one of them, trudging through a never-ending, mind-numbing job.

A few of the people cast curious looks at them.

"Whatchoo lookin' at?" Justine yelled at a particularly nosy old woman. "Mind yer business."

"Move on," Brandt said, shooing the woman. "They're new rehabs, nothing exciting."

At the tracks, the people clumped in groups tossing their cargo onto platforms where strong teens stacked it.

"Keep it moving," Brandt called to everyone in general.

Aside from a few sidelong glances, no one acted like it was odd for a cop to supervise them dumping garbage, so Reid figured it must be fairly normal, though there wasn't another cop to be seen.

Reid stopped the wagon at the tracks and turned to Justine. There was a panic-stricken look on her face.

"*Blades,*" she breathed. She flicked her gaze to the right.

Twenty or so men in uniforms skated across the road at the next intersection.

Brandt walked past, his back to the Blades. "Unload the trash," he said under his breath.

Reid looked at the wagon. *Mia* was in their trashcan. Hadn't Brandt thought of this? What was he supposed to do?

Reid's fingers worked nervously on the yellow nylon cord tied to the wagon, but his palms sweated, making it difficult. When he got the knot untied, Justine grabbed the trash bag and took it to the kid on the platform along with the one she'd be filling.

When she returned, Reid gestured to the can. "What now?"

Justine eyes were wide. Apparently, she didn't have any more answers than he did. Obviously they couldn't empty it.

"You there," Brandt shouted, pointing at Reid. "You done yet? You have to move faster if you're gonna make it out here. Go on, now. Across the tracks."

Reid breathed a sigh of relief and tugged the wagon forward. If anyone noticed he hadn't dumped the can, hopefully they'd attribute it to a newbie afraid to disobey orders from a cop.

Justine trudged beside him, holding her stomach. "I think I might be sick."

"You didn't know that was going to happen?" Reid asked.

"I've never done this either. I had no idea there'd be so many people. When the Blades went by, I almost heaved."

The workers dispersed. After a few dozen yards, they were on their own again. Reid's heart slowed to normal and he wondered how Mia was doing inside the trashcan

Brandt rejoined them. "Tell me this looks familiar and we're going the right way."

Reid looked around, getting his bearings. "I think so. I'm pretty sure."

"You'd better be. You're risking all our lives," Brandt said, scowling.

Reid squinted through the tinted glasses, trying to focus on the road ahead. *Please, please, please . . .* yes! "See that cluster of buildings up to the right? There's a junkyard on the far side. We hid it in the garage there."

"Slow down, we're still in the open. Can't be too spirited in case someone's watching." Brandt resumed his whistling.

Despite the slow pace, Reid's heart rate quickened as they approached the junkyard.

"I don't see anyone around," Brandt said. "But to be safe, pick stuff up and put it in the wagon while I peek inside." He tromped ahead and went into the garage.

Please let Tinker be there, Reid thought over and over as he placed random pieces of metal and debris into the wagon.

After what seemed like an eternity, Brandt poked his head out and beckoned.

Reid pulled the wagon up the slope to the doorway as Justine pushed from behind, helping it over the threshold.

The car was covered with tarps, just as he'd left it.

"Sorry," Brandt said, but Reid already knew.

Tinker wasn't there.

Chapter 64

Aboard the Emancipation

Nikolai couldn't eat, and hoped Finola wouldn't take offense. The problem wasn't her food, but rather the way the pirates were ingesting it. He didn't consider himself a prig, but it was impossible not to find their voraciousness and table manners repulsive. Kennedy, however, didn't seem to have such qualms. He ate his meal while guiding the conversation.

"So the war has gotten worse recently?" Kennedy prompted.

"By a lot," Markoff said, his mouth full of rat.

Nikolai looked away.

"Things escalated when the *Belle* arrived," Markoff continued. "See, when the southern pirates captured the *Belle*, they used it to get in good with Pascal. That's why your boy and his crew are in the Tank instead of being carved up for sport."

Thank God for small favors.

"It was lucky for your guys," Markoff went on, "those southern blaggards saw it as an opportunity to push us northerners further on the outs."

"How?" Kennedy asked.

Markoff harrumphed. "They told Pascal *we* were in cahoots with *outsiders*. That we were deserters, going to leave Lost Angeles waters for San Francisco. That's why he wants my head on a spit."

"*Were* you?" Nikolai asked.

"Hadn't even considered it. But I might now. Pascal not only has a price on my head, he's got an embargo against us. So we have no canned goods, no red meat, and no liquor. Just fish and no way to trade it."

"There's nothing left to hunt or gather where you live?" Kennedy asked.

"Begad, no. Catalina Island hasn't had a live rat or a can of food in my lifetime."

"Can't you look for food farther up the coast, outside Pascal's territory?" Nikolai asked, feeling a bit more sympathetic about their table manners now that he understood their enthusiasm for food other than fish.

"Tried that. Didn't pan out. My people haven't hunted or collected since I was a baby. We've got no idea where it's safe from Pascal's Blades and environmental hazards. Everywhere familiar has already been scavenged clean. Plus, we prefer to fish."

"Then you definitely should consider San Francisco," Kennedy said. "Our colony welcomes fisherman and would be happy to trade with you."

Markoff tipped his head, as if considering. "There's another problem besides food." He paused to fork in more meat before continuing. "We relied on Pascal's Services for pretty much everything other than fish. Of course, we can do fine with our own women, we have plenty of weapons and ammo stockpiled, and we can get by for now with clothing and such. The problem is, we've got no doctors or dentists. Other than a couple of midwives, we don't have any medical help. Is that something you've got in San Francisco?"

"Some," Kennedy said. "Working on getting more."

"Some is better than none." Markoff belched and shoved his chair back from the table. "Compliments to Cook. That was one helluva meal. I don't think I could eat another bite."

"What's that, Captain Marky?" Finola said, bearing another tray of food. "Am I to throw my cinnamon apples to the fishies?"

"Scratch what I said." Markoff rubbed his hands together. "I can absolutely eat more. I haven't had an apple in . . . how long has it been since you last visited, Nikolai?"

"The last time was about two years ago. Remember that all-night poker game when I cleaned you out, and then some? Seems to me you still owe me the rest of my winnings."

"Why do you think I let you live?" Markoff grinned. "In fact, *you* owe *me,* now. And I'll take that payment in Cook's cinnamon apples."

"Apples are another thing we're willing to trade," Kennedy said. "Cider, too."

Markoff's eyes lit up. "What would we have to trade for that? Our women and firstborn children?"

"Just fish," Kennedy said.

"Surely not just fish," Markoff said, his mouth full again.

"My old partner Simon Creighton runs the cider trade out of San Francisco," Nikolai said. "He hates to fish more than anything. He'll gladly trade fish for cider, as much as you can catch for as much as you can drink." Nikolai didn't think he was overstating. There were dozens of apple orchards in Marin County, and they should be producing quite well now.

"Mmm." Markoff shoveled in more apples. "Where would we live? We'd have to have an island. Pirates aren't mainland kinds of people."

"There are a couple of islands you might like," Kennedy said.

"Right," Nikolai chimed in. "Have you heard of Alcatraz?"

Markoff shook his head.

"No? Alcatraz Island holds one of the most notorious prisons of all time," Nikolai said. "It would be perfect for you." Pirates would be a nice addition to San Francisco Bay.

Markoff smiled with apple-covered teeth.

"We'd be willing to give you Alcatraz," Kennedy said. "As a gift. Free and clear. *If* you help us retrieve the *Belle* and her crew. Including Nikolai's daughter."

Markoff's brow furrowed. He put down his fork, pushed his bowl away, and wiped his mouth on his sleeve. "What you're asking . . . going up against Pascal *and* the southern pirates. . . ." He shook his head.

Nikolai's heart sank. Without the aid of the northern pirates, the chances of a successful rescue approached nil.

Markoff belched. "Well . . . we'd have to have a really good plan."

Nikolai's hopes soared. "Absolutely."

"Planning takes cider." Markoff pounded his chest with his fist and belched again. "And I believe I just made room for some."

"You'll have all the cider you can handle, as well as my bottomless thanks," Nikolai said. "I have the beginnings of a plan, but it only works in partnership with you."

"Then bring on the cider!"

Chapter 65

Lost Angeles

"I'm only going to ask you one more time," Pascal said through his teeth. "Where is the vehicle?"

The prisoner smiled.

Pascal backhanded him, sending him careening off the chair. Pascal kicked the old man's ribs and air rushed out with a *whoosh*.

"Get him up," Pascal commanded.

The two guards lifted the prisoner by the arms. The man's head hung limp, his chin resting against his chest.

This was going nowhere fast.

"Take him to the Tank," Pascal said. "The moment he wakes up, I want him worked over. When he talks, don't send a runner. Send a Blade, whoever is fastest."

"Yessir." The guards dragged the man out.

Pascal went to the command post to check on the search. "Tell me someone's got something to report." His demand was met with silence. "Gomez, get me food and coffee."

Pascal returned to Ellianna's desk feeling weary and spent. But he visualized the ugly daughter of the clothier, and that was enough to bring his blood to near boiling again. Mia was not going to best him. She'd be caught, she'd tell him what he needed to know, then he'd show her what happened to anyone who tried to outmaneuver him. Then he'd let her live. Her death would be too easily forgotten, but alive she'd be an enduring visual example to others.

It was just a matter of time, he told himself. A matter of time before he had the vehicle he deserved and Mia had what she deserved.

No one could beat the King of Lost Angeles, least of all the daughter of a clothier.

Chapter 66

Lost Angeles

"**I** won't leave without my grandfather," Reid said.

"Listen to me," Brandt said. "If they have him, he's already spilled his guts about the car, and Blades are on their way here now. We have to leave."

"Please," Mia said, touching his arm. "Brandt knows what he's talking about."

"If he's been captured, we'll have to rescue him," Reid said, glaring at Brandt. He might have to go back to Colorado without seeds, but he wasn't going back without Tinker.

"You have no idea what you're saying, kid," Brandt said. "There's no point attempting a rescue. If he was captured, they put him in the Tank, which means he's already dead, or as good as. People don't come out of there."

"Think about what your grandfather would want you to do," Mia said. "Would he want you to risk your life when there's no hope of winning?"

Reid knew what his grandfather would want. Tinker had told him point-blank what to do if something like this happened. "Forget it. I'm not leaving Ellay without him," Reid said.

"Don't be a fool," Mia said. "You told me you came for seeds, right? Justine can get you seeds. But only if we leave *right now*."

"You're lying," Reid said, not wanting to believe Mia would try to trick him.

"It's true," Justine said. "Where I'm from, my people grow food."

"Why should I believe you?" Reid said.

"I know the woman you met," Justine said. "Cumorah is one of my people."

"You're saying that to get me to leave."

"No, I swear," Justine said. "She has brown hair and brown eyes. She's about my height. Older than me, but not old enough to be my mother."

"That could be a lucky guess," Reid said.

"We don't have time for this," Brandt said.

"Wait," Justine said. "I remember she was married but didn't have any children. I think she couldn't have any. She always had this black dog with her. It followed her everywhere."

Reid bit his lip. This couldn't be coincidence.

"She's telling the truth," Mia said. "If you take her home, you can fill your car with seeds for your people. Can you afford to risk that?"

"Get in the car," Brandt said. "We're going *now*, while we still can."

Mia was right. They were all right. They should go. Kayla, the baby, everyone back home needed those seeds. He looked at the car for a long moment, but he couldn't do it.

"I can't without knowing what's happened to my grandfather," he said.

"*I'm telling you* what's happened to him," Brandt said, throwing his hands in the air.

"You don't know for certain," Reid said. "What if he's hiding? If we find out for sure he's been captured, I'll accept it and we'll go. But I have to know, even if I can't save him."

"Fine, you go find out," Brandt said. "I'll figure out how to drive this thing on my own."

"I'll go," Mia said. "Two minutes inside the Grand and I'll know what happened."

"Absolutely not. You're coming with me and Justine," Brandt said.

"Look," Mia said. "Reid said up front that he was not leaving without his grandfather. Now he just wants to know what's happened to him, so I'm going. It's the decent thing to do."

"Thank you," Reid said, overwhelmed by her compassion.

"When do we decide you've been caught and aren't coming back?" Brandt asked.

"Caught?" Mia said. "Chances are, they're not even looking for me."

"But they could be," Reid said, guilt now overshadowing his gratefulness.

"Trust me, I'll be fine," Mia said. "If I'm not back in two hours, go without me."

"What if you're wrong? It's too risky," Justine said. "Brandt and I will go. No one will suspect us. Brandt can ask another Blade, and we won't have to go all the way to the Grand."

"Who's to say Reid won't take the car and leave without us?" Brandt said. "Besides, I won't have you risking the baby. We're doing this for her."

"You're pregnant?" Reid asked.

"Brandt's right," Mia said. "I'll go."

"I'll go with Mia," Brandt said. "Between the two of us, we'll find out quick."

"Thank you, honey," Justine said, throwing her arms around Brandt's neck.

Reid let out a breath he hadn't realized he was holding. They'd find Tinker and they'd all get out of Ellay. They had to.

"Reid, I want you and Justine to wait in the car, ready to drive out of here," Brandt ordered. "If Blades come, drive over them and keep going. Don't think twice about Mia and me. Get Justine to her people, you understand me, Reid?"

"Hold on," Justine said. "If we have to leave, we'll meet at Anaheim Stadium. I'm not going any farther than that without you."

"I'll take good care of her," Reid said. "Just find out what happened to Tinker."

Mia's hand slid into his. He pulled her close and kissed her.

"Don't leave without me," she whispered.

He couldn't imagine leaving her behind. He kissed her again.

Reid and Justine watched Mia and Brandt walk toward the tracks. Justine stood with her arms crossed, tapping her foot, her face contorted with concern. But every time Brandt glanced back, she smiled and waved. When Mia glanced back, Reid had to stifle the urge to run after her and go in her place. But he bit his lip and stayed put. This was the best plan to find Tinker. He believed that enough to let her go, and he prayed he wouldn't regret it.

After a last wave, Brandt and Mia disappeared around a corner.

Reid turned to Justine. "We'd better get in the car. I'll keep watch, and you can lie down in the back and rest."

"I have a better idea. Why don't you show me how it works?"

Reid was caught off guard. "I, I don't know." If they didn't need him to drive the car, what would prevent them from taking it and leaving him behind?

"No worries," Justine said. "I was just curious. I'm happy to nap."

She gave a little grin and headed for the car.

Was she plotting against him? He wouldn't put it past Brandt.

Justine stood at the car trying to figure out how to open the back door.

"Let me help," Reid said, heading over to her.

Maybe the smart thing would be to make sure she knew how to drive so she could get away if something happened to him. Or maybe that would be incredibly naïve and stupid.

What's your gut telling you? he imagined Tinker saying.

But he'd tried trusting his gut before, and look where it had gotten them.

Chapter 67

The Grand Hotel

Pascal smiled as Brandt shoved Mia into the room.

Mia stumbled but regained her poise quickly. "Chancellor Worth, I'm so pleased to see you again." She held out her hands to him.

Pascal turned to the collectors that Linus had escorted in. "Is this the woman you saw?"

The small man sniffed and stepped closer, taking a long look, enjoying his moment. "That's her, though she smelled better."

"Yeah," the bigger man said. "That's her."

"Take them back to the lobby," Pascal told Linus. "I may have need of them later."

"Will that be all, sir?" Brandt asked.

"Not from you, Brandt," Pascal said. "You and Mia stay. The rest of you are dismissed."

While the other soldiers exited the room, Pascal tried to read Brandt. The man held his shoulders back and looked Pascal in the eyes, but he seemed vaguely nervous, which gave Pascal pause. Was he hiding something?

But Brandt didn't waver under Pascal's scrutinizing stare, so Pascal dismissed his suspicions, attributing the man's nerves to the adrenaline of the pursuit, or perhaps the thrill of being singled out by his commander.

"Chancellor—Pascal—please, let me explain," Mia said. Her voice was low and calm, but her eyes gave away her fear.

Pascal decided to let her continue speaking for the moment, curious how she'd handle herself, what she might say. It would all be lies, of course, but watching her try to wriggle out from under his thumb might prove amusing.

"When I was at World Waste," Mia continued. "You remember

when I went out walking on my own, after you took me on my first train ride?" She looked at him coyly, obviously hoping to remind him of their past intimacies, but the stench of the refuse wafting from her clothing spoiled the effect.

"Yes, you went walking on your own," Pascal murmured.

"I saw those collectors, Frank and Roger."

Nice technique, Pascal thought. Laying the truth as groundwork before peppering it with lies. He nodded, encouraging her to continue.

"It was my own fault," she said. "I wasn't thinking when I told them I was a Ford Girl."

Pascal nodded again, furrowing his brow as if he were concerned. Another nice move on her part, saying it was her fault. It was a terrible waste that she'd betrayed him. She could have gone far.

"They, they cornered me." Her pitch rose as she built to her punch line. "Then they, they *violated* me. Both of them." Her voice cracked with emotion. "I know I should have reported it, but I didn't want to ruin your important meeting with Director Gould. I was wrong not to have told you." She blinked rapidly, and Pascal thought she might produce actual tears. "Pascal, I—"

He slapped her, and she cried out, staggering backward.

He'd seen and heard enough. He turned his attention to Brandt. "You're to be commended for bringing in our little outlaw."

"Thank you, sir," Brandt said.

Pascal enjoyed the venomous glare that Mia turned on Brandt, but the man didn't seem to notice or care. This was a bit of silver lining— Brandt standing by, unflinching and unflappable. It was a small consolation to have found an asset in him, while losing someone who could have been so much more.

"How is that girl of yours?" Pascal asked him. "Justine, isn't it? I understand congratulations are in order. She's expecting a child, correct?" Pascal enjoyed the surprise on Brandt's face.

"Yes, sir. She's well, sir, thank you."

"I've had my eye on you, Brandt. Keep up the exemplary work and you'll go far," Pascal said, feeling all the more satisfied this business was being conducted in front of Mia. Her discomfort was palpable.

"Brandt, you bastard—"

Linus burst in, crashing into Brandt. The two tumbled into Mia. There was a scuffle. *A gunshot.* Brandt propelled Mia backward, slamming her into the wall. He let go and she slumped to the floor.

"Is anyone hurt?" Brandt asked, pointing his handgun at Mia's inert form.

Pascal was stunned, but realized he was unharmed. "Linus, are you hurt?"

"I, I'm fine," Linus stammered. "What happened?"

"When we collided, Mia went for my gun," Brandt said without taking his gaze off Mia. "I couldn't let that happen."

The doorway darkened as armed men poured into the room. "Sir? Sir? Are you okay? We heard a shot." The room was abuzz with commotion as the security forces surrounded Pascal, their weapons searching for a target.

"Stand down," Pascal said. "Officer Brandt discharged his weapon protecting my son from her." He pointed to where Mia lay on the floor.

Brandt holstered his weapon and stepped aside, allowing a medic access to her.

"She's unconscious, but does not appear to have been shot," the medic said.

"When she went for my gun, I must have knocked her out," Brandt said.

"Thank God you did and no one else was hurt," Pascal said, his heart rate slowing. "Medic, take her to the Tank and notify me when she regains consciousness."

"Yessir."

"Brandt, my son and I are in your debt," Pascal said after Mia had been taken away. "In recognition for your actions, I'm promoting you. You'll be my personal deputy, a job that comes with a great number of perks, including a house. Bring Justine to see Mr. Gomez immediately so you can get married and move in. You have the remainder of today to get settled, then report to me for duty first thing tomorrow."

"Thank you very much, sir."

"See you in the morning." Pascal shook Brandt's hand. The man was an asset indeed.

Chapter 68

Lost Angeles, a junkyard

Reid and Justine jumped out of the car and ran toward Brandt.
"Where's Mia?" Reid demanded.

"Get back in the car. We leave now," Brandt said.

"Honey, what happened?" Justine asked. "Where's Mia?"

"The Tank." Brandt shook his head. "The whole city's been looking for her. I wish I'd gotten wind of it on the way, or we might have made it back here. As it was, we were surrounded outside the Grand."

"How'd *you* get away?" Reid asked.

"Pure luck. Since all cops were put on alert to find Mia, everyone assumed I was bringing her in. Though I'm sure Mia thinks I betrayed her."

"How do we know you didn't?"

"Because I'm not here with a team to take you in," Brandt said, coming toward Reid with his chest puffed out. "Now get in the car."

"Oh my God," Justine said. "Mia will tell them where we are."

"If she hasn't already," Brandt said. "I don't know how your grandfather is withstanding interrogation, but Mia can't."

"They have Tinker?" Reid asked.

"I didn't see him, but I heard they've had him since yesterday afternoon. That's a long time for anyone to hold out. He must be a tough old guy."

It had already been too late when Mia left. They'd had Tinker all along. Now they had Mia too.

"Now you know what happened to your grandfather," Brandt said. "Let's get the hell out of here. You gave your word."

"That was before they had Mia," Reid said, squaring up to Brandt.

"There's nothing you can do for her," Brandt said. "We'll all be dead if we don't go."

"I've had it with you acting like you know everything, dictating what we do. Mia and Tinker are alive, which means there's still a chance to save them."

"Reid," Justine said. "Brandt knows what he's talking about. Blades will be here any minute. What good would that do Mia or your grandfather? We need to move."

"Running now's our only chance," Brandt said, steering Justine to the car.

"I said we need to *move*, not *run*." Justine climbed into the back seat. "It's dark enough to move to another hiding place."

"I'm all for that," Reid said, getting in the driver's seat.

"No, someone will see us. Everyone's looking for this car. Once we're in the open, we have to keep going, out of Lost Angeles," Brandt said.

"They might see us, but they can't catch us." Reid started the car. "Let's find a safe hiding place, then come up with a rescue plan."

"How could we live with ourselves if we didn't at least try?" Justine said.

Chapter 69

Newport Harbor, aboard the pirate ship Majestic

"I should be drunk for this," Markoff said. "On the other hand, cider got me into this."

"We shouldn't be in the Tank for long." Nikolai looked around, comforted by how few boats accompanied them. Kennedy needed numbers on the southern pirates at San Clemente, which meant that they— he, Markoff, Olexi, and a handful of Markoff's crew—had to rely on guile.

"It would be better to avoid the Tank altogether," Markoff said. "Are you sure this son of yours is worth it? I have a son I wouldn't mind giving you in his place. It's not too late."

"We're in range to be seen," called the watch from the crow's nest.

"*Now* it's too late," Markoff muttered. "You do know they want my head, right?"

"But you're sure they won't shoot?" Nikolai felt exposed standing at the bow.

"Pascal wants me alive, at least at first," Markoff said. "They'll take our emissary to Pascal and be back to put us in the Tank before you can say Jack Sparrow. I guarantee it."

Nikolai wished they'd figured a way for Olexi to serve as emissary, but it was too risky to use someone who didn't have any cutting scars, so they'd chosen Bud, the recent defector.

The *Majestic* turned to port, rounding the crumbling seawall marking Newport Harbor.

"There she blows," Olexi said, as Nikolai himself spotted the *Belle*. "Her mast looks true."

"She'll be in good condition," Markoff said. "Otherwise no one would trade me for her."

It made sense, but didn't relieve Nikolai's concern. They couldn't risk the *Belle* lagging behind when bullets were flying, which they surely would be, so if she didn't appear seaworthy, they'd have to leave her.

Nikolai looked at his bindings. He'd have been fooled himself if he hadn't known they were rigged. The blouse of his trousers obscured the pistol in his boot, but the feel of it was reassuring. The knife in his waistband, too. He glanced at Olexi and Markoff who were similarly bound and armed. He sure as hell hoped this worked.

Chapter 70

Lost Angeles

R eid drove as fast as he dared.

"Turn right. *Here,*" Brandt shouted.

Reid turned, wheels squealing. "You have to give me more warning."

"Fine. Go straight another three blocks, then turn left."

Reid juked around cars and debris in the road.

"So far so good," Justine said from the back seat. "I haven't seen a soul."

"That doesn't mean no one's seen us," Brandt said.

"Hang on." Reid slowed a little going into the left turn, then as they rounded the corner he stomped hard on the brake pedal.

"*What the——*" Brandt braced his hands against dash as they screeched to a stop.

In the middle of the road, a small cluster of people stood around a fire.

"What do we do?" Reid asked.

"It's too late to do anything but keep going," Brandt said.

Reid moved his foot to the gas pedal and went around the people. "I thought you said no one lived this far out."

"Except for outcasts like them," Justine said.

"Will they report us?" Reid asked.

"They won't go out of their way, but they'll talk if confronted," Brandt said. "Hopefully, Blades won't come across them."

An hour later, Reid sat in the driver's seat gazing across the enormous parking lot at Anaheim Stadium. Brandt said the locals avoided the place, and Reid supposed he understood. A game had been in progress when the sunstorm hit. There'd been panic in the stands. Mass casualties. Bodies everywhere. Now it was an open tomb thought to be haunted, making it a great place to hide.

A quiet had fallen over the car now that they'd settled on a plan. Justine was stretched in the back, snoring softly. Brandt turned sideways in the passenger seat to watch her.

"Let her sleep a few more minutes, okay?" Brandt asked.

"Sure."

A few more minutes wasn't much for them, but he didn't know about Mia. He tried not to imagine the horrors being inflicted on her, and Tinker too. How long could they withstand it? He wished he could tell them it was okay to talk, that he'd moved the car. Then again, as long as they held a secret—even one that was no longer valid—that leverage might keep them alive.

He knew attempting a rescue was foolish. He told himself to leave Mia and Tinker behind, to get out of Ellay with Justine and Brandt, to go get seeds while he still could. That's what Tinker had told him to do. It was the smart thing to do. But he couldn't make himself.

"Okay, we shouldn't wait any longer," Brandt said. "Justine, honey? Time to wake up."

Reid's stomach flip-flopped as he thought about the thin line they planned to walk. One false step would land them in hell.

They left the car in the parking lot and set out on foot. A few blocks away, they found a house that had everything they needed, from food and water to the perfect disguise.

"Are you okay, Justine?" Reid asked. She looked pale.

"Nervous, I guess."

It didn't sound like nerves. It sounded like pain. "Nothing else?" Reid prompted.

"Honey," Brandt said, "if there's something wrong, you've got to tell me."

"I'm fine." Justine winced. "I don't want to mess up the plan."

"Are you cramping?" Reid asked.

"A little," Justine said.

"What about spotting? Have you noticed any blood?" Reid asked.

"Not much."

"Will you let me examine you, just to be safe?"

"What are you, a doctor?" Brandt said.

"A medic. I know what I'm doing."

"That's probably a good idea," Justine said, wincing as she rose from a chair. Brandt took her arm and led her to the couch.

"Lie back and try to relax," Reid said. "I'm going to feel your belly." He was gentle as he placed his hand overtop her overalls, but she flinched anyway. "How far along?"

"I'm not sure."

"Have you ever felt the baby move?"

Justine shook her head. "Is that bad?"

"Not necessarily. Most likely it's because you're still early in your pregnancy." Reid palpated the abdomen, trying to identify the top of the fundus without causing her discomfort. He couldn't say for certain how far along she was, but if he had to guess, maybe ten weeks or so. "Does it hurt where I'm pressing?"

"No. The pain is all across the lower part. My back, too."

"What's wrong? What is it?" Brandt asked.

Reid looked over at Brandt whose face had drained of blood. "Don't worry. It's probably nothing."

"It doesn't feel like nothing," Justine said. "Be straight with me. Is this a miscarriage?"

"Honestly, I don't know." It was true that he didn't know for certain, but it was likely a miscarriage. So many pregnancies were lost in the early months, even in the Before. But now, the odds were definitely not in her favor. "You should try to prepare yourselves for the possibility."

"No, you have to do something," Brandt said. "We can't lose this baby."

"There's not much we *can* do, other than rest," Reid said. "And wait."

"There's got to be something. Please," Justine said, grabbing Reid's arm.

"There is one thing we sometimes do back home," Reid said. "But there are side effects that can be dangerous."

"What is it?" Brandt asked.

"Aspirin."

"Painkillers?" Brandt said. "To make her feel better?"

"It could ease the pain, but that's not why we give it," Reid said. "There's a theory that a high level of toxins in the mother—like we get from all the canned food—can reduce blood flow to the fetus and cause a miscarriage. If this is what's happening, aspirin could help by increasing blood flow to the baby."

"I'll find some." Brandt bolted down the hall.

"But there are side effects?" Justine asked.

"You said you're spotting?"

Justine nodded.

"Aspirin thins the blood. It can make you bleed more."

"I don't know what to do, Reid. What would you do if it was your wife, your baby?" Justine looked at him, eyes pleading.

Reid was about to give her the stock non-answer he gave his patients. But he hesitated, imagining it was Kayla asking. What if it was Brian's baby—the only baby his brother would ever have? "I'd do it. I'd give the baby every possible chance."

Brandt came back. "I found some."

Reid read the label on the bottle. "This is the right stuff, but don't rush into a decision." He was second-guessing himself now. He didn't want to be responsible for her decision. Maybe he shouldn't have said anything.

"I feel a little better now," Justine said. "But if it gets worse, how much do I take?"

"Only one, but you don't need to worry about that. If you decide you want to take it, I'll be right here with you," Reid said.

"No, you two have to go," Justine said. "The sooner the better."

"You shouldn't be alone," Reid said.

"We're not leaving you," Brandt said.

"Listen, I hope I don't lose this baby, but either way, I want to go home. To raise this baby, or the next one. So hurry up and go rescue Mia so we can get out of here."

"One of us should stay," Reid said.

"The plan only works if you both go," Justine said. "I don't want to live in this hellhole anymore, Brandt. Do you?"

"No, but—"

"Then *go*. I'll be fine."

Brandt took a deep breath, then nodded. "I'll be back before you know it."

"Are you sure?" Reid asked.

"We're sure," Justine said, taking Brandt's hand.

Reid went outside to let them say goodbye in private, and he couldn't help wondering about Kayla and her baby, wondering if he'd ever make it home again.

Chapter 71

The Grand Hotel, Pascal's private suite

"Status report," Pascal demanded.

"Mia's still unconscious," Gomez said. "They're still working on the stranger in the Tank, but haven't been able to get a word out of him."

Pascal sighed. This had not been his day. "I'll sleep here so I'm close at hand if anything changes. You're to let me know immediately, is that clear?"

"Perfectly," Gomez replied. "I'll set up outside your door and instruct the command post to bring all news directly to me."

"Notify me of the slightest development, even if I'm asleep." God, he was tired. He looked at his watch, surprised it was still early evening. His usually impeccable sense of time had been perturbed. He hadn't felt like himself since Mia had gone for Brandt's gun.

"Shall I order food, sir?" Gomez suggested.

"Sure."

Gomez looked at him expectantly, but Pascal waved him out. He didn't care what kind of food. There was nothing that could fill the hollow that had formed in his gut when he realized he could have lost his son. Thank God Brandt had been there.

He slumped on the couch, feeling his years in every bone. He hated to admit it, but his mind wasn't as agile as it used to be either. He'd identified Mia's weapons as sex and manipulation, and completely missed the propensity for violence.

There was a knock and Gomez poked his head in.

"Dinner will be here soon. Did Brandt stop by in my absence?"

"No. Why?"

"I was supposed to show him to his new quarters. Strange he hasn't shown. I'll bring your food when it arrives." Gomez vanished behind the door.

Pascal chastised himself. He rarely forgot anything. The brush this afternoon had rattled him. He looked at his watch again. Gomez was right to worry.

He visualized the puzzle and noted Brandt's piece out of place. He shuffled the pieces, trying to form a picture that made sense. It kept coming back to the altercation with Mia. What had he missed? Something about it niggled at his memory.

Resting his head back on the sofa, he replayed the memory, slowing it to observe every detail. He thought he was close to an answer when Gomez placed dinner on the coffee table.

"Gomez, were Mia and Brandt acquainted prior to this afternoon?"

"I don't know, but Ms. Ford might. She's waiting to see you."

"Send her in." He ignored the plate of steaming pasta and stood to receive his guest.

Ellianna entered, poised and polished as always, looking much younger than her years. Pascal sighed, feeling his age all the more.

As soon as the door closed and they were alone, Ellianna's composure crumbled. She fell into his arms sobbing. "My God, you could have been killed."

Pascal was taken aback and held her at arm's length. "I'm fine."

Tears streamed down her cheeks, leaving tracks in her makeup. "I had no idea about Mia, Pascal. I swear. She's scheming and manipulative, but I knew you'd see that. I didn't have any idea she was violent. I'd have staked my life on it. In fact, I did—you are my life. I don't know what I would have done if—oh, Pascal." She clung to him again.

He eased her onto the sofa and sat beside her, moved but impatient as well.

"Elli, I need to ask you something." He handed her a paper napkin from the dinner tray.

She dabbed at her eyes. "Anything."

"Did Mia and Brandt know each other prior to today?"

"Yes, of course they did." Ellianna sniffed and reached for a second napkin. "Brandt's woman, Justine—the pregnant one—she's Mia's best friend."

Pascal went to the door and yanked it open. "Gomez, put out an alert on Brandt. On his woman, too. Make sure every Blade, guard, officer, and director knows. I want Brandt alive so I can kill the traitor myself. *Go.*"

Gomez ran.

Pascal closed the door and tried to calm the zinging of his nerves. He should have listened to his instincts. He'd sensed something unspoken between Brandt and Mia, but had brushed it aside. That mistake might cost him dearly.

Chapter 72

Lost Angeles

Brandt was charging forward so fast, Reid had a hard time keeping up. There weren't many people out, but those they passed stared. Reid felt like a fool, and his feet hurt. "Do I have to wear these shoes the whole way? Let me put them in my purse until we get closer."

"Fine."

"A little help?" Reid extended his handcuffed wrists.

Brandt rolled his eyes and squatted. Reid wobbled on one high heel while Brandt yanked off the other.

"What's wrong, haven't you ever seen a tranny whore before?" Brandt chided a man who was gawking, then dropped the shoes into the purple bag that hung from Reid's elbow.

Reid preferred to think of himself as a Trojan horse. He tried not to think of what he looked like with giant purple swatches of makeup over his eyes, a red wig, and a floral muumuu. The wig was itchy, but bearable. It was the shoes that had almost changed his mind.

He hurried barefoot now and kept silent about the pebbles underfoot lest Brandt make him put the shoes back on.

"Brandt," Reid said. "Hey, are we getting close?"

"What?" Brandt looked around as if seeing it for the first time. "Yeah."

"Well . . ." Reid hesitated. Brandt's face was blank. If he didn't snap out of it, he was going to blow it. "Pay attention or you're going to get us caught."

"I'm fine."

"Really? Because you're running down the street ahead of me. What kind of cop would do that?"

"Fine, I'll lead you, but they're staring because of how you look." Brandt grabbed the chain that linked the cuffs and pulled Reid along, managing a slightly slower pace.

After two blocks, Brandt stopped suddenly, and Reid nearly walked into the back of him.

"Do you hear that?" Brandt asked.

"Hear what?"

"A train. They don't run at night unless there's news. It has to be something important. We should find out what it is." He hurried down a side road pulling Reid with him.

"This might be easier if you let go," Reid said, trying not to step on Brandt's heels.

"All right, but stay close."

Reid's purple purse swung violently on his elbow as he followed Brandt across a yard and between two houses. They emerged onto a narrow street, then cut through another set of yards to the street beyond that. Ahead, the train was pulling to a halt.

"I was hoping it would stop here." Brandt pulled Reid into the shadows. "This is the closest train stop to the chancellor's residence. Look, someone's getting off."

Reid watched a uniform escort a scruffy man from the train.

"Weird," Brandt said under his breath. "That guy with the armband? He's a pirate emissary. Something big is going on. It can't have any connection to us, but it would be nice to know what it is. Might give us an advantage."

"Think you could safely ask?" Reid pointed to a man at the rear of the train.

"Wait here." Brandt strode to the train.

Reid strained to hear, but the train's engine was too loud.

Finally, Brandt returned. "That was a stroke of luck. He isn't the regular conductor, but for some reason, the chancellor has him running messages. He couldn't tell me about the pirate fast enough. Seems the northern pirate king has been captured, and the southern pirates are in the middle of brokering a trade, turning him over to the chancellor in exchange for a ship. That's good news for us."

"How so?"

"The Blades are already stretched thin. With the addition of this pirate business, communications will be a challenge. There's a good chance that even if Mia has told them about me, word hasn't gotten around yet. We might pull this off after all."

Those words echoed in Reid's head, but offered little reassurance.

His heart slammed against his ribs as Brandt led him into the Tank.

"Hey Roy," Brandt said casually. "I picked up this tranny whoring by the south depot."

Roy looked over the top of his glasses at Reid and somehow managed to make him feel guilty. "Haven't seen this one before. Where's the John the he-she was doing?"

"Got away. I'll find him though. I got a good look at him," Brandt said.

"Put it in cellblock five. The entire row's empty, so take your pick."

"You know, Roy." Brandt leaned in conspiratorially. "Solitary's not a bad idea, but I had something else in mind."

Roy glanced at Reid. "Like teaching it a lesson?"

"What do you say?"

"Let's see." Roy paged through some papers. "Stay away from cellblock one. That's where the political detainees are. But block three has a good crowd. Drunk and disorderlies, plus a handful of thieves and the like. That ought to do the trick. Or there's always psycho row." He looked at Reid with a sick grin.

"Three's perfect," Brandt said. "I owe you, Roy."

"This one's on the house."

"Creep," Reid said under his breath.

"Shut up!" Brandt yanked Reid by the cuffs and shoved him into the hall.

Reid almost fell, but got his feet under him and shuffled forward, keeping his mouth shut. They passed through another door and down a long corridor.

"Okay, this is it." Brandt opened the door to cellblock one.

"Authorized personnel only," a guard said in a monotone.

"Hey, Smitty, I'm authorized, unofficially." Brandt chuckled. "Me and Roy thought this tranny should be taught a lesson."

"Sorry, man. I don't go in for that," Smitty said.

"Not you. We're gonna throw it in with the prisoners."

"Not *these* prisoners." Smitty narrowed his eyes.

This was starting to go wrong.

Brandt threw a swift elbow to Smitty's neck and the guard went down.

"Clock's ticking," Brandt said, snatching the key ring off Smitty's belt. He shoved a key in the lock, and swung open the door to a long hall lined by bars.

A man lay huddled against the bars of the closest cell. Blood trailed from his head down the cement floor to a drain.

"Pops!" Reid dropped to his knees and maneuvered his cuffed hands through the bars to check for a pulse. Tears of relief sprung to his eyes. "He's alive."

Brandt unlocked the cell. "Can you carry him? I'll find Mia."

"Uncuff me."

Brandt selected a key from the ring.

"I'll take those."

Roy had a pistol trained on Brandt, and three other men leveled guns at Reid.

Reid's heart thundered and he held his breath, hoping Brandt had some way out of this without turning on him.

"Funny thing," Roy said. "Word just came down you're a wanted man, Brandt. But I guess I can see that for myself now, can't I?"

Reid grabbed the bars to steady himself as his muscles contracted and the walls closed in with tunnel vision. *Fight or flight response,* he thought, almost laughing at his clinical evaluation. But there was nothing funny about this. There would be no fight *or* flight. They were done for.

Chapter 73

The Grand Hotel, Pascal's private suite

Pascal sipped his brandy, savoring the flavor and the moment. It hadn't taken a massage to relax him. It was enough to sit beside Elli on the sofa.

He put his arm across her shoulders. She leaned against him. He buried his face in her hair and breathed in the sweet fragrance. He'd wanted this for so long.

"Father?" Linus stared at them from the doorway.

Pascal had made a point to never let Linus see him compromised. Now he felt exposed—an empty bottle of brandy, the remains of dinner, shoes off, feet propped on the coffee table, Ellianna curled at his side. But perhaps it was okay that Linus see a more human side of him.

"Gomez told me to come in," Linus said. "It's important."

"Of course." Pascal placed his feet on the floor and straightened his shirt. "What is it?"

"Brandt's been caught. He's in the Tank right now."

"That's the news I've been waiting for." Pascal stepped into his loafers.

"What are you going to do, Father?"

"Make him an example. People must see how their leader treats those who cross him."

"Sir?" Gomez said, knocking on the open door. "Sorry to disturb, but there's an emissary from the southern pirates here. He was taken to your residence first, so he's a bit agitated."

"What does he want?"

"He's here for the bounty. He claims to have the northern pirate king in custody at the harbor, as well as two San Franciscans that prove the king's treachery."

Minou arrived beside Gomez, out of breath. "The car has been spotted. Outcasts saw it near Angel Stadium not two hours ago. My men are combing the area now."

The car. Brandt. The pirates. Pascal examined these critical pieces of the puzzle, deciding which to place first. His fury at Brandt's deception burned to be unleashed, but he realized that would be selfish and short-sighted. No, come daylight, he'd deal with Brandt someplace very public—perhaps at the statue of the Founder and his rodent. The pirate business was necessary but could also wait. Which meant he could indulge his desire to find the car.

"Excellent, Minou," he said. "You'll take Ms. Ford and me to the search area at once. Get us skates and wait in the lobby."

"Right away, sir." Minou saluted and left.

Pascal turned to Gomez. "Brandt will face public execution for treason in the morning. The pirates can wait until morning too. Tell the emissary I'll be at the harbor one hour past dawn for the exchange."

Gomez's forehead wrinkled with concern. "Pirates don't wait well, sir. We could have trouble when the emissary gives them the news."

"Then don't tell them," Linus exclaimed. "Put the emissary in the Tank till morning."

"No, that breaks Pirate Code," Pascal said. "It would rile them even more. Send the emissary back to his ship, but assign a Blade to take command of the men guarding the *Belle Jewel*. Their orders are to keep the peace." He hated pulling a Blade off the search for the car, but sending one man to prevent a riot was preferable to sending a platoon to quash one.

"I'll see to it." Gomez hurried away.

"What about me, Father? I'm as fast as any Blade—I can help with the search."

"No, it's late and you need your rest."

"But Father—"

"I need you at your best tomorrow. You'll accompany me to the exchange with the pirates, then I want you by my side for Brandt's public execution. These are critical times in your rise to leadership. I need you at your best. Understood?"

Linus was crestfallen, but he nodded and left.

Pascal took Ellianna's hand "We'll find the car and take the first drive together."

"I'd love that more than anything, but I'm not a good skater—I'd only slow you down."

He knew she was right. "Then I want you waiting here for me when I get back." He looked into her eyes. He wanted to kiss her. He'd wanted her for so long. Why had he been denying himself? It didn't seem important anymore.

He gathered her in his arms and kissed her, and it felt like he'd found a long-lost piece to a puzzle.

Chapter 74

The Tank

Brandt vomited in the metal toilet at the back of the cell. He'd taken the brunt of the guards' animosity. Reid had it easy by comparison. He hadn't fought back, and they'd quickly grown bored with beating him.

He'd been stripped of his costume and the weapons he'd hidden in his purse, so he knelt beside Tinker wearing only red undershorts. In the light of the bare bulb overhead, he saw that Tinker's pupils were fixed and dilated. His breathing was labored, and there was a sickening wheeze each time he inhaled. Reid lifted Tinker's shirt and winced at the bruising on his chest. He gingerly pulled the shirt back down.

Brandt had been right. Tinker wasn't going to make it out of the Tank alive. He would die lying on the cold cement floor, and there wasn't anything Reid could do about it.

"I'm sorry about the old man," one of the men called from the adjacent cell. "We asked the guards to let us help him, but they laughed."

"Has he been conscious?" Reid asked.

"Nah," the man replied. "He's been out since they tossed him in here a couple of hours ago. He means something to you?"

"He's my grandfather." Reid choked back a sob.

"He's one tough old dude," a second man said. "We heard he pissed off the torture guy something wicked. Apparently, he never broke, never said a word."

Reid sat against the wall and stroked Tinker's hair. "You did good, Pops. Real good."

"I hope he'll be okay," the first guy said.

Reid nodded, not wanting to say out loud there was little chance of that. He held Tinker's hand. "Pops, you fought hard. You protected us. I'm the one who screwed the pooch this time."

His eyes stung and he clamped his teeth shut, trying not to cry. It hardly seemed possible that less than two weeks had passed since they left Colorado. They'd been so full of hope that they'd find seeds and return as heroes. Now Tinker wouldn't make it home at all, and the odds didn't look good for him either.

Reid took a deep breath and tried to pull himself together. He had to be strong for Tinker's sake. He had to be there for him, to let him know he was safe to let go if the time came.

He noticed that Brandt had stopped retching and was standing at the bars, talking with the group of men in the adjacent cell.

"Those guards were royally pissed at you, huh?" one of the men said. "Is it 'cause you're impersonating one of them?"

"No, I *am* one of them," Brandt said. "Or I was."

"Fresh!" the first man said. "You're exactly the break I've been waiting for. What do you say we help each other get out of here?"

Was that even possible? If there was any way they could escape . . . Reid told himself not to hope, but it was too late.

Chapter 75

Newport Harbor, aboard the Majestic

"So much for your guarantee we'd be in the Tank by now," Nikolai told Markoff.

The emissary had come back with little information. Nothing about Will or his crew. The whole city was preoccupied with sightings of a car, and apparently that interested the chancellor more than putting the pirate king's head on a pike. There was nothing to be done until the morning when they would make the exchange.

"We should enjoy the reprieve," Markoff said. "Let's splice the mainbrace."

"Pardon?" Nikolai said.

Markoff snorted. "Break out the cider, of course."

Dulling his senses with alcohol was the last thing Nikolai wanted, but it gave him an idea.

"Psst, come here," he called to Markoff's crewman who was impersonating the leader of the southern pirates, another defector with cutting scars.

Their "captor" ambled over. "Yeah? I mean, what d'you want, you grimy barnacle?"

Nikolai spoke in a low voice. "Get the barrels of cider out of the hold."

"That's the spirit," Markoff said.

"Not for us," Nikolai said. "We can use this downtime to make sure the *Belle* is ready to sail. The cider's our ticket aboard."

The first barrel had gotten them on board the *Belle*. Soon after that, a deck of cards had come out. During the second barrel, one of Markoff's men brought out a fiddle. Several others—guards and pirates alike—joined with harmonicas and improvised drumming.

Into the third barrel of cider, the party was going strong. Nikolai slipped out of his bonds and walked the decks unnoticed. The *Belle* was in decent shape. The deck was dirty, but not damaged. The sheets were tidy and the sails were stowed, though a bit unkempt. The jib showed Will's characteristic sharp folds—it probably hadn't been taken out since he'd been aboard. After some minor tuning, she should make it to Catalina at top speed. Then Friday could fix anything that needed fixing before the return voyage to San Francisco.

Friday hadn't liked staying behind on the island but, unlike Cook, Friday had accepted it. Finola had refused to disembark, gripping the rail as if there were stormy seas. She'd argued until the sweat beaded on her wide brow, and nothing Nikolai said could assuage her. Even Kennedy gave up trying to talk sense into her. It was Olexi who was able to close the matter. He was like the father in an unlikely family—Finola, the man-child Friday, and Olexi. After one soft-spoken word from him, Finola stood down, though clearly not happy about it. Whatever Olexi had said worked like magic.

"Captain?"

"Speak of the devil," Nikolai said to Olexi.

"We need three sober men and three hours to make the *Belle* right. Who do we recruit?"

They surveyed the crew dancing and playing cards in the torchlight.

"I'd say that the only one of ours who's shit-faced drunk is Markoff," Olexi said.

"He's not as drunk as he's playing," Nikolai said, "but he's doing the most good where he is, keeping the guards entertained. Grab any three others and let's get to work."

Chapter 76

The Tank

Brandt was engrossed in quiet conversation with the men in the adjacent cell, but Reid stayed with Tinker. He didn't know how long his grandfather had, and he didn't want him to spend his last moments alone.

Tinker's brow furrowed and he moaned, but he didn't rouse. Reid didn't expect him to, and it was better that way. The pain would be worse, and there was nothing he could do to help.

"I'm sorry I got you into this, Pops," he said. "I wish I could take you home. I wish . . . ." He bit his lip to stop it from trembling.

Tinker's breathing was labored. They were running out of time.

"Pops, I've been thinking about what you said in the car. About Kayla and me. And I wish I'd told you then that you were right. I do love her. I've always loved her. But telling her . . . what good would that do? She'll never love me the way she loved Brian, no matter how I feel, no matter what I say." Reid swallowed hard. "But I guess none of that matters now, does it?"

Tears ran down the sides of Reid's nose. Tinker was fading, and soon Reid would be alone, half a world away from the people he loved with no hope of getting home. How long would Kayla and his grandma watch for their return? How long before they gave up hope?

The door to the cellblock creaked open, and a woman entered the hallway that ran between the two rows of cells. Reid had never seen anyone so glamorous—her red dress shimmered with tiny diamonds, she had jewels on every finger, and her purse and shoes looked like they'd been carved out of gold. She couldn't have looked more out of place.

"Brandt?" the woman called in a melodious tone as she approached their cell. "Brandt, I'd like to talk to you."

"Ellianna?" Brandt met her at the bars.

"My dear, how are you?" Ellianna cooed.

"What are you doing here?" Brandt's voice had an edge that Reid hadn't heard before.

"I came to see what I can do to help. You've gotten yourself into quite a fix."

"I've been wondering how that happened. Can I assume Mia gave me up?"

"Mia?" The woman's laugh was cold. "She hasn't said a word since you knocked her unconscious."

"What?" Reid came to his feet. He couldn't have heard that right.

"He didn't tell you?" Ellianna batted her oversized lashes at him.

"What's she talking about, Brandt?" Reid said, coming forward.

"Don't," one of the men called from the adjacent cell. "She's lying. Trying to turn you against each other."

Reid stopped. They had to be right. He didn't completely trust Brandt, but there's no way he would have hurt Mia.

Brandt glanced at Reid then turned back to the woman. "What do you want, Ellianna?"

"I want to help you, Brandt."

"Bullshit. You never even liked me. Whatever you want, you want for your own purposes."

"Listen to me, you idiot," she said through her teeth. "Chancellor Worth is going to publicly execute you tomorrow morning. I'm trying to save your life."

A public execution? For helping a stranger? Reid hoped she was still lying.

"How can *you* save my life?" Brandt's voice practically dripped with disdain for the woman.

"Tell me where the stranger's car is," she said. "And I'll convince the chancellor you deserve another chance. We have to act fast—he got a tip from some outcasts, and he's out right now looking for the car himself. If he finds it before I tell him, we've got nothing."

The outcasts. They'd parked not far from them.

"Go away, Ellianna."

"Be smart. Think about your pretty Justine. If you ever want to see her again, if you want any hope of seeing your baby, you'll tell me."

Brandt walked to the back of the cell.

"Brandt," Reid said close to his ear. "Are you sure about this? Maybe she can help."

"Guard!" Brandt yelled. The cellblock door opened. "Ms. Ford is done here."

"Last chance, Brandt." Ellianna paused, but Brandt didn't say anything. "You're making a mistake."

The guard escorted her out and the door slammed shut.

"What if she's telling the truth?" Reid asked.

"Everything that comes out of that woman's mouth is some form of self-serving lie," Brandt said. "She wouldn't save my life even if she could. If I told her anything, she'd use it to her own advantage, then laugh through her smile as I swing from the noose."

"It doesn't have to be that way," someone called from the other cell.

Reid looked over. It was the same man that kept butting in. He was shorter and younger than the others in the cell, but he carried himself with an air of authority. "What's his story? Can he really help us escape?" Reid asked Brandt under his breath, still clinging to that sliver of hope.

"I don't know. Maybe. His name's Will. He's from up north, and he's pretty motivated to get out of here. You remember that ship the pirates came to claim as bounty? Apparently it's his."

Chapter 77

Newport Harbor, aboard the Belle Jewel

"Yo ho, yo ho, a pirate's life for me," Markoff sang, sloshing cider. Nikolai's sides ached from laughing. "So you're actually descended from carnival workers who worked on a pirate *ride?*"

"Not just a ride," Markoff said. "A *production*. It was the crown jewel of the park's empire. Our ancestors were proud to be pirates, and when the sea called to us, we continued in the tradition. Yo ho!"

"Yo ho!" the pirates echoed, raising their glasses.

"I can't believe you never told me this before," Nikolai said. "Now so much makes sense, you *salty blaggard*."

"*Mutinous landlubber*."

"*Bow-legged scallywag*."

"Well, that one might be true." Markoff nodded, raising his glass.

Nikolai lifted his in response. "A toast to Captain Scallywag!"

"Yo ho!" the crew answered again.

The guards laughed and raised their glasses, as well. They seemed to be enjoying themselves as much as the pirates, now that there was plenty of cider lubricating the boundaries between them.

"Another round!" someone shouted.

Nikolai had brought an ungodly amount of cider, but at this rate there wouldn't be any left to celebrate a successful mission. Assuming they were successful.

The music resumed, giving Nikolai the opportunity to slip away again.

Olexi joined him at the rail. "This is going better than I anticipated, Captain."

"How about you call me Nikolai. Or Niko, even."

"Are you drunk?"

"Sober as a glass." He sighed and gripped the smooth mahogany of the *Belle's* rail, staring west into the black expanse of sea and sky. "I'm not your captain, Olexi. I never will be again. That's the truth of it."

"The future is yet unknown. That's the beauty of it."

"I suppose."

As they stared west, Nikolai's thoughts drifted to Hawaii as they did more and more often. Indulging himself in a sigh, he turned to Olexi. "What do you say we go now?"

"*Chevo?*"

"The *Belle* is nearly ready. The locals are drunk, while most of our men are sober. The authorities are preoccupied. Let's mount the rescue tonight."

Olexi didn't answer. As the silence stretched, Nikolai began to reconsider.

Finally Olexi responded. "Captain, or uh, *Nikolai,*" he began.

"Oh hell," Nikolai said. "You're right. We should stick with the original plan."

"It's a good plan. Or at least the best one we have."

"Thank you, Olexi. You're a good man. A good friend."

"As are you, Nikolai."

"Oh shut up and make yourself useful, sailor." Nikolai laughed as Olexi left.

He stood at the rail a moment longer, trying to clear his head of the sentimental melancholy that gripped him. Leaning over the rail, he spat into the sea, then took a deep breath. Time to get back to work.

Chapter 78

The Tank

R eid cradled Tinker's head in his lap, wishing they were back home.
"We have to do something *now,*" Will said, pacing in the next
cell. "Tomorrow, my ship will be gone, and you'll be dead."

"I realize that," Brandt said. "But I'm telling you, there's no way out
of these cells without a key. On the other side of the bars I've got the
advantage—I know the procedures, where weapons are kept, which
passages lead out. But on this side, I'm as helpless as anyone."

"Hey kid," Will called.

Reid looked up, not appreciating being called a kid. He'd bet he was
older than Will.

"Come join us," Will said. "We could use another brain on this."

Reid looked at Brandt.

"He's right," Brandt said. "If we're going to do something, it has to
be tonight."

"I'll be back in a few minutes," he said, in case some part of his
grandfather was aware of his presence. He joined the men at the bars.

"Good," a brown-skinned man with a round face said. "We could
use something to break the monotony of these two *jefes* banging heads."

"This joker is Gordo." Will indicated the man who'd just spoken.
"This is Sam and Alfonse. Vlad's asleep." He gestured over his shoulder
to a man curled up in the corner. "What we need is a fresh perspective.
Any ideas how we can get those keys?" Will's eyes were intense but not
unkind, and his sun-worn face looked like it was accustomed to smiling.

"You're working the wrong angle," Brandt said. "The guards are
well-trained in every possible contingency. They aren't going to make
some rookie mistake and hand over the keys."

"Wait, we don't actually need *keys,*" Reid said. "We need the guards
to unlock the cells."

"Why didn't I think of that? Let's ask them," Brandt said.

"I'm serious," Reid said. "You said they're well-trained, right? So we figure out a circumstance where their training dictates they open the cells."

"Right." Will nodded. "Like a fire or something. Anyone have matches?"

"Hold up," Brandt said. "The procedure for fire is the guards evacuate *themselves* and don't come back until the fire's out and we're all dead."

"Nice people," Gordo said.

"They won't open the cells because *we're* in danger," Brandt continued. "The procedures are designed to protect *them.*"

"So let's figure it out," Reid said. "Why would the guards *want* to open the cells?"

The outer door to the cellblock rattled then opened, and a guard strode in. "Brandt, at attention. Chancellor Worth wants a word."

"Don't piss him off," Will said in a low voice. "We need you alive."

Brandt met Reid's gaze, and Reid didn't like what he saw. Through all of this, Brandt had never truly looked frightened until now. That chilled Reid to the bone, but he smiled and nodded at Brandt, hoping to give him courage.

"Now," the guard barked.

Brandt went to the front of the cell and stood at attention. Two armed guards entered the cellblock, followed by a clean-shaven silver-haired man in a suit.

The man stopped opposite Brandt, and stood at the bars shaking his head. "I had such trust and affection for you, Brandt. Only to learn you didn't save my son but *endangered* him in your little charade. He could have been killed. Do you know what a son means to a father? If he'd been harmed, do you have any idea what that would have done to me? *Do you?* Answer me!"

"No, Chancellor," Brandt said. "I don't."

"I didn't think so," the chancellor said. "But you should, and I was able to fix that. I found that lovely, pregnant woman of yours. Justine. I slit her throat and I watched her bleed out, knowing that inside her *your* son was suffocating to death."

"You bastard!" Brandt charged the bars and thrust his arms through, grabbing for him.

A guard cocked his weapon. "Stand down, Brandt. Don't think I won't use this."

Reid grabbed Brandt and muscled him away from the bars.

"Noooo!" Brandt cried. "Oh God, no. Justine, *Justine.*"

"Stop, you're going to get yourself killed," Reid whispered, steering Brandt to the back of the cell.

Brandt slumped to the ground, his head on his knees.

"Who are you?" the chancellor boomed. "Come here."

Reid glanced over. The chancellor was looking at him. "Shit," he said under his breath. Cold dread filled his stomach as he went to the front of the cell.

"I'm Chancellor Pascal Worth," the man said in the same placid tone he'd used to deliver Justine's death notice. "And you are?"

"Reid Landers."

"Are you connected to that man there?" He indicated Tinker. "If you lie to me it will be much worse for you."

Reid swallowed. "He's my grandfather."

"I see. Are you the stranger who was at World Waste with Mia?"

"Where's Mia?"

"Ah, yes, I thought so. But let me share a bit of advice with you, stranger. It will go much better for you if you answer my questions."

The man was cold, deadly, worse than Vega could ever be. Reid clenched his fists and swallowed, trying to push down his terror.

"Yes, that was me at World Waste with Mia." Reid took a breath. "Please, sir, where is Mia? I need to know if she's okay."

Pascal smiled the same sick smile as before. "There, I knew you were a man who could be reasoned with. And to show you I'm just as reasonable . . ." He looked over his shoulder toward the guards at the cellblock door. "Is Mia still alive?"

One of the guards stepped forward. "I don't know, sir. Shall I find out?"

"Bring her here. Either way." Pascal turned back to Reid. "I can be your friend or your enemy. Choose wisely."

Reid forced himself to look the man in the eye. "What do you want?"

"I have your vehicle, but I don't know how to turn it on. I'll figure it out eventually, but as a *friend,* you could save me the time and trouble."

"You're lying." Reid hoped he was, but the man's confidence was unnerving.

The guard re-entered with Mia in his arms.

Reid pressed his cheeks to the bars. "Mia!" Her eyes were closed, and she looked unharmed, but he couldn't be sure. "Is she alive?" he asked Pascal.

Pascal pointed to the cell directly across the corridor. "Put her in there so he has a good view."

"Wait, let me see her." Reid strained to see if she was breathing.

A second guard unlocked the cell door, and the first dropped Mia inside.

"No!" Reid cried as Mia's body tumbled to the ground. She lay unmoving in an unnatural heap, her torn gown gaping open. "Is she alive? *Is she alive?*"

The guards didn't answer.

"Mia!" Reid called, gripping the cell bars. "Let me out of here! Let me see her!"

"Is she alive?" Pascal asked the guards.

"Yes sir," one replied.

Thank God. She was unconscious, but at least she was breathing. "Let me help her. Please," Reid said.

"Perhaps that's how things are done where you're from," Pascal said. "Here, friendship is more reciprocal. I did something for you, now it's your turn. How do I turn on the car?" He held up the keycard from the Humvee. "In case you doubted I have the vehicle."

He really did have the car, but he couldn't use it, which meant Reid still had a little leverage. "If you give me medical supplies and let me tend to Mia and my grandfather, I'll show you how to work the car in the morning."

Pascal shook his head. "As I said, it's your turn."

Reid gripped the bars. He needed to get to Mia, but he couldn't reveal how to work the car. As soon as he did, they'd all be dead. "I need to sleep on it."

Pascal raised an eyebrow. "I hope that's not too late for Mia."

Reid prayed he'd find a way to get to her before then.

As soon as the cellblock door closed behind Pascal, Will called out. "Reid, Brandt, we still need to figure out a plan. Come on, it's now or never."

Chapter 79

The Tank

Tinker was gone. Already growing cold. Reid didn't know how long it had been since Tinker had last taken a breath. He'd missed it.

He took Tinker's hand and held it. "I'm sorry. I'm so sorry." He let his tears stream freely as he knelt beside Tinker, wishing everything were different, wishing he hadn't screwed up so badly, wishing they'd never come to Ellay.

In the adjacent cell, Vlad unscrewed the bare light bulb and the cell went dark. Reid could see by the light from his own cell as Vlad leapt down from his perch on Gordo's shoulders.

"It's time," Brandt said. "Get in position."

Reid slid the wedding ring from his grandfather's finger and placed it on his own. He kissed Tinker's forehead. "I'll try to make you proud, Pops. I'll try to make sure this wasn't all in vain."

He took his place at the front of the cell, on his stomach pretending to sleep. He peeked over his arms. Mia hadn't moved from where she'd been dumped. He still couldn't see if she was breathing, and he hoped the guards hadn't lied about her being alive. It was impossible to tell how much of what Pascal said was true, and how much was orchestrated to get what he wanted. He wondered if Pascal had lied about killing Justine to hurt and manipulate Brandt. It didn't seem likely, though. Pascal did have the car.

He peered at Brandt sitting by their cell door. On the surface, he seemed in control, but the news of Justine's death had broken something inside him. Reid understood a little of what that felt like, but there was no time for grieving right now. He hoped Brandt could hold it together. He had to for the plan to work. Reid thought for a moment about saying that Justine could still be alive, but decided it would be too cruel to get his hopes up.

Reid put his head down on his arms and tried to prepare himself. After all their brainstorming, the plan they ended up with was simple. According to Brandt, two guards would soon enter the cellblock on rounds. They'd see the light out in the cell, and protocol dictated they had to change the bulb immediately. They were supposed to move the prisoners to a vacant cell first, but since they were asleep, Brandt was betting the guards would be lazy. If they refused to deviate from protocol and proceeded to move the prisoners, things were going to get ugly fast, and their odds of escaping would be next to zero.

When the door to the cellblock rattled, a surge of adrenaline sent Reid's nerves thrumming. He thought he detected two sets of footsteps, but he resisted the urge to look.

"What in the hell?" a voice said.

"They didn't do anything," Brandt said. "Bulb burned out about twenty minutes ago. None of them even twitched. They're dead to the world."

"I'll get the ladder." The guard didn't sound too happy about it.

Reid heard one set of footsteps receding.

"Protocol sucks, don't it, Matt?" Brandt said.

"You know it," the other guard said. "Or you used to. What are you doing on the wrong side of the bars? It's not like you."

"A misunderstanding. It'll be cleared up soon."

"That's good to hear, but don't wait too long," Matt said. "Damn. I guess I'd better rouse those prisoners."

"Wait, why'd you say not to wait too long?" Brandt asked. "You know something."

"Yeah, but you didn't hear it from me. You're scheduled for execution in the morning."

The footsteps returned. Reid peeked over his arm enough to see that the other guard had returned with the ladder. This was the moment of truth.

"Sorry I haven't moved the prisoners yet," Matt said. "I was catching up with Brandt. He and I served in the same platoon when we were basics."

"I remember Brandt," the other guard said. "I'll move them. Cover my back."

"Is that necessary?" Matt said. "They're out cold."

"You know the rules," the other guard said.

"They dangerous?" Brandt asked. "What are they in for?"

"Official charge is conspiracy and trespassing," Matt said. "But they've been here for weeks and never caused a problem."

"Fine, then. Let's not make trouble where there isn't any," the other guard said. "I'll sneak in and sneak out. No one will know the difference."

"So what are people saying about why I'm here?" Brandt asked, getting Matt's attention.

"That you were in league with Mia in a plot against the chancellor," Matt said. "That she didn't really try to take your gun. That you knocked her out so she couldn't give you up."

Keys rattled and the door to Will's cell swung open. No one moved. The only sound besides snoring was the metallic creak of the ladder opening.

"Seriously?" Brandt said. "How long have you known me, Matt? Do you think I'd hurt a girl? Even to save my own ass?"

The other guard reached the top of the ladder.

"I don't know," Matt said. "If it were me—*hey!*"

Brandt reached through the bars and grabbed Matt's gun at the same moment that Will and his men rose in unison and pulled the guard off the ladder. Reid leapt up, yanked Matt into the bars by his shirt, and slapped a hand over his mouth while Brandt wrestled him for the gun.

Vlad and Sam rushed out of the other cell. Sam took control of Matt's gun, and Vlad snapped Matt's neck and dropped him to the ground.

"You weren't supposed to kill him," Brandt said.

Will unlocked their cell. "Get the old man," he said, turning to unlock Mia's cell.

"He's dead." Reid looked at the guard who had been on the ladder. He was dead, too.

"I've got the girl." Will hoisted Mia to his shoulder and brought her out.

"Give her to me." Reid pulled Mia into his arms. She was alive.

"Take the lead," Will told Brandt, handing him the ring of keys and Matt's gun. "Sam and Alfonse, you're with Brandt. Gordo, stay close to Reid and the girl. Vlad and I will bring up the rear. *Let's go.*"

Brandt opened the cellblock door a crack and looked out. "Clear."

Reid's heart raced as they followed Brandt down a hallway. Their footsteps seemed so loud, he was sure they'd be discovered any moment. They stopped for Brandt to unlock a door, and Reid shifted Mia so her head was on his shoulder and he could hear her breathing.

Brandt cracked the door, then shut it. "Someone's coming."

Reid squeezed Mia to his chest, ready to bolt if the door opened, ready to shield her if bullets started flying.

He didn't trust Will's men. They'd promised not to kill the guards, and now they looked so jumpy they might start shooting even if no one came through the door.

After what felt like an hour, Brandt inched open the door, listened, then peeked through. "Clear." He motioned for them to follow.

Reid let out a big breath and took his place in line. They went down a service corridor lit by yellow bulbs and lined with banks of lockers.

Brandt stopped in front of one of the larger lockers and selected a key from the ring. "Give me cover. Both directions."

Will took Matt's pistol from Brandt and covered the rear, while Sam faced forward with the other guard's gun.

The locker held dozens of guns and boxes of ammo. "Only use them if you have to," Brandt said, doling them out. He thrust the butt of a pistol toward Reid. "It's already loaded."

Reid shook his head. There'd been enough dying.

Brandt set the gun on a bench and took Mia from him. "Put on that uniform." He gestured with his head toward a locker.

Reid pulled on the shirt and pants. The pants were too big, but he cinched up the belt.

"Boots too," Brandt said. "Hurry."

Reid sat and put on a pair of combat boots. The boots were a half size too small, and he was so nervous he kept fumbling the laces.

"Take the gun," Brandt said. "You might need to protect her."

Reid conceded and shoved the pistol into the holster on the belt.

Brandt handed Mia back to Reid. He slung a weapon over his shoulder, but kept it pointed at the ground. "This last part's the lynchpin."

They went through several dim passages that reminded Reid of the Mountain, right down to the smell of rotting garbage.

Finally, Brandt stopped and gathered everyone around. "It takes two keys to open the last door. One on each side. If the door opens, it means they believe us, so *don't shoot.* Understood?"

The men nodded.

"Reid, give Mia to someone else," Brandt continued. "Button your shirt and take two of the big guns so you look like a guard. Everyone else conceal your weapons."

"This whole thing's a waste of time. We should bust our way out the front," Sam said. He was antsy, shifting from foot to foot and fingering his gun like he wanted to shoot it.

Except for Will, the other men seemed just as tightly wound, like the slightest thing would set them off.

"We try it my way first," Brandt said. "If they recognize me, or if I can't convince them to open the door, that's when we shoot our way out the front."

Will put his hand on Sam's shoulder. "There's nothing to lose by trying."

"Reid, bring up the rear," Brandt said. "Everyone else, remember that you're prisoners."

Reid took his place and pointed the automatic at the ground. He still had the pistol in his holster plus a rifle slung across his torso. His arms felt strangely empty without Mia. He prayed Gordo wouldn't let anything happen to her.

Brandt rapped on the steel door three times and stepped back. After a moment, a hatch at head-height opened and a bleary-eyed man looked through.

"What," he said in a sleepy voice. "Who's there?"

"Sorry," Brandt said. "It's Matt Lehman with a prisoner evac."

"No one told me."

"No time," Brandt said. "We just got the order. Something about pirates trying to mount a rescue at the front doors."

The man paused, and Reid thought they were lost. Then the man blinked. "Okay. Try not to wake the morning shift."

"I'm putting my key in now," Brandt said.

"Ready . . . and . . . *turn,*" the man said.

The door opened and the group hustled through. As Reid came across the threshold last, the guard stepped toward him, scowling. Reid nodded like they knew each other, and the man's frown relaxed.

Sweat soaked Reid's shirt as he followed the men across a dark, cavernous kitchen. He didn't dare hope that they might actually make it. He kept waiting for an alarm to go off or a bullet to pierce his back. He chanced a look behind, and the man at the door already had his feet up and a hat covering his face, but that did little to dispel Reid's sense of having a target between his shoulder blades.

At the far side of the kitchen they stopped at a double door. Brandt put his finger to his lips, then pushed on one of the doors. Without looking back, he motioned for them to follow. Again, Reid was the last one through, and he made sure the door closed silently.

In this room there were about ten people asleep on cots. Reid wondered who they were and why they were there. Were they guards on break? Did they have guns tucked under the covers? Were they light sleepers, listening for anything out of the ordinary?

As their group inched through the room, Reid hoped no one would trip or sneeze, and prayed Mia would not choose this moment to wake.

At the far end of the room was another door. Brandt opened it, and relief flooded through Reid. He'd never been so happy to see the moon.

Brandt stood at the door, ushering each person out and sending them toward a dumpster.

Reid clasped Brandt's arm as he went by. "You did it."

"Don't thank me yet."

They regrouped behind the dumpster. Reid breathed a huge sigh of relief as he handed the guns to Will and took Mia from Gordo.

"Okay, hopefully the train is still on the other side of those buildings." Brandt pointed across an open parking lot. "Stick to the periphery. Let's roll."

Reid resumed his place in the middle, choosing his steps carefully on the uneven ground. His arms were already burning, but he wouldn't consider handing Mia to someone else again.

As they passed the halfway point, a couple holding hands came into view on the other side of the lot. The men froze, but it was too late.

"Who's there?" the young man called. "Identify yourselves."

"*Run,*" Brandt said.

Gordo turned, pointing his gun.

"No!" Reid yelled, but there was nothing he could do.

Three shots rang out.

Reid chanced a look back. One person was on the ground.

"Jenna!" the young man cried. "Oh God, Jenna."

"We'll be swarmed by Blades any second," Brandt said. "Get to the train."

Chapter 80

The Grand Hotel, Pascal's private suite

"Imagine, one day we'll have a whole fleet of cars." Pascal laced his fingers behind his head and stared at the ceiling, almost able to see the cars driving past one by one. Driving to the home of the missionaries. Salvation was near. He could feel it.

Ellianna snaked her arms around him.

"Where shall we go?" Pascal continued. "Vegas? Arizona? Mexico? When Linus is in charge, we can travel the world."

"I'd go anywhere with you."

He caressed the smooth skin of her back. Her fingers danced across his chest, dipping lower with each pass. He smiled. "Again already?"

The door banged open and Linus rushed in.

"Father! Father, I—"

Pascal sat up. "What is it? What's wrong?"

Ellianna clutched the covers to her chest.

"The prisoners escaped! I saw them behind the Tank. Brandt and five or more others. I tried to stop them, but they shot at me."

"Are you hurt?" Pascal demanded, springing from the bed and pulling on his slacks.

"I'm fine, but they killed Jenna! I sounded the alarm as fast as I could."

"Did they get away?"

"I don't know. Blades went after them and I came straight here."

"I'll get dressed." Ellianna gathered the sheet around her and closed herself in the bathroom.

"Father, I should never have disobeyed you. I should have gone to sleep, but I wanted to see Jenna. I didn't think anything bad would happen."

"You're certain it was Brandt?"

"Positive. And Mia, too."

Pascal tucked in his shirt and buckled his belt. "They couldn't have done it without help. It appears Brandt is not our only traitor."

"What about *her?*" Linus whispered, pointing to the bathroom.

Pascal frowned. "What about her?"

"She was at the Tank tonight. I saw her. I thought it was weird since you said she was going with you."

"She made an excuse to stay behind," Pascal said. "When I returned, she said she'd been waiting here the whole time."

"Then she lied. She helped them escape. The guards told me she talked to Brandt. She's the traitor."

Pascal shook his head, not wanting to believe it.

"Ask her, Father," Linus said as the bathroom door opened.

Ellianna came out in her red dress and gold shoes.

"Ellianna," Pascal said. "Did you visit someone at the Tank this evening?"

Her smile vanished. "Why I, uh . . . why would you ask that?" Her gaze shifted to Linus.

"Answer the question," Pascal said.

"Well yes, I went to see Brandt to—"

"See, she admits it!" Linus said.

"To try to get Brandt to see reason," Ellianna finished.

"You lied to me." Pascal wasn't asking.

"No, I . . . I'm sorry. I didn't mention it because I didn't think it mattered. Brandt wouldn't listen. My visit didn't do any good. You're right, I should have told you. I should always, even when it's inconsequential."

"*Inconsequential.*" Pascal walked to the bureau and put on his watch. His son was the bright spot in all of this. His son had seen the treachery, the deceit. His son was his true partner and confidant, not some lying whore. He turned and leaned against the dresser. Ellianna was trembling, one hand covering her mouth, the other wrapped around her ribs. *Good,* but fear wasn't enough. Not nearly enough.

"Linus, I want to teach you something," he said. "As a leader, it's important to know how to deal with different *types* of enemies. For example, a gut wound is what you want if you need someone to suffer. With a gut wound, if she doesn't die of the immediate injury, she'll almost always die later from infection. Don't aim for the gut as a rule, though. Too risky if the person is armed."

"Yes, father."

"Are you armed, Ellianna?"

"Pascal?" Ellianna's voice quavered.

"I didn't think so. Okay, Linus, pay attention. This is important." Pascal opened a drawer and pulled out the Ruger revolver that had belonged to his mother, the one he'd killed her with.

He heard a sharp intake of breath from Ellianna.

"The way to deal with traitors . . ." He shot Ellianna in the foot.

She screamed and fell to the ground. Her shoe was gone, and there was a lot of blood, though none spurting.

"For traitors," Pascal continued, raising his voice to be heard over Ellianna's screams. "You want to inflict pain, but not a mortal wound right away. This serves you two-fold. Revenge for the betrayal, plus it allows you to extract information. Because before they die, you need to find out the extent to which you've been betrayed."

"I didn't betray you! I swear it," Ellianna sobbed.

"For some, it takes more convincing than others." Pascal grabbed Ellianna's injured foot and she screamed. "I can apply pressure to staunch the flow of blood if I want to prolong her life. Or I can make it hurt worse. A lot worse." He pressed his thumb into the wound.

Ellianna shrieked and kicked.

Her pain and suffering meant nothing. She was no one to him now. He looked at Linus, and the boy seemed unaffected, too. Excellent. This was an important lesson, and emotional detachment was essential.

"Be careful not to inflict too much pain, though," he said, letting her foot drop. "If she passes out, she can't talk. Are you ready to talk, Elli?"

"Yes, yes."

"You lied to me."

"Yes. I'm sorry."

"You helped Brandt escape."

"No! I was trying to help you. I don't know anything about an escape. I swear."

Pascal shot Ellianna in the stomach. She went quiet. He thought he might feel some measure of loss, but he didn't. He had his son. That was all he needed.

"Is she dead?" Linus asked.

Linus was asking out of curiosity, not concern. The boy was truly a paragon. And now, with Ellianna and Maybelline gone, it would be just the two of them—father and son—conquering the world.

"It doesn't matter, son. I have no use for her anymore."

Chapter 81

Lost Angeles

Reid put every ounce of strength into getting Mia safely to the train. Finally, he saw it. He followed Brandt into the first car and collapsed onto a seat, hugging Mia to his chest.

"Let's go," Brandt shouted at the man he'd talked to earlier.

"I can't," the man said, holding his hands in the air. "I don't know how."

"Where's the driver?" Brandt demanded.

"Taking a leak. Over by that building."

"Find him," Will told his men.

Alfonse and Vlad went, guns pointed.

In the distance, a siren blared.

"Damn it, we don't have time for this," Brandt said. "We have to figure out how to work this thing. Reid, put Mia down and get over here."

"*Mia?*" the man said. "God, what have you done to her?"

"We're trying to *save* her." Reid laid Mia across the seats.

"The poor thing," the man said. "I thought she was such a nice girl. I didn't want to believe what I'd heard."

Reid scoured the instrument panel alongside Will and Brandt, but nothing was familiar.

"Try that button," the man said. "I think the driver presses it to make it start."

Reid scrutinized his face, trying to figure if they should trust him. Will pushed the button. The engine started.

"Men, get back here," Will shouted.

"What next?" Brandt asked. "How do we make it go?"

The man shrugged.

"*Think*," Brandt urged.

"I don't know," the man said. "I swear, I would tell you."

"Fine," Brandt said. "Get out of here."

The man jumped off the train as Will's men returned.

"Let him go," Reid shouted. "Don't shoot, let him go."

The men climbed aboard.

"We didn't find anyone," Vlad said. "If there was a driver, he's long gone."

"Somebody figure out how to work this thing." Brandt pushed and pulled the levers and knobs.

Shouts came from the parking lot. It sounded like dozens of people heading for them.

"Figure it out fast," Reid said.

A moment later the first shot rang out. Reid dove over Mia, shielding her.

Will's men took cover and returned fire through the glassless windows of the train, while Brandt kept at the controls.

Soldiers were everywhere, shooting, running for cover.

"Brandt, behind you!" Reid yelled.

Brandt turned and fired. There was a volley of return fire. At least one soldier fell.

"Cover me." Will handed his weapon to Reid and went to the controls. He stood stock-still at the panel while bullets flew by him.

Reid pointed the gun out of the train. A soldier ran toward him.

"Stop!" Reid called.

The soldier pointed his gun at Reid.

Reid froze, knowing he should shoot before he was shot at, but he couldn't. The gun felt foreign, evil in his hand, and he tossed it on the floor of the train and covered Mia with his body as the soldier fired, the shots so close Reid was sure he could feel them whizzing by.

Finally, the engine engaged and the train inched forward. The soldiers tried to jump aboard, and Brandt shot them, one by one, until the train gained enough speed the soldiers couldn't catch it.

"What was that about, Reid?" Will said, picking his gun up from the floor. "Jesus."

Reid turned away from the accusing glare and cradled Mia's head in his lap. He wouldn't, he *couldn't* take a life, even to save his own.

Chapter 82

The Grand Hotel, Pascal's private suite

Two soldiers stormed into the room, guns drawn. "We heard shots!"

"Took you long enough," Pascal said. "What if I'd been shot? Or my son?"

"Are you okay?"

"We're fine," Pascal said. "Ms. Ford, on the other hand . . ."

"Should we get medical?"

"No, she was involved in the escape. Have the fugitives been recaptured?"

"Not yet. Men are in pursuit."

"I'm going after them myself," Pascal said. "Have everyone assemble downstairs. I want current intel, and skates for me and my son. *Go.* We'll be there momentarily."

Linus turned to him, face aglow. "What are we waiting for?"

"I need to get socks." Pascal took a pair from the bureau. "And finish this." Pascal crossed to Ellianna and nudged her with his toe. She moaned and opened her eyes. "No one betrays me and lives. Not even you." He pointed the muzzle at her face and fired.

He turned to Linus. "She wouldn't have survived that gut wound, but I wanted my face to be the last thing she saw."

"I think the bitch got what she deserved."

Chapter 83

Newport Harbor, aboard the Belle Jewel

The sky showed only the first hint of morning. The chancellor's men weren't due for another hour, but Nikolai believed in being prepared.

Markoff lay sprawled on the deck in a mixed sea of pirates and guards.

"Wake up, friend." Nikolai nudged him with his boot.

"My head." Markoff rolled over, waving him off. "Go away. It's still dark, fool."

"Not for long." Nikolai poked him again. "What would the chancellor say if he found us in bed with our guards?"

Markoff opened one eye. "Eh, I guess you're right." He grunted as he hefted himself up.

"Let's get our men ready before we wake the others."

Markoff stretched and rubbed his face. "*Holy*——" He dropped to the deck, and Nikolai followed suit. "They're here already."

"Already?" Was their ruse blown? Had something given them away? "The men on the *Majestic*—will they be alert to this? Will they be ready?" Nikolai asked.

"They're competent, but not early risers. I'll send a swimmer to rouse them." Markoff shook a young pirate awake.

Nikolai crab-crawled to the rail and looked out. The parking lot was filling with the dark forms of heavily armed men. This didn't look like a prisoner exchange. It looked like a war.

They were losing the cover of darkness. He had to make a decision. His gut said if they continued their ruse, they'd be executed on the dock. But fighting it out looked like suicide too. There had to be another way. He couldn't leave his son to rot—or worse—in the Tank.

Markoff appeared beside him, remarkably stealthy for a man of his size, especially with what must be a brutal hangover. "We need to re-think our plan, old friend."

"I just reached that conclusion myself." Nikolai surveyed the men still asleep on the deck, and an idea coalesced. "How about a ruse of a different nature . . . ?"

Chapter 84

Lost Angeles

The train plowed forward as the sky grew lighter, and Reid tried to figure out how this journey could possibly come to a good end.

"Brandt." Reid motioned him closer. "I know Will wants his ship back," he said quietly. "But we don't have to go with him. It sounds like suicide."

Brandt shook his head. "If we can take the ship, we'll have a much better chance of getting out alive than if we go on foot, especially carrying Mia."

"What about my car?"

"No way," Brandt said. "Pascal will have a whole platoon guarding it, maybe more. We wouldn't be able to get near it."

That's what Reid feared. "But we don't know Will. How can you be sure about this?"

"I know Pascal. Trust me, the ship's our best chance. It may be slim, but it's the only chance we've got."

"Everyone, come here." Will motioned them to the front of the train.

Reid wasn't feeling reassured as their small group gathered. It seemed like there should be some other option. But if Brandt was committed to Will's plan, he and Mia had no choice but to go along. They'd never make it on their own. A slim chance was better than no chance at all.

"We'll be out-manned and out-gunned, but no one knows the *Belle* like we do. If we can get aboard, we can out-maneuver them."

"The question is, how do we get aboard?" Brandt asked. "They're expecting us."

"No, the question is *where*," Will said, leaning in. "Where will they be expecting us?"

"They know we're on the train," Brandt said. "Even though we'll get off before the station, they still know the general direction we're coming from."

"But they're expecting us on land." Will grinned. "We'll take the *Belle* where she's most vulnerable—from the water. That's our advantage."

"That could work," Brandt said. "Some soldiers will be on the ship, but the vast majority should be on the dock and surrounding area."

"Wait—" Reid tried to interject but they talked over him. Were they forgetting about Mia?

"Add in a diversion," Gordo said.

"Yeah, a diversion."

"Good idea."

"I think we have a fighting chance."

"Then we're agreed," Will said. "We board the *Belle* from the water."

"*Hold on,*" Reid said. "Mia's unconscious and I don't know how to swim."

"Trust me, Reid," Will said. "I've got this. I won't let you down."

Reid had no basis for trusting Will, but he also had no choice. He nodded.

"Good man," Will said. "Now, where should we get off the train?"

"Here is good," Brandt said. "Who knows how to stop this thing?"

Reid hoped Brandt wasn't wrong, because so far this plan wasn't inspiring any confidence.

Chapter 85

Newport Harbor

Pascal skidded to a stop at the end of the road. Linus stopped beside him, followed by a dozen Blades. Close to a hundred others were already assembled in the harbor parking lot.

"Get me my boots," Pascal bellowed. "Gather the platoon commanders so I can brief them. Who's got the latest intel? It's getting light, people. Snap to it."

"Sir." Minou skated forward. "The train will be here within minutes."

"Get to the station and position our men out of sight. Let the fugitives head for the dock. Follow, but don't let them see you. Only engage if they turn tail. We want them to think they can take the ship. Understood?"

"Yes sir." Minou skated toward the train station at top speed.

Pascal cinched his boots. "Listen up, commanders." Linus stepped forward with the others, standing tall and confident. Pascal was glad to see him take his place, but he couldn't help feeling some trepidation. This would be a real battle, not as simple as bringing in a thief or surveilling a doctor. "The escapees are going to try to take the *Belle,* and we want them to think it's possible. Our men must be out of sight to lure them into the open. Then we attack and obliterate. We've got five minutes, so look sharp. Delta commander, you've got the best sharpshooters?"

"Yes sir." A thin man saluted.

"Get your men on the roofs. Charlie commander, your men ready the *Vesuvius,* even though we shouldn't need her. Alpha and Bravo, you're on the ground floors, out of sight. Hold fire until I sound the attack. Go."

"Where do you want Echo, sir?" A burly, bearded commander

stepped forward.

"Cover the pirate ship," Pascal said. "Position your men as close as possible. When the shooting starts, if the pirates choose the wrong side, take care of them."

"Understood."

"What about Foxtrot?" Linus asked. His was the only platoon left.

"I need someone to alert our guards on the *Belle,*" Pascal said. "Who's your fastest?"

"Halsey." Linus pointed at a soldier, no hesitation.

"Good," Pascal said. "Halsey, warn our men that the escapees will to try to board. They should be ready, but out of sight. We want the ship to look easy to take."

Halsey saluted and zipped toward the *Belle,* wheels thudding across the splintered boards of the dock. Pascal had considered sending Linus to keep him out of harm's way, but decided it would be safer to keep him close.

"The rest of you," Pascal said to Linus and his men, "come with—"

An explosion rocked the ground.

Pascal dropped, pulling Linus down with him.

Windows shattered, spewing glass. Smoke and dust billowed into the sky.

"Report! Report!" Pascal shouted. "Linus, are you okay?" He looked his son over for injuries while trying to shield him in case there was a second blast.

"I'm fine," Linus said, pushing Pascal's arm aside. "Report! Someone tell the Chancellor what the hell's going on!"

"The train," someone called. "It was the train!"

Chapter 86

Newport Harbor

From the deck of the *Belle Jewel,* Nikolai watched the soldiers gathering and dispersing on the dock. Only one soldier headed toward the *Belle.* Nikolai straightened his "borrowed" uniform, hoping that there were so many soldiers, his unfamiliar face wouldn't be cause for alarm.

"Private Halsey with orders from the chancellor," the soldier called from the dock.

"Come aboard," Nikolai said.

Halsey stepped onto the deck and saluted, still in his skates. "Some prisoners escaped from the Tank and are coming for this ship. We want them to think they can take it, so all your men need to get out of sight."

Will. Nikolai was careful not to reveal his excitement.

An explosion threw them to the deck.

"Get below," Nikolai told the boy, knowing Markoff would strip him of his weapons and tie him up. He staggered to his feet as the ship bobbed violently.

Will, what are you doing? If it were me . . .

"Olexi," he called. "It's a diversion. Will's coming. Spread the word, make sure everyone knows—*don't shoot.* I'm going below to check a hunch."

Nikolai slid down the ladder, nearly colliding with Markoff at the bottom.

"What the hell was that explosion?" Markoff bellowed, rubbing his head.

"I'd bet ten barrels of cider it was my son, and that he and his men will be trying to board us. They'll think we're the enemy. Tell your men not to shoot."

Nikolai rushed to the tender garage and opened the door. A face gazed out of the shadows.

"Dad?"

"Slava bogu." Nikolai grabbed his son, and hugged him fiercely but quickly. "How many with you?"

"Seven, one unconscious."

"Have the injured stay below," Nikolai said. "Those able to help sail, come with me."

"I've never been so glad to see you in all my life," Will said.

"I know the feeling." Nikolai kissed the top of his head. "Now let's get out of here."

Chapter 87

Newport Harbor

"It's a diversion," Pascal yelled. "They're sailing! Get to the ship."
He grabbed Linus by the shirtsleeve and made for the *Vesuvius,*
shouting orders.

"Hoist the sails. Ready the guns."

The pirates had hoisted sails, too. It was all a sham. That had been
their plan all along.

Elli probably had nothing to do with the escape. No matter. It was
done.

He leapt onto his boat, Linus at his side.

"Go, go, go! Faster," he shouted as Blades streamed aboard and
the *Vesuvius* was freed from her dock lines. "Take positions. Get the
grenade launchers. Trim the sails."

They gained on the *Majestic,* but the *Belle Jewel* was faster, pulling
away.

A man brought the launchers and Linus took charge.

"Rodriguez, take starboard," Linus shouted. "Fields, you have port."

The boy had courage, confidence. Authority. Pascal's heart swelled.
His son wasn't just holding his own. He was a leader.

"I'll take point." Linus grabbed a launcher and ran forward.

They closed on the *Majestic.* The pirates were now in range. But,
Pascal realized, that meant the *Vesuvius* was also in range of the pirates'
guns.

"Linus, come back!"

Sheer, cold terror ran through Pascal's veins as a torrent of bullets
pocked the deck around Linus. Linus stood there, taking aim. No fear.
No sense of his own mortality.

"Get down!" Pascal dove, tackling him. The launcher flew as they
tumbled to the deck. Pascal held onto his son, protecting him from the

fusillade while blood sprayed and men fell around them.

Then it was quiet. Had it stopped? Pascal lay still, pressing Linus to his chest. Thank God, at least his son was safe. But why was it so quiet? Why weren't his men shooting? Was it over?

He boosted himself up on one elbow. The sails were luffing. The ship was adrift. Broken, bleeding men littered the deck. Gaping mouths and eyes. The ringing in Pascal's ears faded and sounds came into focus. The men who could were crying out.

It was over. The enemy ships were already receding into the distance.

Pascal's body still buzzed with adrenaline, but he wasn't hurt. He'd been able to react quickly. It was a miracle he and Linus were spared.

"Son, get up. It's over."

He looked down and realized they were covered in blood.

"Oh my God, *Linus!* Open your eyes! Oh God, oh God." *So much blood.* "Medic!"

The color was fading from Linus's face.

God, no! Not his son. He should not have brought his son.

"No, no, no, this can't be happening. *Medic!* My son's been hit. Medic!"

No one was coming. They were all dead or wounded.

He cradled Linus and rocked him, looking down at his angelic face. Still a boy. Not a man after all.

"I will get revenge, son. I swear it."

Chapter 88

Newport Harbor, aboard the Belle Jewel

"Report," Nikolai shouted.

"They're foundering," the watch called from the crow's nest. "They've stopped the chase—it's over!"

A cheer broke out.

"Good job, men." Will smiled broadly.

Nikolai smiled too, but there was a weight in his stomach that would remain until Tatiana was safe. He walked to the rail and sensed Will trailing in his wake, as his son had so often done as a child.

They stood side by side at the rail looking west. Always west.

"I appreciate you coming for me, Dad."

"You saved yourself."

"In part, but you had the *Belle* ready to sail, saving time and countless lives. Thank you." Will turned to him, extending his hand.

Nikolai embraced him. *"Moy zolotoy mal'ch'ik." My golden boy.*

"How much bloodshed was there before I arrived?" Will asked.

"None."

"How'd you manage that?"

"Cider. When the guards passed out, we tied them up. There's a dozen in the hold."

"What are we going to do with them?"

"They'll probably be given the choice to join the pirates or return home. Markoff will figure it out when we get to Catalina."

"Catalina? No, we have to go to San Clemente. Tatiana—"

"Kennedy went with a contingent of northern pirates to rescue her."

"Then let's go help them. What are we waiting for?"

Nikolai ached to do that, but yesterday it had been a sound decision to keep the two parties separate, and it still was. "The plan is to rendezvous on Catalina. Kennedy may already have rescued your sister. They could be on their way to Catalina right now."

"If they're not there when we get there, I'm turning around and heading for San Clemente to get Tatiana. This whole mess happened on my watch. It's my responsibility to make sure she comes home."

Nikolai looked at his son—the lined forehead, the erect posture, the expression of determination. After a moment, he nodded his agreement.

At some point, Will had become a man.

Chapter 89

Aboard the Belle Jewel

Reid tended Mia as best he could in the makeshift infirmary. His stomach turned flips from the motion of the ship, and from the memory of all the men who'd been killed during their escape. He couldn't think about Tinker, or the car, or his failed mission. He couldn't think about his grandmother or Kayla.

He focused on Mia, dabbing her ashen forehead with a cool cloth, talking to her softly about everything and nothing. Her pulse was steady, her breathing regular. There was no external wound, but he was sure she had a concussion. Twice he'd seen her eyes flutter beneath the lids like she was dreaming. Dreaming would be a good sign.

"It's going to be okay," he whispered in her ear. She had to be okay. Nothing else was.

"Mia, it's time to wake up." He held her hand. "Come on, Mia. Squeeze my hand."

There was no response, but he kept talking, trying to stay positive, trying to keep his mind from wandering anywhere else.

"You'll wake up when you're ready, and when you do, I want to know everything about you. Who your parents were. If you grew up in Lost Angeles. What books you like. We'll take walks under the stars, and you'll tell me everything."

He squeezed her hand again, and it could have been his imagination, but he thought he felt the slightest hint of a response. He smiled and kept talking.

"That's right, Mia. Come back to me. I know you can do it." She had to come back, she had to be okay. There's been too much loss already. He couldn't lose her, too.

Chapter 90

Newport Harbor

Twenty years of work. All his hopes and dreams. All his plans. In his mind's eye, Pascal watched a vast inferno burn it down until there was nothing left. None of it mattered anymore. Without Linus, nothing mattered.

"It's time, sir," Minou said.

Pascal hated her reticence, the sympathy in her voice. No, not *hated.* His feelings weren't that strong. His emotions, his thoughts, his very being was muted. Every iota of his existence had been deadened by the loss of his son.

"Sir?" Minou, louder now.

He closed his eyes, blotting out her presence, wishing her gone, wishing to turn back time for a day. Just a day.

Pascal felt the touch of a hand on his, and he jerked away. "No!" He opened his eyes and met Minou's pitying stare.

"Sir, you have to let us take him now."

"Don't tell me what I have to do." He gripped his little boy's hand, already growing cool to the touch. He turned his glare from Minou to Linus. A sleeping child. Anything else was unfathomable.

After a time, Minou addressed him again. "I understand, sir. Take all the time you need. All the other . . . all the others have been prepared for transport. When you're ready we'll take . . . Let me know when you're ready."

The kindness in her voice made him want to rip her throat out. His muscles hummed and twitched beneath his skin, and he thought his body might leap up and strangle her of its own accord. He kept his gaze on Linus until eventually Minou left.

Even then he stayed, looking at his son. He would not let go of his little boy, of this moment. He could not turn back time, but neither did he have to let it progress.

Chapter 91

Pacific Ocean

Nikolai stood in the bow of the *Belle* as they sailed west toward Catalina. He felt the familiar pull of the islands beyond, and realized he'd soon be too old to make the trip alone.

He didn't really want to go alone.

Had it been so long since Jess stood with him at the rail?

"We'll go someday," she'd always said with a wistful smile.

Picturing Jess at the rail brought Tatiana to mind. Mother and daughter, as similar as two drops of water. From their charmingly crooked teeth to their maddening stubbornness. That obstinacy is what got Tatiana into this fix. He prayed Kennedy would be able to rescue her from San Clemente and bring her to Catalina. Maybe they were already there.

He was reluctant to admit it, but Kennedy actually seemed to be a decent man. Perhaps not completely unlike someone he would choose for his daughter.

Approaching the rocky shore of Avalon Harbor, Nikolai scanned for Kennedy's yacht among the silhouettes of the boats, but the *Emancipation* wasn't there.

He felt as old and weathered as the round Casino building—forever the focal point of the harbor—whose iconic red roof had gone missing since his last visit. He let out a long, silent sigh and wiped the melancholy from his face. The *Emancipation* would arrive soon. Neither Tatiana's personality nor Kennedy's would have it any other way.

After checking the crew at the lines and the helm, Nikolai returned to the bow to wave at their welcoming committee—a lone round figure in bright orange.

"You're back!" Cook's voice carried from the pier.

She waited restlessly while the ship eased into dock, alternately clapping and wringing her hands until Olexi leapt onto the pier and planted a kiss on her shiny pink lips.

"Oh *my*." She fanned herself with her hand. "You scamp. You devil." She grabbed him by the shirt and kissed him again.

"That's a sight," Will said, stepping off the ship.

"Will, Will! My little William!" Finola crowed. She pulled him into a smothering hug. "You stupid, *stupid* boy. How could you sail off with your sister like that? You worry us half to death." She rocked him back and forth like she had when he was an infant.

"I'm sorry," Will said.

She boxed his ear. "Sorry? You'll know sorry if your sister doesn't come back safely."

Will glanced at Nikolai, pleading to go after Tatiana.

Nikolai was torn but shook his head. "We give Kennedy until morning. Meanwhile, the *Belle* needs tending. You should enlist Friday's help."

"Friday?"

"Only the best shipwright in the known world," Finola said. "I'll take you to him."

"You coming, Dad?"

"After I check on our passengers. The girl's in bad shape, but that young man seems to know what he's doing."

"His name's Reid," Will said. "He's some kind of doctor."

"Good," Nikolai said. "I'll see if he needs anything."

"Don't be long. I'll need your eye if I'm going to have the *Belle* ready to sail at first light." Will had that look of determination he'd developed as a toddler, but he'd added an air of authority. Of a captain.

Nikolai turned to Olexi. "Join me below?"

The hatch to the makeshift infirmary was open, but one look at the lovesick boy at the bedside told Nikolai they were intruding on a private moment, so he knocked on the open door.

"Excuse us," Nikolai said. "We've come to see how you and your patient are faring. Do you need anything? Bandages? Water? Food?"

Reid grimaced at the mention of food, and Nikolai recognized the look of someone unaccustomed to sea travel.

"We're fine," Reid said. "You've been very kind."

"What's your patient's prognosis?" Nikolai asked.

"Hopeful. She's in a coma, but showing signs of increased brain activity."

"I was wondering," Olexi said. "Would you be willing to take a look at the other injured? Mostly minor on this boat, but on the *Majestic*, there's at least one gunshot and a broken arm."

"Of course," Reid said. "I lost my med kit, so I need to gather some things." He pulled an empty drawer from the nightstand and loaded it with scissors, gauze and bandages.

"What else do you need?" Olexi asked.

"A scalpel or sharp knife, needle and thread, sheets and towels. Antiseptic like peroxide, or hard liquor will work. I'll know better once I see the injuries."

Nikolai was impressed. The kid seemed to know his stuff.

"I'll come with you." Olexi took the drawer and went into the hall.

"Captain, would you stay with Mia while I'm gone?" Reid asked.

"Of course, but I have only the most rudimentary medical skills."

"If she wakes, she may be confused or frightened, so do your best to calm her and send for me. If it sounds like she's struggling to breathe or anything like that, send for me right away." Reid kissed Mia's cheek.

"That I can do," Nikolai assured him.

The boy gave a half-smile and left with Olexi.

Nikolai settled in to keep watch, more accustomed now to having nothing to do, but still not comfortable with it. He stared at the young woman, thinking her beauty was the sort ballads were written for. Dark tresses fanned out on the pillow. Perfect lips, arched brows. Warm mocha skin unlined by age or worry. Like the fabled Sleeping Beauty.

His thoughts wandered to another time he'd sat vigil at a sick bed. Tatiana had been delirious with fever, moaning and thrashing and crying out for her dead mother. Days later, when the fever subsided, the doctor had said there was likely brain damage and she might not wake up.

All anyone could do was wait and pray.

But Nikolai wasn't any good at either, so instead he'd held Tatiana's hand and told stories. Fantastical adventures of knights in shining armor, Hawaiian princesses, mermaids—anything that might entice her back. Eventually, Tatiana had opened her eyes. She had a wicked headache, but had retained her equally wicked wit.

Nikolai took Mia's hand and held it gently. Her parents weren't here to call her back to the living, so he would stand in. "Once upon a time, there was a princess of uncommon beauty, unmatched charm, and rapier wit named Mia. She was beloved by all the kingdom, except for a jealous witch who cast a spell upon her to sleep like the dead for a hundred years. . . ."

Chapter 92

Catalina Island

Despite his name, "Ray the Ruthless" was a shy twelve-year-old. His mom held his hand while Reid cleaned a gash on his leg.

"Rinse it with antiseptic once a day," Reid said. "Then put on a fresh bandage. Do your best to keep it dry, okay?"

Ray grinned, exposing missing front teeth.

"I'm guessing Ray doesn't eat a lot of fruits or vegetables," Reid said to his mother.

"No, doesn't like it much. Seaweed neither."

"Do you like rat?" Reid asked Ray. Ray nodded. "If you bring me one, I'll show you a special part to eat that will keep your teeth from falling out."

"Bless you, Doctor," the mom said. "How can we repay you?"

"I have everything I need, and then some," Reid said. "Just come by later with the rat."

Grateful pirates had been stopping by with gifts all morning—a leather satchel for his supplies, a clean shirt, some delicious fish cakes. Judging by the sun, he'd been working more than four hours. The battle injuries had taken only half that, but the pirates had been cut off from medical support in Lost Angeles and were eager to see a "doc" while they could.

Reid was tucking the remaining supplies in his new bag when Olexi returned.

"How's Mia?"

"The same," Olexi said. "Cook's with her, and I guarantee, there's no safer place than under her watchful eye. Nikolai would like you to join him for a bite to eat."

"Sure, but I want to check on Mia first."

"They're holding lunch for you," Olexi said. "Tell you what. I'll sit with Cook and Mia, and come get you right away if there's any change."

Reid nodded. Olexi wasn't taking "no" for an answer. He hopped off the dock and hurried down the beach to the squat restaurant Olexi indicated.

The restaurant windows no longer had glass, and sand covered the floor. A dozen picnic tables were scattered about. Only one was occupied.

"Glad you're joining us," Nikolai called from the head of the table.

Brandt and Will were seated across from a man and a woman Reid didn't recognize. Will scooted over and Reid slid in beside him.

Reid estimated the woman was on the plus side of fifty, though her hair was jet black and her only wrinkles were at the outer corners of her almond eyes. The graying man next to her looked about the same age but hadn't weathered as well.

"Penny, he's here," the women bellowed over her shoulder.

"Coming," a voice with an odd accent answered from the back of the restaurant.

"You had a busy morning, Doc," the woman said.

"Olexi told me there was a line for your services," Nikolai said.

"Glad to help." Reid picked up his glass, careful to smell the liquid before he drank.

"You're a hero to my people," the woman said.

"Bloody Mary calls things by their names," Nikolai told Reid.

"If that means I don't beat around the bush, you're right," the woman said. "But you can drop the 'Bloody.'"

"Mary runs Avalon," Will explained.

"The whole of Catalina Island, if anyone's keeping track." Mary winked. "It's a fine place to live. Good weather most of the time. Good fishing. Good people. But we don't have a doctor. If you take the job, we'll treat you like royalty."

"I'm flattered," Reid said, not sure how to decline without offending his host.

A plate was placed in front of him, providing a momentary reprieve. "Thank you," he said, looking up. He tried not to appear startled by the toothless face grinning back at him.

"The rest of us are hungry too, Penny," the man said.

"You'll get yours soon enough, Dread." Penny's lack of teeth explained the odd accent. "I can't help if Doc's my favorite."

Reid was surprised to see on his plate a whole fish on leafy stuff greener than anything that ever came out of a can. "Is this *grown food?*"

He poked it with his fork.

"Seaweed? I suppose so." Penny made a face. "Never eat it myself."

"It's not grown food like you're looking for," Brandt said. "It grows in the ocean, but it won't grow anywhere else. Try it—it's not bad."

Reid forked a bit of the ribbony material into his mouth, slurping in the trailing part he couldn't bite off. It was the chewiest thing he'd ever eaten. Salty and bitter, but good. He was unsure how to go about eating the fish though, and poked at the skin with his fork.

"Hang on," Mary said. "We did the meal up real classy to impress you, but there's bones in there. Please, allow me." She reached over and pulled the head of the fish away, extracting the skeleton and leaving the meat behind in one swift motion.

Reid placed a small portion of meat in his mouth. It was tender and practically melted on his tongue. He devoured half the fish before Penny brought Dread's plate.

"I guess you like it," Mary said. "Or you were really hungry."

"Both," Reid said with his mouth full.

"If you're our doctor, we'll supply all the fish you can eat. You tell your girl that neither of you will ever have to go fishing. You'll live in our finest house, too. Want to see it?"

"Mary, let him catch his breath," Nikolai said.

"What am I saying? Your girl will want to see it, too," Mary continued. "Why don't you go get her? We'll feed her some lunch then show you both the house."

"I'm afraid she was injured in Lost Angeles," Nikolai said. "She's unconscious."

Mary frowned. "I hope she'll be all right."

"I hope so, too." Reid wiped his mouth and placed his napkin on the table. "I need to go check on her, so if you'll excuse me . . ." He stood.

"Of course," Mary said. "Please consider my offer."

"Thank you for lunch." Reid grabbed his satchel, nodding goodbyes to Brandt and the others. He heard them continue their conversation as he hastened for the dock.

"What about you, Brandt?" Mary asked. "You think you might stay on Catalina?"

"Thanks, but I have other plans," Brandt said.

Reid briefly wondered what Brandt's plans were, but that could wait. With each minute that passed, he grew more anxious about Mia. He broke into a jog.

Chapter 93

Lost Angeles

Pascal sat in the chair in Linus's bedroom trying to recall memories of his son, but thoughts of Brandt kept intruding.

It was all Brandt's fault. Linus's death. Ellianna's death. The death of his dream. It was Brandt who had put the events into motion, Brandt who was ultimately responsible.

You promised revenge. You swore it as I took my last breath. You swore.

Pascal heard his son's voice as surely as if the boy were speaking, and the message was clear. He had to find Brandt and kill him.

No, not kill him. Brandt should know a loss so deep, so final, his world would never be the same. The lie he'd told Brandt—that Justine and the baby were dead—wasn't enough.

Brandt should watch them die.

Pascal would make sure Brandt sat by helplessly while his future bled out in front of him.

He took Linus's hand, pretending it was not cold. "We will have our revenge, son. I will find Justine and make Brandt watch as I cut the baby out of her. I promise."

Chapter 94

Catalina Island

"Lunch was delicious, Mary," Nikolai said, pushing away his plate. "I hope it impressed that doctor. Think it was fancy enough?"

"Plenty fancy." Dread punctuated his comment with a belch into his fist.

"It was very nice." Nikolai wiped his beard with his napkin.

"I hope it wasn't *too* fancy." Mary scowled. "I think I'll do something else for him. Maybe find him a nice raincoat."

"Mind if I tag along? I need new shoes," Will said.

Mary tossed her napkin on the table. "Sure. What about you boys? Need anything?"

Nikolai looked at the splitting seams of his deck shoes and decided new ones weren't worth what Mary would charge. "No, I'm good."

"You're coming, Dread." Mary tugged on the man's tank top and he stood. "How about you, Brandt?"

Brandt shook his head.

"See you on the *Belle*," Will said as they left.

"Mind if I walk back with you?" Brandt asked Nikolai.

The sun was warm and the breeze cool as they strolled up the beach. They were almost to the pier before Brandt said what was on his mind.

"I was wondering what your plan is for leaving."

"We depart at first light tomorrow," Nikolai said.

"Heading south?"

"That depends on my daughter." Nikolai looked out at the harbor, wishing with all his being that the *Emancipation* would sail into view. "If she's not back, we'll sail to San Clemente. Eventually, we'll head north to San Francisco."

"I'd like to come with you to San Francisco," Brandt said. "But I don't have anything to trade."

"There's no cause for trade. I'm in your debt for helping Will. You and your friends are my guests for as long as you like."

A bell rang from the watch point at the mouth of the harbor, sounding the alert that a ship had been spotted. Nikolai's soul leapt to his throat. He dashed down the pier, dodging men scurrying to their posts.

When he was in range, he cupped his hands and called to the crow's nest of the *Belle*. "What ship?" He prayed to all the gods to allow it to be Kennedy returning with his daughter on board, alive and well.

"The *Emancipation!*"

"What's she flying?" Nikolai held his breath while the watch checked the flag through binoculars.

"*Charlie*. She's flying *Charlie*."

Nikolai let out a whoop.

Before the *Emancipation* had even tied up to the dock, Tatiana leapt into Nikolai's arms.

"*Moy m'ily mal'yish*. My sweet, sweet, girl." He squeezed her, then held her at arm's length. "Are you hurt? Did they cut you?" He hugged her again.

"I'm fine. They didn't catch me." Tatiana's eyes held enough sadness to fill the ocean. "But I was wrong about the seeds. I risked everything for nothing."

"It's over now. You're okay, Will's okay. That's all that matters."

"I'm *so* sorry, Dad. I'll never do anything like that again."

"You'd better not," Kennedy said, joining them on the dock.

"Captain." Nikolai extended his hand. When Kennedy took it, Nikolai clasped his hand tightly between both palms. "I will never be able to adequately thank you for bringing her back."

"No thanks are necessary, sir," Kennedy said. "I love your daughter. I should have been upfront about our relationship from the beginning, and I intend to make up for that mistake."

"No need. All is forgiven. You are family now."

"Whoa, what planet did I come back to?" Tatiana said.

"Tatiana," Will shouted, running down the pier like his hair was on fire. "Thank God." He wrapped his arms around her.

"What's going on here? Have aliens taken over both you and Dad?"

"It's my fault. I could have gotten you killed." Will's voice brimmed with emotion.

"That's BS!" Tatiana said. "I *made* you take me there. What's gotten into everyone?"

"If something had happened to you, I never would have forgiven myself."

"Jesus, Will. Go have a couple ciders and maybe I'll recognize you again." Tatiana shoved him. "And Dad? It's kinda freaking me out that you don't hate my boyfriend."

Kennedy laughed and put his arm around Tatiana's waist. "I'd better take you to see Cook if I want to live to fight another day."

"Maybe take her to see the medic, too," Nikolai suggested. "He could check her over."

"*No thanks*," Tatiana said, letting Kennedy steer her toward the *Belle*. "There's nothing wrong with me a little swamp tea won't cure."

"You actually drink that stuff?" Will said.

"Voluntarily," Kennedy said, making a face over his shoulder.

Nikolai's heart was full watching his daughter walk away, safe and happy, with a man who perhaps was almost good enough for her. And his son— "William, I'm proud of you."

"How can you say that after what I've done?"

"What you've done? I came to rescue a foolish, impulsive boy, but found a man who'd already rescued himself. Everyone makes mistakes, but not everyone learns from them."

"I won't make a mistake like that again."

"Not exactly like that, no. But there will be plenty more mistakes. I wouldn't want it otherwise."

"I never knew you were so smart."

Nikolai laughed. "I remember the day I discovered that my father wasn't an idiot." He grinned thinking how much Will resembled the old man. Everything came full circle eventually. If you lived long enough. "All right, I need to go find Markoff. You coming?"

"I need to check over the *Belle* one more time, make sure I didn't miss anything."

"See? You've become a man. My job is done." Nikolai ruffled Will's hair like he had when he was a child.

Nikolai went in search of Markoff, expecting to find him snoring off a hangover. Instead, he was upright, clean-shaven, and smelled like he'd bathed in cologne.

"My friend," Markoff boomed. "I understand a celebration is in order."

"News travels fast."

"As do the southern pirates. If we're to toast your daughter's return, we best do it now. I'll wager we do battle with those southern scoundrels before my beard grows a shadow."

"That soon?"

"I'm sure they were mighty pissed off."

"Then we'd better make ready for battle or get the hell out of here. Have you given any thought to coming north? Kennedy gave you Alcatraz free and clear. You'd be the only pirates around, and right at the source of the cider."

"Getting out of these muddy waters and starting over—especially where there's plenty of cider—does have appeal. But running from a fight is not the pirate way."

Nikolai raised his eyebrows.

"Well, sometimes it is," Markoff amended. "But not this time."

They strolled to the starboard rail and surveyed Avalon Harbor.

"My friend, a question." Nikolai chose his words carefully. "If you plan to come to Alcatraz, what is the wisdom in risking lives to hold a piece of land you no longer need? We could sail north together, strength in numbers."

Markoff sighed. "I may be captain of my ship and commander of the fleet, but I'm not in charge of shit on dry land. I could leave with the ships and enough men to sail them, but Mary won't go, and twice as many souls are loyal to her than to me. If I left, they'd be unprotected."

"Mary's an intelligent woman. Convince her."

"That's my plan, but even for a man of my extraordinary talents, there's simply not enough time for the parlay and sexual favors it'll take to convince Mary to leave her island."

Nikolai noted the sheepish look on Markoff's face. "Mary's your woman?"

"That she is, and a damn fine one, too. Sweet as your Cook's apple strudel, voracious as a tiger shark in the bunk, and a helluva lot smarter than you or me." Markoff shook his head. "But I've never known a human being—man, woman or child—as stubborn. It'll take more than one afternoon and a barrel of cider to convince her to leave her island."

"I know a little about stubborn women," Nikolai said. "I'll ready my men for battle."

Markoff grabbed his arm. "Don't misunderstand me, old friend. Your offer is generous and much appreciated, but if the southerners see your ships, it won't be a fight, it'll be a *war*. When pirates fight pirates, there's a whole lotta cussing and spitting and farting and hurling of insults, but little bloodshed. We'll see some fistfights and bullets fired in the air, and if anyone gets captured, it might not be pretty, but usually nobody dies. With you here, everything becomes a bit too real."

"Understood," Nikolai said. "My apologies. I'd assumed things had changed since I was last in your waters, what with the southern pirates aligning with Pascal, and their strange new cutting practices."

"Believe me, if the day comes when the southern pirates are our true enemy, it will be ugly. And I'm concerned things may be headed in that direction. But until I know differently, pirates will be pirates and fight like brothers."

"Then I'm glad to leave you to it," Nikolai said. "And I'll hope to see you up in San Francisco Bay waters."

"You're sure there's plenty of cider to go around?"

"Before my wife died—" Nikolai paused, realizing how odd it was he still thought of Jess as his wife. "She planted orchards upon orchards of apple trees across Marin County. They're harvesting well now, enough to make cider for everyone." *Hopefully.* If all the pirates imbibed like their captain, Creighton might not be able to keep up with demand.

"And you're sure all we gotta do is fish?"

"That's the usual arrangement. The brewmaster despises fishing."

"Then I say we have an accord, Captain."

Chapter 95

Catalina Island, aboard the Belle

"Squeeze my hand, Mia." There was still no response, but Reid tried not to let that discourage him. There were plenty of good signs. Her breathing was stronger, he could elicit pain and reflex responses, and she continued showing signs of dreaming. It was only a matter of time before she showed intentional action.

He didn't want to consider the possibility of permanent brain damage, but the thought persisted no matter how staunchly he tried to ignore it.

"Can I come in?" Brandt poked his head in the door.

"I was wondering when you'd stop by."

"I didn't want to intrude," Brandt said. "How is she? Has she woken up?"

"Not yet, but she's showing signs."

"That's good." Brandt stared at Mia. "Nikolai's daughter is back."

"That's terrific. He must be so relieved."

"You should've seen the expression on his face. He didn't look like the same person."

"I bet."

"They're leaving on the Belle for San Francisco soon, and we're welcome to go. I didn't know what you wanted to do, if maybe you were thinking about staying here."

"I haven't thought about anything except Mia." Reid cringed realizing how long it had been since he'd thought of Kayla or home. "What are *you* going to do?"

"Get as far from Lost Angeles as I can."

"What do you think, Mia?" Reid asked. "Does San Francisco sound okay?"

"She can hear us?"

"I believe she can. You should talk to her."

Brandt shook his head. "I, I can't. I feel too guilty. I wouldn't even know where to start."

"Why should you feel guilty? It's my fault this happened. If I'd listened to you from the beginning . . ." *Justine would still be alive.*

"You don't understand . . . I'm the one who did this to her."

"What?"

"I didn't mean to knock her out."

"That woman in the Tank—"

"She was telling the truth." Tears rolled down Brandt's face. "I didn't want to hurt Mia. I was just trying to buy time to get out of there."

Reid bit back the venomous words that filled his throat. He wanted to rail at Brandt for being so selfish, so cowardly, for hurting Mia to save his own skin. But the man was already broken.

"You got her out of there alive," Reid said. "You got us all out."

Chapter 96

Lost Angeles

Pascal hadn't eaten, hadn't showered, hadn't left Linus's room. He'd have no peace until Justine was found, and no one else would, either. Every Blade, every clerk, every available body was searching for her, fanning out and going through every house starting from where they'd found the vehicle. He'd left Gomez in charge of the command post with strict orders for the search to continue around the clock.

There had been some grumbling about burying the dead. But the dead were already dead. What did they care?

The dead.

Linus.

No. His son was sleeping.

A little while ago, Linus had asked for a brandy and they'd discussed the strategy for the search. His son was fine. A little more tired than usual, but otherwise fine.

Pascal turned his thoughts back to Brandt. It was important to keep his focus there.

He imagined his revenge, the images feeding his rage. Fueling it. Stoking the flames until it burned so hot, it kept away the black tendrils of emotion that threatened to twine around him and pull him into the depths.

This was all Brandt's fault. All that mattered now was making Brandt pay.

The door flung open and Gomez burst in, minus his usual decorum and sweater vest.

"We found her. We found Brandt's girl. She's in bad shape, but she's alive. They're taking her to the hospital now."

"Finally! Did you hear that, Linus? Soon, revenge will be ours. What are we waiting for? Let's go to the hospital."

"Is, uh, is Linus coming, too, sir?" Gomez asked.

"What's wrong with you? Of course he's coming. Where would I be without my right-hand man?" Gomez was usually sharp as a tack. Pascal wondered if he should be concerned that the man was slipping.

Despite Gomez's uncharacteristic mental deficiency, he'd managed to rally the troops and move the command post to the hospital in record time. Even so, Pascal was still annoyed. Gomez had asked him twice more about Linus, followed by three different nurses asking to take Linus to his own room.

What was wrong with everyone? Linus was staying right by his side in the command post where he belonged. Pascal had finally obtained a bed for the boy so he could rest, but he'd practically had to threaten a nurse with beheading to get her to bring it.

Linus was his right-hand man. A brilliant strategist. A wise counselor. He was needed for brainstorming and advice. Moving him elsewhere would be inefficient. It was out of the question. The next person to suggest it *would* be beheaded.

Pascal paced beside the bed, talking through his plans with Linus.

"Sir?" Gomez interrupted.

"Leave us alone. We're working. Whatever it is, handle it yourself."

Gomez slunk away, but Pascal's focus would not return. He kept glancing over at Gomez. Mousy Gomez, soft and weak in his sweater and bookish glasses. That dotard had no place running his empire. The empire he built for Linus. The world had never borne a more natural leader than Linus, one with such innate charisma and intellect. With Pascal's tutelage and guidance, there was no limit to his success. There was no one with a greater destiny.

Pascal paced faster, losing himself in his thoughts. He pulled them around himself like the blankets that shrouded Linus, and the sounds and smells of the hospital faded away.

"Sir?"

Pascal looked up to see Gomez. "It had better be important," he growled.

"A report from the pirates, sir. The southern fleet is in the harbor. They were attacked by the northern pirates at their home base on San Clemente."

"By the same pirates who attacked us?"

"No, a separate contingent. The attacks appear to have been orchestrated to occur simultaneously. Now the southern pirates want to retaliate and attack the northern base on Catalina, but they've suffered casualties and are outnumbered. They're awaiting your orders."

Brandt escaped on one of those ships.

"I want him captured alive!"

"Who, sir?"

"*Brandt.* Send everyone to Catalina, every boat that's seaworthy. Arm them to the teeth. Put Minou in command. Have her bring Brandt to me. Alive. And that outsider, too. They're going to pay."

"Yes sir." Gomez pivoted on his heel.

"Wait! Are there any northern pirates in the Tank?"

"I'll find out, sir," Gomez said.

"If there are, send them with Minou. Maybe she can trade for Brandt. Go on, get moving."

Gomez exited and Pascal felt like he could breathe again.

"This is better, eh Linus? Yes, this is good. Now we wait for news. News of Justine and news of Brandt." He drummed his fingers together. "Ah, here's a lesson for you, son: do not listen to those who say waiting is the hardest part. Those are the words of the weak and powerless. What most men call *waiting* is a prime opportunity for planning. We won't *wait* while the doctors patch up Justine and the soldiers fetch Brandt. Instead, we'll use the time to our advantage. To plan their reunion."

Chapter 97

Pacific Ocean, aboard the Belle

Nikolai stretched out his legs and propped up his feet in the cockpit. It was his favorite time to sit the watch, when all was quiet except for the lapping of the sea against the hull, and the stars were his only company.

Getting underway had gone smoothly. Nikolai had placed Will in command of the *Belle,* and Will handled the job so efficiently, there had been little for Nikolai to do. Rather than feeling at loose ends, though, Nikolai found it satisfying. Enjoyable, even.

Their plan had been to take a short sail up the island to a protected cove to loosen out the kinks. They'd spend the night tucked out of sight in case the southern pirates arrived, then begin the long voyage in the morning. But the *Belle* and the *Emancipation* had sailed in concert like they'd been doing it for years, and the sky was so clear even Finola could have navigated, so Will saw no need to stop at the cove. Kennedy agreed, so they'd continued sailing north into the night.

Nikolai always preferred sailing after dark when the sea was deep and the stars were close. This night was particularly sweet. He was content to be back at sea on the *Belle* with his family. No more Democracy, no more bureaucrats. He looked forward to never seeing another manifest again. He was happier than he'd been in years.

"Sir?"

It was Will's friend, Gordo. Nikolai had known him since he was a pudgy toddler. "Is it that time already?"

"Yes sir."

"Then the watch is yours." Nikolai stretched and headed belowdecks.

Though it was late, he wasn't sleepy. Normally he'd pop in for a snack and conversation with Finola, but she'd be with Olexi now. Will's cabin was shut, but the infirmary door was ajar and a light was on. Maybe the medic could use a break or some company.

He poked his head in and saw Reid sitting by the girl's bedside. Nikolai listened for a moment as the young man read aloud. He'd just decided to leave without interrupting when Reid looked up.

"I didn't mean to disturb you," Nikolai said.

"Not at all," Reid said, standing. "What can I do for you?"

"I thought perhaps I could do something for you. I wouldn't mind sitting with her so you can get some rack time. I don't think I could sleep anyway."

"I don't like to leave her, but I will visit the latrine while you're here, if you don't mind."

It took Nikolai a moment to realize what he meant. "Oh, the *head*. Sure, go on."

After Reid stepped out, Nikolai sat and picked up the book.

"*The Secret Garden*. Let's see where you left off." He opened the book to the marker and cleared his throat. "'There was a bright fire on the hearth when she entered his room, and in the daylight she saw it was a very beautiful room indeed. There were rich colors in the rugs and hangings and pictures and books on the walls which made it look glowing and comfortable even in spite of the gray sky and falling rain.'"

When Nikolai reached the end of the chapter, he found Reid sitting on the floor with his head resting against the cabinet, sound asleep. Nikolai was struck by how different he looked without the heavy responsibility he wore when awake.

It reminded him of Will after Jess died. All day, the little boy had carried the burden of grief until he cried himself out at night and slept. Only then did he look like the child Nikolai knew. It had been harder for Tatiana. She'd lain in bed for hours while Nikolai read aloud, her arms wrapped around an old rag doll even though she was almost a teenager. After she fell asleep, Nikolai would often keep reading. He couldn't bear to go to bed where Jess's absence was most keenly felt in the long hours before dawn.

He looked at Mia now, her eyes moving beneath the lids while she dreamt.

"Let's make sure they're pleasant dreams, sleeping beauty."

He settled back in the chair and began the next chapter.

Chapter 98

Aboard the Belle

He was behind the dumpster watching Mia kick a can down the road. Then he heard the low rumble of a man's voice, followed by the tinkle of Mia's laughter.

Somewhere in his mind he realized this was not a memory. He was dreaming. He swam for the surface, forcing himself to open his eyes.

"Mia!" She was awake. Reid pushed himself up off the floor. "Why didn't you wake me?" he barked at the captain. He pushed his way between them, pulling Mia's hand away from Nikolai to take her pulse.

"Mmm, don't be angry." Mia's voice was raspy, her speech lethargic.

"I'm not." Reid kissed her forehead. Relief washed over him. She was going to be okay.

"My head hurts." She hung her arm across her face, covering her eyes.

"It's from a head injury, but you're also dehydrated. Can you drink some water?"

She didn't answer.

"Mia?" He touched her arm.

"Lemme sleep."

"Try to stay awake."

She uncovered her eyes and frowned. "Water?"

He reached for a bottle of sugar-water and noticed the captain was gone. He felt a stab of jealousy that Mia had woken for him. He turned back to Mia. Her eye were closed again.

"Oh no you don't," he said, slipping his arm behind her shoulders and sitting her up.

"Tired."

He held the bottle to her lips. "Take a sip, not too much." She swallowed. "Good. Now one more."

"Let me sleep," she said, her lids drooping.

"But I just got you back."

She touched his cheek, then her arm slipped back to her side and she was out.

Chapter 99

Lost Angeles

Pascal looked out the hospital window. The air still held the grayness of early morning. He checked his watch without reading it. He knew to the minute what time it was. It was premature to expect Minou to return from the pirate battle, but there ought to be news about Justine. He looked at the closed hospital door for the hundredth time—the doctors and nurses had been working on her for hours. If someone didn't come out in the next ten minutes, he was going in.

He looked out the window again. No Minou, but he wasn't concerned. His forces far outnumbered and outclassed the northern band of pirates. Failure was not in the cards.

Motion caught his eye—finally Justine's door was open. A doctor emerged and headed toward Gomez at the desk, but Pascal got his attention and met him in the middle of the room.

"Tell me." Pascal's mind raced as the doctor took a breath. This was a young doctor he'd only met once. Pascal tried to read the news on his face, but he was as expressive as a stone. It took forever for him to speak, and Pascal fought the urge to grab him and shake him.

"She's alive. We're treating for shock, dehydration, hypoglycemia, and blood loss."

"I want to speak to her."

"That's not possible. She was delirious and combative, so we had to sedate her."

"You said blood loss. From what?"

"She may be having a miscarriage."

"May be? That's not good enough. Is she or not?"

The doctor blinked slowly. "I don't know."

"That's not an acceptable answer. Try again."

"Chancellor, I will tell you everything I know. If I don't know, I'll tell you what's likely and what I suspect. But I will not tell you I know something when I don't."

The doctor did not seem intimidated by him. Good. "Very well, what do you know?"

"She either had a miscarriage very recently, or she's having one now. Or there's the chance she could remain pregnant when the bleeding stops. This is not an exact science. We've done all we can for now and we need to give it time."

"How much time?"

"I don't know."

"But you *suspect* . . . ?"

"I'm unable to make an educated guess at this time. I'll monitor her closely and inform you as to any change." The doctor nodded and turned to leave.

"Doctor." Pascal waited while he turned back. "Thank you for the information. Now I have some for you. Number one, Justine is to be kept alive. I don't care what you have to do or how many resources it takes. If the baby lives, that's a bonus, but the woman's life is paramount. Number two, when she wakes, get me immediately. No one speaks to her before I do. Number three, you will be her only doctor and she your only patient. You have no other responsibilities or concerns. You do not leave this ward. When you eat, sleep, or take a piss, you do it here. Are we clear?"

"Yes, Chancellor. Perfectly clear."

"What's your name, doctor?"

"Benjamin Lawrence."

"Doctor Lawrence, do you have a family? I'll get word to them that you're tied up with an emergency so they don't worry."

"Yes, a wife and son. Thank you, sir." A ripple of relief crossed the doctor's face. The stone could be read after all.

"Consider it done. I'll let you get back to work."

When the doctor was halfway to Justine's door, Pascal called out. "Ben? If that woman in there dies, so does your wife. Understand?"

The doctor stopped. Pascal assumed that after a moment of anger, he'd resume walking into Justine's room. He was wrong.

The doctor turned and took large, confident strides back to Pascal. The only indication of anger in his expression was a tic at the corner of his left eye.

"Chancellor," the doctor said, his voice even. "I appreciate you illustrating the gravity of the situation and the value you place on this woman's life. However, I already treat each patient as if it were my only patient, and I value each life equal to that of my own wife or child. So your threats, while cruel and credible, have no impact on the care this particular patient receives."

"Thank you, Ben. That is good to know. Now if there is anything at all you need, anything to help you do your job, tell me and I'll see you have it."

"I'll return when I have something to report." The doctor turned and went toward Justine's room.

Pascal considered calling him back again, just to mess with him, but he let him go. He wouldn't have any trouble with Dr. Ben Lawrence.

He returned to the window. The sun was coming up, burning away the morning haze. He had a clear view of the door into the hospital.

"They should be here soon." He stroked Linus's hair. "Perhaps Minou will arrive with Brandt even before Nathans returns with your breakfast."

Chapter 100

Aboard the Belle

M ia stretched and moaned.

"I'm right here," Reid said, smoothing the scowl from her brow.

She opened her eyes and smiled. "Reid."

"You remember me."

"I couldn't forget you." She held out her hand and he clasped it, bringing it to his lips. "What I don't remember," she said, "is where we are or how we got here."

"We're on a boat—"

"A boat? Why? Where?"

"It's a long story." He smoothed her frown again. "We escaped from the Tank and now we're sailing to San Francisco. Do you remember being in the Tank?"

She shook her head and winced.

"Does your head hurt?" he asked, grabbing a bottle from the nightstand. "Drink this."

She accepted the bottle and took a sip.

"You've been unconscious for a while so you're dehydrated. Plus your head probably hurts from the injury that knocked you unconscious. Do you remember what happened?"

"It's all so hazy." She took another swig from the bottle, then sank back into the pillows.

Maybe it was better she didn't remember that it was Brandt who hurt her. What good would it do for her to know?

"Whose boat?" Mia asked.

"Do you remember the man who was here when you first woke up this morning?"

"No. All I remember is waking up now with you."

Reid knew he shouldn't feel smug about her not remembering Nikolai, but he did. "Well, he's the captain—or maybe his son is, I'm not sure. The son escaped from the Tank with us, and now they're taking us far away from Lost Angeles, like you wanted."

"To San Francisco." Her voice drifted off, a hint of a smile at the corners of her mouth.

Reid sat in the chair by the bed to watch her sleep, but felt his own eyes growing heavy. He couldn't remember the last time he'd had a good night's sleep. He tried to stay awake, but after awhile, he couldn't fight it any more.

"Helloooo. It's me. Yoo hoo. I'm coming in."

Reid rubbed his eyes and stretched, wondering how long he'd napped.

"I heard our girl was awake." Cook waddled across the threshold in a bright yellow dress. She carried a tray of food. "What's she doing back asleep? She needs nourishment! Needs to gain back strength."

Reid reached over and took Mia's pulse with one hand, while he brushed a stray lock of hair away from her face with the other. "Mia, wake up," he said gently. Her color looked good, her pulse was strong. Her breathing was easy and regular. But he had no doubt she was dehydrated, and she had to be hungry.

"Clear a spot for the tray, will you?" Cook instructed, shooing Reid away from the bed and handing him the tray. She plopped into his chair and took Mia's hand in hers. "Mia, my dearie, my love. Time to wake up," she cooed. She patted her hand and made clicking noises with her tongue.

"Hmm?" Mia opened her eyes.

"I brought you some broth," Cook said. "Magical healing broth from a recipe handed down on my mama's side."

"Do I know you?" Mia asked.

Cook laughed. "You and me are old friends. You just don't know it yet."

"It smells good," Mia said, pushing herself up against the pillows.

Reid thought the broth smelled revolting, and he wouldn't be surprised if it was the "swamp tea" everyone complained about. But if Mia thought it smelled good, he didn't care what it was, so long as she drank it.

"Yum yum," Cook said, feeding Mia with a spoon like a baby.

After several loud slurps, Mia and Cook erupted in laughter.

"What's funny?" Reid asked.

"Nothing," Mia said. "I spilled all over myself, that's all."

"That's okay, dearie. Cook will fix you up, good as new."

"I'd love a bath or shower," Mia said.

"I can help you," Reid said.

"Thanks, but I'd like a woman's help," Mia said.

"But I could—"

"Ah ah!" Cook cut him off, thrusting her forefinger in the air. "No buts. A girl needs privacy to work her magic for her man." Cook patted at her upswept hairdo, then looked at Mia out of the corner of her eye. "Am I right?"

Mia smiled. "I knew you'd understand."

Cook pointed her meaty finger at Reid. "Now you get out."

"But I—"

"I said no buts! I take no talk-backs. Out, mister."

"Okay, I give up." Reid held up his hands. "Can I gather my things?"

"What for? Everything you need is in the room next door. You get *yourself* a shower, right? Then eat. Nap. I'll fetch you when it's time to come back."

Heading for the shower, Reid almost turned back three times. He kept thinking of things he should have told Cook, but he made himself keep going. Mia wasn't in any danger. He suspected the same couldn't be said for him if he crossed Cook.

Chapter 101

Lost Angeles

Pascal grew more agitated each hour that passed. He alternated between staring out the window and pacing in front of it, but neither made Minou appear.

The door to Justine's room was still closed and there had been no further update from the doctor. He'd begun to suspect that Ben knew something and was keeping it from him. That was not acceptable, but Minou was his greater concern at the moment.

"What's that, Linus?" Pascal said, leaning closer. "That's kind of you to offer, but the matter of Justine will wait until we've spoken with Minou."

Linus was becoming such a thoughtful and responsible young man, but Pascal would not shuffle off his responsibilities. They would watch for Minou together.

At long last, Minou and her men approached the building. Pascal turned to the interior door and willed himself to remain calm while he waited for Minou to throw Brandt at his feet. Pascal could almost see him huddled on the ground begging for mercy.

The door opened. Minou entered alone. Pascal shook his head to clear his vision, but nothing changed.

"Minou, tell me something that will keep me from ripping out your jugular with my bare hands." He said it in a low, calm voice, as if he were asking the special on today's menu.

"Brandt wasn't on Catalina. Witnesses saw him there an hour before we arrived. We searched the whole island, but he was gone. I'm convinced he left on the *Belle Jewel* with the others who escaped from the Tank."

Minou's uniform was torn and dirty, her boots were caked with mud, there was filth under her nails, and she had a scrape on her cheek crusted with blood.

"The reason for your tardy return?" Pascal asked.

"It's a big island, sir."

"And the question that determines whether you live or die today: where is the *Belle Jewel* now?"

"I don't know, sir, but I brought you the pirate king."

"At least that's one bit of good news."

"If anyone knows where the ship is, it's Markoff," Minou said. "I brought his wife to ensure he's motivated to share that information. They're in the Tank now."

"Congratulations. You've earned yourself the rest of today. Tomorrow will be determined by what you learn from our guests. Dismissed."

"Thank you, sir."

Why wasn't she leaving? "Is there something else?"

"Requesting permission to assign six men to burial detail, sir."

"Request denied. The dead aren't going anywhere."

"Yes sir." Minou double-timed her exit.

Pascal pivoted and nearly collided with the doctor.

"Chancellor," the doctor said. "I have information."

"That is fortunate for you, Ben."

"We resolved the patient's hypoglycemia and dehydration, but when we brought her out of sedation, she was still disoriented. We ran more tests and found she has severe anemia, so we began blood transfusions to raise her iron level."

"Is she alert now? I need to talk to her and I'm not a patient man."

"No, she's not responding as I'd hoped. The type-specific blood supply on hand doesn't have a high enough concentration of iron."

"Then what do you suggest?"

"We need blood from a compatible donor whose diet is higher in iron."

"No one has a better diet than I do." Pascal rolled up his sleeve. "See if I'm a match."

An hour later, he felt fine, despite having given a pint of his own blood. He'd made Ben test and draw his blood right in the command post. He couldn't have his men thinking he was weak or vulnerable. The sharks, they'd take any sign of weakness as opportunity to overthrow him. He sat up straight and looked at each of the people present, making sure they knew he was still fully in control. If anyone had looked the slightest bit skeptical, he'd have shot him right there. Luckily for them, no one did. He was still their commander, the chancellor, the King of Lost Angeles. But he could never let his guard down. He'd be on the lookout lest anyone forget who was in charge.

"You see that, Linus? I make my own destiny." Pascal said. "She needed blood. I gave her my own. Soon we can implement our plan. You'll see, son. We'll have our revenge."

Pascal knew his men thought he was crazy, talking to his son like he was a trusted advisor. He heard them whispering, but he didn't care. The boy was a genius. Making keen observations about seemingly inconsequential details. Catching things even Pascal had not seen. In fact, Linus had recalled the one piece of information that brought the entire plan together.

Now all they needed was for that bitch Justine to stop playing hard to get.

Or maybe she wasn't the problem at all.

He was beginning to think the young doctor wasn't as forthright and uncompromising as he'd portrayed himself to be. Pascal usually saw through false posturing immediately, but something had been clouding his judgment. Unfortunately for the doctor, the clouds had parted.

"Gomez, keep an eye on Linus and send someone to find out what's keeping his lunch."

Pascal charged into Justine's room. She was sitting up in bed, *awake*. She and the delusory doctor were chatting. *Laughing*. She'd probably been fine the whole time, and they'd been conspiring, colluding, making him a fool. He wanted to rip the head from Benjamin Lawrence's neck, but he reined in his anger and put on his most concerned expression.

"Justine, you had us so worried."

"I was about to get you, Chancellor," Ben said. "The transfusion worked beautifully. Justine, the chancellor's blood saved your life."

"Thank God it worked," Pascal said. "I don't know what I would have done, what I would have said to Brandt if . . ."

"Where is he?" Justine asked. "Why isn't he here?"

"Darling, what do you remember?"

"That's enough for now," Ben said. "She needs to rest."

"Of course." Pascal smiled warmly at Justine. "You rest and let me take care of everything. Brandt saved my son's life, which makes you and your baby my highest priority."

"My baby." Her hand went to her abdomen and her eyes welled with tears.

"Your baby is going to be fine," Pascal said.

"But the doctor said . . ." Justine's brow furrowed.

"Dr. Lawrence doesn't like to speculate. Isn't that right, Ben?"

"Yes," Ben said. "It's too early to say."

"Don't you worry, Justine. I've sent for a specialist," Pascal assured her. "Get some sleep. When you wake, the other doctor will be here." He held the door. "After you, Ben."

"As soon I get her blood pressure, Chancellor."

"Ben, I'm sorry to impose, but my son has been waiting to see you. Now that Justine is stable, could you take a moment to check him over? Only if you don't mind, Justine."

"Of course," Justine said.

Pascal ushered Ben out of the room and over to the command post. "You tried to deceive me, Ben."

"No, sir, I—"

"Get out your gun," Pascal told Nathans. He wanted to shoot Ben right there, but he wasn't going to let his anger ruin his plan. If he needed to produce the good doctor later, he wanted him alive and well. Or at least alive. "Nathans, escort Ben to the Tank. Put his wife and kid in a cell where he can see them. Gomez, get me a doctor I can work with."

"Dr. Levine from the Grand?"

"He'd be perfect if he didn't have the bedside manner of a fish."

"What about Dr. Advani?"

"Advani . . . she'll do anything to keep her pretty young daughter from working at the Grand. How a woman that looks like a troll could produce a daughter that attractive is beyond me." He flashed to Mia and her ugly clothier mother, and fury sprang to his chest.

"Sir?" Gomez said. "Dr. Advani?"

"Yes," Pascal said, coming back to himself. "Yes, get her. *Now*. Go."

"Right away, sir." Gomez hurried off.

Pascal looked from Linus across the room to Justine's door. With both Gomez and Nathans gone, he was torn between watching after his son and guarding Justine's door. It was his very distraction over Linus that had permitted Ben to deceive him. He'd need to keep a much closer watch on Advani. This meant, despite his own desires, he needed someone else, someone trustworthy, to be with Linus. It would be best if it were someone Linus *wanted* to spend time with. He couldn't have the boy feel he was being pawned off.

Wait, there was someone. That junior nurse who had a crush on Linus. Linus liked her. Of course it was only a dalliance, not worthy of anything serious, but how perfect that she was a nurse. It was so obvious, he couldn't fathom why he hadn't thought of it sooner.

What was her name? Gomez would know. Gomez would take care of it.

Chapter 102

Aboard the Belle

R eid jerked awake. He'd fallen asleep in the room next to Mia's, and had nightmare after nightmare. In the last dream he'd been working on a patient, performing CPR, but he couldn't revive the man. When he pulled his hands away, they were covered in blood. Kayla was screaming at him—*It's your fault! It's all your fault!* His grandmother was wailing. He looked back at his patient. Now there were three—his father, Tinker, and Brian—all dead. He looked down and the floor was littered with soldiers. They'd all been shot. Everyone was dead and it was his fault.

He took off his sweat-soaked shirt and splashed cold water on his face. It *was* his fault. He could see his grandmother's and Kayla's faces. The horror, the blame. The hate and disgust.

That's how they'd look at him if he went back home. If they could look at him at all.

There was a knock at the door.

"Yeah?" He glanced around the room for a shirt to put on.

"Yoo hoo. Mister Reid, it is Cook." The door swung open. "Why are you not ready! You hurry yourself. Do not make Miss Mia wait." She *hmph*ed and slammed the door.

Seeing Mia was exactly what he needed. When he was with her, the images of home faded, and the guilt and regret kept their distance. He found a clean gray shirt in a drawer, grabbed his bag, and was out the door so fast he could still smell Cook's perfume in the hall.

He knocked on the infirmary door, then entered. Mia was posed on the bed in a white silk robe that showed more of her long slender legs than it covered. It was tied closed but managed to reveal ample cleavage as well. She patted the space next to her.

Reid sat down, unable to take his eyes off her.

"Well?" She looked at him expectantly. "Reid, how do I look?"

Damn, he should have said something right when he opened the door, but he hadn't been able to form a coherent thought. Now that he was close to her, she smelled so good he wasn't doing much better. "I . . . I . . ."

"Good." Her lips curved in a provocative smile. "That's what I was hoping for." She draped her leg over his and grabbed his shirt, pulling him on top of her. She arched against him, her breasts hard against his chest.

He kissed her tenderly, but she dug her fingers into his back and wrapped her legs around him. Frantic, urgent. Moaning, grinding against him.

"Whoa," he said. "It's too soon."

"I'm fine. Better than fine."

He wanted to lose himself in her. "You're not making this easy. I don't want to stop."

"I'm not asking you to."

"Feel how fast your heart is beating?" Reid held his hand to her chest. "This is definitely too much too soon." He rolled to his back and cradled her in the crook of his arm. "Let's take it slow. We have all the time in the world."

"Slow is not what I want. I want you."

"I want you too, but I never should have let it get that far." He knew better.

Mia rolled to her side, turning her back to him.

"You mad?" he asked.

"No, sleepy."

He wasn't sure he believed her, but after a few minutes, her breathing slowed. He snuggled closer, wishing he could fall asleep too, but every time he closed his eyes the dead from his nightmare returned. They pressed against him, sucking the air from the room. He saw Kayla's eyes, accusing.

He slid his arm from under Mia and went to the window, but staring at the ocean didn't vanquish his ghosts. He looked at Mia, but all he could see was Kayla. The guilt was suffocating. He opened the door. He had to get out of there, but he shouldn't leave Mia alone.

"Mister Reid, what can I do for you?" Cook asked, waddling down the hall with a tray.

"I . . . nothing. I'm fine." Reid felt like an idiot, running from ghosts that didn't exist.

"You look like cabin fever," Cook said. "It's time for Miss Mia's tea. You take a walk."

"If you're sure." Reid stepped out of the way so Cook could squeeze into the room.

"Scrambo, mister."

Reid felt better as soon as he filled his lungs with fresh air. A hundred shades of pink and orange clouds floated atop the cobalt water, ushering in the night sky. He'd seen gorgeous sunsets in Colorado, but nothing like this.

As he headed for the bow, he noticed a couple silhouetted at the rail. The man had his arm around the woman's shoulders. Reid turned the other direction, not wanting to disturb them.

"Reid, have you got a moment?"

Reid shielded his eyes and turned back toward the couple. By the time he realized it was Nikolai who'd called to him, it was too late to do anything other than walk over.

"Let me introduce you to my daughter, Tatiana," Nikolai said.

The young woman shook Reid's hand. "Pleased to meet you."

"How is Mia?" Nikolai asked. "I'd like Tatiana to meet her."

"She's doing better," Reid said.

"I brought some clothing for her," Tatiana said. "I'm sure Cook's been doing her best, but there's not much to choose from on the *Belle*."

Reid pictured Mia in the silk robe—he never wanted Nikolai or anyone else to see her in that. She definitely needed some other clothes. "I'm sure she'd appreciate that."

"I'll come by in the morning?" Tatiana asked.

"Great," Reid said.

"See you then." Tatiana took Nikolai's hand and they strolled toward the rear of the boat.

Nikolai seemed like a good dad. It made Reid think of his own father. He wished he could tell him he'd been a good dad, despite what had happened at the end.

Chapter 103

Lost Angeles

Pascal smiled. Doctor Parvati Advani was indeed the perfect replacement for Ben.

"You're *sure* the baby is okay?" Justine held her hands protectively across her stomach.

"Absolutely, one hundred percent," Advani said.

"I told you there was nothing to worry about." Pascal made sure his voice oozed kindness and concern. "She's our best neonatologist. You can rest easy."

"But Dr. Lawrence wasn't sure the baby was still alive." Justine's lip trembled.

"Do you know what the nurses call him?" Advani said. "*Doctor Doom.* Because he always gives the worst case scenario, getting patients worked up over nothing at all."

Nice touch. "You don't have to worry about Dr. Doom anymore," Pascal said. "He's been assigned to another patient."

"Your son?" Justine asked.

Pascal's heart skipped, then he remembered his earlier ruse. "No, no. When he examined Linus he scared me out of my wits with his ominous diagnoses. Thank goodness Dr. Advani provided a more sensible second opinion. It turns out Linus is in no immediate danger. He's suffering from vitamin deficiencies, isn't that right, Doctor?"

"I'm afraid so. Like all the children in Lost Angeles, Linus isn't getting enough nutrients from our food supply. It's something I'm sure you think about with a little one on the way."

"You see, Justine," Pascal said, "even the Chancellor's son is not immune. I'd hoped our scientists would have made more progress by now."

Dr. Advani checked the bottle delivering blood into Justine's arm.

"You're very lucky. The Chancellor saved your life by giving you his blood."

Justine smiled at Pascal. "Thank you."

"I'll give you some time to visit," Advani said. "When I return I'll have a meal for you and I expect you to eat." Advani shook her finger at Justine, then turned it on Pascal. "Do not tire her out."

"Yes ma'am." Pascal closed the door behind her and pulled a chair to the bedside.

"Sweetheart, there's something I need to tell you. About Brandt." Pascal's voice was low and somber. "But if you're not strong enough . . ."

"No, I am. I've been trying to remember. I know something must have happened, otherwise he'd be here."

"What's the last thing you *do* remember?"

"I was cramping. I was scared for the baby. Then Mia's friend, Reid—he's some kind of doctor—he tried to help me."

"Yes, the stranger. I know about him and his grandfather."

"I never saw the grandfather. He was already missing when I met Reid." Justine frowned. "I remember Mia going to look for him. . . ."

"That's right," Pascal soothed. He could tell she remembered more. "It's okay to tell me. You don't need to worry about hurting my feelings or making me angry."

Justine looked at him, then back at her hands. "Reid said you put his grandfather in the Tank. And Mia, too."

"No honey, that's not true at all. Mia is fine. The grandfather too, although addled by dementia. Neither of them is in the Tank."

"Why would Reid lie?"

"Why indeed? I don't understand his agenda. For whatever reason, when his grandfather wandered off, Reid claimed I kidnapped him. I inadvertently made things worse when I sounded the Intruder Alert. Do you remember the Alert?"

She nodded. He could see her latch onto that small truth. She was so easy to read.

He continued. "Of course, I only did it to mobilize my men to help find the old man. It worked—we found him wandering the streets with a gash on his head, so we took him to the hospital—but in hindsight, perhaps I shouldn't have tried to help, because from that point things went from bad to worse. Reid turned Mia against me, and that's when she tried to hurt Linus, and Brandt saved his life."

"Yes, I remember something about that."

She wanted to believe him.

"Then Reid turned Brandt against me. He told him—" Pascal's voice broke. He took a deep breath. "I don't know how to tell you this . . . Reid told him I killed you."

Justine gasped. "He thinks I'm dead. That's why he didn't come back to get me at the house. Oh my God, why would Reid say that? Why would someone do such a terrible thing? We have to tell Brandt I'm alive, that I'm here."

"I want that more than anything, and believe me, I've tried. I assigned my best men and we searched and searched, but . . ." Pascal paused for effect. "I'm afraid he's gone, Justine. And there's no way to tell him that you're okay."

Justine began sobbing. Nothing he said served to calm her, so he instructed Advani to administer a mild sedative without Justine knowing.

He returned to Linus's bedside and sent Gomez to find Linus's young lady friend. It would be good for his son to spend time with a friend.

"I'm here," he said, stroking Linus's hair. "I thought you'd appreciate an update. Things are going much better now that we're rid of Dr. Doom. The new doctor is perceptive to my cues and adept at improvising. What she said about the vitamins could not have been better if I'd scripted it. The foundation for our plan is in place, son. Now the real work begins."

"Chancellor?" Advani said, approaching. "This must be your son. I didn't realize he was actually ill. Shall I have a look?"

"That won't be necessary," Pascal said.

"It's no trouble." Advani grasped Linus's wrist before he could stop her.

"I said *no*." Pascal stepped between them, forcing Advani to withdraw her hand. "My son is fine. He doesn't need a doctor."

"My apologies." She stepped back.

"I wanted to compliment you on your performance with Justine. Keep up the good work and your daughter will enjoy my continued protection."

"Thank you, Chancellor."

"From this point forward, you're not to leave Justine for even a moment. No one else is to see her without my express permission. You'll sit at her door yourself to make sure. If you sleep, do it blocking her door. I'll send word that you won't be coming home. Someone's watching your daughter?"

The doctor nodded curtly. "My mother." Pascal analyzed her expression, pleased there wasn't a hint of rebellion. Just determination. Her child was everything to her. She'd do what needed to be done. That was something they had in common.

"If there's any change in Justine's condition, I want to know immediately."

"Understood, Chancellor."

"Parvati?" He paused until she made eye contact. "Do not tell Justine anything about my son."

The doctor cast a furtive glance at Linus, then headed back to Justine's room.

He couldn't have Justine thinking he was distracted by his son, a child, being there in the command post. Of course there was no way she could know how valuable Linus was to his operation, despite his age. But Justine might think him a hindrance, or worse, she might think he was in the hospital because he was ill with something more than a vitamin deficiency. No, Pascal couldn't have that. He couldn't have her thinking there was any weakness there. Advani had better keep her mouth shut if she knew what was good for her and that daughter of hers.

Chapter 104

Aboard the Belle

Reid started down the steps to go belowdecks, only to meet Brandt on his way up.

"Hey how's it going?" Reid asked, backing up to let him by.

Brandt's face was blanched, his expression flat. "I'm sorry."

"For what? What's wrong?"

"I heard she was awake, and . . ." Brandt held out his hands and looked at his empty palms. "I didn't mean to. I never meant to . . ."

Reid pushed Brandt aside and jumped down the stairs. What had Brandt said to her? What had he *done?* He ran to the room. He didn't want to think that Brandt would hurt Mia. But he'd done it before. He reached the door and flung it open.

Mia was on the floor, hugging her knees, rocking.

Reid slid to her side. "What happened? What's wrong?" He looked her over, but didn't see anything out of place. Still, Brandt had clearly done something to hurt her. And Reid wanted to hurt him for it. "Mia, what is it? Tell me what's wrong."

She emitted a low keening as she rocked, but she didn't answer.

He pushed her hair aside and studied her face for signs Brandt had hit her. Tears leaked from the corners of her eyes, twin rivulets running down her cheeks, but there was no blood, no bruising. He cupped her face gently in his hands and wiped her tears with his thumbs.

"Tell me," he said softly.

"He . . . he . . . he told me."

"That he hurt you?"

"*What?*"

"Wait, what did he tell you?"

"That she's dead. Justine's *dead.*" She sobbed.

He wrapped his arms around her and held her as tight as he could.

He wished Brandt had told her a lie, something he could dispute. But there was nothing he could do about the truth. Nothing he could say to make it better. So he held her.

It was black outside the portal when she cried herself out.

She took a shuddering breath. "He hates me," she said, her head resting on his shoulder. "He blames me for Justine."

"How could he? If it's anyone's fault, it's mine."

"No, he blames me. He said so."

He held her by the shoulders so he could see her face. "I'm sure it's a misunderstanding. I'll talk to him in the morning." He tucked a lock of her hair behind her ear.

"No, you can't talk to him!"

"Why?" He didn't understand the heat behind her response.

"Because he'll tell you lies, he'll turn you against me."

"That's not possible."

"He'll try. He'll tell you horrible things. Promise me you won't talk to him. I couldn't take it if you hated me, too."

"Shhh." He kissed her cheek. "He could never turn me against you. I could never hate you, no matter what he said." He kissed her other cheek.

"*Promise* you won't talk to him."

"I promise." He kissed the tip of her nose.

"Swear?"

"I swear." He kissed her lips, her cheek, her temple. "I swear," he whispered in her ear, then tickled her lobe with the tip of his tongue. She emitted the tiniest laugh, and he pulled back to see her face. She was smiling.

She leaned toward him, and he kissed her softly, taking his time.

"Take me to bed," she whispered.

He picked her up and placed her on the bed.

She looked up at him. "I love you."

The way she said it, the look in her eyes, he knew she meant it. And the way it made him feel in his chest, in his gut—he loved her too.

She reached for him and he took her hand and climbed in beside her. She clung to him like she couldn't get close enough.

He felt the same, like he wanted to be so close nothing could ever get between them.

Chapter 105

Lost Angeles

Pascal had slept off and on all night in the chair beside Linus's bed in the command post. He hadn't gotten much rest, but it was morning, and there was a lot that needed to be done.

He rubbed his hands across his face, noticing the scrape of stubble. He couldn't remember the last time he'd shaved or taken care of any personal necessaries. What he needed was a shower and a toothbrush.

Gomez sat at the desk, running things in his gray sweater vest. It was strange not to feel any curiosity about the decisions Gomez was making on his behalf, the affairs of the city, the status of the dentist or the Grand. Nothing inside him stirred when he thought about it. Nothing.

The thought of Brandt, though, that got the blood flowing.

He patted Linus on the leg. "Let's see what Gomez found out about your friend. What did you say her name was? *Jenna.* That's right, I remember now. I'll make sure she's available to spend the day with you. No, no, I want to spend the day with you myself, but I have business to take care of. What's that? Yes, of course—I'll fill you in on everything."

Pascal stretched and headed to the desk.

"Good morning, sir," Gomez said, peering over his glasses.

"Any luck locating Linus's junior nurse friend from the spa?"

"I looked into it, but couldn't be certain without her name."

"Linus reminded me. It's Jenna. I don't know the last name."

"No need. I found only one Jenna who worked at the spa. I know where she is."

"Would you arrange for her to spend the day with Linus? Not here, though. The hospital is no place for young people."

"I'll see to it."

"Let me know when you have it arranged, and I'll take him myself. For now, would you stay with him while I get cleaned up?"

"Why don't I take Linus to Jenna now? Justine is sleeping, and Dr. Advani guards her door fiercely. You'd be free to do whatever you need to do." Gomez's dark eyebrows were raised clear above his reading glasses. He seemed overeager, and Pascal wasn't sure why.

Pascal glanced at Linus. "I suppose he'd feel comfortable going with you."

"Linus and I have always been comfortable with each other, sir. I promise to take excellent care of him, and he'll be in good company with Jenna."

"I suppose you're right." Pascal looked hard at his secretary, trying to see what it was that was off. But he decided it was nothing. Gomez was simply taking care of things, as he always did. "Yes, of course you're right. Fine. Go ahead. But when I see them later, everything had better be . . . as it should be."

"I understand, sir. When you're ready, I had a room prepared for you. It's down the hall on the left, marked 'private.' Your personal items, clothing, toiletries, etcetera are laid out near the shower. I took the liberty of stocking your favorite brandy."

"You take better care of me than any wife, Gomez."

"Kind of you to say, sir."

"Have Nathans man your post while you're gone, and make sure he knows where to find me. I want to know right away if anything should change with Justine, or if Minou comes with information from the prisoners."

"Understood. Shall I bring the daily reports to your quarters?"

"That's not necessary. Do whatever you think is right and sign my name."

Pascal kissed Linus's forehead then headed to his room. He thought perhaps he'd feel differently about the affairs of Lost Angeles after the business with Brandt was concluded, but it was hard to imagine ever wanting to see another report again.

An hour later, Pascal strode down the hospital hall in a fresh suit, feeling alert and focused. The news Minou had brought from the Tank was scant but good—the pirate king had broken and revealed that Brandt and the stranger had gone north. The missionaries were from the north. He was sure that's where Brandt was heading.

He arrived at Justine's door. "Dr. Advani, how's our patient?"

Advani rubbed her bleary eyes. "Improved. Alert. Iron levels are good. She's eating."

"Take ten minutes for yourself while I talk to her."

"Yes, sir." Advani shuffled down the hall.

"Good morning," Pascal said as he entered. "I hear you're doing better, so why the sad look on your face? Is Dr. Advani treating you well? I won't tolerate a repeat of Dr. Doom."

"She's fine. It's Brandt. I can't stand that he thinks I'm dead."

"You poor dear." Pascal sat in the chair beside the bed. "That's been eating at me, too. I keep coming back to the fact that he believes I'm the enemy. How could he think I'd ever harm you?"

"We have to find him. I've been trying to figure out where he'd be. Did you check the stadium? Or the house where you found me? He could be waiting for me."

"Justine." Pascal patted her hand. "I'm sorry to have to tell you, but I know why we can't find him. I received a report this morning that Brandt left the city with Reid."

"Oh." Her face fell.

"Do you know where they might have gone?"

"No," Justine said without looking up.

"I don't want to cause you any more stress, but . . . with Brandt believing that you're dead and I'm the enemy, I don't know why he'd ever come back." He went to the window and looked out, letting her reflect for a moment. He sighed and turned toward her. "If only we had some idea where they're heading . . . we could focus our search efforts in the right direction."

"I wish I knew." Justine glanced up, and Pascal could see the gears turning. She knew something. She wouldn't tell him right away, but she'd get there.

"I've asked the old man—Reid's grandfather—where they might have gone, but nothing he says makes sense. Like I told you, he's suffering from dementia."

"Reid left without his grandfather?"

"Yes, isn't that odd?" Pascal said. "I can't think of a reason Reid would take Brandt and leave his grandfather. You let me puzzle over it, though. Your job is to rest." He patted her leg in a fatherly way. "I must go see how Linus and his friend are getting along. I'll be back later."

He left the room, waited a moment, then stepped back in.

"Justine, there is one way you might be able to help. If you know how to work Reid's vehicle, we could cover a lot more ground looking for Brandt."

"They didn't take the car?"

"No, they left on a ship."

"That makes no sense."

"I hope they didn't leave the car behind because it's broken. Do you know how to run it? It would speed up our search considerably."

"I, I don't. I'm sorry."

Pascal shook his head sadly, then let the door fall shut.

He could tell she knew something about the car, as well as some idea where Brandt and Reid were headed. She'd come around if he didn't press.

First she'd ask for some kind of concession—proof he was on her side.

Whatever she wanted, he would give it to her.

Chapter 106

Aboard the Belle

"I ran into Will yesterday at the shower," Reid said, pushing aside the medical supplies on the counter to make room for his empty breakfast plate.

"Sounds kinky." Mia raised an eyebrow. She was sitting on the bed with the breakfast tray Cook had made, her plate still full.

Reid laughed. "He told me a little about the San Francisco settlement. Sounds interesting. They don't have seeds there though, or in the settlements farther north. Except for apples."

Mia picked at her food. At least she'd finished Cook's tea.

"It's too quiet here. Did Will say if they have music?" Mia asked.

"He didn't say."

"Did he say if they stay on the boats all the time, even when they're not out sailing around?" She made a face. "I'm not wild about boats."

"I think they use them for fishing. I'd like to try fishing. Nobody fishes in Colorado. They used to, back in the Before. There's no fish now."

He had a pang thinking about Colorado, but he pushed it away.

"I wouldn't mind trying fishing." Mia spun the apple on her plate. "I'd like to see how apples grow, too. I can't even imagine what that looks like." She held her apple up in the air.

"Will said it takes ten years for a tree to make apples." As he stared at the apple, his mind involuntarily went to Colorado again. Finding apples wasn't enough. His people didn't have ten years. He shook his head, forcing himself to return to the present. He snatched the apple from Mia's hand. "Hey, do you think the apple starts out tiny and takes ten years to grow to this size?"

"I think there's nothing for ten years, then *pop,* there it is." Mia grabbed the apple back.

He plopped on the bed beside her and tried to take the apple again. She giggled, and he loved the sound, so he tickled her until they were both laughing.

Reid stared at the slanted ceiling. He was in no hurry to leave their little sanctuary. "I'm going to miss it here."

"Not me. I can't wait to walk around without the ground moving under my feet. It'll be nice to be out in the sun. Oh, and the rain! I've heard it rains in San Francisco. I've hardly ever seen rain. I'd love to take a walk in the rain."

He propped himself up on one elbow. "You're up for a walk?"

"I'm dying for a walk. Aren't you feeling cooped up? I want to get out and see new things, meet new people."

"You know, when you're completely better, we could take a long walk and see lots of new things. I could take you to Colorado." As much as Reid dreaded facing his grandmother, it would be better than the crushing guilt of not telling her. And he thought he could handle seeing Kayla with Mia by his side. "What do you think?"

"Right. Walk to Colorado. Sure."

"It would take a while, but we'd be together. We'll sleep out under the stars, and I'll tell you the stories of the constellations. You'll tell me everything about your childhood and your family. I don't even know if you went to school, or what your favorite color is."

"You're serious."

"If you want to see new things, Colorado is nothing like Lost Angeles. The Rocky Mountains are enormous, and hey—I bet you've never seen snow."

"I haven't even seen San Francisco yet. How can I think about walking clear across the country?" Someone knocked at the door, and Mia couldn't open it fast enough.

"Did you eat your breakfast?" Cook pushed her way in, scowling at the full breakfast tray. "Miss Mia, being sad about your friend is no excuse not to eat my delicious food. But I do understand the sadness. I truly do. That's why I brought someone to cheer you up."

Tatiana poked her head in the doorway. "Hi, I'm Tatiana, Nikolai's daughter."

"Please, come in," Mia said.

Reid nodded. "Nice to see you again."

"I brought some clothing," Tatiana told Mia, indicating the duffle over her shoulder. "I thought you might like some new things since we're arriving in San Francisco today and you'll be meeting everyone."

"I'd love that," Mia said.

"Young man." Cook tapped his shoulder. "You need to scram. Us girls have girl things to do. Don't come back for at least two hours, understand?"

"See you in a while," he said to Mia from the doorway, but she was already absorbed going through the clothes Tatiana dumped on the bed.

"You could do with new clothing, too," Cook called after him, eyeing his ratty sweats. "Go see Will. He's got things to fit you. Nice things. Bright colors. Go." Cook shooed him out.

Reid showered, then went to Will's cabin.

"Come on in."

"Cook said I should ask you for some clothes," Reid said. "Apparently these sweat pants I found are not up to her standards for arriving in San Francisco."

"Here's some jeans." Will tossed him a pair. "See if those fit."

Reid stripped off the sweats, thinking he'd be happy never to see them again, and pulled on the jeans. "These work fine."

"Shirts are in the closet. Take whatever you want."

Reid chose a collared T-shirt that was the least obnoxious in color— a blue bordering on purple. He didn't want to offend Will, but he wasn't accustomed to men wearing pink or orange.

"What about regular shoes?" Reid asked. All he'd been able to find on the boat—Will's closet included—were flip flop sandals.

"We'll scavenge some when we go ashore. You'll want something better for dancing."

"Dancing?"

"My aunt throws a party with music and dancing almost every night."

"Mia asked if there would be music."

"Damn straight, there's music. Piano, guitar, harmonica. Banjo when Creighton is around. It's not a party without music."

Reid was excited to tell Mia, but the thought of dancing made him nervous. He'd seen dancing a few times, but he'd never tried.

"When we get your shoes, we'll find you some other clothes, too. Don't worry about packing anything from here, unless you *like* those colors."

"You don't?"

"Are you kidding? That's all Cook."

Reid smiled. Maybe folks weren't all that different here.

He looked around, unsure what to do next. He had more than an hour before Cook would let him back in the room. He spotted a chessboard in the corner. "Have you got pieces for that?"

"Chess or checkers?"

"Chess, of course."

Will grinned. "Are we talking a friendly game, or would you care to place a wager?"

Chapter 107

Lost Angeles

Pascal decided to give Justine some time to stew. Perhaps he'd take Linus and Jenna to Club Three. He hoped there was no red wine, just so he would witness Linus deal with that pompous wine steward.

"I'd like to speak to Linus," Pascal told Gomez.

"Are you sure you want to interrupt his date?" Gomez asked, pushing his glasses up on his nose. "I'm sure they're having a wonderful time."

"I'd like to see for myself. Where can I find them?"

"I'll take you." Gomez came around the desk.

"That's not necessary, just tell me where."

"Really, it's no trouble," Gomez said, already heading down the hallway.

Pascal wondered why Gomez was being uncharacteristically cagey, but he didn't care enough to ask. After following Gomez down two flights of stairs to the hospital basement, Pascal was becoming irritated—he'd specified that Linus go somewhere outside the hospital.

Gomez stopped at a large door, and turned to him, his expression grave.

Poor serious Gomez. Laughter bubbled in Pascal's chest, though he didn't know why.

"Ready, sir?" Gomez asked.

"Yes, of course." Why wouldn't he be?

Gomez muscled open the giant door. "I'll wait here."

"No need. I can find my way back." Pascal stepped inside. It was chilly. Silent. No windows, but lights were on. Cold light. Cold cement floors. An odd choice for young people.

He walked down the side of the room, avoiding the center, though he couldn't say why. He knew he could figure it out if he thought about it, but he didn't want to think. He didn't want to know. Better to avoid looking.

But the center of the room called to him. He glanced without seeing.

A wave of nausea swept over him. The ground pitched like he was at sea, and he planted his feet wide to steady himself. He couldn't move, but he knew he had to. Keeping his gaze locked on the floor, he took one step closer. Then another. His feet continued of their own volition. When they stopped, he closed his eyes and took a deep breath.

When he opened his eyes he saw Linus and Jenna. They were on their backs, side-by-side but not touching. A red and white checked blanket covered the cold metal table where they lay. Almost like they were at a picnic. Like they were staring up at the summer sky, trying to find pictures in the clouds.

Except that they are dead.

The weight of that knowledge crushed the air from his lungs, his ears rang hollow, and his vision blackened. He gripped the table to keep from collapsing.

"No!" He closed his eyes against the truth, but he couldn't deny it any longer. He laid his head on Linus's feet and sobbed until his throat was raw.

When he had nothing left, he straightened and took a ragged breath, wiping the mucus and tears from his face with his sleeve.

His little boy was dead.

He could admit that now. He'd known, of course. He'd simply needed time to accept it. A cushion between life and death. A veil over reality while he prepared himself.

Now he could face the truth without it destroying him.

"Linus?" He took his boy's hand. "This is not what I wanted for you. Not what I dreamt of for my only child. Not at all what I envisioned." He closed his eyes, not wanting to face the whole truth, but knowing he had to. He took a deep breath and squeezed Linus's hand, then looked his boy in the face. "I did this to you, Linus. I'm sorry, son. I'm so very, very sorry."

He looked at the girl. *Jenna.* Wholesome. Pretty. She'd been kind to Linus. Clearly she'd been smitten. They both had. Perhaps he'd judged her too harshly. Did any of the trappings of station or intellect matter now?

It was good they were together. It was good Linus had a friend. Especially in this cold, unforgiving place.

He reached over and placed Jenna's hand in Linus's.

"There," he said. "Keep each other company until I return. It won't be long. It won't seem like any time at all. I'll take care of everything. When I come back, you'll be able to rest."

He returned to the door and found Gomez waiting as he said he'd be. Stolid, dependable Gomez, looking at him expectantly, if a bit apprehensively, through his little spectacles.

"Thank you, Gomez. I'm okay now."

"Very good, sir. Shall we?" He gestured to the staircase.

Pascal's mood lightened as they climbed because each step took him that much closer to making things right for his son. At the top of the stairs, Pascal turned toward the hospital room that held the girl who would fix everything so his son could rest.

"Gomez, now that I'm back, we've got work to do. I need to see Minou right away."

"Yes, sir. At the command post?"

"This needs to be private." He remembered the bottle of brandy in his room. "My temporary quarters. Don't keep me waiting."

Chapter 108

Aboard the Belle

"Yoo hoo, Captain. Knock, knock."

Nikolai opened the door for Cook.

"A message from the sleeping beauty," she said. "She summons you to her chambers."

"I never should have told you that."

"I'd think you'd know better by now."

"Apparently I'm not as smart as I look. What does Mia want?"

"Her highness did not say, but you'd better get on your magic carpet and zip over there before she turns you into a rat or something."

"You're mixing up your fairy tales, Finny."

"What tales? I'm serious." She winked and stepped out of his way.

"You're not coming with me?"

"I don't wanna be turned into a rat."

Nikolai walked to the other end of the *Belle* and knocked at Mia's door.

"Captain, I'm glad you came." Mia sat on the edge of the bed looking radiant in a pink dress. Her hair and makeup were artfully done, but not by Finola if he were to guess based on subtlety alone.

"What can I do for you?" he asked.

"Keep me company?" She patted the bed.

Nikolai nodded but opted for the chair. Mia produced an exaggerated pout.

"Where's Reid?" Nikolai assumed Mia had dolled herself up for the young man who was so obviously in love with her.

She shifted, giving him a long look at her slender legs. "I don't know. Off doing something. I was lonely, so I asked Cook to see if you'd pay me a visit."

"I'm glad you're feeling better," he said. "You had us worried. I was beginning to think you'd sleep all the way to San Francisco."

She smiled. "Cook says you thought I looked like Sleeping Beauty."

"I'm making a mental note not to tell Cook anything anymore." Nikolai hoped Mia couldn't tell that under his beard he was blushing.

"I've been meaning to tell you," Mia said in a low voice. "I'm glad you were with me when I first woke up. I felt safe the moment I saw you. And the sound of your voice . . . it was somehow familiar, comforting."

"I'm sure my voice was familiar because I read to you while you were sleeping. I used to read to my daughter while she slept. In the morning, she'd say my voice was in her dreams."

"I hope she knows how lucky she is to have a father like you. I never knew my father."

"I'm the one who's lucky to have a daughter like Tatiana. Especially after her most recent escapade. Did she tell you about her pirate adventures?"

"I want to hear you tell it. I love the sound of your voice."

Was she looking for a father figure, or was she flirting? "I'm afraid that will have to wait. I need to help my son prepare the ship for arrival."

"You have a son on board?"

"Yes. He escaped from the Tank with you and Brandt and Reid."

"Is he handsome like you?"

"I'll introduce you after we land, and you can see for yourself." He stood.

She grabbed his hand. "Stay a little longer? I'm not afraid when you're here." Her lower lip trembled. "Tell me about San Francisco. If I know what to expect, maybe I won't be so scared."

The frightened look on her face reminded him of Tatiana as a child, and he couldn't say no. He sat beside her, telling himself she wasn't angling for anything more than the comfort of a father, though he wasn't altogether certain.

Chapter 109

Aboard the Belle

Reid stood at the bow with Will and Brandt, straining to see through the gray mist. The fog lifted, and Reid gasped at the enormity of the bridge before them.

"That's the Golden Gate," Will said.

"It's phenomenal," Reid said.

"Wow," Brandt said. "There's nothing left like this in Lost Angeles."

"If you look close, you can see glimmers of red paint," Will said. "When the sun hits it just right, it glows."

The fog continued to dissipate, revealing patches of bright green between the rocky gray shoreline and jagged brown mountains.

"That green . . . what is it?" Reid asked.

"Apple orchards," Will said. "When my mom was alive, we came once a year to plant. There's an orchard for every spring. There are big ones on the west side of the peninsula. This is what we could fit into the little valleys where good soil collected from rain runoff."

"I never thought . . . It's so beautiful." Reid's chest constricted as he thought of his brother. Brian should be the one seeing this.

"Where is the city?" Brandt asked.

"Actually, there are cities all around us," Will said. "See those houses? That was a suburb of San Francisco. The city of San Francisco itself is ahead on the right. It will come into view in a moment or two. Our settlement is in Sausalito, on the left side of the bay."

"I thought it was *in* San Francisco," Reid said.

Will shook his head. "Too dangerous. My dad says survivors lived there at first, but it hasn't been safe in my lifetime. Too many collapsed and unstable buildings."

"I wish Mia was seeing this," Reid said.

"She and my sister are taking forever to get ready," Will said.

"I saw your sister in the kitchen with Cook," Brandt said. "But I didn't see Mia."

"That's odd," Reid said. "I'd better go check on her."

"Mind if I come?" Brandt asked. "I want to talk to you about something."

"Not now," Reid said, remembering his promise to Mia. "She might not be feeling well."

He hurried down alone, wondering what Brandt wanted to talk about. Was it possible he actually blamed Mia for Justine's death?

From the hallway outside Mia's room, he heard the tinkle of her laughter. He smiled and swung open the door. The last thing he expected was Nikolai sitting on the bed holding Mia's hand.

Mia looked up, her face beaming. "Reid!"

Nikolai stood and straightened his shirt. "I'm glad you're here. I was keeping Mia company while she waited for you, but I have business to take care of."

Reid remembered they were his guests and bit back what he wanted to say. "Thank you," he said instead, but he sounded disingenuous, even to himself.

Nikolai nodded. "See you topside."

Reid closed the door behind him and leaned against it, finding it hard to string words together. "I interrupted something." His voice was strangled.

"Not really," Mia said. "He was telling me about San Francisco. I'm excited to see it."

"He needed to hold your hand for that?"

"Don't be silly. He wasn't holding my hand, he was reading my palm."

"Right." Did she think he'd believe that?

"It's fun. You should ask him to read yours."

That was safe to offer, since he'd never ask in a million years. "What was your fortune?"

"Oh, riches of course. Everyone gets told that. A sea voyage—easy since we're already at sea." She giggled. "And he said there were many men who had come and gone from my life, but that my one true love had finally found me."

Reid clenched his teeth. "I suppose he said *he* is that one true love."

Mia rolled her eyes. "It's sweet you're jealous, but he thinks of me as a daughter." She crooked her finger, beckoning him, but he stayed at the door, holding on to his anger. "Oh, you want me to come to you, is that it?" She walked over and ran her fingers down his chest. "It's sexy when you're angry."

He grabbed her wrist. "Don't."

"Oooh, that's what I mean. You like it rough?"

"Knock it off." He stepped around her. "I'm not an idiot."

"That's not fair. I wanted to get pretty for you, so we could be together. I was ready early, and I didn't know where you were, and . . ." Her voice trailed off and she pressed her fingers to her temples.

Reid caught her before she hit the ground. He placed her on the bed and held a glass of water to her lips. "Sip. Real slow. Now lay back." The timing of her faint was awfully convenient. If he had to bet, he'd say she faked it, but he couldn't tell for sure.

"I don't feel good."

"You'll be fine in a minute."

"Please, don't be mad." Her lip quivered and her eyes welled with tears.

"I won't have you play me for a fool, Mia."

"I'm not, I swear." She sniffed and wiped away a tear. "I promise you, Nikolai treats me like a daughter, nothing more. I never had a father. But I won't see him anymore if it bothers you."

She took his hand and kissed it. He was mad at himself for letting her, but he didn't pull it away. She was saying exactly what he needed to hear.

"I have you, Reid, and that's all that matters. You're all I need. You're everything. I love you." She looked at him, her big eyes dewy with tears. "Please? Forgive me?"

A little voice in the back of his mind told him that her words were too perfect, her timing too convenient, but he chose not to listen.

He pulled her close and he kissed her. "I love you, too."

Chapter 110

San Francisco Bay

Nikolai usually loved to sail across the bay, but he caught himself clenching his fists, reopening his sores. He was more anxious about seeing Marseille and Creighton than he wanted to admit, Creighton more so than his sister. He'd work things out with Marseille, as they always did. But with Simon . . . Nikolai was still furious and wouldn't be quick to get over it.

He tried to enjoy himself as Will and Tatiana took turns pointing things out.

"We've almost got Horseshoe Bay cleared," Will said. "It'll be our main point of export."

"The orchards are producing, businesses are thriving, people are renovating houses to live in. It's become a real community." Tatiana glowed like when she was eight years old and completed her first solo sail. "Wait till you see where you're staying, Dad."

"You haven't had enough time to restore Cavello Point . . . *have* you? Exactly how long have you been coming here?"

Tatiana laughed. "Not *that* long. Besides, it's better than that."

"Hmm . . . The Inn Above Tide?" Nikolai craned his neck trying to see it.

"No, it was too far gone, but that's part of the surprise—we tore it down."

Tatiana grinned, and Nikolai knew immediately what the surprise was. "The Hotel Sausalito."

"Yes! It's a guesthouse for new arrivals. Where we tore down The Inn, that's Aunt Marseille's new party spot. She calls it 'The Landing.'"

"I bet she started planning a party for tonight the minute the *Belle* was spotted. *Look*." Will pointed. "She's waving to us."

Nikolai saw the brilliant shock of red hair, so like their mother's. If that were the only way they were alike, the two women might have gotten along better. But there had always been friction, particularly over the business. He understood why Marseille left Washington, and he'd acknowledge that, right after he chewed her out for not handling her exit more gracefully.

The crewmen eased the *Belle* up to the freshly rebuilt dock.

Marseille held out her arms. "Niko, I've missed you!"

Nikolai stepped onto the dock and hugged her tightly, lifting her off her feet. "I've missed you more."

She laughed, and just like that, everything between them was healed. With some, it was that easy. With others? Creighton hadn't even bothered to meet them. That didn't bode well.

There was a touch at his elbow.

"Hello, I'm Mia." Mia extended her hand past him to Marseille.

Marseille shook Mia's hand and appraised her with exaggerated affect. "They don't make them prettier than this one, do they Nikolai?"

Mia giggled, snaking her arm into the crook of his elbow.

"Mia, this is my sister, Marseille."

"I'm so happy to be here," Mia said. "All the trees—it's gorgeous." Her smile seemed to radiate from the inside, and Nikolai had to admit she was an exceptional beauty.

"I have your bag, Mia." Reid approached, his expression strained.

Nikolai realized Mia was still holding his elbow, so he reached for the bag. "Here, let me help with that. Do you have your balance, my dear?" he asked Mia.

"Yes, I'm fine now, thank you." She transferred her grasp to Reid's arm.

"She had a recent head injury," Nikolai explained to Marseille.

Reid looked relieved, but Mia's smile may have been less genuine. Nikolai hoped it was his imagination.

"Marseille, this is Reid," Nikolai said. "He's a medic and has taken excellent care of Mia. He's here all the way from Colorado."

"Colorado?" Marseille said. "I've met people from a lot of places, but none as far as Colorado. I'd love to hear about it."

"Yes ma'am," Reid replied.

"Call me Marseille. 'Ma'am' sounds much older than I feel."

"Follow me, everyone," Tatiana called out.

Nikolai waited for the crowd to trail after Tatiana before he headed toward the hotel. Creighton wasn't the only one missing. He still hadn't caught sight of the person he most hoped to see, and Kennedy didn't seem to be around either.

As everyone filed into the hotel, Nikolai stopped to admire the crumbling city of San Francisco across the water. The skyline was still identifiable, if a little malformed, and even in its advanced state of decay, Nikolai found it a view to behold.

Before going inside, he took a last look at the dock to make sure no one had been left behind. From there, he had a full view of "The Landing" and appreciated the improvements on Marseille's design from back home. A huge bonfire was ready for lighting, precisely the right distance from the bar. There was a cooking area, tables and benches, torches, a dance floor with a stage for the band, and a gazebo off at a distance. The shed behind the stage brought a smile to his face—he was sure he knew what was inside.

He'd gone too long without music or dancing. A party would do his heart good.

Nikolai entered the lobby to find the crowd had already dispersed. He climbed the stairs and caught up with Tatiana who was showing Reid and Mia to their room.

"There you are, Dad. I was just saying, this is the communal washroom, and that's your room there." She pointed to a door.

"Excellent," he said. "If you'll excuse me, I'm going to rest up before the festivities tonight. Oh, this is Mia's bag." He handed it to Reid. "I wonder what I did with mine?"

"I believe *someone* already put it in your room," Tatiana said with a conspiratorial grin.

Nikolai understood and braced himself. He opened the door and Josh barreled into his arms. "My golden boy. Now this day is perfect."

Chapter 111

Lost Angeles

Pascal found his quarters tidied—bed made, bathroom cleaned, toiletries and clothing stowed. The brandy was on the nightstand with two clean glasses. He splashed water on his face, then poured a small glass. Not too much. He needed to keep his thoughts clear. He sat and stared out the window. Everything he saw was his, but it didn't feel the same without Linus. He wondered if it ever would. Maybe once he found Brandt.

It would feel damn satisfying to inflict pain on Brandt and that stranger, Reid.

Each moment that passed brought Justine closer to revealing where they'd gone. Pascal was certain he already knew the truth as surely as if she'd said it: she'd sent Brandt to her home, the home of the missionaries, where he could have a life of ease and plenty.

Ellianna had been right—Justine wasn't like the other missionary girls he'd tortured over the years. They had no idea how to get home, other than to find a church and pray for salvation. Justine was different. Special. She knew, and she'd told Brandt. Soon, she would tell him, too.

There was a rap at the door. Minou stepped in and stood ramrod straight at the door.

"Come sit. I have another mission for you. Brandy?"

"No thank you." She sat in the chair opposite him.

"I'm about to tell you my most guarded secret. You won't speak of it to another soul."

"Sir, you have my word."

"How do I know your word is good?"

"I have no family or friends. My work is my life, and that only continues at your pleasure. Without your trust, I have nothing. So my word is everything."

Pascal already knew Minou was right for the job, but her commitment was gratifying to hear. "I've trained an elite platoon for long-range missions. They ride *bicycles*."

Minou's eyes widened, but she said nothing.

"My scientists are using a newly discovered supply of tires that, for reasons unknown, don't disintegrate. I'll use them on motorcycles and cars eventually, but until then, bikes can travel faster and longer than the best Blades. It was to be a surprise for Linus's birthday."

He paused. Minou wisely did not say anything while he gathered himself.

"I'm placing the Travelers in your command," he continued. "Your first mission is imminent. You have a day, two at most, to learn to ride a bike and organize your troops."

"I'll master the bike by sun-up, sir. The men will be ready to leave at your command."

Pascal didn't doubt she'd be true to her word. "We're going after Brandt and the stranger. I'll drive the vehicle, and your platoon will follow in secret. You'll face long hours and rough terrain in unknown territory, but at the end is the home of the missionaries."

"You know where it is?" Minou's tone was incredulous, and Pascal enjoyed seeing the flare of emotion.

"Not yet, but Justine does. The trip will be no easy task, especially with green soldiers, but I know you're good for it. And you will be rewarded appropriately. If we succeed."

"We'll succeed. I guarantee it."

Pascal sent Minou to Gomez for further instructions, and he went to see Justine. As he stood outside her door, he almost felt sorry for her. He'd faced his demons and emerged stronger. It was hardly a fair fight.

He opened the door to find her dressed and sitting by the window.

"Hello, Justine. It's good to see you up."

She glared at him. "Why do you want to find Brandt?"

"Apparently we're dispensing with the pleasantries," he said. "Okay, I want to find Brandt to reunite you two, of course. What other reason would there be?"

"What's in it for you?"

He sat on the foot of the bed across from her. "I don't like him thinking I killed you. I want to show him you're alive and well."

"That's not all."

"I don't like unpaid debts. He saved my child's life. I want him to know I saved his. Then we'll be even." He could see she wasn't completely satisfied. "It's not enough that I want to help you find him?"

"There's a lot more at stake than that."

"You're a perceptive woman."

"How about you dispense with the bullshit and tell me the deal."

Pascal found this refreshing after the sappy, sentimental conversations they'd been having. "All right, stop me if I get something wrong. The strangers were looking for seeds. You're a missionary—your people grow food; they have seeds. You know how to get home, and you sent Brandt and Reid there, to get seeds. Does that sound about right?"

"You're right about one thing: I came here as a missionary. But so have lots of girls. What on earth makes you think I know how to get home any more than the rest of them?"

"You're different. I haven't figured out how or why yet, but for whatever reason, they don't know how to get home, while you do. No use denying—I can see on your face I'm right. So let's stop wasting our time with this dance of lies and half-truths, shall we? You want to go home. You want your baby to grow up where there's food, where she has a daddy. I can help you get there. I'm the only one who can."

Her brow furrowed. Pascal schooled his own face, though he was smiling inside. She would come around. She was coming around now.

"For argument's sake, let's say you're right," she said. "Let's say I want to go home, that I know how to get there, and Brandt is there waiting for me. If I took you there, there's nothing to stop you from taking everything and leaving my people with nothing. Even if you were my only chance of getting home, I couldn't risk it because it's not just about me and what I want. There are hundreds of lives at stake."

"We're talking about more than hundreds of lives. Not just your people, but the rest of mankind. It's time you saw past the brainwashing, Justine. Your people believe that to protect what's theirs, they need to keep it for themselves. They're wrong. Seeds are not a finite resource. The more you give away, the more there will be."

He could see the gears turning.

"You're a bright woman," he continued. "So I'm sure you've considered the possibility of a blight or fire wiping out your people's food stores. By holding all the resources in one location, you're placing the existence of mankind at risk. Don't you see that sharing with others would protect your people, not harm them?" He paused while she processed this. "Blindfold me or sedate me or whatever it is your people do to keep their location secret, but don't keep the seeds from me. Let me feed my child. In the long run, it will ensure you can feed yours."

It was nearly impossible for Pascal not to react as her thoughts played across her face.

"I'll think about it," she said.

"See that you do. I'll return tomorrow morning for your answer."

After the door closed behind him, he allowed himself a smile.

"Has there been a breakthrough?" Advani asked.

"You could say that," he said. "Gomez, watch Justine's door. I need to speak to the doctor in private."

He strode to his quarters, hearing the uneven clip-clop of Advani's heels behind him.

Pascal held the door for her. "Sit down." He indicated the pair of chairs at the window.

Advani sat, crossing her ankles and folding her hands in her lap.

He turned the lock on the door, then crossed to the other chair. He sat and looked the doctor over for any signs of apprehension. Her expression was of mild curiosity, expectation. But no fear. That was good.

"Parvati, we're embarking on an important mission, you and I. One with far-reaching implications, not only for our community, but for the future of humanity." He paused to let that sink in. "We're going to the home of the missionaries. Do you know what that means?"

Chapter 112

Hotel Sausalito

"I don't want you to overdo it." Reid hated being the bad guy, hated disappointing Mia.

"Please?" she pleaded. "It's just dinner. I want to meet everyone and listen to the music."

"If it means that much to you . . ."

Mia clapped her hands. "And a few dances." She rushed to the closet where she'd hung the clothing Tatiana gave her. "What am I going to wear?"

"You don't take anything slow, do you." Reid laughed to conceal his discomfort. He was worried about her over-exerting herself, plus he didn't know how to dance and didn't like the idea of her dancing with anyone else. Especially Nikolai. She'd sworn that his interest was fatherly, but Reid still seethed when he pictured Nikolai holding her hand.

"What do you think of this?" Mia asked, holding up a black and white blouse.

"You look great already." He'd never seen anything prettier than her in that pink dress.

"This is rumpled." She ran her hands down the sides of the dress. "But it does twirl nicely." She spun and the skirt flared.

There was a knock at the door. Mia ran on her tiptoes and opened it.

"Your dinner?" A pimple-faced boy held a tray.

Mia turned away without saying anything.

"Thank you." Reid quickly went over, took the tray, and closed the door. "Mia, I'm sorry. I arranged for this earlier, but we don't have to eat it. We can still go down to dinner."

"No, it would be wrong to waste it." She sank into the couch across from the window.

"We could go down after we eat." Reid placed the tray on the coffee table and sat beside her. "Hey, think of it like this—now you don't need to expend any energy visiting over dinner. You can save it for sitting at the bonfire and listening to the music."

"And dancing." Mia grinned. "Let's hurry."

Reid removed the silver domes that covered the food, releasing an enticing aroma.

"Curry!" Mia grabbed a fork. "I love curry."

"I've never had it." He'd missed lunch and was glad for the huge portion of fish and whatever else was soaking in the thick red sauce.

"Delicious, isn't it?"

Reid nodded, not wanting to stop eating to talk.

After a few bites, Mia set down her fork. "Can you believe this view?"

Reid cleaned his plate, savoring each bite, while they watched the sky turn red.

"Dessert?" he asked, but Mia had fallen asleep.

As he savored warm cinnamon apples, his thoughts turned to Brandt. Maybe Brandt did blame Mia for Justine's death. Maybe he blamed them both. Brandt had every right to blame him—it was his fault that Justine was dead, and Reid knew it better than anyone. He carried the burden for her death, and Tinker's, and all those who had died during their escape. But there was no way Brandt should blame Mia. She'd done nothing except try to help. He wished she'd change her mind about him talking to Brandt. The man was grieving, but Reid thought he could get him to see reason.

The sky was black when he heard the music start. He considered letting Mia sleep, but was sure she wouldn't forgive him. "Mia? We can go to the party now if you want."

"Leave me alone," she mumbled.

He was relieved. "I'll put you in bed." He tucked his arm under her knees, but she kicked him and curled up in a ball.

Reid covered her with a blanket and climbed into bed alone. The moment his head touched the pillow, his guilt hit him full force, like it had been lying in wait for his guard to drop.

I should be trying to find seeds, trying to get home.

He imagined telling his grandmother about Tinker. The look on Kayla's face.

They'd be right to blame him. To despise him.

Pressure built behind his eyes and his throat constricted.

He couldn't go home. Especially if Mia didn't go with him.

Maybe Kayla and his grandmother were better off not knowing what had happened. If he never went home, they'd live out their days with a small measure of hope.

But the thought didn't assuage his guilt.

He tossed and turned until a particular strand of music caught his attention. The music had been wafting up from the party for hours, but this song was different. He had no idea what instrument it was, and he'd never heard the melody before, but something about it relaxed him. Breathing came easier, and he felt himself drifting off.

Reid woke with a start and it took a moment to remember where he was. A sliver of orange light appeared—the light from the hall as the door opened.

"Mia?"

"Going to the bathroom," she whispered.

"I'll come with you."

"I can do it myself. Go back to sleep."

He felt ridiculous. Of course she could go down the hall by herself. He'd been acting like—what did Tinker call it, a mother goose?

He tried to go back to sleep, but he couldn't while she was gone. How long had it been? It seemed like a long time, but he was sure it had only been minutes. He told himself she was fine. She was down the hall, not wandering the Burn or swimming in the ocean.

He squeezed his eyes shut and rolled over. He refused to be a mother goose.

Chapter 113

Hotel Sausalito

"It's the middle of the night. Go away," Nikolai called.

The knocking continued. It was probably Marseille, finally come for Josh.

"Josh is fine," Nikolai yelled. "Let him sleep until morning."

He put the pillow over his head, but the doorknob rattled.

"*Damn it,* Marseille." He slid out of bed and yanked open the door. "Mia? Sorry, I thought you were my sister coming for Josh."

He looked over at the boy who was still asleep despite the commotion, his head and shoulders hanging out of the "tent" they'd constructed in the middle of the room.

"Sorry to bother you." The makeup around Mia's eyes was smudged and tears had drawn charcoal trails down her cheeks. She was still wearing Tatiana's pink sundress. "I shouldn't have come." She turned away, her shoulders heaving with silent sobs.

"Wait." He touched her arm. "Tell me what's wrong. What can I do?"

She turned and flung her arms around him, burying her wet face in his neck.

He was suddenly aware of his bare chest, and thankful he at least had on a pair of shorts. "Did you and Reid have an argument?" he said into her hair.

"Uh huh." She tried to catch her breath. "He, he hurt me." She clung to him, her body shaking.

Nikolai was at a loss. He saw how Reid looked at her. The boy doted on her. Too much, if anything. It was obvious he cherished her. Nikolai couldn't imagine he'd hurt her.

He stroked Mia's hair and made shushing noises, reminding himself that the face people showed in public could be quite different than the one they wore in private. He'd known men who hurt women. Men who seemed normal and kind, but who humiliated and beat their women when no one was around to stop them.

"Did he hit you?"

Mia looked up at him. He saw no cuts or bruises, but there was plenty a man could do that wouldn't leave a mark. If Reid hurt this girl, Nikolai would make sure it was the last time he touched her.

"Tell me," he insisted. "Did he hit you?"

"He doesn't let me out of his sight. I can't go dancing or be with other people. . . . He says it's because I need to rest. And he's probably right, but . . ."

"But what?"

"He's taking me to Colorado. I don't want to go, but I don't want to make him angry."

"Don't go if you don't want to."

"I have nowhere else to go, I have no one else."

"That's not true. You have me and Tatiana and Cook. Plus I know Marseille will adore you. We're not going to let anyone take you against your will."

"I can stay with you?"

"Of course. As long as you want."

"I mean right now?"

She was so vulnerable, he didn't want to hurt her but he shook his head. "I'll get you your own room. You don't have to go back to him."

"No, don't. I mean, I don't want to trouble anyone. Besides, if I disappear in the middle of the night, Reid will worry. He saved my life. I can't do that to him."

"If he hit you—"

"No, it's not like that. He'd never hit me. I'm being overly emotional. It's just, so much has happened. I'm not myself. I shouldn't have bothered you."

"You're not a bother." He took her face in his hands. "You can always come to me."

Chapter 114

Hotel Sausalito

Reid pulled on his jeans. Mia wasn't back yet, and he couldn't sleep without knowing she was okay. He went into the hall, squinting as his eyes adjusted. He heard voices in the direction of the bathroom. It was the middle of the night. Who had Mia stopped to chat with?

He rounded the corner and stopped dead. Mia was with Nikolai in his doorway.

Nikolai was half-naked. His hands cupped Mia's face.

He's going to kiss her.

Reid couldn't look.

He went back to his room and sat on the couch in the dark. The stars usually gave him comfort, but now they were distant and cold. The longer he sat, the more images filled his mind. He saw Mia in a white shirt pushing Nikolai into a chair and climbing astride him.

He'd been a fool, an idiot. Too naïve, too trusting. Of course Mia had been snowing him with that bullshit about Nikolai being a father figure. The signs were all there. He should have listened to his instincts.

The door opened.

"Reid?"

He didn't answer. After a moment, Mia's silhouette blocked the stars.

"There you are." She knelt. "Are you okay? Why aren't you answering me?"

"Leave me alone."

"What's wrong? Are you missing your grandfather? Are you sick? It's okay, you can tell me." She put her hand on his knee.

He got up and crossed the room. He had to get out of there. He grabbed his shirt and shoes and headed for the door.

"What are you doing? Reid, stop. Talk to me."

He hesitated. He didn't *want* to go, but there was no point talking. She would lie.

"*Oh no,*" Mia breathed. "You saw me, didn't you. You saw me in the hall with Nikolai."

"You're not denying it?"

"Of course not." She crossed to him. "Let me explain?"

"I know what I saw."

"It wasn't what it looked like."

"Right." He turned the doorknob.

"Fine, go," she said. "But you'll always wonder. You'll ask yourself what you *really* saw, and if there could be some other explanation. You'll never know for sure if you threw away the best thing that ever happened to you over a simple misunderstanding. Every day you'll ask yourself if you'd only stayed to listen, if you'd still have me."

Reid rested his forehead against the door. What *had* he seen? Would he always wonder? She was the best thing in his life. The only thing in his life. Could he toss that away without hearing what she had to say?

After a long moment, he turned to face her. "Don't lie to me."

She took his hand and led him back to the couch.

Chapter 115

Lost Angeles

Pascal woke feeling rested for the first time since Linus— His mind balked, but he made himself face it. *Since Linus died.* He took a deep breath and realized he was okay. In fact, he felt so much like his old self, he considered asking Gomez for the daily reports. But he decided against it. Without Linus, Lost Angeles meant nothing.

The only thing he cared about was the one gift he could still give his son. Closure. In the form of Brandt's head on a platter, with Reid's alongside it.

This morning Justine would agree to the plan, and make some demands, of course. He was looking forward to it. It felt good to have something to look forward to.

He took a brisk shower and dressed, then headed to Justine's room.

Advani dozed in a chair blocking Justine's door. She roused without him saying a word.

"Status?" he asked.

"She's alert. She's eaten. Her vitals are good." Advani leaned forward and lowered her voice. "She asked when she can leave the hospital."

"What did you tell her?"

"That she was clear to leave any time, as long as she remained under a doctor's care."

"Well done." Pascal smiled. He'd made a good choice in Advani. "Take twenty minutes for yourself. I'll stay with her until you return."

He rapped on Justine's door, then opened it. "Good morning. I thought it time we had another chat."

Justine was sitting up in bed. "I've been expecting you."

"You've thought about my offer?"

"Offer? Is that how you see it?"

"What else would it be?" Pascal sat in the chair beside the bed. "You want something. I've offered to help you get it. It's your choice to accept or not."

"It's not much of a choice."

Pascal could see she'd already decided. "I'm not going to force you."

"I have some conditions."

"Of course."

"I'm not going anywhere until I know it's safe for me and the baby to travel."

"Has the doctor said when that will be?"

"*Your* doctor has. I want a second opinion from Dr. Lawrence."

"Doctor Doom?"

"He's not afraid to tell the truth, even if *you* don't like it."

"If that's what you want, I'll see to it. I assume there's more?"

"Yes. I need to know when the full moon is. After I've spoken to Dr. Lawrence—in private—I'll tell you what's next."

"I'll get busy with my assignments." He saluted and left the room.

In the hall, he motioned Gomez over. "I need to know when the next full moon will be."

"I'll find out right away, sir."

Pascal watched Gomez scurry away, taking the odd request in stride. He was truly better than any wife.

Chapter 116

Hotel Sausalito

"Good morning, sleepyhead." Mia pulled open the drapes.

Reid stretched. "It's bright out."

"I let you sleep in." Mia crawled across the bed and planted kisses all over his face. "Are you hungry? I brought you something." She hopped off the bed and retrieved a paper bag.

Reid sat up against the headboard and scrubbed his face with his hands. "I feel like I slept a whole day. I guess I needed it." In the light of day, he felt ridiculous about distrusting Mia. He'd been overtired, that was all. That, and feeling like he didn't deserve her, didn't deserve to be happy because of everything he'd done wrong. She'd told him that. Told him he was seeing things that weren't there because of his own demons. He was thankful he'd listened. "What time is it?"

"It's only mid-morning. I would have let you sleep longer, but Tatiana offered to show me around before lunch and I thought you might want to come." She sat beside him and reached into the bag. "I had Cook pack you the most amazing breakfast."

She pulled out an apple, a paring knife and a small bowl of something brown. She sliced off a chunk of apple and spread the brown goo on it.

It smelled good. He opened his mouth. "*Oh wow,* that's delicious."

"I know! Here, have more." She fed it to him. "Oops, I got a little on your chin." She grinned and licked it off.

"What is this stuff?"

"Peanut butter and honey. I can't believe I never had it before. Cook says honey never goes bad."

"We eat honey at home, but never peanut butter. It can make people really sick."

"Cook says the trick is to avoid jars that have been opened. The sealed ones are okay."

"I hope she's right. Give me another bite."

"So, do you want to go out? Or close the drapes and stay here."

"Can we do both?"

"If we hurry."

Twenty minutes later, Reid sent Mia off to find Tatiana. He showered and dressed quickly, then headed out to meet the girls. On his way downstairs, Nikolai stopped him.

"I'd like a word," Nikolai said.

Reid didn't feel particularly friendly toward him, despite Mia's reassurance about the nature of their middle-of-the-night conversation. That little voice inside whispered to him that this was his chance to find out if Mia had told the truth. He wished he could ignore it. He wished he could just trust her and tell Nikolai to buzz off. But he didn't. "What can I do for you?"

"I should probably mind my own business," Nikolai said. "But I haven't seen Mia today and I'm wondering if she's okay."

"She's fine. Why?"

"I saw her here in the hall last night, and she was upset."

"Oh?"

"She was pretty broken up. Scared. Grieving. She's fragile, and emotional. But she's a fine young woman, and she really cares about you."

This wasn't at all what Reid had expected. "I appreciate you saying that."

"My advice—not that you asked for it—is to give her some time to heal and process things. You've been taking good care of her. Maybe too good. I think she'd benefit from the freedom to explore this new place and who she is in it. If you can give her a little space, she may eventually go to Colorado with you. I'd hate for you to lose her because you push her too fast."

"I'll definitely think about that." Mia *had* told the truth. "I'd better go. She's waiting."

Reid flew down the stairs, happier than he'd been in a long time. Nikolai wasn't interested in taking Mia from him; he was trying to help them stay together.

From the front door, he saw Mia. She stood under a tree looking carefree and gorgeous like the people he'd seen in magazines. He always thought those people looked happier and more beautiful than any real people he'd known. Now it was like the girl in the magazine had walked off the page and chosen him.

He jogged over, and when she saw him, her face lit up.

"Hi." She kissed his cheek. "Tatiana will be back in a sec. She went to get us sun hats. Her house is right up there." She pointed. "She said people get to pick any house they want and fix it up to live in." She looked at him out of the corner of her eye. "You know . . . if we had our own place, we wouldn't have to be so quiet or put on clothes to walk to the bathroom."

He made up his mind instantly. "Sounds good to me. Pick a house nearby so we can come to the parties." He'd give her as much time as she needed.

"Really?" She clapped her hands. "Maybe there will be another party tonight."

"You didn't get much sleep last night."

Her brow furrowed, and Reid realized he'd done the very thing Nikolai warned against.

"Wait," he said. "Forget I said that. Go with Tatiana and find us a house, then we can dance all night if you want. Whatever you feel like doing. You're the boss."

"You don't mean it. You don't want a house here. You want to go to Colorado."

"Mia." He tipped up her chin with his finger. "I mean it."

She smiled.

It was better this way. They'd go when they were both ready.

She kissed him quick on the lips, then turned to Tatiana who was walking down the hill. "Guess what? We want to pick a house to live in! Is there a good one close to yours?"

"There are several right across the street. Do you want to see them now?"

"Yes, let's go." Mia headed toward her.

"Aren't you coming, Reid?" Tatiana called.

"Nope, I'll like any house Mia chooses."

Reid stayed under the tree watching the girls walk away. Halfway up the hill, Mia turned and blew him a kiss. Nikolai had given him good advice.

"Reid, I'm glad I found you." Brandt came down the hotel steps. "Have a minute?"

Great. "Sure, I guess." He wouldn't be able to avoid him forever.

Might as well get it over with while Mia was occupied.

"Have you tried the cider yet? The pub's over here." Brandt pointed opposite the direction Mia had gone.

"Why not?" Reid gestured for Brandt to lead.

"This is where I'm staying," Brandt said as they entered the tall, narrow building. "It's Marseille's place. The pub's on this floor, she lives on the top story, and there's guest rooms on the floors in between." He held up two fingers to the girl behind the bar.

The place was empty. "Mind if we sit back here?" Reid asked Brandt, indicating a table far from the window. He didn't want to chance Mia seeing them together.

Brandt nodded and they sat.

"Where is everyone?" Reid asked.

"Left for the orchards at sun-up," Brandt said. "The growing operation sure takes a lot of labor. And they say this is the slow time."

The girl from behind the bar brought over two tall glasses of amber liquid.

"Are we supposed to pay?" Reid asked. He didn't have anything to barter, unless the bar girl needed medical care.

The girl smiled. "Brandt's tab is already taken care of. Have as much as you want."

"Thanks," Brandt said. He watched her walk back to the bar, then turned to Reid. "I've been wanting to apologize for upsetting Mia before. I assumed she knew about Justine." He drank down a third of the cider, then wiped his mouth with the back of his hand.

"It wasn't your fault. I should have realized. I should have told her myself." Reid took a sip of cider, relieved this was what Brandt wanted to discuss.

"What do you think of it here?" Brandt asked. "San Francisco or Sausalito or wherever we are." He took another long pull from his glass.

"It seems nice enough, from what I've seen."

"Have you decided what you'll do next? Will you go back to Colorado?"

"When Mia's stronger."

"She said she'd go with you?"

"I won't go without her."

"But she didn't exactly say she'd go, did she."

Reid pushed his glass aside. "What's this about, Brandt?"

"Have you given up on finding seeds?"

377

"Not by choice. I don't know where to look."

"Well, we know they don't have them here. Except for apple seeds. So I thought you might want to come with me when I leave."

"Wait." Reid came forward on his chair. There was something odd about the expression on Brandt's face. "Do you know where Justine's people are?" That would change everything.

Brandt shook his head. "No, but I'm going to look for them. There's evil in the world. Pascal and others like him. A long time ago someone wise said, 'all that's necessary for evil to triumph is for good men to stand by and do nothing.' Well, I'm not going to stand by. I'm going to find Justine's people and warn them, tell them that Justine died trying to get back to them. Besides, what else have I got to do? I heard Sacramento's inhabited. I figure I'll start there, and you're welcome to come."

Reid let out the breath he'd been holding and slumped in his chair. "Like I said, Mia's not ready yet. But thanks. I wish you luck."

"You're sure about this? About Mia?"

Reid nodded. "When I'm with her, nothing else matters."

Brandt finished his drink and stood. "That's all I needed to know. I wish you luck, too." He extended his hand. "It's been good knowing you."

Reid watched Brandt go, hoping he'd find peace even if he never found Justine's people. Halfway to the door, Brandt turned and came back.

"Forget something?" Reid asked.

"More like I changed my mind."

"About going?"

"About Mia. There's something you need to know."

Chapter 117

Lost Angeles

Pascal was back on his game and looking forward to a little banter with the good doctor, Benjamin Lawrence. Maybe Ben's time in the Tank was tempering his moralistic proclivities and he'd be a bit more practical-minded.

"How precious," Pascal said at the door to the doctor's cell. "Do you enjoy playing with your little boy through the bars, Ben?"

Ben's face was no longer a stone. His eyes smoldered and tension worked bulges in his jaw. "Chancellor."

"What do you want?" Pascal asked.

"You came to me. What do *you* want?"

"I'm the man who can give you everything. Or take everything away," Pascal said with a pointed glance at the doctor's family. "Tell me what you want, Doctor Lawrence, and I'll tell you how to get it."

"I want my family out of here."

"Is that all? No lofty dreams of being chief of the hospital? A private suite at the Grand? Extra food rations? A mansion, perhaps?"

"I'd settle for things going back to the way they were."

"The doctor at the spa tragically died recently. Would you like his job?"

"You asked me what I wanted. I want my old life back."

"Very well. Help me get what I want and it's yours."

"What do I have to do?"

"Lie to a patient."

Ben's gaze lingered on his son, and then his wife, before coming back to Pascal. "Go on."

When Pascal was confident that he and Ben had an understanding, he and a guard escorted Ben to the hospital to see Justine. The two of them had been alone in her room for more than ten minutes now, and

Pascal was beginning to run out of patience.

Ben had better not disappoint.

Finally, Ben stepped out and pulled the door closed behind him.

"We'll be in my quarters," Pascal told Advani.

Advani took her place by Justine's door, and Pascal marched ahead of Ben down the hall. He was anxious to hear about the conversation with Justine, but more anxious to keep it private.

As the door to his quarters closed behind them, he turned to Ben. "What did she want?"

"Shall we sit down?" Ben gestured to the chairs by the window.

Pascal wanted to slap the smirk off Ben's face. "No. You're not my guest. Tell me."

"As you expected, she asked if she was still pregnant. I told her I had already reviewed her chart, then I gave her a cursory exam and told her she was definitely still pregnant."

"She believed you?"

"By all indications. What about you? Do you want to know if she's still pregnant?"

"I couldn't care less. Tell me what else she said."

"You were correct that she wants to travel. As you instructed, I told her it was safe as long as she stretches her legs regularly and sleeps in a bed each night."

"I assume she asked you to come with us?"

"No, you were wrong about that." Ben looked like he enjoyed that. "She said Advani would be traveling with her, and wanted to know if she was a decent doctor. I assured her she was. Then she asked about your son."

Pascal's heart stopped for a second. "What about him?"

"She remembered you asked me to examine him. She wanted to know if he was okay."

"You didn't tell her—"

"That Linus was dead before she got here? No, I said he was stable and in no danger. She mentioned that Advani diagnosed him with malnutrition. I told her I concurred."

Pascal exhaled silently. "Why did she want to know?"

"She said she doesn't trust you, but your love for your son seems genuine. She wants to believe your motivation is to give your son a better life, even if you don't actually care about the rest of the people in Lost Angeles."

"Interesting." Pascal's estimation of Justine rose. He'd need to remember not to underestimate her intelligence. "Did she request drugs or supplies?"

"She asked if we had Lorazepam. She wanted to know if it would still be potent after fifty years on the shelf, and what the dosage would be to induce amnesia. But she didn't ask me to provide any. Does she plan to take it herself?"

"That's none of your concern. Did she tell you where we're going?" Not that it mattered. He'd know soon enough.

"Only that she was going to see the baby's father."

Everything appeared to be coming together nicely. Ben had better not be hiding anything. "Did she say anything else? You've done well so far, Ben. Don't screw it up by leaving out any detail, no matter how inconsequential it may seem."

"There was nothing more."

Pascal studied the doctor's face for any indication of deception, but only found resignation and regret. "We're through here. Go home, and don't mention this to anyone, not even your wife."

"My family's at home?"

"They will be as soon as I authorize it. Go home and wait for them. But don't get too comfortable. If you've lied, your family won't be safe, even in my absence."

Chapter 118

Sausalito

Nikolai stood on the dock looking out at the water. His children were safe and accounted for, the sun was out, and he was taking Josh fishing.

What could be better?

"Are you *whistling?*" Creighton asked, coming up behind him. "When was the last time you did that?"

"It's been a while."

"So you're happy."

"Not about everything. But right now, in this moment, yes, I'm happy." Nikolai rocked on his heels. "Today is a good day."

"But you're still pissed as hell at me."

"That sums it up."

"I'm pissed as hell at you, too," Creighton said. "What are we going to do about it?"

"What are the options?"

"We could ignore each other."

"Too late."

"Yeah, I see that now." Creighton scratched his head, jostling his unruly locks. "We could stay mad and not talk about it. Or we could talk about it. Or you could punch me again. I'd probably punch you back this time, though."

"Is that it?"

Creighton shrugged. "We could get drunk and talk a whole lot about it, not resolve anything—or resolve everything—then not remember any of it in the morning."

"Seems like a waste of time and cider."

"Yeah."

They stood in silence a moment.

"*Or* . . ." Nikolai said.

"Or what?"

"We could take Josh fishing."

"I hate fishing."

"I'm saying it's an option."

"Eh, it's an option. Not my favorite, though."

"Are you going to hit me?" Nikolai asked. "If so, could you do it now? Because I can't be late to pick up Josh."

"I was thinking about it. That or apologizing."

"What?"

"Yeah, I was thinking I could apologize for not paying attention when Will needed me, and not telling you when your kids were in trouble, and in general being a selfish dick and a rotten friend."

"You forgot the part about not telling me Tatiana was sleeping with Kennedy."

"Right. I was thinking I'd apologize for all that, including the part about Kennedy, and maybe we'd grab a couple of ciders and take Josh fishing."

"If I were hearing this from my oldest friend Simon Creighton, I'd accept the apology and render one of my own. However, I have no idea who you are. You're obviously not Simon Creighton because the Simon Creighton I know and love would never, ever willingly go fishing."

Out on the boat, Nikolai and Creighton joked and bantered like nothing had ever come between them, completely neglecting to police their language. It took promises of sailing, camping, and lots more fishing before Josh agreed not to tell his mother. He probably knew Nikolai would have done those things with him anyway, but it was good for him to practice his negotiating skills. Creighton called it blackmail, but that was in the eye of the beholder.

They sent Josh to Cook with the string of fish, and ambled over to Marseille's pub. Marseille herself was behind the bar.

"It's nice to see you boys together," she said. "What can I get you? Humble pie? Crow? Or are you too busy eating your words?"

"Nothing for me. I'm full," Creighton said.

"A couple of ciders?" Nikolai asked.

"You got it, sailor." She delivered them, along with one for herself. "To a full cup, keeping your nose to the wind, and women of easy behavior."

"Aye, to good fortune, good sense, and good women." Nikolai

raised his glass.

"And good friends," Creighton said. "Even when they're selfish dicks."

"To selfish dicks," Marseille said.

"I'll drink to that." Nikolai downed half his glass and slammed it on the bar. "Speaking of drinking, is there a party tonight?"

"If you want one, you'll have to host it," Marseille said. "I'm on call—two girls in labor and only one midwife. I'm sure I'll be needed one place or the other."

"Tomorrow then? I have a big announcement to make, and I want everyone to be there."

"Sounds interesting," Creighton said. "You getting ready to settle down? Going to introduce your bride-to-be?"

"You'll have to wait like everyone else. Or try to pry it out of me while we're fishing."

"No more fishing," Creighton said. "I've got to draw the line. Out of self-respect, you understand?"

"Let's plan on a party tomorrow night," Marseille said. "I'll have at least one of those babies birthed by then. I can always call on the new medic if the midwife needs help, right?"

"He's a good kid," Nikolai said. "Very competent. I'm sure he'd be glad to help."

"Then it's settled. Spread the word—there's a big shindig at The Landing tomorrow." Marseille raised her glass.

"Works for me," Nikolai said, clinking his glass against hers.

"You know me. Always up for a party," Creighton said.

Chapter 119

Hotel Sausalito

M ia bounded into the room. "I found the perfect house. Are you sleeping? Get up! I want to show you the house." She pulled on Reid's arm.

He sat up but didn't get off the bed. He'd been staring at the ceiling for hours, going over and over what Brandt had told him. He'd tried to convince himself Brandt was lying, that Brandt blamed Mia for Justine's death and was trying to destroy any chance Mia had for happiness. But it hadn't seemed like that. It had seemed like Brandt didn't want to tell him, that it had pained him greatly to tell him.

"Come here a minute." He scooted to make room for Mia. "There's something I need to ask you."

She sat beside him. "What's wrong?"

"I talked to Brandt."

She leapt to her feet. "Damn you! I told you not to."

"I tried to avoid him, but he insisted. He's leaving soon and he felt he had to tell me what happened with my grandfather."

"I can't believe you went behind my back." Mia stormed to the door, turned around, and stormed back. Her cheeks were flushed, eyes narrowed. "You promised me. You *promised.*"

"I know, and I'm sorry." He didn't break promises, and part of him wished he hadn't broken this one. "Mia, Brandt told me something about you. I don't want to believe it but . . . I need to ask, I need to know if it's true."

"Of course it's not true. He's trying to hurt me. Whatever he told you, I can guarantee it was a lie."

"I hope so. But I have to be sure. He said . . . " Reid swallowed, not wanting to say it, not wanting to allow for the slightest possibility it could be true. But he couldn't let it go. He had to ask. "He said that when you went to find out if Tinker had been captured, you never intended to learn the truth. That you planned to wait awhile, then come back and say he was in the Tank."

"He *was* in the Tank."

"Brandt said you didn't want to risk your life for the truth when I'd believe anything you said." It stung that the part about him was true. He would have believed Mia, whatever she'd told him. "He said that you wanted out of Lost Angeles, and the fastest way was to tell me Tinker was in the Tank. Whether he was or not."

"I *did* risk my life. Tinker *was* in the Tank. You were there, you know it's true."

"But were you *planning* to lie?" So far she hadn't denied it.

"How can you even ask that?" She stormed to the door and wheeled around again. "I might be able to forgive you for breaking your promise, but I don't think I can ever forgive you for believing Brandt over me. I almost *died* for you."

"Stop it, Mia. Just answer the—"

There was a rapid knock at the door. "Reid, it's Marseille. There's an emergency."

Mia opened the door, edged past Marseille, and ran down the hall.

"What is it?" Reid asked, slipping on his shoes.

"A young woman, her first pregnancy. She's in labor, but something's wrong. It's beyond my capabilities, and the midwife's away on another call."

He pushed all thoughts of Mia from his mind. "I'll grab my bag."

Chapter 120

Sausalito, aboard the Belle Jewel

Mia held her hands out in the rain. "Let's go for a walk." She turned to Nikolai and eased closer. "No, I have a better idea—make love to me in the rain."

"You don't have to try so hard."

"I don't know what you mean."

He gentled his voice to soften the message. "You can stop playing me."

"Who's playing?" She slid her arms around him and pressed her breasts against his chest. "I want you, and you can have me right here on the deck of your boat."

"Mia." He took her wrists and extracted himself. "I know what you're doing, and it's not going to work on me. I know the difference."

"Just because this is what I do, doesn't mean it's always business. And Brandt had no right to tell you."

"No one told me. I didn't know until now."

"So you admit it. You don't want me because of my job. Well, you can go to hell. I'm not ashamed. I chose it and I do it well. I won't apologize to you or anyone else."

Her eyes flashed with rage as she turned away, but Nikolai knew it was a mask for her fear. He grabbed her arm and spun her around.

"That's not why," he said.

"You're all a bunch of prudes. Let me go."

Nikolai laughed. "Do you have any idea what my mother does? And my sister? I grew up in a whorehouse. I have nothing against what you do. I understand you, perhaps better than you understand yourself. And I know what you really want now is not a fuck in the rain."

She looked up at him, soaked to the bone, her soul naked and vulnerable. This was the real Mia—a frightened, lost child. "I'm all alone here. I have no one." She wasn't playing him now.

"You're not alone. I meant what I told you last night. I'm not going to abandon you. You don't need to flatter me or play me or fuck me. I give you my friendship freely."

He held out his arms to her. She hesitated a moment, then stepped forward and let him envelope her. She was stiff. Tense and unsure. So he waited, giving her time to realize there was nothing sexual about his embrace. After a moment, she slid her arms around him and rested her forehead in the crook of his neck, the way Tatiana did when she needed to feel safe. As he held her, he wondered if Mia had ever known the love of a father, or of any man who didn't want something from her in return.

Chapter 121

Sausalito

The sun was coming up when Reid left the new mother and baby. The ground was wet, but the sky was clear. He'd missed the chance to take that walk in the rain with Mia.

Maybe he'd ask her to go for a walk anyway. They needed to finish their conversation.

All night he'd tried not to think about what Brandt told him, or the fact that Mia hadn't denied it. It had been easy to forget during the delivery itself. A breech baby was all-consuming under the best of circumstances, but this one had gotten hung up on the umbilical cord and entered the world blue and still. Reid refused to give up, though, and when he'd finally handed over the baby, pink and squalling, the new mother said it was a miracle.

Miracle. That's what she named the baby.

An image of Kayla flashed in Reid's mind, the way she'd look in a few months' time, her belly round and full with Brian's baby. Then a realization hit him like a physical blow—he wouldn't be there for the baby's birth, the naming, for any of it.

He wouldn't be there for Kayla if the baby didn't make it.

The guilt nearly drove him to his knees. How could he live with himself if he didn't go back? He owed it to Kayla. He owed it to his grandmother. They shouldn't spend the rest of their lives waiting and wondering. They deserved to know Tinker had died, even if they hated him for it. They needed to know there were others in the world, people thriving on fish, and seaweed, and apples.

He absolutely had to go home. *But,* he realized, he didn't have to stay there. He could come back to Sausalito and bring anyone who wanted to join him. They'd be free from malnutrition and have a better life than was ever possible in the Mountain.

He pictured himself returning to Sausalito with dozens of people from Colorado. He could imagine the astonishment on their faces as they saw the green of the trees for the first time, and the warm welcome they'd receive from the colonists. He could see Mia standing there in her pink dress, squealing with delight as she saw him, running to meet him with love in her eyes that was meant for him and him alone.

For the first time since Tinker died, he knew exactly what to do. And when he came back from Colorado, he'd settle down with Mia. She was beautiful, and sexy, and she loved *him,* wanted *him.* He could be happy with her. Brandt had lied, and Reid never should have believed him.

He hurried to town, anxious to find Mia and apologize. He'd beg and grovel until she had no choice but to forgive him, then they'd make up.

When he got to the hotel, he bolted up the stairs and down the hall to their room. As he reached for the doorknob, he heard a man's voice.

"You got what you wanted. You don't need him anymore."

Nikolai? Reid opened the door.

Brandt stood toe-to-toe with Mia.

"What's going on?" Reid said.

"Tell him the truth," Brandt told Mia. "You owe him that." Brandt met Reid's gaze, then strode past him through the doorway.

Reid shut the door and held out his hand to Mia. "I never should have listened to him. Please, forgive me."

Mia turned away and went to the window.

"I was wrong," Reid continued, crossing to her. He touched her shoulder. She didn't turn, didn't say anything. He slipped his arms around her and nuzzled her ear. "I love you."

"*Don't.*" She pushed him away. "Take your stuff and go. Please, go. I'm trying to do the right thing here."

"What do you mean, the *right thing?*" He tried to make eye contact, but she wouldn't look at him.

"I'm not going to Colorado with you."

"That's okay." He touched her arm. "I have to go, but I'll come back."

"You don't understand. I'm trying to say *I don't love you.*"

"You don't mean that." What had Brandt said to do this to her? "Whatever Brandt said, he was trying to hurt you, like you said he would. He doesn't want you to be happy. But we love each other. I'm not going to let you push me away."

"*Listen.* You don't love me any more than I love you. I needed you to believe you loved me. I had to make sure you wanted me, needed me, couldn't live without me. So that when you left Lost Angeles you didn't leave me behind. But you don't love me. Not really."

"Why would you say that? You know I love you."

"Believe me, you're not the first to leave my bed thinking you were in love." She shook her head, a smirk curling her lips. "That's what I do, and I'm good at my job."

"What . . . what are you talking about?"

She took a breath as if to speak, but then stared at him, eyebrows raised. The longer she was silent, the sicker he felt and the more he wanted her to keep the words inside, and not speak them. Not ever speak them. He didn't want to know. But it was already too late.

"That was your job?" he whispered.

"You had to have known."

"That *sex* was your *job?* How would I know that? Where I'm from, that's not a job." Embarrassment spread from his cheeks down his neck. It all added up now—the elaborate set-up with the shower and doctor's exam. Mia coming onto him so quickly. *God.* How many men had she been with? Did it take a lot of practice to become so good at pretending?

She shrugged. "It's better than being a seamstress or a cook."

"So everything between us, you didn't mean any of it. It was all a lie."

She shrugged again.

"And my grandfather?" Reid asked, his stomach clenching. "You were going to lie about that, too?"

"As it turned out, I didn't need to."

She didn't have any trouble looking him in the eye now. This was the real Mia. How had he not seen it before? It was right there in front of him. The manipulation, the cunning, the guile, the outright lies. She didn't love him. She'd used him. She'd been using him all along.

He couldn't look at her any more. He turned away, but it didn't help. The real Mia was etched on his retinas, her callous smirk and remorseless eyes perpetuating his pain and humiliation.

Chapter 122

Lost Angeles

Pascal cleared his throat and entered Justine's room. "The full moon is in three days."

"Three days?" Justine exclaimed. "We need to leave right away."

"Then we will. Tell me what you need. I'm at your command."

"I need to set some ground rules. First, I'm the only one who drives."

"Is that wise? In your condition?"

"I'll be fine. Second, I'm not going to tell you where we're going."

"I didn't expect you to."

"Third, Dr. Advani is the only one coming with us. No soldiers, no weapons. And finally, I'll need to drug you and Dr. Advani when we get close to our destination. You agreed I could sedate you, so no arguing. It's the only way I can protect my people. Without that, we don't go."

"I understand. I will instruct Dr. Advani to bring whatever drugs you request, but I insist on a handgun for protection." He had to make her feel like there was a little give and take. She was no half-wit. If he agreed to everything, she'd know something was wrong.

"Fine, one gun. Now, shall we get the car?"

Pascal nodded, carefully concealing his joy. "Absolutely, my dear, as long as you're feeling strong enough." Finally the vehicle. One step closer to having his revenge.

It was a challenge to remain patient while Dr. Advani got Justine situated in a chariot for the ride out to Anaheim stadium. The woman kept fussing with blankets and pillows, making sure Justine was comfortable, giving her a bottle of water. It nearly broke him when, after Justine was settled, the doctor asked if she had to empty her bladder. Luckily for all concerned, Justine declined.

He and Advani both sat with Justine for the ride, making the cart that much heavier for the Blades to haul. He hadn't intended for Advani to accompany them, but she'd parked herself beside Justine uninvited. When he'd looked at her quizzically, she'd scowled and turned back to arranging Justine's pillows. Perhaps it wasn't a terrible situation. He did want Justine to think that her health was paramount.

Finally, they pulled into the stadium parking lot, and the Blades slid to a stop near the Humvee. The leader set the brake on the chariot, then assisted Advani and Justine to the ground.

Justine drew in a sharp breath as she stepped down.

"Are you all right?" Advani steadied Justine by the elbow as Pascal leapt from the chariot and took her other arm.

"I'll be fine." Pain creased Justine's brow as she walked to the car. "If we don't leave tomorrow, we have to wait a month."

Ah, the phase of the moon.

Justine opened the car door and climbed into the driver's seat. "The key?"

Pascal took the card from his pocket and placed it in her hand.

"Step back," Justine said. "Your men, too. No one sees how I start it. Non-negotiable."

"Men!" he shouted. "Form a twenty-foot perimeter around the vehicle. If it moves, shoot her." He smiled at Justine and stepped back, hoping he could see what she did to start the car. She put the key in the reader—that much he'd done himself. It looked like she was entering a code, but it was impossible to see which digits or how many.

The engine came to life.

The window lowered. "Get in, Chancellor."

Pascal allowed himself to grin back at her. This was indeed a moment to be celebrated, more than Justine even knew.

Chapter 123

Sausalito

Reid found Brandt in Marseille's pub. "I'm going with you."

Brandt looked up from his cider. "What happened?"

"You were right about Mia."

"I'm sorry. I wish I'd been wrong."

Reid collapsed in the chair across from him. "I wish I'd seen it sooner. Maybe things would have turned out different."

Brandt took a swig of his cider and wiped the froth from his mouth. "It wasn't your fault, Reid. I know Mia told you I blame you for Justine's death. But I don't."

She didn't have to—I blame myself. "Let's not talk about Mia."

Brandt nodded. "I can live with that."

"So, when do we leave?"

"Tomorrow soon enough?"

"*Now* isn't soon enough, but tomorrow gives me time to pack. I just need a minute, then I'll get to work." He propped his elbows on the table and rested his head in his hands, trying to put his jumbled thoughts in order.

"You look wrecked," Brandt said.

"Before things went bad with Mia, I was up all night delivering a baby. I need a couple of hours sleep, but there's no way in hell I'm going back to my room."

"Go crash upstairs in my room."

"Yeah? That would be great, because right now I can't think straight. I'd end up packing six left boots and nothing else."

"Go get some sleep, and don't sweat the packing. Everything will make more sense when you wake up."

Reid hoped so, but he doubted anything could help him make sense of Mia's job.

Chapter 124

San Francisco Bay, aboard the Belle

Nikolai stood shoulder to shoulder with Will looking out at the Bay. "Son, I have something for you." Nikolai pulled his father's pipe from his breast pocket and held it out. "This doesn't mean I want you to take up smoking."

"Wow, Dad. It's beautiful. You sure?"

Nikolai nodded, and Will took the pipe, turning it over in his hands.

"It came on the sub with your grandfather all the way from Russia," Nikolai said. "It was his father's before him, and I want it to stay in the family. It's yours now, and I hope someday you will pass it down to your own child."

"Thank you. I'll treasure it," Will said.

Nikolai pulled him into a hug. "I'm proud of you *moy zolotoy mal'ch'ik.*"

"*Yah vahs lyoo-blyoo, Papa.*"

"Who taught you that?"

"You did."

"When you were *five.*"

"I have a good memory."

"Hmph. Go find your sister. I have something for her, too."

Will went belowdecks, and Nikolai hurried to the bow where Kennedy was checking the riggings.

"There's something I need to say to you privately, but with my nosey daughter on board, we have to make it quick."

"Yes sir?"

"You asked me something once, and I gave you a less than pleasant answer."

"I'm afraid you'll have to be more specific."

Nikolai laughed, realizing that statement could apply to multiple occasions. "I'm talking about when you asked to marry my daughter."

"Ah yes, I believe your answer was, *no fu*—"

"If you'll allow me," Nikolai interrupted, smiling despite himself. Kennedy was already feeling like a son. "I'd appreciate the chance to answer you differently . . ." Nikolai pulled a small box from his pocket and opened it. "I'd like for you to have this, along with my blessing."

"What are you doing?" Tatiana called.

"Damn, not quick enough," Nikolai said.

"Is that mom's ring?" Tatiana exclaimed. "Will said you gave him Grandpa's pipe. Are you going to kill yourself?"

"*What?*" After a split second of shock, Nikolai roared with laughter. He laughed and howled and snorted until his sides hurt and he had to sit down on a barrel and blow his nose. No one else was laughing. "Tatiana, you are the most direct person I've ever met."

Tatiana glared, hands on her hips. "This isn't funny."

"I'm not going to kill myself," he said. "I can't imagine why you'd think that, but you don't have to worry. It's the furthest thing from my mind."

"I'm sorry, but when a person *changes* and gets all emotional and gives away their most prized possessions, then it's logical to think that maybe they're planning to, *you know*."

"I don't know about logical," Will said, coming up behind her. "It's not the first thing that came to my mind."

"You've never been known as the most logical person," Tatiana said.

"Hey! Not nice," Will said.

"Well, what did *you* think was going on?" Tatiana demanded. Then she gasped and turned back to Nikolai. "Oh no, don't tell me you're having a midlife crisis and you're going to marry someone half your age. Oh God that's it! That's why you have mom's ring out. That's what the big announcement is going to be at the party tonight."

Nikolai couldn't help grinning.

"No, no, no," Tatiana said. "That is so wrong, so terribly horribly wrong. Do something, Will."

"Like what? What can I do? It's not like giving back the pipe will change his mind."

Nikolai looked at Kennedy, pleading with him for help.

"Guys," Kennedy said, getting their attention. "I don't know what your father's big announcement is about, but I know why he has the ring, and I'm afraid it *is* for a young woman. Someone your age, Tati."

"I knew it," Tatiana said.

"Way to go, Dad," Will said, socking him in the arm.

Kennedy held out his hand. "Sir, may I?"

Nikolai whispered, "Now?" When Kennedy nodded, Nikolai handed him the ring.

Kennedy turned to Tatiana and bent down on one knee. "Tatiana Grace Petrov, you are the most incredible creature on this planet. You make my life interesting every moment of every day, and I want to spend the rest of my life trying to keep up with you. Will you marry me?"

"Oh my God, *that's* what this is about?" Tatiana said. "You let me think my dad was committing suicide or marrying a teenager so you could surprise me?"

Nikolai was incredulous. "Is this how you answer his proposal?"

Kennedy's grin was wide. "I wouldn't have it any other way, sir."

"Oh, stop it," Tatiana said. "Don't worry, Dad. He already proposed quite romantically, and I already accepted."

"I guess I shouldn't be surprised," Nikolai said shaking his head. "Don't tell me you're already married, too."

"Married? No, I didn't want to get married without Mom's ring. I figured it would take you a while to come around, so I planned on an extra-long engagement."

"Am I that old and stodgy and stuck in my ways?" Nikolai asked.

"Not as much as I thought," Tatiana said. "I told Kennedy it would take over a year for you to accept him, but apparently the whole pirate thing put us on the accelerated plan."

Nikolai looked at Kennedy with new respect. "You were willing to endure that for a year?"

"I'm in it for the long haul, sir. Besides, you weren't all that bad."

"Kiss-ass." Nikolai thumped Kennedy on the back, perhaps a little harder than necessary.

"Okay, I give up," Will said. "What's the big announcement tonight? If it's not about any of you getting married, and I know *I'm* not getting married, and Dad's not announcing he's going to kill himself, then I'm stumped. What is it?"

"I did ask you all out here to tell you my news in private. And I shall open my soul to you all . . . " He looked from face to face, all flushed with curiosity. "*Tonight.*"

"*Dad,*" Will scolded.

"You're a tease!" Tatiana laughed.

"I'm enjoying your anticipation far too much to let it go now," Nikolai said. "You'll find out at the party tonight along with everyone else."

"But you *swear* you're not getting married," Tatiana said, with her hands on her hips and a stern look on her face, just like when she was six years old scolding her "classroom" of dolls.

Nikolai raised his eyebrows and shrugged.

Chapter 125

Sausalito

Reid sat up, still half in a dream. He looked around trying to remember where he was. Was he in the Mountain? Tinker's house? The Tank? *Brandt's room*. The present came rushing back, and he wished it hadn't. *Mia*. The horrible truth. His shame and humiliation.

He didn't want to be in the present. He closed his eyes to go back to his dream, but then he remembered: he was going home. There were feelings of guilt and shame there, too, but also a sense of rightness and purpose.

The door opened, and Brandt entered. "Hey, you're awake."

The curtains were drawn but Reid could tell it was light out. "What time is it?"

"Afternoon."

Reid groaned. "I've got to check on my patient, and then I still have to pack." His stomach knotted at the thought of going to his room, but he needed his med kit.

"I already got your things from your room." Brandt indicated a pack by the door. "And I gathered up most of the other stuff we'll need—bedrolls, food, matches. Will gave me apples and apple seeds. They'll come in handy for trading, and for you to take home if we don't find Justine's people. All we need now is to find you a knife and gun."

"I have a knife. I don't want a gun." He opened the pack and pulled out his med kit.

"Trust me, you need a handgun," Brandt said.

"Trust me, I don't."

Brandt stared at him, and Reid stared back. He wasn't backing down.

Finally Brandt shook his head. "All right. Up to you."

"What I *do* need is a place to sleep tonight."

"I already talked to Marseille. She said you can have a room here with the girl of your choice."

"What?"

"It might help."

"What are you talking about?"

Brandt's brow furrowed. "Marseille's place, it's like the Grand."

"And the women are . . . *like Mia?*"

Brandt nodded.

"What the hell?" Reid stormed to the window and wheeled around. "What is wrong with the world? How did sex suddenly become a job?"

"Whoa," Brandt said. "That's been around forever. The oldest profession."

"Not where I come from. I never even heard of such a thing. I only found out about Mia this morning. Now it turns out it's everywhere. Is Marseille?"

"Marseille? Yeah, sure. She runs the place."

Reid opened the curtains and leaned against the windowsill, trying to make sense of something that made no sense at all.

"Sorry, man," Brandt said. "I didn't mean to upset you."

Reid's cheeks burned. "I feel like an idiot."

"Don't beat yourself up. You didn't know."

"What I don't understand is why a woman would choose that as a job."

"Not everyone chooses," Brandt said. "Here they have other options, but most women at the Grand didn't have the choice. Justine didn't."

"*Justine?*" Reid turned. "I had no idea."

"It's the way things are in Lost Angeles," Brandt said. "But not where Justine came from. It was hell for her."

"Was Mia forced too?" Reid thought it wouldn't be as bad if she didn't have the choice, but felt horrible for wishing that.

Brandt shook his head. "Mia chose."

"Of course she did." Reid turned back to the window. He wasn't surprised. Yet he was the slightest bit disappointed, and he didn't understand why he still cared at all.

"Look, forget I said anything," Brandt said. "Sleep in my room tonight. We'll leave first thing in the morning and put all this behind us."

Seeing his patients was a respite for Reid. He knew what to do, what to think. Plus today he had the added benefit of company—Josh had asked to tag along, and the boy was a nice distraction.

The visit didn't take long. The new mom was healthy, and the baby was nursing well. The midwife arrived shortly after Reid, so he briefed her then headed back to town with Josh.

The kid never stopped asking questions, but Reid didn't mind. It kept his thoughts from venturing where he'd rather not go.

"Do you like being a medic?" Josh asked.

"I can't imagine not being one."

"Did you get to choose it or did other people choose for you?"

"I chose it, when I was about your age."

"I've been thinking a lot about what I'm going to choose." Josh's brows were drawn in concentration, his tone serious.

"There's no rush."

"I know. I'm collecting options. Mom says anything you choose is okay, but if you don't have any options, it's not really a choice."

The observation was insightful. "Your mom sounds like a smart woman." *So why did she choose sex as her job?*

"Yeah, mom's pretty smart. Uncle Niko too, and Tatiana. My grandma is *really* smart. I don't know how smart Uncle Simon and Will are, but I'm trying to learn from everybody, even if they're not that smart, because I want to know all the options."

"That makes you pretty smart."

"Why did you choose being a medic? Because, from what I saw back there with the baby, it's pretty gross."

Reid laughed. "Uh oh, what did you see?" He'd made sure Josh wasn't in the room when he'd examined the mother.

"The shriveled-up black thing sticking out of the baby's tummy— what the hell was that?"

Reid tried not to smile. "The umbilical cord. Is your mom okay with you swearing?"

"Nah, it's a guy thing. Me and my uncles do it when there's no girls around. You won't tell my mom, will you?"

"Nope. It's between us guys."

"Fresh." Josh grinned.

They entered the lobby adjacent to Marseille's pub.

"I'm heading to the kitchen," Josh said. "Want to come?"

"Thanks, but I'll go up to Brandt's room." He'd rather not chance running into Marseille.

"If you come with me, I bet Cook will give us a treat. Maybe even chocolate if you tell her I helped you. Please?"

"Okay, you talked me into it." There was no need to disappoint Josh. Marseille probably wouldn't be in the kitchen anyway.

"Hello, you two," Marseille said as they entered the kitchen.

"Uh oh, Mom's here," Josh said behind a cupped hand. "That means no chocolate."

"How is the new mother?" Marseille asked.

"Doing great. The baby, too," Reid said, hoping he didn't look as awkward as he felt. "Josh helped."

"What did you think?" Marseille asked Josh.

"Disgusting."

"Tactful as ever." Marseille ruffled his hair. "At least thank Reid for taking you."

"Thank you, Reid," Josh said. "I think you're one of the smart ones, but I don't like your option. Too much disgusting baby poop and black cord things."

"Josh," Marseille admonished, unable to keep the grin from her lips. "Cook's out back shucking clams for tonight. Why don't you see if you can help?"

"Mom! You know I don't like her option."

"But you like her chocolate, and she's got some in her apron."

Josh ran out the door without a backward glance.

"I hope you're not sorry you agreed to take him," Marseille said.

"Not at all. Although if I'd known he was checking out my 'option,' I might have done something more interesting than changing a new-born's diaper."

"I think it was the perfect introduction. Much better than if he'd seen you deliver our little Miracle." Marseille smiled, and it transformed her. She was pretty to begin with, but her smile made her extraordinary. "If it weren't for you, Miracle might not be with us. Have you considered settling down here? We could use a man with your talents."

"I appreciate that, but I've decided to leave with Brandt." Reid shifted, uncomfortable with Marseille now that he knew what she did for a living.

"That's too bad. I'm sure Josh is disappointed."

"He doesn't know yet. I should find him and tell him myself."

"He'll be at the party tonight. You can tell him then."

"I won't be there."

"No? Nikolai's making some big announcement, so Cook's preparing a feast. The instruments will be out. Tomorrow's a day off from the orchards, so the party could go all night."

"We're leaving early tomorrow." Reid had no interest in hearing Nikolai's announcement. It probably had to do with Mia.

"If you change your mind, come find me. I'd like a dance to remember you by."

Reid looked into her eyes, trying to understand how she could have sex with men she didn't love, perhaps men she didn't even know. It was too foreign, too incomprehensible.

Marseille took his hand. "I'm sorry for what you've been through, Reid. You're a good man, and I hope you find what you're looking for."

"Thank you." He squeezed her hand, then let it go and headed out of the kitchen.

"You've made a difference here," she called. "Whatever life brings, that cannot be undone. If you are ever in need of a safe harbor, you will always be welcome."

He continued to Brandt's room, feeling the warmth of Marseille's words, feeling valued and appreciated, but at the same time wondering if manipulating his feelings was part of her job.

Chapter 126

Lost Angeles

While Justine napped, Pascal oversaw preparations for their journey. Minou assured him she could ride a bike as well as any of the Travelers, and the men were outfitted and standing by. Nathans fetched spray paint from Supply, too intimidated to ask what it was for. Gomez took care of the food, gear, and weapons, and Advani guarded Justine's room while packing medical supplies. Everything would be ready for a morning departure.

Pascal went home and put some clothing and toiletries into a duffle, then stopped by his private suite in the Grand to retrieve his mother's Ruger. He declined to spend any time there despite a nice offer from Ellianna's replacement. Instead, he returned to his room at the hospital.

He considered visiting Linus, but decided against it. He had nothing to offer him. Not yet. The thought of finding Brandt and Reid had his blood pumping. He'd take great pleasure in giving Linus the closure he deserved.

Maybe after that he'd be inclined to start over. With the car and seeds, there would be no limit to what he could accomplish. It wasn't too late to raise another son, and this time he'd be more careful whom he chose to bear his child.

"Sir?"

"Come in, Gomez."

"Everything is ready."

"Thank you. I couldn't have done this without you."

"I appreciate you saying so, sir."

"I don't know how long I'll be away, but I trust you'll manage my affairs well in my absence. Continue as you have been. I know you'll do what's best."

"Yes sir."

"One thing . . . I'd like to see Linus when I return. Can you do whatever is necessary?"

Gomez looked at him wide-eyed, and the requisite "yes sir" did not roll from his tongue.

"Don't worry, Gomez. I know he's dead," Pascal said, noting the relief evident on Gomez's face. "I meant I want you to delay the decaying process. Have him embalmed or something. Jenna, too, so Linus won't be alone."

"Of course, sir. Anything else?"

"Dinner. I seem to be getting my appetite back, and who knows when I'll have another decent meal. Too bad I can't take Chef with me."

Chapter 127

Hotel Sausalito

Reid sat at the window watching the sky rush through every trick it knew—from blue to pink, orange to red, purple to cobalt, and finally to black. The whole world changed in the space of a few heartbeats, and you couldn't go back.

Yesterday he and Mia had made love and planned for a future together. Then, in the time it took for the sun to set, his world had gone from bright to black.

How had he not seen Mia for who she was? Was he really so gullible, so naïve? Or had he not seen the truth because he hadn't wanted to? Had he been complicit in her charade?

The room pushed in on him. He couldn't breathe. He threw open the door and half-ran down the stairs, breaking into a sprint as soon as he reached the night air.

The orange glow of the bonfire lit the party down by the water. He turned in the opposite direction and ran until his chest heaved and the only light was from stars peeking through a gap in the clouds. He slowed to a walk, pressing a fist to the stitch in his side. As the pain dissipated, his head cleared.

He'd be glad to leave all this behind him. He'd forget about Mia and focus his energy where it should be. Cumorah's people—Justine's people—were out there somewhere. He hadn't *imagined* the grown food. Seeds did exist, and he was going to find them and bring them back to Colorado, no matter what it took.

The clouds were low and moving fast, and thunder grumbled as Reid tried to make his way back to Marseille's building. He wasn't sure exactly where it was, but he could tell he was going in the right direction because of the occasional snippet of music drifting on the air.

Down a cross street, he saw an orange glow indicating he was nearing the bonfire. He turned and headed toward it, hearing the music faintly but steadily now.

The road dead-ended at a clearing where he could see a gazebo outlined by the bonfire. The sky grumbled again and let go of a sprinkle of rain. As Reid jogged toward the gazebo for cover, the moon broke free of the clouds, illuminating two figures already inside the structure. Then the sky went dark again and started to pour.

Mia? Reid stopped. He'd only caught a brief glimpse, so he wasn't sure. Then he heard laughter and knew it was her. She was *laughing.* Like nothing had happened.

Who was she with? It had to be Nikolai. Mia had probably been seeing him all along.

Reid told himself to walk away, but he kept watching.

The two in the gazebo continued murmuring, laughing. Their silhouettes became one. They were kissing. Bile rose in Reid's throat. Why was he doing this to himself?

The two pulled apart.

"You're sure?" the man asked. It was *Will.*

"It's definitely over," Mia said. "It was never serious."

"I don't think Reid saw it that way," Will said.

"Don't feel too bad for him," Mia said. "I may have been using him, but he was using me too."

Reid's protest caught in his throat. Mia was right. He *had* been using her. To avoid facing the truth. To avoid admitting his failure. He'd never loved her. She'd been his anesthetic to help him forget. Did the Mia he'd been obsessed with even exist? Or had he projected onto her exactly what he'd wanted to see, what he'd *needed* to see to make sure he could see nothing else?

Yes, he'd been as guilty of using her as she was of using him. But not any longer. It was time to stop hiding from the truth.

Reid gave the gazebo a wide berth, and made it to the far side of The Landing without being seen. The rain had stopped and the party was in full swing, with people dancing and singing and drinking, but he wasn't in the mood. He wanted to sleep so tomorrow would come sooner.

He skirted the edge of the dance floor, heading for the stairs that led up to the hotel and Marseille's place.

The music stopped and the dancers applauded. "Encore!" someone shouted.

Reid kept walking, but stopped abruptly when he saw who was sitting behind the piano. Nikolai smiled and waved to the crowd, then began to play again. The song was upbeat and joyous, and totally captivating. Reid sank onto an empty bench at a table with a view of the piano.

The dancing resumed in earnest, and Reid felt part of it as the vibrations from instruments and stomping feet reverberated through him. He was mesmerized as the dancers spun across the floor. The swirling colors of skirts, the swish and swoosh of long hair, flashes of smiles and bare skin. He decided dancing made every woman beautiful.

He thought he might like to try it, but the idea of going on the dance floor alone was terrifying. He'd just about decided it was time to leave the party when his gaze landed on Marseille dancing in the center of the crowd. Her red hair tumbled down her back, the light from the fire turning it the color of glowing embers. She wore a tank top and a flowing skirt in shades of amber that caressed her hips as she moved. She wasn't doing flashy steps or twirls like the couples, but Reid was mesmerized by the sensuality of her movements. Her eyes were closed, her face upturned and serene. She had no partner except for the music—it seemed to be all she needed. He still wasn't comfortable with what she did for her job, but he couldn't stop watching her dance.

When the song ended and the applause stopped, Marseille shouted something. Nikolai's gaze snapped in her direction, and a smile spread across his face. A hush fell when the song began, one sad, haunting note followed by another. The other musicians lowered their instruments, then Nikolai began to sing. Such a clear, strong voice. Powerful and loud, then soft on what seemed like just the right notes. He looked as lost in the music as his sister in dance.

Reid glanced back at Marseille, but she was gone. He scanned for her amidst the couples dancing in each other's arms, but couldn't find her.

There was a tap on his shoulder. "I'm glad you changed your mind," Marseille said. "Are you going to dance with me?"

Reid's mouth went dry. No words would come out.

She took his hand and he followed her to the next table where she whispered something in the ear of a man with shaggy blond hair. The man grabbed a guitar-like instrument from the table and walked toward the stage, playing as he went.

Nikolai's expression turned mischievous and the music changed, issuing a challenge to the other man. The man countered with a faster, louder riff, which Nikolai answered with another of his own. Other musicians joined in, and the song grew louder and more lively. The mass of bodies and colors on the dance floor seemed alive, ebbing and flowing with the music.

Marseille pulled Reid in among the dancers and turned to face him. He tried to tell her he didn't know what to do, but she placed her hands lightly on his hips and started to dance. He was self-conscious, but watching Marseille completely give herself up to the experience, he decided not to care how he looked. He surrendered to the music that thrummed through his body, and lost himself in the moment.

The song ended too soon. When the applause stopped, Marseille looked up at him. "Shall we dance another?"

"Hell yes," he said, lifting her and spinning around. His chest was full with something like joy. He'd never experienced that kind of emotion when he'd heard hymns back home. He placed Marseille back on her feet, anxious for the next song.

"Everyone, can I have your attention?" Nikolai's voice rang out over the hubbub of the crowd. "I have an announcement."

Reid had assumed that Nikolai'd made his big announcement earlier. His first instinct was to leave, but then he realized it didn't matter what Nikolai announced. It made no difference now, and he wanted to dance some more.

As Marseille turned to face the stage, Reid kept his arms circled around her waist and she leaned back against his chest.

"I have decided," Nikolai said, looking across the rapt audience. "To retire." His face drew into a wide smile. "As many of you know, it's long been my dream to sail west. But of course, there is always work to be done, trials and tribulations, obligations, children to raise, children to rescue . . ." He paused as a ripple of laughter went through the crowd. "And all the joys and sorrows that make life rich and full. You are so busy living your life, you don't realize until too late that it's coming to an end, and you've missed your chance. Your chance to sail west, or whatever it is you've always dreamed of doing.

"For those who are lucky," he continued. "There comes a day when the tide turns. It's your children who are doing the work, raising the young, and rescuing you. The children have become the adults, and for better or for worse, they are running the world.

"For those who are very lucky, when that day comes, you're not too old or infirm to take the chance, to chase after your dreams. That day has come for me. When I see my children and the thriving community they are building with you, I'm proud beyond measure. It's their turn to run the world."

There was a smattering of applause, but Nikolai held up his hands. He had more to say.

"Soon, I'll sail west to answer the question that has burned in my soul for more years than I can remember. So please, raise your glasses."

People scrambled for drinks, and someone handed mugs to Marseille and Reid.

"Join me in a toast," Nikolai said. "To sailing west."

"To sailing west!"

"And to family!"

"To family!"

"Aloha, my friends." Nikolai bowed, and the crowd erupted in cheers and applause.

"Music!" someone shouted.

Nikolai stepped off the stage, but other musicians began to play.

Marseille took Reid's mug and deposited it on a table, along with hers, then ran back to him. Reid hadn't noticed before that she was barefoot except for tiny strings of bells around her ankles. The faint jingling as she moved made him smile. She closed her eyes and gave herself up to the music and motion. In that perfect moment, he knew her. He couldn't put it into words, but he felt it. A profound sense of understanding and acceptance.

Hours later, Marseille coaxed him off the dance floor with the promise of a drink of water. The fire had died down, the crowd had thinned to almost nothing, and the last two musicians were packing their instruments, but Reid wasn't ready for it to end.

The man with the shaggy hair waved them over. "Excellent party, Marseille. It's a shame it's ending so early."

Reid was sure it was after two in the morning, but he agreed. It was definitely too early.

"Why don't you do something about it, Simon?" Marseille said.

"I'm about to."

Simon crossed to one of the few tables still occupied. A moment later he ushered Nikolai to the piano and sat beside him on the bench. Nikolai began to play, and then to sing. Simon joined in. After a moment, Marseille began to sing too, with a voice as beautiful and joyous as her dancing. As the song continued, more people joined in, their voices melding together as one.

Marseille took Reid's hand and walked toward the stage, drawing him with her. She stopped behind Nikolai and placed her hands on his shoulders, belting out the song. Reid felt odd being there without knowing the words, but Nikolai winked at him. Simon motioned for others to come up, and everyone who remained at The Landing gathered around the piano.

When the song ended, Nikolai launched into another tune. By the end of the third song, the group had dwindled to a handful.

Simon stood and turned to Marseille. "Despite my noblest efforts, it appears this party is over." He kissed her cheek and departed.

Nikolai pushed himself back from the piano.

"One more?" Marseille asked. "This young man owes me a dance to remember him by."

Nikolai gave a nod and began to play.

Reid knew right away it was the haunting song he'd heard before, and he didn't care that they were the only ones on the dance floor. Marseille draped her arms around his shoulders.

"What is this song?" he asked.

"My brother wrote it for me. It's called *Marseille*."

He looked into Marseille's face, her expression pure joy. He wanted to remember her just like that. He wanted to remember all of it—the dancing, the music, Marseille, how he felt—forever. She'd said she wanted a dance to remember him by, but she had given him one.

He pulled her close, and they leaned against each other, moving as one until the last note died away.

Chapter 128

Lost Angeles

As per her instructions, Justine was the driver. Pascal sat in the other front seat, relegating Advani to the back. Now that they were outside the park, the road was full of obstacles. Pascal felt ill from the constant swerving as Justine avoided other cars and the bigger potholes. He put down the window and took a deep breath, hoping the feeling would soon pass, as it usually did in rough seas.

"How are you doing, Justine?" Advani called from the back seat.

"I'm fine, like the last time you asked me," Justine said.

"This is awfully bumpy," Advani said. "Are you sure you're not cramping? Maybe you should drive slower."

"I said I'm fine," Justine retorted.

"Justine," Pascal said. "This jarring can't be good for the baby. Why bring the doctor if you're not going to heed her advice?"

She slowed down, albeit not by much, and they drove north on the I-5 in silence. Pascal tried to distract himself from his nausea by looking at the surroundings, but it was all the same—rusted vehicles, crumbling buildings, all decaying in various shades of gray and brown. As much as he'd anticipated traveling by car, he found he preferred sailing. Perhaps he'd feel differently when he was the driver.

After an interminable hour ticked by on his Rolex, he informed Justine it was time to stop and stretch her legs.

"I feel fine," she said. "Let's keep going."

Pascal considered it. He needed to mark the way for the Travelers if they altered course, but since he had no idea where they were going, he didn't know when that might be. If he had Justine stop now, and then ten minutes down the road she took a turn, he couldn't very well have her stop again without arousing suspicion.

"Doctor," he said. "I think it's fine to keep going if she's feeling well, don't you?"

"A little longer," Advani said. "But not another hour."

After fifteen more minutes, Pascal was growing anxious about how many miles they'd put between themselves and the Travelers. He couldn't keep waiting for a turn. The I-5 highway went all the way to Canada—they might stay on it for days on end.

"It's time to stop, Justine," he said.

"Look up ahead," she said. "Can you tell what that is?"

"I don't know," Pascal said, squinting. "An overpass? Another highway?"

"Whatever it is, it looks huge," Advani said.

"Let's stop there," Justine said. "I want to look at the map anyway."

After a few minutes, they stopped at the juncture of a massive cluster of overpasses.

"Dr. Advani, can you give me the map?" Justine asked.

Advani handed it up, then got out of the car and stretched.

Justine opened the map, placed her finger on the city of Anaheim and traced I-5 north.

"This is where we are?" Pascal asked, touching the map.

"It has to be," Justine said. "The last sign we passed said this highway number."

"Are we getting on that highway, or staying on this one?" Pascal asked.

Justine scowled. "I'm not telling you that."

"I'm not asking our *destination*," Pascal said. "I need to know which of these roads to check out. For safety."

"Oh. We stay on I-5."

"Thank you. Now turn off the car and hand me the key."

"Why?"

"Let's not pretend we trust each other," Pascal said.

He tucked the key card in his pocket, then took handcuffs out of his bag and secured Justine to the steering wheel.

He walked up the highway examining the structure, noting they had to turn to stay on I-5. It would be confusing to the Travelers if he didn't mark it. He hiked back to the car and opened Justine's door.

"Looks structurally sound, as far as I can tell," he said. "To be on the safe side, we're going to stop and check any time we cross an interchange like this."

"Fine, whatever," Justine said under her breath.

Pascal unlocked the cuffs from the steering wheel and left them dangling from Justine's wrist. "Get out."

"Are you going to take these off?" Justine held out her arm.

"No." He helped Justine down from the vehicle. "Doctor, come here."

Advani circled around the car and Pascal attached the other cuff to her wrist.

"You've got to be kidding," Justine said. "It's not like I'm going to run away out here in the middle of nowhere."

"Let's go, Justine," Advani said. "We'll walk ten minutes to help circulation. Let's head over there for a little privacy. I'm sure you need to empty your bladder."

"I have to pee attached to her? This is ridiculous."

After Advani led Justine away, Pascal grabbed his bag and walked along the highway in the direction they'd come. When he was a good distance from the vehicle, he stopped. He'd given Advani clear instructions to keep Justine where she could not see him, but he still scanned the surroundings before pulling a can of spray paint from his bag.

He shook the can and painted "stay on I-5" on the asphalt in bright red letters, adding an arrow for good measure.

Chapter 129

Hotel Sausalito

A t sunup, Reid shrugged on his pack and headed to the dock. Brandt was already aboard the small sailboat that would take them across the bay.

"You didn't come back to the room last night," Brandt said, grinning. "Maybe now you appreciate the benefits of a professsional, huh?"

Reid grinned back, letting Brandt think what he would. The truth was, he'd been tempted by Marseille's offer to make him forget about everything but her. But in the end, he'd slept on her couch, not because of her profession, but because he was done forgetting.

He climbed aboard the boat, glad to be leaving Sausalito, though there were things he'd miss. The fresh apples, fish, and seaweed. The friends he'd made. The dancing. He liked contributing, using his skills. Under other circumstances he could see himself living there and helping to develop the colony. As it was, his only focus was finding seeds, but he'd like to think maybe he'd return one day.

He'd already said his goodbyes to Marseille and Josh, Tatiana and Kennedy, Olexi and Cook. He'd wanted to thank Will and Nikolai for their help, but decided it was better to avoid them. It wasn't his place to warn them about Mia, and he didn't think he'd be able to hold his tongue.

"So you're our captain, eh Friday?" Reid asked the little man who sat in the bow.

Friday's creased face pinched into a smile, but he didn't say anything.

Reid remembered Friday didn't speak.

"I guess we're ready to go," Brandt said. "Shall I?" He gestured to the ropes that held the boat to the dock.

Friday shook his head and pointed.

Reid looked up the hill. A lone person walked down from the hotel. Nikolai.

"Good morning," Nikolai called, holding up a hand in greeting.

"Morning, Captain," Brandt said. "Come to see us off?"

"On the contrary. It's a beautiful day for a sail, so I thought I'd take you myself."

Reid drew in a deep breath and sighed as Nikolai boarded.

"Is my company that difficult to stomach?" Nikolai asked.

Reid winced.

Nikolai laughed. "I know the water between us is muddy, but perhaps I can clear it a bit, if you'll allow me."

Reid wasn't sure what he meant, but he nodded, not wishing to be any ruder.

"Let me start with a gift," Nikolai said. "The wind is excellent and I think I can save you a day of walking by sailing you up the Delta rather than across the bay."

"Yeah?" Brandt said, raising his brow. He unfolded a map he had stashed in his pocket and held it flat on his knees. "I planned to head across Berkeley, and take this road east through the mountains, making our way toward Sacramento." He traced the path with his finger. "How close can you get us?"

"We should have clear passage up the Delta at least through the Carquinez Strait," Nikolai said. "Friday, how much farther do you think we can go?"

Friday looked at the map, pointed, then shrugged.

"Antioch? That's farther than I thought," Nikolai said. "Of course it depends on the wind, and on the waterway being wide enough for a tack. But it's still better time than you can make walking."

"Sounds good to me," Brandt said. "Reid, you okay with that?"

"Why not." Reid didn't relish the idea of spending the day with Nikolai, but it would spare his feet a fair number of miles.

Friday untied the ropes from the dock, then hoisted a sail as Nikolai manned the tiller. Wind filled the sail and they eased out into the bay.

"I heard you're heading to the Hawaiian Islands," Brandt said to Nikolai.

"It's as if they've been beckoning me since I was a small boy."

"Leaving soon?" Brandt asked.

"Not as soon as I'd like. Preparations to the *Belle* will take me and Will several weeks."

"Will's going with you?" Reid asked, figuring that meant Mia would be too.

"No, he's helping me prep, then I'm dropping him in Seattle," Nikolai said. "He gave the *Belle* back to me—says he doesn't want to be a sailor anymore."

"I'm surprised Will's leaving," Brandt said. "He seems so passionate about the colony."

"The colony's a relatively new interest," Nikolai said. "What surprises *me* is he's giving up sailing. It's all he ever wanted from the time he could toddle after me. Now he says he's had enough adventure. He wants to settle down."

Reid glanced toward the hotel where Will was surely in bed with the source of his sudden career change. *Same game. Different player.* He should have warned Will.

"But why settle in Seattle? Why not here?" Brandt asked.

"He's taken an interest in the family business," Nikolai said.

"I guess I could see Will running a cider-making empire." Brandt grinned.

"Oh, cider is a side venture," Nikolai said. "The real family business is my mother's whorehouse."

"Will's going to be a *whore?*" Brandt blurted.

Nikolai laughed. "No, he'll take over the management."

Reid snorted. "Perfect. His new girlfriend should feel right at home."

"You're right," Nikolai said. "My mother's retiring, and I can't think of a better apprentice than Mia. She's very like my mother—shrewd and cunning with a keen ability to read and manipulate. And no moral qualms about the nature of the business. The role will fit Mia like a glove."

"That's fine for Mia, but what about Will?" Reid knew he should keep quiet, but he couldn't help it. "You can't stand by while she manipulates him into giving up his dreams."

"Not long ago, I would have agreed with you," Nikolai said. "But my children are adults now. It's not my place to steer them where I think they should go. A person must chart his own course if the journey is to mean anything."

"I should have warned him," Reid said. "I wish someone had warned me."

"Would you have listened?" Brandt asked. "Besides, Mia's not all bad."

"How can you say that?" Reid asked. "You know better than anyone what she's like. You're the one who made her come clean with me."

"I didn't make her," Brandt said. "All I did was point out what you'd be sacrificing to stay with her. She chose to do the right thing and let you go."

Reid heard Brandt's words, but he was having a hard time digesting them. Was it possible Mia had made a choice out of concern for someone other than herself?

"I appreciate your concern for Will," Nikolai said, clapping Reid's shoulder. "But when a man feels the siren's song, there's nothing anyone can say to keep him from following. It's up to the man whether he goes blindly or opens his eyes. I think Will's eyes are wide open and he sees the real Mia. Whether he follows her siren song because of that or in spite of it, who can say?"

Chapter 130

Santa Clarita, California

"We should stop for the night, don't you think, Doctor?" Pascal was concerned about the bicycles keeping up in the mountains.

"No," Justine said. "We've hardly gone any distance at all."

It had taken half a day to cover less than a hundred miles. Of course stopping every hour to walk hadn't helped, but it was necessary given the Travelers' pace.

"Justine." Advani placed her hand on Justine's shoulder. "You and the baby need a full night's sleep. We must find lodging and make a meal before it gets dark."

"I'm not stopping yet," Justine insisted. "We have at least two more hours of sunlight, and we're on a deadline."

"Tell me about this deadline. What happens on the full moon?" Pascal asked.

"If I tell you, can I keep driving?" Justine asked.

"That seems fair," Pascal said, not promising anything.

"Okay," Justine said. "If we don't reach a particular meeting place by the full moon, we'll have to wait there until the next full moon."

"Why have I never heard this?" Pascal asked. "Not one of the missionaries I've questioned over the years mentioned it."

"They can't tell you what they don't know."

"How does it work if they don't know?"

"We're trained from a young age that when we find a husband, we to go to church and pray for instructions from Heavenly Father."

"A specific church?"

"No, He can hear prayers in any church."

That part fit with the bits of information he'd obtained previously. The girls were supposed to go to church, pray, and wait. Now he understood that someone came by to collect them on the full moon, but there was a disturbing implication. "There must be thousands of churches to monitor—how many people are in your community?"

"My people don't monitor them."

She hadn't answered the question, but he didn't want to make her suspicious by pressing. "You can't expect me to believe God actually speaks to the women."

"I don't care what you believe," Justine said.

"It's time for a walk," Advani said.

"But we're not stopping for the night," Justine said.

"I haven't agreed to that," Pascal said.

"Be reasonable," Justine pleaded. "I explained the deadline like you asked. We have to keep going. I know how far we need to get each day, and we're not even close."

"I can be reasonable," Pascal said. "To a point. How much farther do you want to go?"

"Bakersfield."

That's useful information. Pascal opened the map. "Bakersfield's still a long way off."

"Right, that's why we can't stop yet."

"Take a quick walk, then we'll drive awhile longer," Pascal said. "I'm not promising Bakersfield tonight. Unless you let me drive while you sleep."

"No deal," Justine said.

"It's your call," Pascal said.

Justine stopped the car. Pascal cuffed her to Advani and sent them on their way.

When they were out of sight, Pascal went behind the car and painted "Bakersfield" on the ground. He settled himself in the car and closed his eyes until he heard the women approach.

"What's that smell?" Justine said.

The paint. He'd forgotten what a keen sense of smell pregnancy brought on. He should have gone farther from the car.

"It's nothing," he said. He got out and uncuffed the women. "I knocked over a can of some chemical when I went to empty my bladder." He returned to his side of the car and got in.

Justine climbed into the driver's seat while Advani resumed her place in back.

"Turn away, please," Justine said.

Pascal faced the window while Justine entered numbers on the keypad. He hoped Advani had sense enough to try to see the code.

Chapter 131

Oakley, California

Reid was glad to be back on dry ground. To keep the peace with Nikolai, he'd kept his eyes closed for the bulk of the journey, pretending to sleep, but the resulting motion sickness made him wish he'd found some other way. He understood Nikolai didn't think it was his place to interfere with Will's decisions, but Reid didn't agree.

"We'd help you set up a night camp," Nikolai said, "but we're already cutting it close if we're going to make it home before dark, even going with the wind."

"That's okay. I'd like to cover more ground before dark anyway." Brandt looked at Reid. "If you're up for it."

Reid nodded.

Friday grinned and handed Brandt a string of fish. He bowed, then returned to where he'd tied the boat to a half-submerged pier.

"Thank you, Captain," Brandt said.

Nikolai clasped his hand and pulled him into a hug.

Brandt laughed, struggling with his pack and string of fish.

"Thank you," Reid said, extending his hand to Nikolai.

Nikolai grasped his hand and held onto it, staring at him. The pause had become awkward when he finally spoke.

"I'll speak to Will, if you want me to."

"Yes! Thank you—"

"Wait," Nikolai said, squeezing his hand. "I want you to be certain."

"If you can spare Will the pain—"

"I've tried before to spare my loved ones pain," Nikolai said. "But pain is inevitable. It's an inextricable part of living. It's how we learn. How we grow. To protect my children from pain would be more of a disservice than outright killing them. Because it is only through experiencing pain and adversity that we become human. That we become alive."

"But—"

"Who were you before you met Mia, and who are you now? I don't mean what you felt or what you lost, but how it changed you. Would you be who you are without pain?"

"I don't know." Reid tried to pull his hand from Nikolai's grasp, but Nikolai held firm. Reid didn't like to admit Nikolai was right, but he was. He swallowed and nodded.

Nikolai pulled him into a hug, thumping him firmly on the back with his other hand. "It's been good to know you."

"Thanks," Reid said. "For everything."

Nikolai stood back. "My friends, I wish you neither fur nor feather."

"What?" Brandt exclaimed. "What does that mean?"

"I have no idea," Nikolai said, chuckling. "My father always said it for luck. I hope you find what you seek. Be safe and be well."

Reid and Brandt watched the boat sail out of sight.

"That was intense," Brandt said. "You still up for walking?"

"Absolutely." He'd had his fill of talking. It was time to get moving.

Chapter 132

Grapevine, California

A t dusk Justine drove into a tiny town with a sign proclaiming "Grapevine."

The mountains were much steeper than Pascal had anticipated. It would be tough-going for the Travelers, especially in the dark. He needed to give them time to catch up.

"We're stopping here for the night," he said.

"But it's not much farther to Bakersfield," Justine said.

"You need a hot meal and a bed for the baby's sake," Advani said.

"I am willing to revisit my earlier offer," Pascal said. "If I drive, we can continue to Bakersfield after dinner."

"No," Justine said.

"Then stop in that parking lot. There's a convenience store, a restaurant, and a motel. Everything we need for the night."

Justine sighed and exited the highway. She turned off the engine in front of the motel and handed the key to Pascal.

"Advani, find two adjoining rooms while Justine and I stretch our legs." Pascal nodded and Advani nodded back, indicating she knew what must be done.

"What, no handcuffs?" Justine asked.

"Do you need them?"

She was silent.

"Shall we peruse the convenience store?" Pascal asked. "We have plenty of supplies, but there might be something useful or interesting."

Justine shrugged.

"Where's your spirit of adventure?" Pascal continued. "How about a hat that says 'Grapevine'?"

"That's not allowed at home."

He hadn't been fishing for information, but this was interesting.

"Why not?"

"Missionaries can't bring back souvenirs. We're not allowed to talk about anything that happened on our missions, or even reveal where we served."

"That seems odd," Pascal said, passing the entrance to the convenience store.

"The elders say it's because the only important lessons are those we've internalized. Charity, generosity, appreciation. Not physical things. But I think it's more than that. They're trying to keep the community separate from the outside world to preserve our way of life."

Pascal processed this. Their leaders kept them isolated, insulated. Not dissimilar to how he ran Lost Angeles. "Do you agree with that?"

"Yes and no. On the one hand, I don't believe our people are the only ones deserving of seeds and animals. But on the other hand, after seeing what I've seen, I know better than to mix your world with mine. Mine would disappear."

"I can respect that," Pascal said. "I promise to keep our worlds separate, so long as I get the resources I need for my people. But there's something I'm not clear about. How can you promise me seeds when your leaders are so dead-set against sharing with outsiders?"

"Let's say I have good reason."

"Not good enough." Pascal stopped. He resisted the urge to yank Justine around to face him, and instead waited for her to stop on her own. When she did, he continued. "I've agreed to go into your community impaired by drugs and unarmed. I don't think it's unreasonable to ask how I'm going to get out alive with the items you've promised."

"My people are entirely nonviolent. That's why we go to such extremes to keep our location secret. There are no weapons or military. You'll be fine."

That jived with what other missionaries had told him. If true, that would make taking over far easier. But the more he could learn, the better. "So even if they don't kill me, what's to keep them from locking me up? I can't imagine they'll simply load me up with seeds and send me back to Lost Angeles with their blessings."

Justine folded her arms and chewed on her lip. Pascal waited.

"Okay," she said. "The truth is, I'm not a missionary."

The bottom dropped out of Pascal's stomach. "What do you mean?"

"You were right about me being different," Justine continued. "My father is the Prophet, the leader of my people. Because of that, I didn't need to go on a mission to find a husband—I was supposed to marry an important man in our community. I did not leave my home willingly. I was kidnapped. My father will be so happy you brought me home, he'll give you anything."

This was an interesting twist. "Who kidnapped you? Was it someone from the outside?"

"No, one of our own elders. He said he loved me and that Heavenly Father meant for us to be together. But he was married, and divorce isn't allowed."

"Did you share his feelings?"

"No! He was like a grizzled old uncle. Kind, harmless. I trusted him. I had no idea he had feelings for me, so it was easy for him to slip me the herb we use for the missionary rituals. It put me in a trance and he led me away from my parents, my friends, my home, from everything I'd ever known. And I have no memory of him doing it. The next thing I knew, I was in a strange house in bed with him naked on top of me."

"How terrible."

"You can't imagine. All I ever thought about was getting away from him. He never left me alone, but even if he had, I had no idea how to get back home. If I was ever going to see my family again, I had to gain his trust. So I made him believe I loved him. Eventually, he told me things. Things that are kept secret from our women about the elders and the missions and the rituals. That's how I know things missionaries don't."

"He told you how to get home?"

Justine shook her head, a far-away look in her eyes. "No, but he told me where the meeting is on the full moon. That's why it's so important we make it on time. I don't know where to go from there, and I can't wait a month with Brandt thinking I'm dead." Justine stared blankly into the night sky, tears streaming down her cheeks.

"We'll make it there on time, Justine," he said. "Out of curiosity, how did you end up in Lost Angeles? Obviously you escaped from that man and went to the meeting place. What happened? Why didn't you return home?"

"I never went to the meeting place. I couldn't. Not after what I'd done."

"Because you'd pretended to love him?"

Her focus came back to him, and she locked her gaze on his. "Because I killed him."

426

Chapter 133

Knightsen, California

R eid and Brandt walked as long as they could, only stopping when it grew too dark to continue safely. The ground was dry and the sky was clear, so they set up camp outside in a rural area rather than in a house.

They hadn't seen any sign of other people. Still, they scanned for lights before building a small fire, and kept their guns at hand.

Brandt gutted the fish, skewered them on sharpened sticks, and handed one to Reid. They held them over the flames.

Neither had said much since they'd parted ways with Nikolai. Reid welcomed the quiet—he'd hardly had a moment to himself since he left the Mountain—but he did wonder if Brandt was giving him space, or if something was bothering him.

Reid picked all the fish off the bones, then ate an apple before laying his bedroll near the fire. He stretched out, using his coat for cover, and keeping his boots on to be safe.

Brandt sat staring at the fire.

"Wake me when it's my turn for the watch," Reid said.

"There's something I need to tell you."

"Yeah?"

"I lied about Justine's people."

What the hell? Why did everyone lie to him? He took a breath and tried to sound calm. "They don't have seeds?"

"No, they have seeds. I lied about not knowing where they are."

"What?" Reid bolted upright. "That's great!"

"There is a catch. A big one."

"Okay." How bad could it be? There were seeds, and Brandt knew how to find them.

"If Justine's people see you, they won't let you leave. Justine and I figured we'd give you and Mia the choice before it was too late. You could either come with us, knowing you could never leave. Or you could go back to Colorado without seeds."

"Why didn't you tell me before?"

"Couldn't take the risk word would get out and someone would follow. I don't want anyone else to die."

"But people *are* going to die, Brandt. The people who don't have fish and seaweed and apples need those seeds." He thought of Kayla, and the baby, and his grandmother, and all the others in Colorado, New Mexico, and who knew where else. "We have to go back to Sausalito and get help. There's too much at stake not to. We'll try to get Justine's people to see reason first, but if they don't, we'll have the numbers to take the seeds by force."

"I agree about the seeds, but I don't want any more bloodshed. I think I have a way that no one else has to die."

"I'm listening."

"Justine didn't leave home like other missionaries. She fell in love with a married man, and they escaped so they could be together. They were on their own for about a year, then when he died, she didn't want to go back home. That's when she came to Lost Angeles."

"I don't understand how this helps."

"She *escaped,* and she told me how. Once I'm in the compound, I know how to sneak back out with seeds. Then you take some to Colorado, and I take some to San Francisco. No one else ever knows where the seeds came from."

"What if those seeds die, or aren't the right ones?"

"*Then* we come back with force. But not before."

Reid wanted to like the plan, but it was too much of a risk. "No. If we don't make it, the location of the seeds dies with us. We'd be risking everyone's future, not just our own."

"Please, Reid," Brandt said. "There's been enough death, too much of it at my own hands. I don't want to be responsible for any more."

What hung in the air unspoken was that only Brandt knew the location of the seeds. Reid could amass an army, but without Brandt's cooperation, there was nowhere to take the fight.

Reid looked at Brandt across the dying embers. "Do you really think your plan will work?"

"I think it's a long shot, but I'm going to try."

Chapter 134

Grapevine, California

As they walked to the motel, Pascal wanted Justine to keep talking. The more information he gathered, the more prepared he'd be for contingencies. But she didn't say another word, and he thought it better to let it lie. Besides, he already had a lot of new information to mull over. Justine as the kidnapped daughter of the leader. Justine as a killer. Those were unexpected pieces of the puzzle. He needed to ponder how they fit into the bigger picture. How they changed the puzzle as a whole.

One of the motel doors was hanging open. Inside, he could see the room lit dimly by two lanterns and the blue glow of the canned fuel Advani was using to heat their food.

Pascal steered Justine to a chair.

Justine sat. "I'm not hungry."

"You need to eat," Advani said. "If not for you, then for the baby."

Pascal took a place at the table while Advani scooped something thick and brown from a pot and portioned it onto plates. He sniffed it, then wished he hadn't.

"What is it?" he asked.

"Stew. It's not bad if you put enough salt on it." Advani handed him the salt.

Pascal salted his food and took a bite. "This is awful."

"It's the best I can do without fresh meat or fish." Advani shoveled stew into her mouth.

Pascal was sure Chef could have done better, but he didn't say so. He choked down several mouthfuls without chewing.

Justine pushed the food around with her fork.

"You must eat," Advani told her.

"Don't nag her," Pascal snapped. "It's only a few days. Give her vitamins. She'll be fine." He took another bite and washed the taste from his palate with a whole bottle of water.

Advani continued eating.

"Don't sit there," Pascal growled. "I told you to get vitamins."

Advani swallowed visibly, then pushed back from the table and went into the other room. After a moment she returned and handed Justine a small cup of pills.

Justine looked at Pascal, then took the cup and tossed back the pills. She followed them with a few sips of water from her bottle. "I'd like to go to sleep now."

"Cuff her to the bed," Pascal said, handing Advani the cuffs.

"I'll need the key," Advani said. "In case she needs to urinate."

"Give her a bucket."

Advani took one of the lanterns and led Justine into the adjacent bedroom.

"Don't close the door," Pascal called.

He took the other lantern to the bedside table, and placed his mother's Ruger and the other contents of his pockets beside it. He slipped off his shoes and pants, leaving them neatly at the foot of the bed, then extinguished the lamp and slid under the covers.

He watched the flickers and shadows through the open door as the women moved about, getting ready for bed. He almost felt bad handcuffing Justine and treating her like a hostage after what he'd learned about her past, but if anything, it was more necessary now. He hadn't seen her as a killer. She was far more complex than he'd estimated, and he wondered if this lapse in his abilities was temporary, or if he'd been permanently damaged by the loss of his son.

He took the key card for the vehicle from the nightstand and placed it under his pillow. His last thought as he drifted to sleep was that, even with Justine sedated and handcuffed, it would be a mistake to underestimate her.

Pascal awoke before dawn, but he didn't get out of the lumpy bed. He hadn't slept well. Something had niggled at the back of his mind all night, but he couldn't quite grasp what it was. He watched the sky grow lighter through the gap in the curtains. Perhaps if he had a few more minutes' peace before he woke the women, he could resolve whatever was nagging at him.

When his bladder would no longer permit him to wait, he put on his clothes and shoes, tucked the key card and Ruger in his pocket, and stepped outside. He took a deep breath of the cool morning air and was about unzip his slacks when he heard a noise. It sounded like . . .

The Travelers.

Frantically, he scanned the roads. He couldn't see them, but the sound of bicycle tires on pavement was similar enough to that of the wooden chariot wheels to ruin everything. If Justine heard it, she'd know they were being followed and the jig would be up.

He listened at the women's door and heard murmuring. They were awake. *Shit.* He had to cover the sound of the bikes, so he did the only thing he could think of.

"*Fair Genevieve, my early love! The years but make the dearer far,*" he sang as he returned to his room and closed the door. "*My heart shall never, never rove; thou art my only guiding star.*"

He crossed to the adjoining room while launching loudly into the second verse.

"*I see thy face in ev'ry dream, my waking thoughts are full of thee. Thy glance is in the starry beam that falls along the summer sea.*"

Justine gaped at him from her bed, and Advani looked like she'd seen a ghost.

"*O Genevieve, Sweet Genevieve,*" he sang as he paraded dramatically into their room. "*The days may come, the days may go. But still the hands of mem'ry weave the blissful dreams of long ago.*"

He stopped near the window and listened while he took a breath. It was quiet. The bikes had passed.

"Sir, I had no idea you sang," Advani said.

Justine narrowed her eyes. "Why the sudden serenade?"

"No reason other than it's morning," he said. "Time to rise and shine, as my mother used to say. Doctor, come get the key to the handcuffs so Justine can get dressed."

He motioned Advani into his room ahead of him.

"What was that about?" Advani asked in a hushed tone.

He yanked her close. "Bicycles," he said directly into her ear.

Her eyes widened.

He leaned close again, ignoring the stench of her breath. "Forget something last night?"

She drew in a sharp breath. "I thought you . . ."

"Me? You were supposed to handle that when I took Justine for the walk."

"I didn't know. You didn't say."

"I couldn't exactly say, now could I. That's why we pre-arranged it. In the future, I'll take care of marking all the stops. Right now we have something more pressing to deal with."

"What?"

"They're ahead of us now, you idiot. How will we get past them without Justine seeing?"

"I suppose I'll give her a sedative," Advani said.

"Make it a strong one. If she sees them, your trip is over."

An hour later, Pascal was nearing the end of his patience. If Justine didn't pass out soon, he might very well have to knock her out with his bare hands.

"I'm almost ready!" the doctor called. She'd taken an exorbitant amount of time loading the car, pretending to misplace various items to prolong the chore, but the ruse was beginning to wear thin.

"Justine, I believe it's finally time to get in the car," Pascal said.

"I don't feel well," Justine said, holding her head. "I'm dizzy. Queasy." Justine stood, but her knees buckled and she sat down hard in the chair.

"Doctor, come here," Pascal called.

Advani rushed in from outside.

"What did you give me?" Justine accused.

"Vitamins, because you're not eating," Advani said. "Why, what's wrong? Are you feeling ill?"

"It doesn't feel like vitamins," Justine said. "Are you sure? I feel, I feel drugged."

"Maybe you should rest a bit longer," Advani said.

"No, we have to go." Justine stood again, grabbing Pascal's arm to steady herself.

"You can barely stand," Pascal said. "How can you drive?"

"I can't wait another month." Justine gripped his arm, nails biting into flesh. "You drive."

Pascal turned to Advani. "Doctor, is that safe?" She'd better not improvise.

"Perfectly safe," Advani said. "We'll make the car comfortable with pillows and blankets. It will be like sleeping in a bed."

Pascal breathed a silent sigh of relief that they were leaving. And he would finally get to drive. He would actually be glad for the doctor's blunder, provided they made it past the Travelers without incident.

He helped Justine into the driver's seat while Advani made a bed for her in back. Justine was so out of it, Pascal caught a peek of the code, but not the whole thing. As soon as the engine was running, Justine climbed into the back seat and Advani tucked her in.

"She's already out," Advani whispered. "The sedative hit harder than I expected."

"It took long enough," Pascal muttered, settling in behind the steering wheel.

Advani climbed into the passenger seat. "I doubt I can rouse her, so I hope you know how to work this thing."

"I've watched her for hours. I know what to do."

Pascal put the car into gear and pushed the pedal with his toe. The car lurched forward and Advani's head slammed against the headrest. He let off the pedal and tried again with less pressure.

It didn't take long for him to get the feel of the controls, and by the time they got to the freeway, he'd mastered it. From Interstate 5, he took the exit for Highway 99 toward Bakersfield. Hopefully his troops had done the same. With Minou in charge, he felt confident they had.

Soon he saw a sign proclaiming Bakersfield. Clumped at the base of it was a mass of soldiers on bicycles. He looked at Justine in the rear-view mirror. "She'd better not wake up."

"I can't guarantee it," Advani said. "But at the very least, anything she sees or hears will be distorted and difficult to recall."

Pascal pointed to the Travelers. "Can I risk talking to them?"

Advani shrugged.

Pascal struggled with the decision as he slowed alongside them. The stunned look on Minou's face made up his mind. He pushed the button that lowered the passenger window.

"Sir?" Minou asked.

Pascal put his finger to his lips and indicated Justine in the backseat. "A mistake. It won't happen again."

"Our destination?" Minou whispered.

"Unknown, except that we're supposed to arrive tomorrow night, and we're behind schedule. Could be anywhere in northern California or Nevada. San Francisco seems unlikely with the recent colonizing, plus we'd have stayed on I-5. So I'm thinking Reno maybe, or Sacramento."

Justine mumbled something that sounded like "marmalade fur lock."

"We should go," Advani said.

"Everything according to plan on your end?" Pascal asked Minou.

"No problems we can't handle," she said. "Your markings have been good."

Except for the absence of the one last night.

Pascal put up the window and eased the car forward. "Doctor, all bets are off if Justine remembers this."

Advani looked concerned but nodded.

Pascal pushed hard on the pedal, increasing speed as much as he dared with his new driving skills. He knew he should slow down and give Justine as much time as possible to warp her drug-induced dreams around reality before it was necessary to wake her for directions, but to hell with it. He liked the speed.

Chapter 135

Byron Highway, California

"Am I going too fast?" Brandt asked.

"Not at all." Reid cinched his pack tighter to minimize bouncing.

"Good, because I wasn't telling the truth about going to Sacramento. I didn't want Nikolai to know we're actually heading for Stockton. I'd like to make it there before dark, so we need to get a move on."

"Do Justine's people live in Stockton, or is that the meeting place?"

"Neither."

"Then what?"

"I'd rather not say."

"Why not?" Reid said. "We have a plan, what difference does it make?"

"The less you know, the better. You could still change your mind, and this way I don't have to worry you'll return with an army."

"There's nothing more important to me than getting seeds. I'm not changing my mind."

Brandt raised his eyebrows.

"Oh, come on!" Reid said. "I was temporarily insane when it came to Mia. I never stopped wanting to find seeds. I just didn't think it was possible, and I couldn't face going home empty-handed."

"Still . . ."

"Hey." Reid grabbed Brandt's arm. "I admit I was an idiot, but I'm not the same person now. Nikolai was right. I learned a whole lot from what happened with Mia. I have a responsibility to my people, and hiding from that truth doesn't change it. Without seeds, they're going to die, and a lot sooner than the people out here. I can't live with that on my conscience. I'm not changing my mind."

"Okay." Brandt resumed walking. "But neither am I. The less you know, the better. I'll stash you in a safe place while I go get the seeds."

"Let me go with you. I can help."

"I won't risk it," Brandt said. "Justine's people have lived in secret for generations protecting their plants and animals. I can't take the chance you'll tell others where they are. Everything could be lost."

Brandt seemed dead-set, so Reid dropped the subject. For now. "How did they manage to save plants and animals? Any danger in me knowing that?"

"I guess not," Brandt said. "About ten years before the disaster, a religious man, a Mormon, claimed an angel warned him of a coming apocalypse. He said God was sending a flood, like in the Noah's Ark story, but this time it would be fire, not water. The angel called this man the 'new Noah,' and gave him instructions for how to prepare."

"So he built an ark?"

"Of sorts. He bought a mine and created an underground repository of seeds and animals. He tried to convince the Mormon church to support it and help choose families to populate it, but the church didn't believe it was real prophecy. The man ended up splitting from the church and choosing families himself that he deemed moral and worthy of joining him."

"That would sound really kooky, if you didn't know there actually was an apocalypse."

"It gets weirder. When the apocalypse occurred, everything inside the mine was protected from the radiation like the angel predicted—the seeds, the animals, the women and children, and Noah himself. But there had been no warning, so almost all the men were working the fields at the time and didn't survive. They needed more men, so Noah modified the Mormon custom of missionary work and sent women to find worthy husbands among the survivors. When word got out about their community, outsiders poured in. The supplies couldn't support everyone. When Noah realized their survival was in jeopardy, he ordered the deaths of all outsiders and created an elaborate system to keep their location secret."

"Justine said her people were nonviolent," Reid said.

"Yeah, but it's not true. The women are taught that, but in actuality, there's a big fence surrounding the community. It goes for miles and took years to construct. It's topped with razor wire, and protected by armed men and vicious animals. Once you get inside the perimeter, it's still miles before you reach the fields where they grow the crops and keep the animals. Women aren't allowed beyond the fields except on the way to and from their missions, and then they're given drugs that affect their memories. That's further protection against outsiders—the women can't reveal how to get home, even under torture."

"Then how did Justine know?"

"The man she ran away with. He'd been privy to the secrets, and figured there was no harm telling her since they could never return home."

"They left knowing they couldn't go back? Knowing they'd never see their families again?"

"Justine didn't have a family. Her mother died when she was five, and she never knew who her father was."

Chapter 136

Fresno, California

Pascal gripped the steering wheel as he pulled into the outskirts of Fresno. Both women were sleeping, and Justine's snoring was almost as irritating as the high-pitched whistle emitting from Advani's hooked nose.

He loved the speed of driving, but he would have enjoyed it even more if he hadn't had to drive in circles for hours coaxing directions out of Justine. It had taken longer to get her to say "Fresno" than it had taken to drive there. He hoped she'd slept off enough of the drug to be of use now, but before he woke her, he needed to leave a message for the Travelers.

There was a large park alongside the highway that looked like a decent place for the Travelers to wait. Pascal stopped the car, but was careful to leave it running while he painted a large "X" on the asphalt, and an arrow pointing toward the park. Minou would know what to do.

Pascal drove down the off-ramp, bypassing the roadside motels to provide the Travelers a wide berth. He turned into a residential neighborhood and parked in front of a modest house, then pocketed the keycard.

He nudged Advani's shoulder. "Wake up."

Advani wiped drool from the corner of her mouth. "Huh?"

"Watch her," Pascal said. "I'll be back in a minute."

He pulled out the Ruger as he approached the house. The neighborhood didn't appear inhabited, but no sense taking unnecessary risks.

The back door was unlocked. He went through the house room by room, but didn't find any sign of recent occupants. When he went back outside, Justine and Advani were standing beside the car.

"What the hell are you doing?" he growled. "I told you to watch her."

"It's not like she's going to get away from me," Advani said.

"You idiot," Pascal said. "Get the food bags."

"What are we doing here?" Justine asked, scratching her head. "What time is it?"

Pascal ushered Justine to the house. "It's afternoon. We're stopping to eat."

"My legs feel weak," Justine said. "Did I sleep all day? What about my regular walks?"

"We got you up every hour," Pascal lied. He took her inside and deposited her on a green velvet sofa. "You don't remember?"

"All I remember is my mother's voice, and something about a boat. I must have been dreaming."

"Maybe you heard the doctor telling me about her childhood. Did you know her father was a pirate? Maybe that's why you dreamt of a boat."

"Maybe." Justine's eyelids drooped and her head tipped back against the couch.

Advani brought in the bags containing foodstuffs. "She's asleep again?"

Pascal pulled Advani into the kitchen. "What concerns me," he said in a low voice, "is what happens if she won't sleep tonight."

"Handcuff her to the bed again."

"I can't sleep unless she sleeps. When can you give her more sedatives?"

"Not anytime soon. It could harm the baby."

"I don't *care* about the baby. She might not even be pregnant. My only concern is that she wakes up in the morning. Otherwise, we'll have come all this way for nothing."

Advani frowned and her nostrils flared. "If she eats, I can give her a small dose."

"Fine, make some food." Pascal balked at the thought of Advani cooking, but he needed time to discern what Justine remembered.

He returned to the couch. "Wake up." He sat beside Justine and patted her hand, but she didn't stir. "Justine, wake up." He gave her cheek a light slap.

She snorted like she'd swallowed her tongue, and her eyes opened wide. "What? What is it? Where am I?"

"We're in Fresno, remember?"

"Fresno?" She looked confused. "How did we get here?"

"You were sick in Bakersfield. You had me drive here."

"I wouldn't do that."

"You said it was urgent we get to Fresno, but you were too ill to drive."

"Oh my God, what day is it?" Justine came forward on the couch, hands clutching at the fabric. "Is it the full moon?"

"Not until tomorrow."

"Good, there's still time. I need to see the map. Where's the map?"

"Doctor," Pascal called. "Get the map from the car."

Advani came out, rolling her eyes as she wiped her hands on a towel. She sighed as she went through the door, like she'd been assigned a monumental task. He looked forward to when she was no longer necessary.

"Justine," Pascal said. "What do you remember from today?"

"Nothing." Justine narrowed her eyes. "Did the doctor give me sedatives?"

"Not to my knowledge," Pascal said. "That could harm the baby."

"I *feel* drugged. I'm groggy and nauseated, and my head hurts. She's been giving me a lot of pills. She says they're vitamins, but I don't believe it."

"So don't take them. It's your body. It's up to you."

"You won't force me?"

"To what purpose?"

Justine's brow furrowed. "Maybe I misread the situation."

Advani came in and thrust the map book at Justine, then huffed into the kitchen.

Justine thumbed through to a map of Fresno. "Show me where we are."

Pascal pointed.

She studied the page for a moment. "Okay, I know where we need to go." She stood, swayed, and sat back down.

"You should eat first."

"I can't." Justine grimaced and held her stomach. "And I can't sit wasting time. The meeting place could have changed in the last two years. I need to go to church right now and pray about the location. Then, even if they've moved it, we should still have time to get there."

There was obviously something to the praying thing, some kind of code or hidden message. "How far to the church?"

Justine looked at the map again. "About five miles."

"We'll leave the doctor to finish cooking. Maybe you'll be hungry when we get back."

Justine nodded and stood, using Pascal's arm for support.

"We're going out," Pascal called.

"What?" Advani said, poking her head out of the kitchen. "We're leaving?"

"Not you," Pascal said. "We'll be back soon."

Advani looked alarmed, but wisely kept silent. He would love to leave her there and not come back, but he still needed her to direct the Travelers to the meeting place once he was "drugged." Besides, abandoning her wouldn't be nearly as satisfying as killing her.

Justine leaned on Pascal as they went down the walk.

"Shall I drive again?" Pascal asked.

"I'll be fine."

Pascal helped her into the car, then settled in his seat before handing her the key.

"Look away," she said, inserting the card.

Pascal stared out the side window as she punched in the code. There was a momentary pause, then he heard the tapping of her finger on the keypad again.

"What did you do?" Justine demanded. "You broke it. It's not working."

"I didn't do anything. Try again."

Justine pressed the start button, but nothing happened. She did it twice more with the same result. "Don't look. I'm going to try the code again."

Pascal shielded his face, but took the chance of peeking through a crack between his fingers, hoping Justine was too stressed to notice.

She entered 8-6-7. He'd seen that before.

0-3-0-1. These numbers were new to him.

8-4-2. Enter. Now he had all the numbers.

Justine pressed the start button again, but the engine remained silent.

"Ugh! Did you enter a code?" she demanded. "I don't know what happens if you enter the wrong code."

"You entered the code for me. I didn't enter anything," Pascal said, keeping his tone even. "Think. Is there something you're forgetting? Did Reid mention anything that might help?"

"No! You must have done something."

"I didn't, so calm down and let's figure this out."

Justine glared at him. "I'm not missing that meeting tomorrow, even if I have to walk."

"Focus," Pascal said. "How does the vehicle get power? Maybe we need to refuel it."

"I have no idea. Reid never said."

"There's got to be a power source. Try to remember."

"There's nothing to remember," Justine shouted. "I don't know a damn thing other than it won't start." She opened the door.

Pascal grasped her arm. "Where are you going?"

"Church."

"Walking? Be reasonable," Pascal said in his most soothing tone. "It makes more sense to figure out how to fix the car."

"We can't fix it! We don't have any idea what to do. I need to start walking now if there's any hope of making it to the meeting place by tomorrow night."

"How far is it? Assuming it hasn't changed."

"About a hundred miles."

"You can't walk that in a day, Justine."

"I don't have a choice."

"You'll never make it without the car. Maybe all it needs is a cooling down period. It could be as simple as waiting until morning."

"I can't wait." She got out of the car and headed down the road.

He caught up to her easily. "You're not thinking clearly."

"Leave me alone."

"You don't have water, food, a coat. You didn't even bring the map."

Justine's face contorted. One loud sob escaped her lips.

He was by no means glad that the car had stopped working, but it did seem to be pushing her to a breaking point. He sensed she was close. Just one more little nudge. "I'm here to help you, Justine. Let me help." He put his arm around her shoulders. "We can figure this out, but you must tell me everything." He steered her to the house and sat her on the porch steps. "Start with what happens at the church. Why do you need to go there?"

She wiped her nose on her sleeve and let out a jagged breath. "To pray."

"Justine, we don't have time for any more lies."

Justine met Pascal's gaze, then looked down at her lap. He could feel her resignation, could almost taste victory. He waited. Five seconds, ten, twenty. It stretched out like an eternity until she finally looked back up at him.

"We're taught to open the Bible to a certain passage of scripture. The meeting place is written on that page."

He took a breath, forcing himself to go slowly. He didn't want to scare her now that he was so close. "Okay, that's good. How do you know which church to go to? Your people can't put the message in every church."

"Any church *could* have the message, but the Temples always do. The church I chose is the only Temple in the region. If the meeting place changed, I guarantee the message will be there."

"See? That wasn't so hard, was it? Come, let's get some water from inside and we'll walk to the Temple together. Hopefully the car will work when we get back."

Pascal led her inside.

"You're back already?" Advani said, running out of the kitchen.

"Shut up and get us a couple bottles of water," Pascal said. He steered Justine into the bedroom. "Sit down here a moment while I pack up some things." He patted her on the shoulder and went to get his handcuffs.

Chapter 137

Fresno, California

Pascal cuffed Justine to the bed. "It's for your own good."

"Damn you!" Justine yanked her arm, clanking the cuffs against the metal bedframe. "I shouldn't have trusted you. I never should have told you anything."

"I'm doing what's best for you and the baby," Pascal said. "I only hope we can still make the deadline tomorrow. I'd hate to wait another month."

"Let me come with you," Justine pleaded.

"Tell me where to look in the Bible."

"If I did, what would prevent you from going to the meeting place without me?"

"Absolutely nothing. But why would I? My chances of getting what I want are far greater if you're with me. Besides, I'd be stupid not to come back to try the vehicle. However, time is short, Justine. Even if the car starts, we could miss the deadline if I take too long looking through the Bible at the church. Why don't you save us time and tell me where to look for the message."

"I guess you'll eventually find it, and either you'll come back or you won't." Justine pursed her lips. "Fine. Book of Mark, chapter ten, verse six."

Pascal made sure the key to the cuffs was securely in his pocket with the keycard, then slung a small pack of provisions over his shoulder and left.

He slid behind the steering wheel, inserted the keycard, and entered the code. He took a deep breath then pushed the start button. Nothing happened. He tried twice more, then got out.

He wasn't taking the car to the church, but neither was he walking. The Traveler's camp wasn't far, and it felt good to stretch his legs after being cooped up in the car. He arrived at the outskirts of the park in no time and could see his men gathered under a pavilion.

"Halt!" a soldier shouted, pointing a gun at him.

"Stand down," Pascal commanded. "It's Chancellor Worth. I need to see Minou."

"Yes, sir," the soldier said. "My apologies. I recognize you now." He pointed across the park to the pavilion. "She's there, sir. Shall I stay at my post?"

"Yes, dismissed." Pascal continued toward the makeshift base camp.

Before he reached the pavilion, Minou headed toward him.

"Sir?" Minou said with an uncharacteristic look of surprise on her face.

"No need for alarm," Pascal said. "I need a bike. Put someone else in charge—you're coming with me."

"Yes, sir." Minou turned toward the pavilion. "Heinz!" she shouted.

A soldier broke away from a group and headed toward them.

"We may have a problem with the vehicle," Pascal told Minou. "Who are your most technically-minded?"

"Zakarian and Sinclair," she said without hesitation.

"Get them and whatever tools they have, plus munitions and bikes for the four of us. We leave immediately."

Minou saluted and jogged toward the pavilion, already shouting orders.

"Heinz," Pascal said. "I need Minou for a short mission. You're in command while we're gone. Pack up camp and wait at the ready until we return.

Pascal opened the Bible and smiled. He didn't need the doctor anymore. He didn't have to hide the Travelers. He was no longer at Justine's mercy. He had the location of the meeting.

A church in Oakdale, California. The exact address.

He pulled the map from his pack and flipped to the page Justine had last used. Oakdale was less than a hundred miles. Even if the car didn't start, they could cover that on the bikes before sunset tomorrow. Whoever waited at that church would be no match for his Travelers.

Everything was falling neatly into place.

Back at the house where the women were waiting, Pascal laid the bike on the driveway and motioned for Minou to join him. He pulled the Ruger from his pack and went to the car. He had a feeling it was going to start this time, and he didn't want to take the chance of anyone getting the grandiose notion to overthrow him. Not that he thought that likely, but now was no time to get complacent.

He pulled the keycard from his pocket and slid behind the wheel. After switching off the Ruger's safety, he placed the gun on the center console in easy reach, then shoved the card into the reader. If he believed in a god, now would be the time to pray. But if there was a god, Pascal had no use for him. Pascal believed in no one but himself.

Shielding the keypad, he punched in the numbers. Then, without hesitation he punched the start button. The motor whirred to life.

"Ha!" he exclaimed, beating his hands on the steering wheel. "Yes!"

Minou smiled. "Well done, sir."

"Go get the women. They're inside the house." Pascal pulled the key to the handcuffs from his pocket and handed it to Minou through the window.

Something like joy bubbled up in his chest and came out as a laugh. He looked in the mirror and rubbed his hand across the gray stubble on his face. He looked good—the smile, the sun-kissed skin, the burgeoning beard. He felt good. Powerful. Unstoppable. He felt like himself for the first time since Brandt and Reid murdered his son.

"You bastard!" Justine shouted, struggling between the two soldiers who brought her out.

"Put her in the backseat," Pascal said. "Get in with her, one on each side."

Justine fought as they shoved her in.

"Hey, she bit me!" one of the soldiers said.

"Put the cuffs back on," Minou said. "I'll get some tape for her mouth."

"Will that be necessary, Justine?" Pascal looked at her in the rearview mirror. She shook her head. "Minou, get in the front seat."

Advani stood on the walk with the bags of supplies. Her ugly face contorted in a scowl. "Where am I supposed to sit?"

Pascal picked up the Ruger and shot her in the chest.

Justine screamed.

"Aaahh. I've been waiting a long time for that." Pascal placed the gun back on the center console and put the car in gear.

—

Chapter 138

Stockton, California

The nearly-full moon lit the road, but not well enough to keep Reid from tripping over a rock. His hands were scraped and his knees were bruised from several falls, but he kept on. He'd long since stopped wondering how far they had to go, concentrating instead on placing one aching foot in front of the other.

He found himself thinking about bathing his sore muscles in the hot shower at his grandparents' house, and his mind wandered to Kayla. It felt like an eternity since he'd really let himself think about her. He'd used his infatuation with Mia to crowd out his feelings for Kayla, but it hadn't made those feelings go away. He pictured Kayla now, her belly full with the baby, though in reality, she'd barely be showing. How could it be that so much had changed and he hadn't even been gone a month?

He remembered how it felt to hold Kayla in his arms. The smell of her hair. The sound of her breathing. He still loved her. He'd never stopped.

He recalled Tinker's advice to tell Kayla how he felt, and he realized—

Brian was gone. There was no reason to keep his promise to his brother anymore. He was free to tell Kayla, but did he want to? If she could never return his love, wouldn't it be better not to know?

He imagined Kayla looking at him with green eyes full of love and longing. Was it possible she could look at him that way and not imagine Brian?

He twisted Tinker's wedding ring on his finger. He had to take the chance.

I'll tell her, Pops. I'll get back home and I'll tell her. I promise.

Reid tripped again. "Damn!"

"Did you find a way to sleep while you're walking?" Brandt asked.

"Huh?"

"That rock," Brandt said. "You had to have your eyes closed not to see it. You okay?"

"Yeah, fine." Reid wiped his eyes. "But I *will* end up sleeping on my feet if we don't stop soon. How much farther?"

"You really did have your eyes closed," Brandt said. "We passed a sign a ways back that said 'Stockton city limits.' We're here."

Reid looked around, registering the buildings, the side streets, the increased number of cars. He hadn't even realized they'd entered a city.

"I think we're almost to the church," Brandt said. "What's that sign say?"

"Mar . . ." Reid squinted. "Mariposa Road?"

"Good, that's what I thought. The church is a mile down that road. We'll sleep there."

"This is the meeting place?"

"No, that's still a day away. At least I hope it's not more than that. I'm supposed to check here for a message, in case the meeting place changed."

"I don't understand why we have to go to the meeting place at all if you know where Justine's people live."

"It's not like I can follow a map and stroll into their community," Brandt said. "If I'm not escorted in, I'll never make it past the gate."

"I thought Justine told you how she did it."

"She told me how she got *out,* not how to get in," Brandt said. "I have to be at the meeting place when the elders arrive to escort the missionaries home. That was the plan when Justine and I thought we'd be doing this together. I'm still going through with it, but it's a bit iffy now that I'm showing up without a missionary to claim me as her husband."

"Why didn't you and Justine go sooner?"

"At first she didn't want to go home. There were all the reasons she'd left in the first place—the strict rules, the religious dogma. But more than that, she was afraid to return because of the way she'd left. The man she escaped with had a wife and children, a high position in the church. Justine didn't have any family or any standing. She'd be a pariah, worse than a nobody if she went back."

"What changed?"

"The baby." Brandt's voice broke. After a pause he continued.

"We'd been talking about it even before she knew she was pregnant. We didn't want our children growing up in Lost Angeles. Justine said that, as bad as things were at home, it was better than where we were. She didn't think her people would ever fully accept or forgive her, but they wouldn't throw us out, and our child would grow up safe and well fed. She was willing to sacrifice her own freedom and happiness for that."

"And you?"

"There's nothing I wouldn't sacrifice for her and the baby. Of course, I hoped that her people would see what a good person she was, that eventually she'd be forgiven. But even if we were never accepted, at least our child would have a future and Justine would have a say over what happened to her own body."

"I take it her people don't condone sex as a job?" Reid asked.

"Hardly," Brandt said. "If they had any idea that's what happened to the missionaries in Lost Angeles, they'd never let them go there."

"Don't the girls tell them when they go back?"

"Missionaries who return aren't allowed to talk about their missions, including the location. But Justine didn't think any missionaries ever made it home from Lost Angeles. Pascal makes it impossible. That's why your vehicle was such a Godsend."

"I'm sorry she didn't make it out," Reid said.

"I can tell you one thing," Brandt said. "When I meet her people, I'm not keeping my mouth shut about Lost Angeles. No other woman will go through what Justine did." Brandt turned down a side street. "We should be almost there."

Reid tried not to think about how nice it would be to sit down. "How do you know where this place is?"

"Justine said we'd need to check if the meeting place had changed, so in Sausalito I looked up the churches in this region where Justine's people leave messages and marked them on my map."

"Do you want to stop and check it?" Reid asked. "I know it's dark, but I don't see anything that resembles a church."

"I can't believe you doubt me," Brandt said, acting offended. "Turn here. You'll see in a minute." They walked another half a block. "There it is."

Brandt pointed at an unassuming building in a large parking lot. There were no crosses or fancy architecture except for a lone spire.

"You sure this is it?"

"Yep."

The parking lot was full of cars, and Reid figured the church would be full of skeletons. Maybe he'd sleep outside again.

Brandt pulled open the front door and held a finger to his lips. They listened to the silence for several long moments before Brandt nodded.

Reid held the door open so the moon could wash a few feet of the interior with its gray light. Brandt stepped inside and struck a match, illuminating a table that held a dozen or more candles. He lit one and handed it to Reid, then lit another for himself.

They crossed to a set of double doors. Brandt pulled one open, and it creaked in protest. Rows of benches flanked a center aisle. The men followed it to a lone podium on the altar.

Brandt handed Reid his candle. "Hold them up so I can see." He set aside two smaller books and opened a large Bible. "I don't suppose you know where the book of Mark is?"

"Actually, I do." Reid never expected his mandatory Bible studies to have a real-world application. He handed the candles to Brandt and flipped to the New Testament. "What am I looking for?"

"Chapter ten. There should be a handwritten message."

Reid flipped through the pages to Mark, chapter ten. There was a handwritten message in the margin next to verse six. "*1111 A Street, Oakdale.* Does that mean something to you?"

"It sure as shit does," Brandt said. "It means we can get a decent night's sleep."

"Maybe we should sleep outside." Reid squinted at the rows of benches, expecting to see an audience of skeletons, but the place appeared vacant.

"Up to you," Brandt said, handing Reid a candle. "But let me show you something before you decide."

Reid followed Brandt back through the lobby and down a long hallway. He stopped at a door labeled "nursery," a grin on his face. "Go in."

Reid opened the door, holding up his candle to illuminate the interior. The walls of the room were lined with beds and cribs, each draped in a white sheet. Brandt entered and pulled off one of the drapes, revealing a bed made with a patchwork quilt and puffy pillows.

"Not bad, huh?" Brandt said. "Most of the Mormon churches are fixed up like this for missionaries traveling through. Pick whatever bed you want, unless you want to sleep outside."

"No, this is great." Reid pulled away a protective sheet and collapsed onto the bed.

"Leave your pack and we'll get some food."

"I'm too tired to eat." Reid's eyes were already closed. His limbs were leaden, but he knew he should at least take off his boots, so he forced himself to sit up. "How many miles do you think we did today?"

"Something close to thirty, according to the map."

"No shit?" He tossed his boots on the ground and flopped back onto the pillow. "No wonder I'm exhausted." How many more miles was it to Colorado? He couldn't even think about it. Instead, he closed his eyes and drifted off, picturing the carrots and the nuts and the aloe stuff Cumorah had in her pack. There was more in the world besides grown apples, and he was getting close. He could feel it.

Chapter 139

Turlock, California

"This is where we turn," Minou said.

Pascal turned the car, grateful Minou's younger eyes could read the map by the light of the moon. "How much farther?" He was at the brink of exhaustion, but he couldn't sleep yet. He didn't want to risk shutting off the car until he was in walking distance of the meeting place, just in case it wouldn't start again.

"Maybe twenty miles," Minou said.

The guards in the backseat had been dozing for hours, as had Justine, but Minou stayed awake. Her silent company was a hundred times better than the doctor's drivel.

Pascal glanced in the rearview mirror. Moonlight glinted off the metal of the Travelers' bikes. It was nice having them where he could see them.

"Can your team make it another two hours?" he asked.

"Yes, sir. They'll do what they have to."

"The sun will be coming up about then. You should get some shut-eye now."

Minou leaned against the door, leaving him with only Justine's snoring for company.

Chapter 140

Stockton, California

R eid woke with a start.

"Sorry," Brandt said. "I dropped my boot. Didn't mean to wake you."

"S'okay," Reid said. His mouth was dry, his teeth sticky. "What time is it?"

"Still early. Go back to sleep."

"Might as well get going." Reid swung his legs off the bed. His feet hit the floor and he winced. He'd never make it to Colorado with his feet intact if he continued doing thirty-mile days.

"I think you should wait here," Brandt said.

"You were going to leave without telling me, weren't you. Damn it, Brandt, we had a deal."

"You knew this was coming. If you learn where Justine's people are, you can't go home." Brandt tied his boot and slung his pack over one shoulder. "There's plenty of supplies here. Give me ten days. If I'm not back, leave for Colorado."

"Ten days?"

"It's a day to the meeting place, then time to get from there to the community, more time to gather up seeds and escape. I hope to be back sooner, but I'm trying to be realistic."

"If it's a whole day to the meeting place, let me come with you part of the way."

"I can't risk you knowing where it is."

"Come *on*. It'll shave some time off my wait. And if you're still going east, it will get me that much closer to home."

"Shit, I hadn't thought about your route home." Brandt scratched his head. "I *have* to take you farther east. Otherwise, you could accidentally pass too close to the meeting place and someone could see you. I can't have you getting yourself shot after we've come all this way."

"I agree, getting shot would be a bummer."

"Fine. Pack up your shit. I'll grab some more supplies from the kitchen."

"You won't regret it." Reid fingered the water-blisters on his heels and gingerly pulled on socks and boots. He was beginning to understand how Cumorah's feet ended up the way they did. How long had it taken her to get to Colorado? He wished he'd been able to learn more from her. He had no idea if there was enough time to make it over the Rocky Mountains on foot before winter.

Brandt came back with Reid's canteen. "I filled it for you."

Reid remembered Kayla saying the same words after their first night on brevet. He saw her in his memory as clearly as if she were standing in front of him—hair back in a ponytail, the sadness in her eyes. He ached to see her again. He knew now that he had to tell her how he felt. How he'd always felt.

"What's with the stupid grin?" Brandt asked.

Reid laughed. "Was I grinning? I was thinking about my girl back home." It felt weird to say that out loud. Kayla had always been Brian's girl to the rest of the world.

"What the hell, man. You have a girl back home?"

"Not exactly. It's a long story. Do we need to clean up here before we go?"

"No. Are you trying to avoid telling me the story?"

"Actually I wouldn't mind telling someone," Reid said as he slung his pack on and they exited the room. "I've kept it to myself since I was nine years old."

"Does *she* know?"

"No one knew, but I think my grandfather figured it out."

"Why keep it a secret?"

"She was in love with my brother."

"Shit."

"He loved her too, but I loved her first." Reid took a deep breath of early morning air as they left the building. "I remember the first time I noticed her. I'd known her my whole life, of course. Our community isn't that big. But that day in church I really *saw* her. I was seven and she was eight—an older woman, and totally out of my league. But I couldn't help how I felt. She was the most beautiful thing I'd ever seen."

"Geez, Reid. You've been in love with this girl your whole life."

"I didn't know what love was then. I only knew that when I was with her, I couldn't think straight, and when I tried to talk to her, I always sounded stupid."

"That sounds like love, all right," Brandt said.

"Then when I was nine, we both got the chickenpox and were quarantined in the infirmary. Just me and her. We had a nurse, but she ignored us. At least, that's how I remember it. Like there was no one else in the world but Kayla."

"Chickenpox? Where you get really itchy bumps?"

"Yeah. We told stories to keep each other from scratching. The itchier we got, the crazier the stories got. We spent most of the time laughing. I can still picture her with red spots all over her face, telling a story about living on the moon together, just the two of us. That's when I knew I loved her."

"So what happened?

"My brother. He came down with the chickenpox a couple of days later and they put him in the room with us. From the minute he arrived, it was like I didn't exist. I hated him for that."

"Did you fight for her?"

"It wouldn't have made any difference. All her stories became about Brian. So I wished as hard as I could that Brian wasn't there. I wished he was dead so I could have Kayla to myself again." He paused, surprised how painful the memory still was. "Then Brian got sicker, much worse than me and Kayla. The doctor sent for my dad because Brian wasn't going to make it."

"And you thought it was your fault."

"I knew it was. When it looked like Brian was on the verge of death, my dad called me over to say goodbye and I whispered in Brian's ear that if he lived he could have Kayla. I meant it. So when he got better, I kept my promise. Eventually, they got married. I tried to go on with my life. I even married someone else. But I never stopped loving Kayla."

"And she never knew?"

Reid shook his head. "Brian died a month ago. She's pregnant with his baby. I was supposed to marry her, but I couldn't do it."

"Why the hell not?

"I was sure she could never love me the way she loved Brian, and I didn't think I could handle that. But now, I need to know. Funny I had to come all this way to change my mind."

Chapter 141

Oakdale, California

"**P**lease," Justine said. "Don't do this."

Pascal turned off the car and looked at her in the rearview mirror. "You've become expendable, and you're getting on my nerves."

He wasn't going to kill her yet—he wanted Brandt to watch the life drain out of her—but she didn't need to know that.

"It's not too late," she said. "You can still get what you want without hurting anyone."

"You have no idea what I want."

"Leave your men here," Justine continued. "Let's stick to the original plan. We'll go in, just me and you."

"Shut her up," he told Minou. "There's tape in my bag."

"It's a good plan." Justine's voice was shrill. "Please, it can still work!"

He wished they'd hurry and muzzle her. He'd had about all he could take, and it would be a shame to have come this far only to shoot her before he reached the finish line.

Minou handed a roll of gray tape to Heinz in the back seat.

"Listen to me," Justine pleaded.

Pascal watched in the rearview mirror as Heinz put tape across Justine's mouth, muffling her protests. "Cuff her, too. Stay in the car with her. I'll send for you if I need you."

It was better to be one man down than to risk Justine ruining the element of surprise.

He went to the back of the car. The Travelers stashed their bikes alongside an industrial building, then gathered around as he pulled up the floor of the vehicle's rear compartment, revealing a cache of guns and ammunition.

Pascal doled out semi-automatic rifles and the ammo to go with them, as well as the supplemental ammo he'd packed for the handguns the Travelers carried.

"Take a couple men on recon," he told Minou. "We'll be ready when you return."

As the Travelers checked and loaded their weapons, Pascal tucked his Ruger in the waistband of his pants and loaded the M4 he'd set aside for himself, then he sat back to wait.

When Minou returned twenty minutes later, she reported seeing a dozen men inside the church, ranging from twenty to sixty years old. No women or children visible, though one of her men had heard a baby crying. There were no weapons in sight, which could mean that Justine had told the truth about them being nonviolent, or it could just as easily mean they were well concealed. Either way, Pascal was confident they were no match for his soldiers. He'd come at those assholes so fast and hard, even if they were armed, they'd have no idea what hit them.

Minou led a contingent to the back door, while Pascal and the bulk of the men waited to go in the front. He held long enough for Minou to get into position, then gave the order.

"Subdue and contain. I need some alive," he said. "Team leaders . . . *go.*"

His men poured into the church. Pascal joined ranks with the last of them, hearing gunfire and shouting before he even went through the front door. Immediately inside, two bloody strangers lay still. His men continued through a set of double doors into a larger room.

"Hold the lobby," Pascal shouted, pointing at two of his soldiers.

He went through the double doors and ducked behind a row of chairs. The scene was chaos and he sorted the sounds into categories, laying them out like puzzle pieces on a table. Gunfire. M4s and multiple pistols. The rapid-fire of an assault gun he didn't recognize—the enemy was returning fire. Men shouting. Women screaming. Moans and cries.

One voice penetrated the din. "Hold your fire! Hold your fire," Minou shouted from the opposite end of the room.

The shooting ceased, leaving only the moans and cries of the wounded. Pascal assessed the situation from his point of cover, then stood. "We've got you surrounded," he said, striding forward so the enemy could see who was in charge. "You're outmanned and outgunned. Do as I say and no one else has to die today."

In addition to the two dead in the lobby, two more of the enemy lay still and silent, and another two were down, bloody and out of the fight.

The rest—seven of them, all men—had been disarmed and subdued by his Travelers.

Wait . . . he had heard women screaming during the fight, and one of his soldiers had heard a baby cry earlier. There were others in the building.

"Where are the women and children?" Pascal demanded.

"I have them back here, Chancellor," a voice called.

"Bring them out," Pascal replied.

After a moment, a woman appeared from the shadows of a hallway. She clutched a baby to her chest. Behind her came two more strangers—a tall man bleeding from a gash on his cheek, and another woman. A Traveler with an M4 herded them toward Minou.

As they approached, Minou glanced over at Pascal. In that split second, the tall man lurched, grabbing Minou and putting a knife to her throat.

"Put down your guns," the man said, "or I'll—"

Pascal squeezed the trigger on his M4, spraying bullets in the general direction of the man with the knife. The man fell. Minou fell. The woman and the infant fell.

The Traveler who'd been ushering them stood frozen with his weapon half raised. The remaining woman shrieked hysterically. Pascal shot her.

He went to Minou, hoping she wasn't dead, but he knew she was. He stepped over the dead baby and picked up the stranger's knife.

"You didn't check for weapons?" Pascal asked the Traveler, holding out the knife.

"No sir, I—"

"You cost me my best man." Pascal thrust the knife into the soldier's gut and twisted.

The Traveler dropped his gun, his eyes wide, mouth agape. Pascal withdrew the knife and the man went down, blood pouring between the fingers he pressed to his belly.

Pascal looked at the rapt strangers. "He was one of my own, so he died quickly. Imagine what I'll do if *you* displease me."

He walked toward the lobby as he let that sink in. Even the wounded were silent now. He stopped at the double doors and turned, assessing the resources that remained. Seven prisoners. That should be plenty.

"You." Pascal pointed at one of the older prisoners. "Who else is here? How many?"

"I . . . none. No one else," the man stammered.

Pascal shot him. The remaining men gasped as the body fell.

"I didn't believe him," Pascal said. "Now you," he said, pointing with the muzzle of his gun. "You tell me, how many others in the building?"

"I, I, please, I don't know of any. Please," the man whined.

"I want to believe you," Pascal said.

"It's the truth!"

"We'll see." Pascal opened one of the double doors. "Carter, Watson, report."

"All quiet here, sir."

"Carter, keep watch," Pascal said. "Watson, take two other Travelers and check the rest of the building. Kill anyone you find."

Watson nodded and double-timed it out of the lobby.

"Search the prisoners again for weapons," Pascal ordered to his men at large. "Then sit them in the front row. Someone go out back and check on the watch. Do it!"

Pascal went to Minou and stripped her body of weapons. It was a shame, such good help gone to waste. But someone else would rise in her place before long.

He climbed the stairs to the stage and placed his Ruger on the lectern. The prisoners were situated in the front row as he'd instructed, with armed Travelers positioned strategically behind them. Pascal's gaze landed on the last prisoner he'd questioned. He glared at him until the man squirmed, then paced behind the lectern until Watson reappeared.

"All clear, sir," Watson said.

Pascal picked up his Ruger and went to the squirming prisoner. "You told the truth."

"Yes sir," the man said.

"Thus you are still alive. Do you wish to continue breathing?"

The man nodded.

"Then continue telling the truth," Pascal said. "All I want is the location of your home."

The man looked down.

"Well?" Pascal asked.

The man shook his head without looking up.

"I will not ask you again."

The man kept his head bowed, his shoulders jerking with silent sobs.

Good. Pascal would have been disappointed if he'd talked. It was better he serve as a lesson to the others. He put the muzzle of the gun to the man's temple and squeezed the trigger.

The man on the opposite side was sprayed with blood, bone, and brain. He wailed as he tried to wipe the gore from his face. Pascal turned from him and faced the prisoner on the other side of the body.

"You," Pascal said. "You're next."

"Go ahead and kill me, because I'm not going to tell you anything." The young man's eyes blazed with defiance.

"You're ready to die?" Pascal asked.

"A thousand times to keep my people safe from you."

"Then it's a shame I'm not going to kill you." Pascal slowly and deliberately pulled the knife from the sheath on his belt.

"Fine, torture me," the man said. "Give it your best. I won't break."

Pascal leaned close and spoke into his ear. "Good. It's not you I'm breaking." He looked over at the man whimpering and quivering in his seat, the man who still had bits of human flesh in his hair.

Chapter 142

Highway 4, north of Oakdale, California

They'd been heading east for hours on a pocked and pitted highway that reminded Reid of the road outside Cheyenne Mountain. He let his mind drift to the day he and Kayla left the Mountain. It was such a short time ago, but so much had happened. He wondered what Kayla was doing now, if she was sick, if she was still pregnant. If she missed him. Thinking about her kept him going when his feet hurt so bad he thought he couldn't take another step. He watched the ground, careful not to get so lost in thought he'd trip again. Every so often, he glanced ahead to where the road disappeared into the mountains.

Finally they turned south. The road was equally marred, but the horizon was flat. After several minutes of walking, Reid's thoughts started to drift back to Kayla when he realized something looked different.

He squinted his eyes, staring into the distance. "What do you make of that?" He pointed at a blob far ahead on the road. "Was that there a minute ago?"

Brandt shielded his eyes and looked. "Move!" He dove off the road onto his belly.

Reid hit the ground and slid down the dirt embankment. "What is it?"

"Whatever it is, it's coming toward us," Brandt said. "We need to hide."

Reid lifted his head and looked around. "There's nowhere to go."

"This way," Brandt said, low-crawling back the way they'd come. "I saw a drainage pipe. It's not far. Stay low. And hurry."

They scrambled toward a pile of bramble and garbage that had collected in the depression where a pipe went under the road. "You first,"

Brandt said.

Reid pushed prickly tumbleweeds aside. "It's too full of dirt. No way we can fit."

"We have to. I'll hide the packs under the trash, but we need to get inside."

Reid clawed at the dirt.

"Hurry," Brandt urged. "It's coming fast. I can hear it."

Reid pulled out two more armloads of dirt, then crawled in, wedging himself nose to knees as far inside the pipe as he could go. "Brandt, get in."

Brandt backed into the opening, somehow curling his body into the impossibly small space between Reid and the outside world, filling the opening and blocking the light.

Reid felt like he was going to suffocate, like the earth was swallowing him. He fought to quell the panic, focusing on the gap of light between Brandt and the wall of the tunnel. His arms quivered and his breathing grew rapid, every cell in his body screaming for that outside air. He didn't trust himself not to shove Brandt out of the way, so he closed his eyes, blocking out the light to remove the temptation.

He imagined he was home in the Mountain and the power had gone out. It happened so often, it was routine. All he had to do was be still and wait. His breathing slowed and he heard the mechanical whir of things restarting in the Mountain. *No,* it wasn't his imagination. The sound was real. Coming from the road.

It grew louder. Buzzing, whirring. It sounded like something back home, but he couldn't place it. Almost like the sound of the units restarting . . . but not quite. He could discern a low-pitched hum beneath the other sounds, also familiar.

The whirring slowed, then stopped, leaving just the hum. It reminded him of . . .

"What is it, Chancellor?" a voice called.

"I thought I saw something," another voice answered. A pause, then, "It was probably nothing. A shadow or a trick of the eye. Let's move out."

The hum changed tone slightly and Reid realized what it was. *Tinker's car.* The hum faded and was replaced by crunching gravel, creaking, voices, grunting. Reid's heart felt like it was going to pound out of his chest. It seemed like an eternity before the noises receded.

"Brandt," Reid whispered. "That was—"

"Pascal."

"The car. Wait, that was Pascal's voice?"

"I'd know it anywhere," Brandt said. "Those other sounds were the car?"

"Do you think it's safe to look yet?"

"I'll give it a shot."

After a moment of rustling, Reid could see light again.

"You were right," Brandt said. "It's definitely the car. And . . . something else."

Reid scrambled out of the tunnel and crouched beside Brandt. The Humvee was quite a ways down the road but clearly recognizable amidst a pack of *bikes,* probably the source of the hum he'd heard.

"Those are bicycles," Reid said. "We use stationary ones back at the Mountain to supplement the hydro-electric power when battery reserves run low. You're sure it was Pascal?"

"Dead sure," Brandt said.

"How did he start the car? He couldn't have known the code, unless—"

"Unless Justine told him," Brandt said. "Justine's alive."

"Justine must have told him," Reid said. "But don't get your hopes up. It doesn't mean she's still alive."

"She is. I feel it. I'm going after them."

"What about the meeting place?"

"It's still miles in the opposite direction. Besides, Pascal probably came from there. If so, there's no one left alive."

"We'll never keep up."

"I know where they're going." Brandt held out his hand. "This is where we say goodbye, Reid. Don't bother waiting. I doubt I'm coming back."

"I'm going with you."

"Don't be an idiot. If you come with me, you're not going home. If Pascal wins, you're dead. If Justine's people win, they won't ever let you leave."

"We can figure that out later. Right now you need my help, and I'm not leaving you."

"Reid, there's no guarantee—"

"Are there ever any guarantees? Besides, that jackass stole my car, and I want it back."

Chapter 143

Outside Copperopolis, California

The man covered in brain matter was named Jacob, and he was beginning to smell bad.

"How much farther?" Pascal asked.

"I, I'm not sure," Jacob said. "It's hard to tell when I'm not walking."

"Would you rather walk?" Pascal was tempted to allow it, if only to get his sniveling, stinking ass out of the car.

"There! There!" Jacob was manic, almost gleeful. "I recognize that building." Jacob pointed with the hand that wasn't taped down.

"Good," Pascal said from between clenched teeth. "And that means . . . ?"

"We're almost there. Almost to the gate. Almost home."

Pascal hoped so. Jacob's mental state was deteriorating to the point where he'd no longer be useful. He stopped the car and turned to Justine who sat in the back seat, seething.

"Do *you* recognize the area?" he asked her.

She glared at him, then gave a nod.

"Talk to me, Justine. The more I know, the higher the odds we'll survive."

Justine stared, eyes narrowed, her hatred palpable. But he could see she wanted to live.

"This is the last town before we get to the fence that surrounds the compound," she said. "If we stay on this road, we'll come to a gate. There will be armed men. Guard dogs. If we make it past them, the road curves around out of sight. In a couple of miles, we'll start seeing crops and orchards. Then the compound isn't far."

Pascal motioned out the window for Carter, who was leading the Travelers since Minou's demise. After relaying the plan to Carter, he leaned back in the driver's seat and took a deep breath. He could almost smell the freshly harvested food, and he imagined it would taste sublime served alongside his revenge.

A short time later, the compound was his. It was almost too easy.

The idiots had gotten complacent and the gate had only the dogs protecting it. He'd taken care of two problems at once by slicing Jacob's throat, then sprinkling the bloody corpse with sedative and feeding it to the dogs. Not a single shot had been fired, preserving the element of surprise.

They'd driven up the road around a bend, as Justine had described. After a distance Pascal had seen green, and it was as if he were seeing the color for the first time. Green like seaweed only . . . fresher. More vibrant. More alive. Tree after tree, field after field, different shades and shapes of green. He breathed deeply of cool air thick with the smell of living, growing things.

As they'd neared what Justine referred to as "the compound," there were pens of animals. Finally, something besides rats and fish! He recognized the sheep by their wool and the pigs by their snouts. But the cows and horses, they were bigger and more muscular with eyes more intelligent than he could have dreamed. It seemed utterly foolish now to think his scientists could have created such animals working from rats and degraded DNA in a lab. But none of that mattered. Here they were, flesh and blood, and his for the taking.

Amidst all the life, oddly, there wasn't a human soul in sight. Justine directed them to the largest of the buildings, a low white structure that she said was their church.

All the people were inside, singing hymns, every last one of them. Not a single guard at the door. No one on watch. Not a weapon in sight.

There were more people than he had expected. But even if they hadn't been corralled into one building, his Travelers would have taken them easily. Granted, it would have been bloodier. As it was, he simply walked into the church and wiped out the leadership, who'd thoughtfully clustered themselves at the front of the church. They even conveniently fell face up, making the next order of business that much easier.

"Bring her in," he told Heinz.

The sound of children crying grated on his nerves. These people had an abundance of snot-nosed brats. Each woman had four or more clinging to her, smearing mucus and tears on her fancy church clothes. For the number of women and children, there were few adult men, and none of them was Brandt.

Pascal walked up and down the center aisle, looking over all the faces again, hoping he'd missed him the first time, but Brandt wasn't there. He strode to the podium. "Shut those children up, or I'll do it for you."

"Let the children go."

Pascal turned toward the voice. A woman in the front row. He pointed his gun at her. "What did you say?"

"The children are no threat," she said in a steady voice. "Send them to their Sunday school classrooms. Then you can tell us what you want without all this distraction."

Pascal hesitated, noting the hopefulness in the faces of the other adults. This woman had authority. People listened to her.

"Come here." He motioned her up to the podium with his Ruger.

As she approached, he saw concern lining her brow, but not terror. She had some moxie. She might prove useful, for a time.

"What's your name?" he asked.

"Sister Odekirk."

"Sergeant Carter," Pascal called out. "*Sister Odekirk* is going to show you the largest classroom. Assess it for security and report back."

"Yes, sir." Carter pointed his weapon and followed the woman out a side door.

"You see, I can be reasonable," Pascal announced. "So don't be stupid. Cooperate and perhaps I'll spare your children."

"Sir?" Heinz appeared in the main doorway with Justine.

"Bring her here." Pascal watched the audience, noting murmurings as Justine was led in.

"What have you done?" Justine wailed as she saw the bodies of the twelve men at the front of the church. "Why? You didn't have to do this!"

"Which one is your father? This one?" He pointed at the oldest man with his Ruger.

"None of them," Justine said. "I lied. I never knew my father."

"What's she doing here?" Sister Odekirk exclaimed as she returned through the side door.

"You know this woman?" Pascal asked Sister Odekirk, pointing at Justine.

"Know her? She's the adulteress who ran away with my husband."

The pieces shifted and fell into place. "You lying bitch," he said to

Justine. "What else did you lie about? *Brandt?*"

"Hell yes, I lied." Justine thrust out her chin. "Brandt doesn't know about this place. He's not coming. I lied about all of it."

Pascal smiled. He could see it in her eyes now, the difference between a lie and the truth. Brandt was on his way. Pascal could sit back and wait. Brandt would come to him.

"The children," Sister Odekirk said. "Can they go to the classroom now?"

"It's secure, sir," Carter said.

Pascal considered. He wanted the sniveling and crying and fidgeting to stop, and killing the children would *eliminate* the problem rather than shuffling it off to be dealt with later.

"Please," Sister Odekirk said. "We'll cooperate when we know our children are safe."

"I don't need your cooperation," Pascal said. "There's nothing I need from you. What I need is revenge on Justine's man, Brandt."

"Revenge?" Justine said. "For what?"

"Sister Odekirk," Pascal continued. "Brandt is going to show up here whether you and your people are alive or dead. I think dead would be easier, but you're welcome to try to prove me wrong."

Chapter 144

Copperopolis, California

"Copperopolis. Population 2363." Brandt pointed to a sign half hanging off its post. "This is the last chance you'll have to change your mind."

"I'm not changing my mind," Reid said.

"Okay, if you're sure," Brandt said. "According to the map, about twelve more miles into the mountains is Angels Camp. That's where Justine's people are."

"The City of Angels," Reid said. "The woman I met, Cumorah, she said she came from the City of Angels. At first I thought she was delirious, but I remembered my grandfather's stories about Ellay—Lost Angeles—being the 'city of angels.' That's why we came west."

"Funny thing is, that woman probably *was* delirious," Brandt said. "Justine told me that the women are never told the name 'Angels Camp' so they can't reveal it under torture."

"That's *not* funny." Reid didn't want to think the entire journey hinged on a coincidence.

"My guess is, Pascal headed straight up this highway to the gate to take it by force."

"You think Justine's people can hold him off at the gate?"

"I don't have any idea," Brandt said. "We'll try to find a vantage point to scout the gate without being seen. If Pascal controls it, we'll follow the fence to the south and hope to find where Justine cut through it."

"If we don't find where she cut it, can't we just cut it ourselves? Or climb over?"

"Sure, but getting past the fence isn't the problem. It's figuring out where to go once we're on the other side. If Pascal controls the road, we'll have to try to retrace Justine's route from the hole she made in the fence to the compound, and then enter through the mineshaft she used to escape."

By the time they approached the gate, it was well past dark, but the full moon was bright enough to see by. From their vantage point, they could see the gate hanging wide open. After surveilling it for thirty minutes, they'd seen no hint of movement or sound. No sign of the car, or people, or animals.

"It's still possible someone's inside that shack," Brandt said.

"I doubt a guard would go this long without patrolling, especially with the gate open," Reid said. "I say we risk it."

Brandt nodded and stood.

As Reid straightened upright, he caught movement in his peripheral vision. He dropped back to the ground, yanking Brandt with him.

A lone figure crept along the fence line toward the gate. The person was small, a boy.

They watched him sneak past the guard shack and through the gate, then bolt down the road toward where they hid. As the boy was about to pass, Brandt stepped into the path and grabbed him, clamping one hand over his mouth to mute his cry.

"We're not going to hurt you," Reid said as Brandt pulled the boy into their hiding place.

Reid figured he couldn't be more than ten years old.

"Don't yell, okay?" Brandt said.

The boy nodded, and Brandt removed his hand.

"Some bad men came, and you're going to get help, right?" Brandt asked.

"My mom sneaked me out. I'm supposed to get the elders," the boy said.

"There are no more elders," Brandt said. "But we're going to help you."

"But the bad men have guns!" the boy said. "They're killing people."

"It's going to be okay," Reid said, hoping he sounded convincing. "We'll take care of the bad men if you can sneak us inside. Do you think you can take us back the way you got out?"

The boy nodded.

"Good," Brandt said. "We need you to tell us everything you remember. How many there are, where they are, what demands they're making."

"Brandt," the boy said. "They're looking for someone named

Brandt."

———————

The boy's name was Luke, and he was wiser and braver and bigger and healthier than any eight-year-old Reid had ever seen. If it hadn't been for him, they'd have no idea what was going on inside. Now they had a plan. A plan that could actually work. As long as Reid did his part.

"If you follow the road, you'll come right up to the compound," Luke said. "There are men guarding it. They will definitely see you."

"This whole thing goes to hell if they shoot you on sight, Brandt," Reid said.

"Pascal wants me *alive*. Right, Luke?"

The boy nodded.

"He wants me, "Brandt said, "so that's what we're going to give him. Me and just me. He'll think he's won and his guard will be down. He'll never see you coming. But this only works if you can take the shot."

"I know what I have to do." Reid touched the hard, cool metal of the gun at his belt, and swallowed down the butterflies.

"You're *sure?*" Brandt asked, looking doubtful. "Because back at the train . . . We need to be sure."

Reid pushed away the last of his doubts. This was different. *He* was different now. "I've got this, Brandt. You don't need to worry." He knew it in his gut, in his soul, in every part of him—he could do what had to be done.

"Good, then all that's left is the timing. How long do I wait before waltzing into town?"

"Luke," Reid asked. "How long will it take to get me into place?"

The boy's brow furrowed. "I'm not sure. It'll take awhile to get back to the mineshaft, and then a little while longer to get to the church where the bad men are."

"And you think they'll still be there?" Reid asked. "In the church?" It just took one variable out of place for everything to go wrong.

Luke shrugged. "The head bad guy hasn't left the church since he got here. He even sleeps there."

"Luke, it's probably about midnight," Brandt said. "Do you think you can get Reid into place before morning? Before it gets light? That's about six hours."

"Yeah, I think so," Luke said.

"I'll be there by dawn," Reid told Brandt. "I'll be ready. You can count on me."

"I know I can," Brandt said, gripping Reid's shoulder. "Just remember, you can't negotiate with him. Don't even try."

"I understand."

"Then I'll see you in there," Brandt said, extending his hand.

"See you on the flip-side, as my grandpa used to say." Reid grasped Brandt's hand and hugged him. They thumped each other on the back.

Reid followed Luke out of their hiding place. Reid crouched as they headed down the road toward the gate. He felt bare and exposed in the moonlight, as if Pascal's men were about to descend on them, but there was no sound of anything other than Luke's footfalls and his own on the pavement.

They crossed through the gate to the guard shack. Reid risked a glance in, expecting to see a body, but it was empty. On the other side of the shack, however, were dark masses on the ground and the smell of death.

"They killed the dogs," Luke said, his voice low and somber.

"What's that buzzing sound?" Reid whispered.

"Bugs. They eat the dead."

"*Oh.*" That was something he'd never thought of.

"Come on," Luke said, motioning. "This way."

Luke led him away from the road into the moon shadows of the tall, long-dead trees. They followed the fence for what felt like miles to Reid's blistered feet, until finally Luke turned with purpose and headed into the dead forest.

The going was tougher and slower as they ascended, and it wasn't long before Reid's thighs and calves burned, but he kept pushing. He had to be there in time or Brandt was dead, and a lot of other people, too. This time the plan hinged solely on him, and he wasn't going to fail.

After a couple of hours, they emerged from the forest into an open field. Reid took a swig from his canteen and a deep breath of night air. It smelled different. Earthy and damp, not unlike the apple orchards in Sausalito.

Squatting down, he touched the ground and gasped. *Plants.* He was sure of it.

"Psst, Luke," he whispered.

The boy turned and came back to Reid. "What's wrong?"

"What is this?" Reid asked, indicating the field.

The boy knelt down and felt the plants. "Green beans."

"*Really?*"

Luke snapped something off the plant and handed it to him. "See?"

Reid took the bean, turning it over in his hands. It was firm but bendable, and more than twice as long as any green bean Reid had seen in a can.

"You can try it," Luke said.

"You mean eat it? You don't have to cook it or anything first?"

"Just eat it." Luke snapped another bean off the plant and took a bite. "See?"

Reid put the bean in his mouth. The sound of the crunch was like he'd bit into a bone, but the bean gave way between his teeth, filling his mouth with tangy, slightly sweet flesh, moist though nothing like the mushiness he'd always known to be green beans. He couldn't help but think that Brian should be with him. This was *his* dream.

He looked up to the sky, wanting to believe there was a heaven, wanting to believe his brother was watching him, and his parents and Tinker, too. That they knew he'd finally found seeds, and that they were proud of him. He didn't know if they would still be proud after he did what he'd come to do—he didn't think he could be proud of himself—but he'd made his decision. What was at stake was a whole lot bigger than him being able to live with himself.

"Reid?" Luke touched his shoulder, jolting him alert. "You okay?"

"Yeah, sorry." He stood, only then realizing that the sky he'd been staring at was turning the slightest bit lighter. "We should go. How much farther?"

"Not real far, but we should probably hurry."

As Reid followed Luke across the bean field, he tried his best not to crush any of the plants. Each one was like a self-contained miracle, a dream come true all wrapped up in a little green package. He thought about taking one home to Kayla, even just one grown bean. To see the look on her face as she bit into it. To see, as the sweet freshness washed over her tongue, her realization that Brian's hope was a reality. That there *were* seeds in the world, and their baby would have a future to grow up in.

If there was any way he could make it home to her, to deliver that news, that hope, that future, he was determined to find it. Even if she couldn't love him, even if she couldn't face him after what he was about to do.

Chapter 145

Angels Camp, California

It was barely dawn, but Pascal couldn't wait any longer for breakfast. Not after everything he'd eaten the day before—chicken and waffles, watermelon, beets, lemonade. Corn and green beans and tomatoes. He recognized the names of the foods, but they didn't taste like anything he'd ever eaten. Some foods he'd never even heard of, like pumpkin pie and whipped cream. Those had been his favorites until this morning's bacon and eggs.

He chewed slowly, savoring the hearty, creamy, salty freshness. He took another bite of bread, warm and spongy, dripping with butter, then washed it down with cow's milk, letting the sweetness linger on his tongue.

When he couldn't eat another bite, he pushed back from the table and motioned for the women to clear the dishes—they were proving useful enough. For now. He dabbed his mouth with a napkin, then looked at Justine who had long ago finished eating.

Justine looked past him, her eyes wide, her mouth forming a silent exclamation.

Pascal snapped his head around to see what she was looking at. "*Brandt.*"

"What are you doing here?" Justine cried as she leapt from her chair and ran to Brandt. She threw her arms around him. "You shouldn't have come. You shouldn't have come."

Brandt's hands were held behind his back by one of the Travelers. Watson.

Watson looked at Pascal, questioning. Pascal nodded, and Watson yanked Brandt from Justine's grasp.

"I heard you were looking for me," Brandt said, glaring at him.

"Yes, I've been expecting you," Pascal said.

"You should have stayed away," Justine said. She cupped Brandt's face in her hands and kissed him.

"Remove her," Pascal said to Heinz who he kept stationed nearby in case Justine tried to make a break for it.

"I'm staying right here." Justine clung to Brandt and looked at Pascal defiantly. "I'm tired of your games. Do what you've got to do, but I'm not budging."

"You have no idea what you're asking," Pascal said.

"Whatever you're planning to do to me," Brandt said, "why don't you come over here and do it yourself? Quit hiding behind your soldiers and be a man."

Pascal's hand went to his Ruger, and he considered shooting them and being done with it. But that would be far too fleeting. Not at all what they deserved.

He leaned back and kicked his feet up on the table. He was going to savor this.

Chapter 146

Angels Camp, California

Reid's hand was steady as he held the gun, waiting for the shot. He was well hidden about twenty yards behind Pascal, but Brandt knew he was there, waiting and watching for the right moment. That's why Brandt was goading Pascal—he was trying to get him to stand up so Reid could take him out.

Reid knew he could do it. He'd looked inside himself, really looked, and he knew he could do what had to be done. He didn't even care if he had to shoot Pascal in the back. He just didn't want to miss. Sure, it would be hard to live with, but given the big picture, his own feelings didn't matter. He couldn't allow the hope of the world to fall under the control of an evil, power-driven despot.

That meant he had to take a life, so that's what he would to do.

It was for the greater good.

Now if only the bastard would stand up.

"There's no question," Pascal said, leaning back in his chair. "I'm going to kill you both with my own hands. But it's not going to be quick, or painless, or on your terms."

"Just get it over with," Justine said. "You already have everything you want."

"My dear," Pascal said, "what do you think I want?"

"The crops, the animals, the seeds," Justine said. "You have it all, and there's nothing we can do, so put me out of my misery."

Justine was wrong. There *was* something they could do. Reid gripped the gun tighter, careful not to put pressure on the trigger. He'd wait for the right moment. He had to make the first shot count.

"I didn't come here for the resources," Pascal said. "Though I am enjoying them. No, I came to exact revenge on those responsible for my son's death: Brandt and Reid."

"Your son is dead?" Justine exclaimed. "But I thought . . ."

"He was killed in the pirate battle when Brandt and Reid escaped," Pascal said. "If you think about it, this is all *Reid's* fault. If it weren't for him, where would you two be right now? You'd be in Lost Angeles in a beautiful home, with all your needs met, preparing for your baby's arrival. And I . . . I would be at Club Three having breakfast with my son. Instead, here we are—me childless, and you about to die. But not until I find out where Reid is."

"Reid's already dead," Brandt said.

"Don't lie," Pascal growled. "Markoff's in the Tank. He told me that you, Reid, and Mia sailed from Catalina with that northern ship captain."

"That's true," Brandt said. "But right after that, Mia betrayed Reid. She left him for the ship captain. Mia was all he had to live for after you killed his grandfather, stole his car, and took away his hope of saving his people. He killed himself."

"*Oh my God.*" Justine said.

"I don't suppose you have any proof," Pascal said.

"You know Mia," Brandt said. "That's all the proof you need."

Pascal chuckled. "You're right."

"I'm the only one left to blame, so get on with it," Brandt said.

Come on, Reid thought. *Stand up, you sonovabitch.*

"I don't know why you're in such a hurry to die," Pascal said. "You might want to reconsider, because I'm not simply going to kill you. That would be far too easy."

"Why?" Justine said. "Why not just get it over with?"

"It was because of you that I watched my son die," Pascal said through clenched teeth. "There are no words sufficient to describe that agony. The only way for you to understand is to experience it for yourself. It's only fair, don't you think?"

"Our baby isn't even born yet," Justine said.

Reid could hear the horror in her voice.

"Leave her out of it," Brandt said. "She's done nothing to you."

"You're right," Pascal said. "In fact, she's been quite helpful to me. I've even grown a bit fond of her. I can try to save her, but once I cut the baby out, the odds are against her."

"No!" Justine cried.

"You can't, you wouldn't," Brandt said, coming forward. The guard yanked him back.

"I can and I will," Pascal said.

Reid blew out a steadying breath and aimed at Pascal's back, ready to shoot through the chair if he had to.

"But first, I want to know something," Pascal said. "Tell me, Justine. How have you been able to live with yourself knowing all this food is here? All this plenty, and a whole world of people out there who never have enough."

"What do you want me to say?" Justine said. "That I'm sorry? That I felt bad about it? If I apologize, will you spare my baby?"

"What I don't understand," Pascal said, "is the rationale for not sharing this food with the rest of the world. It makes no sense. The more you share, the more there will be."

"Our bounty is not meant to be shared." An older woman stepped forward, addressing Pascal. "Heavenly Father meant it for His chosen. We're to keep it hidden until the time is right to take it into the world again."

"Oh, the time is right, Sister Odekirk. That's why I'm here," Pascal said. "To spread the seeds to the rest of the world. The time has come. In fact, it's long overdue."

Could that be true? What if Pascal really wants to spread the seeds to the world? Wouldn't that be better, even under someone like Pascal?

"You're wrong," the woman said. "The time has not come. Not until the world has been cleansed of the wicked and unworthy."

"The world is full of the wicked. Look at me." Pascal pushed his chair away from the table and stood, his arms spread wide, presenting a perfect target.

Reid knew he should take the shot, but he hesitated.

"I'm as wicked as they come," Pascal continued. "Does that mean I'm not worthy of the basic human necessities, like food? What about innocent children like my son? How are they less worthy than your sons and daughters? I say the time has come for this bounty to be delivered into the world, and that's what I'm going to do. Right after I cut the baby out of Justine's womb and Brandt watches it die." Pascal pulled a knife from his belt, grabbed Justine by the arm and yanked her to him.

"Stop!" Reid shouted, rising from his hiding place. He needed time to think, time to process what Pascal had said, time to figure out what to do.

"*Reid, no!*" Brandt shouted.

The soldiers turned their weapons on Reid, and Pascal's look of shock transformed into a smile. In that moment, time slowed and Reid saw his life pass before his eyes, the way his patients described it before they died. Only to Reid, it felt like his past was rushing forward, colliding with the present.

"I'm as wicked as they come."

"You can't negotiate with him."

"Once you've walked in the sunshine, you can never go back to living in the dark."

"Bring back seeds. It's what Brian lived for."

"It's for the greater good, son."

As Pascal pointed his knife at Justine's belly, Reid understood why his father had made the choice he'd made, why he'd sided with Vega even though it meant an innocent woman would die. And Reid knew what he had to do.

All that's necessary for evil to triumph is for good men to stand by and do nothing.

Reid wasn't going to stand by. The greater good wasn't good enough. He wanted a *better* good. He wanted hope and goodness and sunshine, even if it was only for a few.

As he pulled the trigger, he said a prayer to a God he didn't fully believe in.

Please let my aim be true.

Justine screamed. Pascal fell, the knife dropping harmlessly to the ground. Brandt shouted. Shots rang out.

A bullet tore through Reid's shoulder, sending him reeling. Another shot ripped through his thigh, and he slammed backward into the ground. He cried out in agony, tumbling to his side and curling into himself. He could see the gaping wound in his leg, the femoral artery pumping blood into the morning air. Pascal was dead. But so was he.

There was screaming and shouting, but Reid couldn't grasp their meaning. The words floated down through the air like flakes of snow.

Stranger.

Prophecy.

Savior.

Death.

The pain was gone. He was bleeding out. He hoped there was a God, because that meant he would soon see Brian, his mother, his father, and Tinker. He let out his breath and closed his eyes. He'd done the right thing. His one regret was Kayla. He'd never told her he loved her.

epilogue

"How will we know when the time is right to send seeds back into the world?" the new Noah had asked the angel.

"It will come to pass," the angel had replied, *"that a barren woman of your people will travel an arduous road to a glorious red garden to beg God for a child. Her prayer will be heard and, in time, a woman with a baby in her womb will return to your people, followed by a rolling tide of evil that threatens not only the unborn babe but everything you have built. Finally, your fate will lie in the hands of a stranger who will have to choose between saving this baby or saving himself and his own people. If the baby dies, it shall mark the end of your way of life, Noah. But if the baby survives, she shall be a great Prophet and her birth shall mark a new beginning—the time to share God's bounty with all the earth's creatures."*

Manitou Springs, Colorado, eight months later

Reid stood at the top of the hill looking down at his grandparents' house. He couldn't tear his gaze from a lone wooden cross planted atop a fresh mound of dirt in the yard.

Who was buried there? The baby? His grandmother? Kayla? All he had to do was go down the hill to find out. But he couldn't bring himself to do it.

He knew that either Kayla was alive, or she wasn't, and nothing he did would change that. But as long as he stood there not knowing, there was still the hope, the possibility, she was alive. The moment he knew the truth, he could never go back to not knowing.

He twisted Tinker's ring on his finger, remembering his promise. It was time.

Steeling his courage, he started the slow walk down the hill. The closer he got, the more he was sure. He wasn't going to get to keep his promise. It was Kayla's body in that grave. Kayla's soul was with Tinker now, and the old man would have spilled Reid's secret. Or maybe Kayla had already known. Maybe she always knew.

As Reid reached the grave he fell to his knees, tears streaming down his face.

The front door of the house swung open. "Reid?"

He looked up. "Kay?"

"My God, it *is* you!" Kayla ran to him across the yard.

Reid stood and caught her as she leapt into his arms. "I can't believe it," he said, his face buried in her hair.

"I thought I'd never see you again." She squeezed him hard then looked at him, her eyes flowing with tears, too.

"The baby?" Reid asked, glancing at the grave.

"No, he's fine. Look," Kayla gestured to the front door where Reid's grandmother held a swaddled infant.

"Thank God," he said, hugging her tighter. "Then who . . . ?"

"Zeke. I guess he was old. One morning he didn't wake up."

"I'm sorry," Reid said, remembering how much the dog had adored her. "I know nothing can replace him, but . . . I did bring you something."

"Seeds?" she asked.

Reid gestured to the top of the hill where the rest of his travel party waited. There were a couple dozen strong, young men and women, including Brandt and Justine who'd insisted on coming with their baby girl. There were dogs, goats, and chickens. Horses drawing wagons full of grown food. And seeds.

Kayla gasped.

"It's everything we hoped we'd find, and more," Reid said. "Except . . ." He looked at his grandmother who had joined them, the baby cradled in her arms.

"Tinker?" she asked.

"I'm so sorry." More tears filled Reid's eyes as he pulled Tinker's ring from his finger and handed it to her.

His grandmother kissed it and slid it on her finger next to her own ring.

"He loved you," Reid said. "He loved you both, and he would have loved this baby more than anything." Reid touched the silky cheek of the baby boy.

"He had a long, full life," his grandmother said. "And he died making sure this baby would have one, too. That's the way he would have wanted to go."

"I promised him something," Reid said, swallowing hard. He turned to Kayla. "That if I made it home I'd tell you how I feel, Kay. How I've always felt. I love you."

Kayla looked into his eyes and he knew she saw him. *Him,* not Brian. And she smiled.

Acknowledgements

The "seed" for this book came from a National Public Radio story about the Svalbard Global Seed Vault. My husband heard the story while driving to work and called me to insist I write a book about it. At first I resisted (I do have my own ideas, after all) but once the seed germinated, I couldn't stop it from growing. So I owe a debt of gratitude to NPR, the "Doomsday Vault," and my husband, as well as the inventors of cars, radios, and phones. And I greatly appreciate the seemingly infinite supply of seeds-related puns and analogies, though I'm not sure anyone else does.

While any errors in this book are my own, I owe enormous thanks to friends, family, writers, readers, agents, editors, doctors, lawyers, scientists, Mormons, and mentors for their contributions and support. Whether you're named here or not, you have my gratitude.

Thank you to:

My family: my husband Jody; my sons Kit, Jack, and Duncan; Judy Sawicki; Bill, Nan, & Jessica May; Walt & Margaret Mandeville; Kathy Santelli; Kerry Quirk; and all of the many aunts, in-laws, cousins, and nephews

My critique partners: Todd Fahnestock and Aaron Brown who were with me from beginning to end providing invaluable brainstorming, critical feedback, and encouragement; and the other awesome Sparkling Hammers, Giles Carwyn, Leslie Hedrick, and Morgen Leigh

Early draft readers: Kirsten Akens, Geoff Andersen, Jodi Anderson, Michelle Baker, Trai Cartwright, Ron Cree, Megan Foss, Bonnie Hagan, Debbie Harris, Karen Lin, Tiffany Yates Martin, Chris Myers, Julia Pierce

Beta readers extraordinaire: Aaron Brown and Mandy Houk, for your generosity of time and spirit

Advance Readers: for your support and enthusiasm

Matt Lehman for the tires

Andrea Somberg and Michelle Johnson for believing in the project and in me as a writer

Deb Courtney for being an incredible advisor, reader, critiquer, and supporter

Celebrity casting directors: J. Rose and K. Julia

Friends, colleagues, and mentors at Pikes Peak Writers, Castle Rock Writers, Delve Writing, Superstars Writing Seminars, and Rocky Mountain Fiction Writers

Scientists: Kurt Brueske, Derek Buzasi, Jody Mandeville, Geoff McHarg, Brent Morris, Brian Patterson, Heather Preston

Cheyenne Mountain advisors and facilitators: Tom and Michelle Zwally, John Brtis, Susan Luenser, Martin Douglas

Mormon friends from the Church of Jesus Christ of Latter Day Saints, who understandably wish to remain unnamed, but whose open sharing of their beliefs was critical in my development of the fictitious Second Noah prophecy and church

And finally, I am beyond grateful for the crew at Parker Hayden Media, in particular my phenomenal editor, Pam McCutcheon, and the incomparable cover designer-slash-everything advisor, LB Hayden.

My greatest thanks go to you, the reader, for reading this book. You have so many books to choose from, and I'm grateful you chose this one. If you enjoyed it, the best way to show the love is to leave a review on Amazon, Barnes & Noble, Goodreads, or Kobo. I would greatly appreciate it (although puppies and cookies are also welcome!), plus it lets other readers know that this is a book they might want to choose, too. Thank you!

To learn more about the *Seeds* "world" and the science behind it, please visit my website at ChrisMandeville.com.

About the Author

 After growing up in California and graduating from the University of California at Berkeley, Chris married a U.S. Air Force officer and moved from state to state, as well as to British Columbia, before settling in Colorado. She now lives in the woods of the Rocky Mountains with her family and her service dog Finn. Chris is a writer of science fiction and fantasy novels and short stories, as well as nonfiction books for writers. Her other works include the young adult time travel series, "In Real Time," which debuted with *Quake* in 2018, *Undercurrents: an Anthology of What Lies Beneath*, and *52 Ways to Get Unstuck: Exercises to Break Through Writer's Block*. Learn more and become a member of her Reader Group at ChrisMandeville.com.